A THOUSAND VEILS

D J MURPHY

A THOUSAND VEILS

a novel

Illustration by Janice Lawrence.
Copyright © 2007 by www. janicelawrence.com.

Poem, "Enrich me with the flood of love . . . ," by Umar ibn al Farid (at pp. 371-372), from *Music of a Distant Drum: Classical Arabic, Persian, Turkish, and Hebrew Poems* by Bernard Lewis © 2001 by Princeton University Press. Reprinted by permission of Princeton University Press.

Published 2007 by www.lulu.com.

ISBN: 978-1-4357-0531-9
LLCN: 2007909854

Printed in the United States of America

To Mary Elizabeth Murphy,
my mother,

1919–2005

A woman of unsurpassed vision

THE UNVEILED MAID

by Umar ibn Rabi'a (died 728 A.D.)
translated by W. Gifford Palgrave

In the valley of Mohassib
I beheld her where she stood:
Caution bade me turn aside,
but love forbade and fixed me there.
Was it sunlight? or the windows
of a gleaming mosque at eve,
Lighted up for festal worship?
or was all my fancy's dream?
Ah, those earrings! ah, that necklace!
Naufel's daughter sure the maid,
Or of Hashim's princely lineage,
and the Servant of the Sun!
But a moment flashed the splendor,
as the o'er-hasty handmaids drew
Round her with a jealous hand
the jealous curtains of the tent.
Speech nor greeting passed between us;
but she saw me, and I saw
Face the loveliest of all faces,
hands the fairest of all hands.
Daughter of a better earth, and
nurtured by a brighter sky;
Would I ne'er had seen thy beauty!
Hope is fled, but love remains.

PROLOGUE

Baghdad
Saturday, Sept. 7, 2002

The sandstorm began in the early morning. For hours it had besieged the city, the final, in–your–face affront of an uncommonly brutish summer. From the west it came, out of the Syrian desert—the earth itself wafting skyward in great swaths, in huge diaphanous clouds, the hot, swirling wind whipping itself into a mad frenzy, driving the freighted air across the sky. Its coarse, particled cargo now had fallen upon every house and shop and café in Baghdad, and, in spite of the ramparts erected by man against it, the laden wind had found its way through infinitesimal cracks in window frames, through minute fissures in tiled walls, and through tiny breaches in wooden doors in every building around the city.

Over all Allah's faithful alike, from the high and mighty to the humblest of beggars—mattering not whether they resided in grand palaces, in mud abodes, or out on the street itself—the dust and dirt and sand had sifted down and down upon them, veiling them all with a sparkling sediment that soon became a suffocating chokehold. There was simply no escaping it; the wind would only pause now and then to gather up yet more of its grimy consignment. It seemed to do so now as the first light brightened the sky in the east, suffusing it with an alien glow. A strange hush had descended on the entombed city. In the amber air, mists of grit still drifted, curling lazily around the city, a yellow dog that no stick, no curse, could chase away.

From somewhere in the souk, the raucous chant of a muezzin, calling the faithful to prayer, broke the sepulchral stillness. Almost at once, a cat in the courtyard, as if by design, countered with a falsetto wail. The two cries became one, a dissonant duet of man and beast—each, in its own way, praising Allah.

Fatima Shihabi blinked open her eyes, dry from the dust that had infiltrated her bedroom, that now filled her nostrils with its gritty pungency. Outside, the chorus grew even more strident. Then, suddenly, the muezzin stopped, and, as if on cue, so did the cat, leaving a stunning silence. Only then did she hear the ring of the phone on her writing table, on the other side of the room. She sat up, threw her legs over the side of the bed, and ran to the desk. Who would be calling her, she wondered, at such an early hour? With a heart full of premonition, she picked up the phone. "Hello," she said softly. There was no sound. "Hello . . . hello," she repeated. "Is anyone there? Hello?"

The phone clicked dead at the other end. She stood on the tile floor, feeling the grit of the storm on the soles of her feet, and waited. After a moment, the phone rang again. Just once. Her premonition was even stronger now, and she didn't answer. Another pause, and it rang a third time, but this time twice. Then it stopped.

A sudden hiss of sand drew her eyes to the window facing on the street. A menacing hiss, as if a viper lay seething somewhere in the haze, taunting her to venture outside. Along the sill the wind had piled a ridge of sand in a miniature dune. And now, it seemed, the wind was picking up again, relentless in its mindless mission to desertify the city. The air was so thick with dust she could barely see the front gate. Beyond, a rusty beige blanked the walled houses on the other side of Zankat al Hudh. The headlights of a passing car glimmered dimly through the dust. It would be a hard day for going about, for travel, she reflected. No, the entire city would be shut down. It could be an advantage.

She turned back to the phone. The calls had been a code. It meant that Ibrahim had been picked up by Mukhabarat. It would be just hours, a day or two at the most, until torture would work its charms. He would reveal her name. And he would tell them how much she knew. Then they would come for her. She knew them well. They would wait for another pause in the storm, but by then she would be long gone. For over two years she had expected this day to come. She had prepared for it. She had steeled herself for it.

Two years ago it had been "Sami," then "Massoud," and finally, a month ago, "Khalid" who was her designated escort, their names no doubt among the many *noms de guerre* of the makeshift corps of the Iraqi underground. "One hour, no more no less, after you get the call," Ibrahim had told her, she was to rendezvous with "Khalid." It would be the first step on the journey that would lead her to the West, to her brother Omar, and to freedom. She would travel on a Canadian passport her escort was to give her, since her Iraqi passport had been taken. Their route wouldn't be easy. It would pass through desert country she knew in the south, across the Saudi border, then on to Riyadh, by plane to Munich, connecting to Montreal. There she would work and wait until this stupefying repression ended. It wouldn't be long, she told herself. The UN inspectors would know. It was only a matter of time before they learned the truth—in spite of Saddam's diabolical stratagem to hide the facts. And then the American planes would come back. In the meantime, her writing, the wellspring of her life, was being choked off. She was suffocating. And now she had no choice but to run for her life.

The back of her tongue felt gritty. She went into the bathroom and bent over the sink. She made herself cough, and spat a dirty brown mass into the bowl. Hurrying back into the bedroom, she threw on a loose-fitting, black cotton dress, with flowing sleeves that came down to her wrists, then put a few things into a small cloth satchel. Ibrahim had cautioned her to travel light, so she packed only a few clothes—a black silk dress with long sleeves, similar in style to the one she wore, a change of undergarments, a small black head scarf, and a cotton sweater in case it got cool in Montreal before she could get to a shop. And since her sandals surely would be roughed up on the way to Riyadh, at the last minute she decided to add a sturdy pair of black oxfords. After these items, it wasn't hard to decide what else to bring or leave behind. For most of her life she had lived simply, with only a few possessions besides her clothing—several books, including her father's well-fingered copy of the Holy Koran, a gilt comb her grandmother had given her, a strip of brown ribbon, once ochre red, that had bound her mother's silky raven hair. The last was the only thing she still had from her mother, who had died of cholera long ago, when they were all living in Kassim, in the desert, an almost forgotten time before the Great War, before Saddam's treachery and American weaponry had devastated their lives.

She drew her father's Holy Koran from its place on her bookcase and, for several minutes, cradled it in her hands. Then she went over to her writing table and set the book down. From the drawer she took her mother's ribbon and her grandmother's comb and placed them in the book, just inside the front cover. Then she slowly closed the book, and left it in the center of the table. She picked up the satchel, pulled its strap over her left shoulder, and draped the large black fabric of the abayah over her head and shoulders, letting it fall around her. As she left her bedroom, she spotted a small Arabic–English dictionary on the bookcase and tucked it into her things. She then closed the door behind her and headed for the stairs.

Soon Iraq would be but a memory. She would free herself from this place of unspeakable fear, of unimaginable acts, of unbearable repression. Her life was now taking a turn, she believed, down a path leading only Fate could know where. And, as at the outset of all journeys, she calmed herself with the thought that, no matter what might happen, no matter what risks she would face, she would be the better for it in the end. And in the end she would survive, and, at the very least, she would be able to write.

The hardest thing of all was leaving her daughter Latifa behind. As she passed her daughter's chamber, she paused and gazed at her treasure, whose spidery limbs were splayed across the bed. She had wanted to bring Latifa with her, but her brother Abdeljelil considered the trip too long and dangerous, especially across the desert, and insisted that it would be better if Latifa stayed with him for a time. "You can always send for her once you're settled," he told Fatima. Children were often arrested and tortured when their parents fled abroad, but Latifa would remain in his household, directly under his protection, and safe by virtue of his position in the ministry and the party, not to mention the prominence of the Azizes, his wife's family. His wife, Zhaleh, the only Christian Fatima had ever known, had taken a particular interest in Latifa. Nevertheless, it would be no small chore for Abdeljelil and his wife to look after a twelve-year-old, whose nerves seemed wound even more tightly than her mother's.

It wouldn't be all that long, Fatima consoled herself, before she would see her daughter again. Meanwhile, she would miss her daughter like nothing else, she thought, no less than the blind beggar at the entrance to the souk missed her sight or the gnarled cripple who lived at the end of Zankat al Hudh missed his good leg. For a few moments she wavered, then went on down the stairs. Better to let her dear child sleep.

She tightened the abayah around her head, leaving only a slit for her eyes. Then, with her right shoulder, she leaned against the front door, heavy with the sand that had piled against it during the night, forcing it open. She emerged onto the portico, into a storm once again in full fury, and pushed the door closed behind her.

Hesitating momentarily, as if to summon her resolve, she stood tall and erect, a black-shrouded shadow at the top of the staircase. The wind tugged insistently at her abayah and the hot desert sand stung her eyelids as she took a deep breath behind the folds of her veil. Then she went down the cement steps and out the front gate, into the maelstrom.

ONE

Fatima Shihabi was, both by birth and by her very nature, a *bint asa-hara*, a child of the desert. As her Bedouin forebears, she was taken in by the desert's veiled promises, its haunting vastness, its ceaseless sameness, and its inapproachability. She loved its clean, tasteless air, unleavened by vegetal scents, air that yielded no clue to its origins. Colorless and feature-less, the desert might even have been noiseless had it not been for the swishing and whooshing wind, which remorselessly thrust her back again and again into this world, its gentle yet firm hand nudging her as one might a toddler learning to walk. And as a child, she had relished the unruly exhalations of its summer storms, the unrelenting breath of what Omar called "the lungs of nature." How small she had felt before the desert's magnificence—especially at night, when, the winds having calmed, she and her father would stand beneath the great dome of the heavens, calling on the stars, as if greeting old friends, trying to puzzle out the words they faintly blinked.

Early on, the desert had worked its magic over her. It was as a child when she first heeded the whispers of its winds, which tutored her in a mysterious idiom whose urgings she imagined she could divine. When she began to write, it was the desert proscenium, clean-scoured by the parching wind and searing sun, that offered a wide and inviting setting for her stories and her poetry. And it beckoned her into its realm of endless possibility.

As she matured, the desert became for her a place of *fitna*, of seduc-tion. She thrilled at its bold caresses when she and her father would ride on horseback over the scrubbed and sandy terrain. And where others considered the desert a mere empire of emptiness, she found high drama—in the desert's infinity of sand, its bestial sun, its wells, its plants, its storms and its demons. She rather imagined the desert to be a rich and generous woman, who loved her as much as the mother she had lost in her infancy. It was, as a Bedouin friend of her father used to call it, "a bountiful orphan child, which was begat from the union of man and Allah and from which comes all earthly existence." Even so, for her, the desert would also stand as irrefutable proof of the fragility of that existence, as the desert's evanescent images and mirages filled her eyes, as they did those of all Allah's creatures, with their illusions. As she grew older and tried ever harder to comprehend its murmured counsel, the desert would take on a different, even larger significance. It became a metaphor for her fate, a fate in which she instinctively trusted and yet which she ultimately saw for what it was: essentially Delphic and irreproachable as the desert itself.

It was her family, especially the companionship of her four brothers, that offered Fatima a human foil to the desert's austere beneficence. She loved her family, every one of them. She loved her older brother Majid for his rectitude and piety, her brother Abdeljelil for his unfailing kindness to her, and her younger brother Dawud for his loyal companionship. But it was her eldest brother Omar who was her favorite. He was the one who first discerned her artistic temperament and, from as early as she could remember, nurtured it. He would read to her endless passages from the Holy Koran, saying, "You must lose yourself in these cadences, Fatima, the exquisiteness of these lines. There's no greater beauty in the world."

Omar's exhortations had the effect of inspiring her to write. At first she composed a few simple stories based on the maxims and parables of the Holy Koran. Then came the verses, mostly extolling Mohammad or his cousin and son-in-law the Holy Imam Ali or their Shiite brethren in ancient Arabia. And from the beginning, words came easily to her. She began to write poetry the way the ancients of Arabia propounded algebraic theorems. She had a special power to concentrate her thoughts, virtually at will, veer them off into worlds of startling profundity but then ultimately bring them back to absolute simplicity. Her father once joked that she seemed to read her Koranic poetry from a copybook engraved on her eyelids. She would pause, become very serious, and then, with surprising gravity, she would pronounce the words as if, at that very moment, Allah himself had made her his vessel.

In spite of the isolation of their hamlet, Kassim, the Shihabi children were educated. They attended a regional primary school in a nearby village, organized under the general auspices of the imam of Najaf to propagate study of the Holy Koran. As each of her brothers turned twelve, their father sent them to attend one of the large middle schools in Najaf. They lived there for months at a time, with their cousin Abdul and his family, returning to Kassim for their vacations and for the month of Ramadan and other holy days. Their stories of the "big city" served as an opening for Fatima to the larger world that lay beyond the circumscribed life of their settlement. Omar in particular would regale her with tales of daily life in Najaf.

Thus, it was hardly surprising that she credited Omar with her need to write about what he would call the "Others." "A writer has to mirror the concerns of ordinary people," he told her. "Force humanity to look itself in the face, so that maybe, one day, one glorious day, it may decide to tidy itself up, make itself right." Many years would pass before the concerns of women became her special domain, but the importance of expressing her ideas on the issues of the day was never lost upon her. Just before Omar departed for America, she crafted a few lines for him, explaining that they were "simply to sum up what you've told me so often, my dear brother." She delivered them in a playful, singsong Arabic, a sort of private parlance she and Omar would sometimes use, her dark eyes flashing with merriment.

"Life, in all its fullness,
Experience, the writer's bread,
Need I but the morsels
Each evening . . .
And a bed."

Omar left to study in America the day after her tenth birthday, a day for her of overwhelming sadness. For years after that, she wrote to him almost every week, enclosing bits of verse with her letters. He typically responded with high praise but also with insights that both surprised and delighted her. As she and her poetry matured, she found that he, more than her other brothers, understood and appreciated her work. Through their letters she drew very close to him, and after he became a teaching fellow and eventually a full professor, she even tried to fathom what it would be like to be his student, in his classes at Columbia University in New York City, where he taught computer science. How she would have liked to visit him, she thought.

The independence of mind that Omar instilled in Fatima was in stark contradiction to the extreme isolation of their home. Some fifty kilometers northwest of Najaf, Kassim was, even to Iraqis who knew the region, exceedingly remote, accessible only by a rutted track that led off the main highway north to Baghdad. It comprised only a few houses, a small herd of camels, and a temperamental well that gave good water most of the time. But as a young girl, in the days when only the occasional Bedouin clan would chance upon their hamlet, Fatima found its seclusion provoking and invigorating. It was a place where she found herself free as the desert blackbird to assert herself and her increasingly self-reliant spirit. She drew from its solitude the life-long lesson that she too could stand alone. Forever after, she would remain a creature apart, removed from the common course of human existence, always observing the "Others" so as to be better able to take them to task.

The only exception she made was for her brothers. With them she played, argued, fought, won, lost and lived—unquestionably as an equal to be reckoned with, a comrade to be vouched for, a confidante to be cherished, and a worthy protagonist to be admired. To them, and to herself, she was just another sibling whose gender was no more relevant than the color of her hair. With them she was blood-bound, and at their side she would engage the world, invincible against its fiends. And so she believed until her father decided they should move to the Holy City of Najaf.

TWO

Najaf, Iraq
1980–1990

The Holy City of Najaf had always captivated her father. When she was eleven and ready to attend middle school, her father decided to take her—to better her chances one day for a worthy suitor, she thought at the time—together with her youngest brother Dawud, from their secluded hamlet and move into the bustling center of the city. He was a clever merchant, and he opened a small shop there, not far from Ali's mosque. He sold gold and silver jewelry, mostly old Bedouin pieces, all intricately designed and beautifully crafted. "It's to distract the pilgrims from their piousness," he would joke, which was about as far as he went with humor about religious matters.

It was in Najaf, when she was twelve, where the two defining events of her childhood took place. First, there was the onset of menstruation, and the dawning that organic differences between her and her brothers ran deep, far deeper than she could have imagined. Then, on top of that, the modalities of her public persona changed. As did almost all Muslim girls in the city, she took the veil, the long black *abayah* draped around the body, concealing its lines in shapeless fabric, and drawn around the face. At first she resisted, mostly because her superabundant spirit resisted definition of any sort—but also out of the simple desire not to be treated differently from her brothers. In the end, her father convinced her that it was a sign of her coming–of–age, to be worn proudly. "It is your invitation to take up the honored role of your mother," he said, "and your mother's mother, in Islamic society. You have an indefinable but sacred element, your womanhood, that you and our Muslim community, together, must safeguard."

After she began to wear the veil, she still engaged her brothers as before (even more so, she told herself, lest they think that her abayah had stilled her spirit as it cloaked her body). But, when she looked back upon those years, it seemed clear that, from that moment, they felt differently about her, and she about them. She remembered how, the first time she wore the abayah, her brother Dawud, with both regret and disdain, said to her, "Ah, Fatima, now you won't be able to play soccer with us any more. You'll be good for nothing but changing diapers." She had been secretly pleased that she had beaten him so severely her father had had to get the doctor. Ever after, the memory of his comment riled her.

Long before her adolescence was over, she came to perceive the subtle irony of draping a black cloth over a sentient being whose very identity was associated with self-expression. After all, it was not simply to hold a mirror to humanity that she wrote, but to change it, if only by degrees. Thus, once having accepted the veil, she soon resolved to renounce it, at least in spirit, and reinvigorate her efforts to observe and engage the Others. Although she obediently heeded her father's advice regarding the abayah, by her mid-teens she found the duality of her veiled and unveiled identities increasingly disturbing. She could hardly reconcile her soaring imagination with the physical confines of a black cloth.

Her marriage to Abdul set for her constraints of a different, invidious kind. She should have threatened to maim herself horribly or follow through with her suicide plan rather than marrying him, she decided soon after the wedding. It was as if the evil eye followed her ever after. But it was not as if she had had a choice. The marriage was her brother Majid's idea. One day, six months after their father's death, he announced he had arranged for her to marry Abdul Shihabi.

"I'm not ready to get married," she cried. "First I want to finish high school. My teachers are pleased with my work, especially my writing. But most of all, I don't want to marry this man."

"Whom else would you marry? Abdul is our first cousin, the son of our father's own brother. How can you possibly refuse him? He naturally has first claim on you."

"Nobody, my brother, nobody has a claim on me. I would rather die than marry him. Besides, he's old, fifty years old, more than three times my age."

"You would be his only wife. I'm sure of that. He never could afford a second wife. And his first wife died two years ago, you know."

"I know, Majid, I know. But he already has five daughters, and four of them are older than I am. He'll just treat me as he would another daughter, not as his wife. It's impossible. I just won't do it. I won't. I'll kill myself before I'd marry him." She threw herself on a divan in their living quarters.

"Look, Fatima, he just married off his youngest daughter. It would be just the two of you, living together. And he's a good man. He's got a good job, a high post in the Najaf constabulary. And he's told me he understands it might be difficult for you. So he's willing to pay a substantial bride price."

She raised her head and shouted, "Don't make me do it, Majid! Our father never would have agreed to it."

"Bah, what do you know our father wanted for you? Without Omar here, I'm the head of this family, and I know what our father and Allah in heaven would want: And that is to have our father's only daughter, eligible, in good health, ready to bear children, and at the proper age for marriage, to marry the man who has the right under law and under Allah to claim her." He paused and stood over her heaving body. "*Khloss.* You will marry Abdul."

Fatima rose from the couch, and without even deigning to glance at her brother, ran upstairs to her room. For an entire week, she refused to leave it, even for meals. Yet, in the end there was nothing she could do. A month before her seventeenth birthday, she was married to her cousin Abdul Shihabi.

From the outset, their home life—such as it was—was scarcely toler-able. Deeply religious, Abdul steeped himself and his new wife in the traditional customs and practices of Islam. He forced her to stay home alone most of the time; the few times she was permitted to go out in public, she had to cover herself—not only with an abayah but also with a veil that covered the lower part of her face. She was one of the few women even in the conservative city of Najaf who still had to wear one.

During their marriage Abdul enjoyed some modicum of success in his work, although he never discussed his work with her. In spite of his age, he rose steadily in the ranks of the police force, as she discerned from small changes in his uniform and his greater liberality with money. Then one day, after three years of marriage, he arrived home puffed up like a rooster and announced that he had received a major promotion. A few days later, she was looking for more writing paper in a drawer when she came across the letter appointing him to a position in Mukhabarat, the Iraqi Secret Service. Devastated, she had to read the letter three times before she could believe the news. How could her own husband, she brooded, enlist in an organization so notorious for its vile practices, its wanton brutality, and its extreme vindictiveness? She began to sink farther into the depths of depression and despair.

Her only solace came from writing poetry. She spent the long days at home lost in her verses. Most of her poems mirrored happy memories from her childhood, but many hinted at darker emotions, and dealt with her unhappy life with Abdul. The rage she felt, she transmuted into a mad creativity. She wrote every moment she could find, always hiding her work from him. He would never have abided her writing poetry, even about her childhood. And he would have murdered her if he discovered that, however subtly, she had written about their relationship, about him.

After a few years of marriage, when she still had not become preg-nant, Abdul began to abuse her, beating and cursing her for her barren-ness. He desperately wanted a son and worried that he would die before he would have a male heir. But she too wanted a child, a child who would be an image of herself, whom she could love and who would love her. She longed for love, which, she now felt, only a child could give her.

At last, one day, after almost four miserable years of marriage, she announced to Abdul that she was pregnant. He was exhilarated. The beatings stopped, although he forbade her to leave their house during her pregnancy. Latifa was born on January 5, 1990. When Abdul received the news that he had yet another daughter, he did not return home that evening. Or the next. Then, two days later, Fatima received a formal letter from the mullah that Abdul had divorced her in the traditional way, repeating three times before witnesses the words "I divorce thee." In Najaf those words virtually condemned her to a life of poverty, social isolation, and despair. When she first read the letter from the mullah, she was consumed with a profound wrath. She vowed she would never let herself or her daughter fall into a similar predicament. And then it occurred to her that in some measure she now was freer than before: There would be no more beatings, and she would be able to pursue her writing.

THREE

Baghdad
1990–1998

After her divorce Fatima had no idea what to do. Abdul threatened to beat her if she and Latifa, whom he continually referred to as "your daughter," remained in what he called "his" house. Fatima had no money of her own, and no one among her few friends would take in a divorced woman, even for a short while. Desperate, she asked Majif, her only brother who still lived in Najaf, to permit them to live with him. He agreed, although grudgingly and only until she could get settled elsewhere. He had by then assumed a teaching position in the Al Hawza al 'Ilmiya, the famous theology institute in Najaf where he had once studied, and he informed her that it would not be proper for a divorced woman, even his own sister, and her baby daughter, his own niece, to live with him.

Thus, Fatima now had to find a permanent residence where she and her daughter would be sheltered and cared for. After a few weeks in Majid's house, she found such a place in the family compound of her brother Abdeljelil in Mansour, a wealthy section of Baghdad, where, now married with two small children, he graciously welcomed them. Four years older than Fatima, Abdeljelil had always adored and protected his sister. After attending the University of Baghdad, he had married the daughter of an Aziz, one of Iraq's most prestigious and wealthiest families. His father-in-law's connections secured him a high-ranking post in the Ministry of the Interior and kept him out of the army. At the age of twenty-five, he was already perceived as a promising younger member of the Baathe party.

When Fatima arrived in Baghdad in the spring of 1990, it was her first time in the capital. She was awed by the huge, modern city, its wide avenues, luxurious hotels, and beautiful bridges traversing the Tigris River. Almost everywhere she turned, there were statues and posters honoring President Saddam Hussein. Most surprising to her was that the majority of women did not wear the abayah. And women walked alone, flouting their chic, Western-style clothes, something that no respectable women would ever do in Najaf. There were many women doctors, lawyers and engineers, and when she visited the university, almost half the students she saw were female. She couldn't believe her eyes.

Abdeljelil helped her and Latifa move into a villa he owned in his family's compound on Zankat al Hudh Street. Then, after a month or so, he told her that she herself could attend the university if she wanted. It was a fantasy she had only entertained in her dreams. Because of her marriage, she hadn't completed high school, but inasmuch as she had proved herself an excellent student and even skipped a level in primary school, she felt she was adequately qualified to enter the university and with extra diligence could catch up. Abdeljelil spoke to the admissions office on her behalf, they agreed to waive the usual prerequisites, and so she applied. He also promised that Latifa would be cared for in his household as if she were his own. Fatima decided to major in journalism, with other courses in literature and English. She entered the University of Baghdad in September 1990, a month after Iraq invaded Kuwait.

The times were grim. With the imposition of the UN sanctions, supplies that normally would have been taken for granted, such as paper, pencils, and books, were scarce or nonexistent. But all the inconveniences were hardly bothersome to her, she was so taken up with her courses. It was not until the night of January 17 of the following year, when the American bombing began, that she began to comprehend the gravity of the situation. She had been preparing a class assignment in her room, in Abdeljelil's villa in Mansour, when the first bomb hit. The sound pounded her ears so forcefully she thought her head would burst. She quickly grabbed Latifa and ran to hide beneath the stairs.

Day after day the bombing continued. Abdeljelil's villa was not far from the center of the city, although well away from any direct hits. She lived in constant fear. There was no electricity or running water. They had to cut the trees in the garden for fuel in order to bake bread and cook what little food they could buy in the nearby souk. By the time the bombing was over, 42 days later, most of the bridges in the city, major government buildings, many factories, the telephone exchange building, the main power plant, and an oil refinery were in ruins.

Then the horror continued—in another guise. Uprisings broke out around Najaf, in the Shiite south, as well as in the Kurdish north, in futile efforts to overthrow Saddam. The government's response was ruthless. Many people were killed, their decaying bodies left abandoned in the streets, relatives of the dead too afraid to bury them. In the ancient city of Kufa, not far from Najaf, Shiite mosques and holy sites were stripped of their treasures, and university buildings and libraries ransacked. The Grand Ayatollah Abdul Qasin al Khoel, whom her father and Majid both knew and admired, and 108 of his followers were arrested in Najaf. The ayatollah died under house arrest, but nothing was ever heard of the fate of the others. She later learned that her favorite cousin, Assia, was among those who had disappeared.

When her classes finally resumed after several months, she was relieved. She had to get her mind off the horrors of the bombings and their aftermath and settle back into some sort of normalcy. She worked hard on her studies. Even though it had been more than five years since she had attended high school in Najaf, she excelled. Language was a special interest for her. She delighted in her native Arabic, how it endowed speech, whether the simplest utterances of vendors in the souk or the most abstruse analyses of verses in the Koran, with a sort of natural eloquence. And, in her English courses, she labored at building her vocabulary and perfecting her accent. She read everything she could lay her hands on, including books and magazines from the West, some that, due to Omar's efforts, a Jordanian trader smuggled to her, others that Abdeljelil spirited into the country, and a few she found on the black market.

Her journalism instructor, Professor Khalifa, took a special interest in her. To foster her creative writing skills, he gave her exercises, such as writing a poem about the timelessness of love, or the character of her father, or an episode from her childhood. "You write verse as the ancients did," he once said to her. "Your poems are grounded, yet lyrical, and always, always pointed."

"I have others, you know, ones I wrote secretly while I was married," she replied hesitantly.

"If you'd like to show them to me, I'd be happy to give you some comments you might find helpful."

"Oh, no. No. They're a little . . . , well, . . . intimate. I wrote them while I was having some hard times with my husband. I wrote them for myself. I never expected to show them to anyone."

"Oh, come now, Fatima. Good poetry is always a gift meant to be shared with others, to help them cope with the pain of existence. What if the great poets all had felt that way? Humanity would have lost one of the only enduring ways that the ages can offer solace to one another. And good poets like yourself have a special responsibility, you know."

"Thank you, professor. Thank you. I'll think about it."

Finally, after weeks more of gentle pressure from Professor Khalifa, she gave in. She brought him her poems—all of them.

He wept when he read them. It was the poetry of a woman who had endured the abuse of a man, often psychological, occasionally physical. She had skirted the jagged edge of depression, but her abundance of spirit and love of life had led her back from the chasm. Her poetry spoke of her profound longing for freedom and of her overwhelming need for self-expression. A pervasive sadness—but also a transcendent hope—infused her work.

"Fatima, your poetry is extraordinary," Professor Khalifa enthused. "It has to be published. I have some connections at the *Nour Review*. Please let me send them at least one poem, just one."

The *Nour Review* was a well-respected women's literary journal in Cairo. Flattered though she was, Fatima at first declined. Professor

Khalifa persisted, and finally Fatima agreed, but only if the piece would be published under a pseudonym or anonymously. The editor replied at once, by return post, asking if there might be other poems by the same poet that she might also like to have published. Fatima carefully screened the hundreds of poems that she had written during her marriage and picked eighty. They were published in an anthology that was received enthusiastically in Arab-speaking countries. It was later translated into French and Spanish.

As a university student, she shed the many evanescent veils that had cloaked her adolescent mind. She read widely—Solzhenitzen's novels of oppression, feminist literature from America, Arthur Koestler, Ayn Rand, Günter Grass, Yukio Mishima, and Nawal El Saadawi. She bared her intellect to a thousand influences. And once again her capacious spirit flew upward like a house bird released from its cage. She pined to open herself to even more of what life had to offer. Since Latifa seemed to be thriving in Abdeljelil's household, Fatima felt free to take a dramatically new direction in her life, by the grace of merciful Allah and, *inshallah*, with his guidance.

Just before her graduation, she asked Professor Khalifa to help her find a paying job. With unemployment in Baghdad running at fifty percent, she knew it would be hard to find work. The professor introduced her to one of his former students, a close friend of Uday Hussein, the President's eldest son. Uday, who controlled almost all media in Iraq and headed the Iraqi Journalists Union, agreed to hire her as a reporter for *Babel*, Iraq's most influential daily newspaper, of which he was the owner and editor-in-chief. She was to report on women's and children's topics. Before she started her job, Professor Khalifa cautioned her to be circumspect about what she wrote. By no means, he warned, should she produce anything critical of the Hussein family.

Until that time her life had been severely constrained—first hemmed in by the natural limits of life in the desert, then by her husband's coercive arrogance and continual abuse, also by her status as a mother in a traditional Muslim community, and most recently by the pressures of her life as a university student coping with a young child. She knew little of the desolation, the abject human suffering, to which her job now exposed her. After the devastation of the war with Iran and the privation caused by the UN sanctions, Iraq's medical and educational systems, once the pride of the Middle East, were now among the worst in the developing world. Thus, it seemed only right to her, at the start, to compose a few stories about the children of Iraq, about the effects of the sanctions upon them, the marked decline in their welfare, and the soaring increase in their death rate.

Addressing in her first article the plummeting enrollment rate in primary schools, she spoke with families forced to send their children out to sell trinkets, to shine shoes, or to beg in the streets in order to earn a few extra dinars to buy bread. One school she visited had only one teacher for the entire school; all the others had quit because they could not survive on their paltry teachers' salaries—which remained fixed even as they were being devoured by inflation. "It is women," she wrote in the article, "who must carry the brunt of the burden during these times of misery. As little girls, they are denied the opportunity of schooling; as adolescents, they are deprived of a future by being married off as young as possible so their families won't have to provide for them; and as mothers, they are given all the responsibility for their households and their children but scarcely any dinars or support from their men." She followed this article with ones on the soaring mortality rates for infants and young children. Soon, women began to approach her on the street or in the souk, distraught women, women furious that their children were dying from what should have been curable diseases. She hardly knew what to say.

With Professor Khalifa's words in mind, she took extreme care in everything she wrote, making sure that her articles reflected no hint of criticism of the government. Indeed, like all the other reporters, she praised the regime continually and, setting aside her chagrin, obsequiously. "Even the poor," she wrote in one article, "those few in Iraq whose mental or physical handicaps make them unemployable, can take pride in the palaces being built in Baghdad, such magnificent edifices in homage to Saddam, the light of our land." How amazed she was, after only six months on the job, when Uday Hussein singled her out for special praise for her reporting. In the next two years she received top awards for journalism from Iraqi panels and a glowing commendation from the Journalists Union. She was vaguely aware that portions of her expository articles, which treated social issues created in part by the UN trade sanctions, were being disseminated worldwide by the Iraqi Ministry of Culture and Information in its ongoing campaign to gain support for the elimination of the sanctions.

Encouraged as she was by the awards she had received, she chose to devote a feature article in *Babel* to a topic that she had been pondering for many months. More than seven years after the bombings, the reconstruction of Baghdad was truly phenomenal. No signs of destruction were apparent. Splendid buildings were being built throughout the city and the country—huge mosques, ornate palaces for Saddam, monumental government buildings. Many more statues and memorials in Saddam's honor were being commissioned—besides the twelve hundred statues of Hussein already in place across the country.

But even as major bridges and many buildings in Baghdad were reconstructed, many within two years, the misery of the people only intensified. As a result of the sanctions, even the most basic necessities, such as baby formula and medicines, could hardly be found anywhere. Once Latifa contracted an ear infection and almost died. It was only through Abdeljelil's contacts that they had gotten antibiotics. Inflation soared. Even by 1995 an egg cost hundreds of times what it had prior to the war. People were selling everything they had—their jewelry, precious family heirlooms, television sets, clothing—in order to feed their families. Cars, if they ran at all, ran on fourth-hand parts and a prayer. University professors moonlighted as taxi drivers. Many professionals fled into exile. Although the middle class was fast disappearing, the wealthy and the privileged were mainly untouched. Only the wealth and position of Abdeljelil and his father-in-law shielded Fatima and her family from much of the misery.

And the plight of the lower and middle classes grew even more dire. The poor desperately needed lower-cost housing. Hospitals, schools, and other public buildings had become so dilapidated as to be dangerous. Ceilings fell in on patients, walls collapsed on families, and whole apartment buildings crumbled beneath their inhabitants. Water purification and sewage treatment systems still had not been repaired, so most Iraqis lacked clean water.

With a calm resolve, Fatima decided to proceed with the article. She carefully organized it so as to highlight those public works projects that needed immediate attention. She labored over the article for days, rewriting parts susceptible to challenge, refining her statements to avoid mistakes in meaning, until she thought the article as neutral as she could possibly make it. In the end, she buried in the text the words, "Some have suggested that if perhaps surplus funds ever remained from the less critical construction projects, they might even be applied to upgrade the fine medical clinics that can be found on the outskirts of Baghdad." She was relieved when the censor passed the piece without comment.

The day after the article appeared in *Babel*, two burly men confronted her as she was leaving her office. They pushed her into the back of a car and drove her to the Al Radhwaniya jail, the detention center for the Feda'iyye Saddam, Uday Hussein's militia force. They took her passport and identity card. She was thrown into a block sandstone room, where she lay on her side, two soldiers standing over her. One pulled a long pole from a rack on the wall and connected it to a wall socket. He poked it against the middle of her spinal column. Pain convulsed her muscles, making her arch her back. She forced her mind to go blank, distancing it from the distress of her body. For many hours, so many she lost track of the time, they interrogated her. "You are worse than the vermin in a charnel house," one menacing soldier said. "You have the stink of sedition all about you," said another. "Don't think we can't read the hidden meaning behind your rosy words. Traitor to our country, you are."

The guards, who rotated every few hours, wouldn't let her escape into unconsciousness. They rested the lit ends of cigarettes on her body, especially on sensitive parts like the soles of her feet, the small of her back and the inside of her thighs. One particularly sadistic guard told her, "You are beautiful, you know," as he held a cigarette against her left cheek, "but we are powerful—and power can always destroy beauty." The wound, which festered, marred her translucent skin. After three days of beatings, denunciations and threats, they were done with her. They threw her battered body into a van and took her to the Al Khatabi Women's Prison.

Al Khatabi Women's Prison faced on Al Farook bin Salim Square, in a poor residential area of the city. A crumbling stone and red brick structure constructed in the early 1950's, it had held hundreds of female criminals, three or four to a cell—most of them the common kind but also some prisoners of conscience and politics and even a few prisoners of war—from the earliest days of Saddam Hussein's regime. Naturally most of the political prisoners in Iraq were men, but an increasing number were women, and Al Khatabi was one of a half-dozen women's prisons in Baghdad where they were kept. Only a few guards were detailed for prisoners no more dangerous than prostitutes, common thieves, and the occasional wife who had murdered her husband in a fit of anger. Political prisoners generally were so cowed by the prison's regimen of torture that they posed no risk of escape.

Obsolete even as its construction was finished, the prison had never been modernized, though it possessed all the paraphernalia needed by a latter-day dictatorship to extract truth, or what passed for truth, from its inmates. No one had ever escaped from the low-security prison—nor had anyone given any thought that a woman would try to escape—though a few women, desperate beyond caring, did try. And it was said that no prisoner ever left Al Khatabi Women's Prison without bearing some conspicuous scar or some permanent disfigurement, a constant reminder of the endless beatings, the diabolical tortures, or, often far worse, the psychological terror visited upon her by the prison's heartless interrogators.

Thus, when she was half-dragged, half-pushed up the cement stairs and through the revolving doors of the old prison building, Fatima naturally assumed that she would die there like so many others.

Nevertheless, she tried to make light of her plight. To pass the time, she wrote poetry on small slips of paper that she hid in her clothing. She felt fortunate to be allowed a visit from Latifa. It would have been quite different, she figured, if she had been held in Al Kelab al Sayba, "Loose Dogs" Prison, where a barbed wire apparatus was kept in place to facilitate the rape of the female prisoners, or even Al Rashad prison, where children of female prisoners were routinely tortured worse than their mothers, who were forced to witness the horror, or the newest women's prison, a fortress of fear being built in the center of Baghdad. And worst of all would have been the notorious Abu Ghraib prison, which held 9,000 male and some female prisoners in space intended for only 1,250. Overcrowding had a simple solution: Prisoners were executed. In 1998, on a single day, 2,000 inmates were killed at Abu Ghraib—to make room for the others.

Her torture at Al Khatabi also could have been worse. It had been trifling—at least relative to what she had heard was inflicted at other prisons, on both men and women. The guards routinely applied electric shocks to sensitive parts of the body or extracted fingernails or beat prisoners on the soles of their feet (a torture called *falaqa*) or hung them from rotating ceiling fans or confined them in narrow, closed coffins for all but a few minutes a day. Army defectors, if caught and sent to prison would have one or both ears cut off; it was another crime to have the disfigurement corrected by plastic surgery, and the wounds often would become infected because of the low standards of medical care available after the UN sanctions. To get a prisoner to confess, other members of the prisoner's family would be arrested, brought to the prison, and tortured as well. Guards would frequently rape the wife in front of the husband. And members of the Hussein family, sometimes Saddam himself, would come to witness the grisly proceedings.

Especially diabolical at Al Khatabi was Mr. Pest—Killer or what prisoners dubbed "the blackbird," a mode of torture that some interrogators applied to recalcitrant prisoners. The plaintive screams of the victim, all but overcome by the breath-stopping, noxious stench of a powerful pesticide sprayed into a burlap bag tied over the head, resembled, it was said, the bird's piteous wail. Many victims survived, although some could barely breathe, and hardly speak, for months afterward because of the trauma to their respiratory systems.

After three months, through her brother Abdeljelil's intercession, Fatima was suddenly released from the prison, without explanation and without charges ever having been lodged against her. Trembling with the after-effects of constant fear and privation, she walked out the prison's revolving doors and down its long stone staircase to the street. When she arrived home, Abdeljelil was waiting for her. He was compassionate but firm. "I was able to save you this time, my sister, only by pleading for mercy from the highest authority, from Saddam himself. Uday was ready to let you die in prison. But even I have my constraints. Think only of yourself, of your dear daughter. The next time I won't be able to intercede on your behalf."

"Dear brother," she had said, "I promise you. I vow never again to write about controversial subjects or direct even the vaguest criticism against Saddam, his family or his regime."

Two days later, she ventured back to *Babel*, to her old desk. She expected to be called to the fourth floor, into Uday Hussein's office, where she would be told to pack her things and go. But nothing happened. Neither did anyone ask where she had spent the last three months. No one dared. They knew better. And the implication of their silence was clear to her. They knew that she would never make the same mistake again. Not if she valued her life. Not if she loved her daughter. Not if . . . and so on and so forth. So she bent her sinewy body, thin from prison, over the wooden table, and, day after day, wrote articles about the most innocuous subjects she could think of. A girl's school in Tarabuls with pen pals in Jordan. A children's bus trip from Al Yarmuk to the Baghdad zoo, recently restored. Special dishes for feasts during the *Id al Fitr* holiday after Ramadan. She would not attract attention. She would pull over herself the veil of anonymity.

She let herself be distracted by the flowering of her daughter's artistry. A child for whom creativity came instinctually, Latifa began to write poetry as her mother had during her disastrous marriage—verses severe and stark, so serious that at times it was hard to imagine that a child had written them. And Latifa's talents took flight in visual form too. With ease she could capture the character of a person in a simple line drawing. Everywhere she went, she carried her notebook so that she could write or sketch what she felt at any particular moment. And always slung over her shoulder was a small radio, of ancient vintage, from which blared music as loud as her mother would permit. She loved all kinds of music and would even compose simple melodies for the piano, of ineffable purity and startling originality.

Latifa helped Fatima regain an intimacy of feeling that she had lost years before. Not since the death of her father had she felt this deep and unconditional love. She had been only sixteen and still living in the family home in Najaf when he died of the lung disease. By then Dawud had been killed in the war, and Majid had been wounded on the Iran–Iraqi battlefront, his right foot blown off in a mine explosion. When he returned from the war, soon after her father's death, Fatima lived in his house for six months until her marriage, but she never again felt the warmth toward him she had felt as a child; his irascible temperament— brought on, she thought, by war wounds and reversals in her father's business—kept her at a distance. Even after she moved to Baghdad to live in Abdeljelil's family compound, she rarely saw Abdeljelil himself, as he was often away on business. And her confidant Omar had stayed in the United States after he received his Ph.D., out of a justified fear of being drafted into the Iraqi army. So, quite naturally, it was her daughter Latifa to whom she gave all the reserves of loving attention she could summon. It was enough to let her forget her past fears and close her eyes to the present-day travesties of life under Saddam.

But after almost a year of half-consciously disregarding facts, facts that would pester her as insistently as flyspecks of sand stuck fast in the eye, she was appalled by a series of horrors—killings of people she knew well, and others she knew about, as well as their families. Still others fled, their lives destroyed, before Saddam's scimitar. To her it was tragedy beyond belief. She could not contain her anger, and the memory of her father's stubbornness nagged at her.

She did not—indeed, could not—hold her tongue for long.

FOUR

Baghdad
1999–2002

In February 1999, the Shiite cleric Grand Ayatollah Muhammad Sadeq al Sadr and his two sons were assassinated in Fatima's home city of Najaf. The government prohibited a funeral in public, but thousands of mourners gathered spontaneously in the streets. The government then attacked them with automatic weapons and armored vehicles, killing hundreds. The writer Hamid al Mukhtar, Fatima's close friend, organized a religious service in his home in bereavement of the ayatollah's death. The police stormed his house, taking him and the other participants away; most were never heard from again. In April 1999 the government tried to prevent worshippers, mainly Shiites, from participating in Friday prayer at a Baghdad mosque. Again, the government used tanks against them and later exiled 4,000 Shiite families from Baghdad. Over that summer, hundreds of followers of Ayatollah al Sadr were arrested, tortured, and some killed. Among them were students at Al Hawza al 'Ilmiya, the theology institute in Najaf where Majid had studied and now taught.

In those days Fatima considered herself a devout Muslim. Although she had scant sympathy for the more extremist elements in her *umma* or community, as a Shiite Muslim she felt as if the incidents in Najaf were directed at her personally. The Shiites were the largest religious group in Iraq, constituting slightly over 60 percent of the population, versus about 35 percent for the Sunni Muslims. However, it was obvious to her that the killings and other horrors were directed at Shiites.

The split between Shiites and Sunnis was undeniable, which she had always known. But it was ironic, she felt, that the two groups were indistinguishable by race, by nationality, or by any other distinctions that commonly divide peoples. The division had started in the seventh century purely over a question of power: who was the legitimate fourth successor to the Prophet Muhammad? The Shiite Muslims recognized Ali, Muhammad's cousin and son-in-law, while the Sunni Muslims thought that the successor should be elected and so chose Mu'awiyah, the governor of Syria, and his successors. Even more ironic, Fatima felt, was how for centuries the Sunnis had dominated the government and the economy— even though most people in Iraq were Shiite. It was undeniable that the two sects had worked together in the 1920's to establish Iraq as an independent country in 1932. Many Shiites even joined the Baathe party, and Shiites formed the bulk of the army in the Iran–Iraq War. But for 20 years, and particularly in the last few years, the government had tried to stifle the Shiite clerics. In light of all this, as Fatima turned out pabulum for *Babel*'s readership, she fumed at the systematic campaign of repression that the regime was perpetrating on the Shiite community and its leadership.

With this new violence she began to listen in earnest. She listened to stories of political persecution, especially persecution directed against women. A female obstetrician whom she had consulted on medical stories for *Babel* was beheaded on charges of prostitution. The charges were quite obviously fabricated: as was widely known, the doctor had been investigating corruption in the medical system. A portion of the country's supply of medicine, already scarce, the doctor had learned, was being diverted by corrupt government officials—either for their own personal use or for sale on the black market. In this onslaught of terrorism directed against women, Feda'iyye Saddam, Uday Hussein's militia, beheaded dozens of other women—all without judicial process. One woman, whose husband had escaped abroad, was beheaded on the street in front of her children and mother-in-law, who were then taken away by the authorities and vanished into the archipelago.

Fatima felt an overwhelming anger surge within her, most of it now directed at Saddam Hussein himself. What else—what new horror against humanity—was this monster capable of? she asked herself. Although Saddam was starting to age, his two sons were as malevolent as their father, and one of them would likely assume power when his father died. What sort of future did this promise for her daughter? Fatima felt power-less. Exile was impossible, as she could not—at least not legally—leave the country. Journalists were restricted from traveling abroad without special permission, which she certainly wouldn't get after time in prison. Also, her passport had been seized. But in any case, she worried that if she left Iraq, the government might attempt to hold Latifa as a guarantee of Fatima's good conduct abroad. Only her brother's high position in the Ministry gave them the assurance that that the responsible functionary could be induced to look the other way.

The final and decisive tragedy was the disappearance of her dear friend, Professor Khalifa. In October 1999 he decided that it would be best to leave the country. He had declined Uday Hussein's disingenuous request that he take over the editorship of a government magazine. Knowing what Uday's wrath could mean, the professor requested permis-sion to travel abroad. Uday assured him that there would be no problem. Professor Khalifa applied for an exit visa and, with funds from his mort-gaged house, posted the expensive bond required. On the Iraqi side of the border with Jordan, he was arrested. As so many others, he disappeared, and his family was forced to vacate their house.

She knew that she had to do something. Otherwise, she could never live with herself. The only weapon she had was her pen. Through friends, she found a contact in the Shiite underground organization called SCIRI, the Supreme Council for the Islamic Revolution in Iraq. She knew him only as "Ibrahim." "With your contacts in education, medicine, the Shiite community, and among women," he told her, "you would be an invalu-able ally in getting the real story about Iraq to the outside world. Any report you write, I'll get to Iraq Press, an independent news agency based in London."

"I have to be careful. I have a daughter, you know. I could get my brother in trouble too." She was mindful of Abdeljelil's earlier words of warning.

"The reports would be anonymous. No one will know. Look, Fatima, you have to do it—for yourself, for your daughter, and for the future of the people of Iraq."

She hardly needed convincing. Even if something happened to her, she rationalized, Abdeljelil's privileged position surely would protect him, his family, and Latifa. So she began to write detailed accounts of what she heard and saw in her travels as a benign reporter of matters of interest to women and children. For two years her clandestine mission was to get word to the rest of the world about what was really happening in her country.

Then, a week ago Friday after she had returned from the mosque, a slight woman, wearing a brown chador that all but covered her face, was waiting as she approached their front gate on Zankat al Hudh. She immediately recognized the woman, whom she had interviewed in early August at a health clinic in the Al Kazimiyah district, a Baghdad suburb. The woman seemed agitated, beside herself, glancing up and down the street.

"I need to speak with you," she said, the fear of a beaten dog in her eyes.

Without thinking, Fatima pushed open the gate, and the two women practically tripped over each other as they entered the courtyard in front of her family's villas. At the foot of the stairs to the villa where Abdeljelil lived with his family, his daughter Aisha was arranging her playthings. Fatima waved at her, asking, "Is your father home yet?"

"No, father go take plane. Mother go to souk. She come back soon."

Fatima breathed a sigh of relief. "I live over there," she whispered, pointing to the other villa, "with my daughter Latifa. Let's go inside." She guided the woman up the stairs to the portico. Then she unlocked the door and bade the woman to enter.

When they came into the main salon, she called for Latifa, but there was no answer. "My daughter must be out, playing with her friends," she said, trying to put the woman at ease. "May I offer you some tea, some dates perhaps?"

"No, no thank you. I have just a few minutes, and then I must go."

"Please have a seat. How can I be of service to you?" They sat on a small sofa well away from a window facing on the courtyard.

"Madame, you must excuse me. You will remember me from the clinic perhaps. You were so kind that day to listen to all of us. About our problems I mean."

"Certainly, I remember you very well. Your husband was sick, and your family had no money to care for him. I couldn't write an article about him. The government would not have been happy, and I could have gotten into a lot of trouble."

"I'm sorry for that, but that is not why I have come."

"Go on."

"I could not tell you that day, but my dear husband was very, very sick. Only ten days ago he died a horrible, painful death. Without medication. Before my eyes. May merciful Allah care for him now." The woman's eyes teared, and she bowed her head in her sorrow. After a minute she composed herself, drew herself up, straightened her shoulders, then gazed solemnly into Fatima's eyes.

"My husband had been a professor of physics at the University of Baghdad. In April Saddam sent him to work at a secret laboratory just north of the city. Deep underground it was. Only a handful of people in all of Iraq knew about it. Saddam told them that if anyone else ever found out about it, they would all be murdered, along with every member of their family, and their family's family. To protect me, for a long time my husband wouldn't tell me what sort of work he did. It was only later, after an accident at the laboratory, that he told me."

"What sort of laboratory was it?"

"He and his three research assistants from the university were working to develop . . . what did my husband call it? Oh, yes, a 'dirty' . . . 'dirty bomb.'"

"What is a 'dirty bomb'?"

"It's a conventional bomb, but it has some sort of nuclear material in it. When the bomb explodes, it scatters the nuclear material—contaminating the site and naturally all the people around it."

"How could Saddam get his hands on nuclear material, with the weapons inspectors scouring the country?"

She paused and pursed her lips. "My husband said the laboratory tried to extract it from radioactive isotopes in medical equipment—like x-ray machines. He said the bomb itself was to be small, to fit inside a briefcase. The inspectors would never have found it."

"Of course, Saddam has been telling everyone that we're not developing such weapons."

"That, and flying carpets can take you to the moon." The woman managed a sardonic smile. "Saddam himself supervised their work. He wanted the bomb, he said, to use in case our country was ever attacked by our enemies."

"Look what he did to the Kurds. He'd stop at nothing."

"Yes, I know. My husband's mother was Kurdish."

"What happened to your husband then?"

"Sometime in late June, Saddam came to the plant. He arrived suddenly and was in a great anger. He gathered my husband and his staff in the laboratory's conference room. For over an hour he ranted at them, becoming more and more abusive and insulting. He claimed that they were incompetent, that they were traitors, that they had deliberately subverted the project's mission and on and on. Finally he told them that unless the work was finished by such and such a date—I think it was August 15—he would simply kill them all as well as their families, that he personally would force down their throats the radioactive material they were using for the bomb."

"So that's what happened to your husband?"

"Not exactly. But what happened was just as bad. My husband worked night and day for weeks, without rest. I brought all his food to him, to a gas station about a kilometer from the laboratory. He wasn't supposed to tell me, he could have been killed for it, but their facility was underground, far beneath an ordinary school building, its entrance cleverly concealed beneath a smelly toilet in the basement, with access through a badger hole in the floor. Saddam kept him and the others as virtual prisoners there, permitting them to leave for just fifteen minutes each day, at 8:00 p.m., so their families could give them provisions for the next day. Then one time, in late July, as I was delivering the meals, the soldier guarding my husband was distracted by something—some commotion on the street, I think it was—and my husband whispered to me that, on account of their haste, one of his assistants had become sloppy. The day before, the radioactive substances—in concentrated form—had leaked from certain equipment. My husband seemed very worried, fearful even.

"Soon after that, he began to develop skin problems. And his health began to deteriorate. Very seriously. His hair fell out. He became jaundiced. Hemorrhages all over his body. In early August, just after I met you, he was allowed to leave the laboratory to see a doctor. But it was too late. Just before he died, he told me he was sick from radiation." She paused and placed her head in her hands.

"Have you tried to find out what happened at the laboratory?"

The woman raised her head. "My husband thought that at least one of his assistants might have been poisoned by the radiation as he was. I've tried to reach the wife of one of the assistants, but I couldn't. No one answers their phone, and when I went to their house, no one came to the door. Who knows what Saddam might have done out of his vindictiveness? I've moved into my brother's house, tried to stay out of sight. You see, I too have a young daughter." The woman hesitated, as if weighing her words.

"I see," Fatima responded, holding herself in check. She suspected the woman knew she didn't have a chance. Better at least to get the word to a sympathetic audience.

The woman reached into the folds of her dress, unhooked a strap, and drew forth a cloth satchel she had concealed against her body. "Before my husband died, he gave me these." She held out a sheaf of what appeared to be charts, drawings, and diagrams of technical equipment. "He made me promise that I would give these papers to someone who could tell people what happened to him. I could only think of you."

"Give me them, then. But say nothing to anyone that you have come to see me. I will do what I can."

"You are a courageous woman, Mrs. Shihabi."

"You are braver still," Fatima replied. "You could have stayed silent, but you have done something very important, something that humanity will long remember. And now you must go home and not think of this any more. I will do what is necessary."

The woman took her leave, but not before handing Fatima a slip of paper on which the woman had written her telephone number, "in case," she said, "you have further questions for me."

Fatima then returned to the main salon of the villa. She picked up the parcel of documents and riffled through them. There were diagrams, drawings, technical notes, a few photographs of equipment, all meaningless to her. Resting them in the crook of her arm, she went over to the front window of the villa. She stared blankly through the grille of the front gate, out across the dusty, littered stretch of Zankat al Hudh Street, to the mud walls that encased the abodes beyond.

She had been right to take them. The papers were the woman's only hope that her husband's death was not without some larger significance. And yet, Fatima knew she could not keep them. Not without jeopardizing everything in her own life that was dear to her. If the house were searched, the papers would surely be found. If she gave them to Ibrahim or even told him about them, they might both be arrested. And if she were to leave Iraq, she would have to leave them behind, lest they be found on her person en route. In any event, she and almost certainly Latifa would be murdered—if not on the spot, then after gruesome torture. In the highly charged environment of allegations, accusations, and threats by the Americans against Saddam Hussein, the papers were far too dangerous for her—or anyone for that matter—to keep.

She took some matches from the kitchen and went out into the garden. She knelt before a small brazier with a rusty grill, once used for cooking, and crushed the papers, then stuffed them into the opening for fuel. The fire caught on the first try, and she waited until the documents were entirely consumed. She then carefully stirred the embers, ensuring that there were no unburned spots. After glancing around her to be sure she had not been observed, she went back inside. She locked the door and peered out, through the curtains, at the small mound of ash. She had an unsettling premonition that from this day on, in spite of her precautions, the world would never again be a safe place for her or her daughter.

A few days later, she noticed that when she returned from her morning visit to the souk, the door to her bedroom was ajar. She was sure that she had closed the door before she left. She caught a faint whiff of cheap Indian cologne in the air of the salon, of the same kind Abdul used to wear. It could have been a servant, she thought. But it was good that she had destroyed the papers that the woman brought her. Then she remembered that the woman had left her telephone number.

She tried the number several times. Each time, the message was the same. The number had been disconnected.

The following day she arranged to see Ibrahim, her contact with the underground, to find out if she was about to be picked up by Mukhabarat. They met in a shadowed alley off Wazeer Street. "I'll check with my friend," he replied a bit cryptically, "and one of our members will alert you by phone if there is any danger. Remember: If you answer the phone, there is silence on the other end, and the phone clicks dead, be prepared. If this is followed by two single rings, with a pause in between, that will mean that your name has been placed on the arrest list. At least you'll have a few days to disappear. But, don't forget, if the phone rings twice on the third call, it will mean that Mukhabarat has penetrated our cell, that I myself have been arrested, and that you'll have to flee at once. An hour after the phone rings, no more no less, you must be at the Al Taeshi Apothecary on Wazeer Street, near the souk. You'll ask for Khalid." He paused to let her register the words. "Clear?"

"Yes, very clear. Thank you, Ibrahim."

"Good luck," he answered brusquely, then abruptly departed, leaving her alone in the shadows.

So when the phone rang, that morning of September 7, she was by no means taken aback. She knew at once what she had to do.

FIVE

Sahra al Hijarah Desert, Iraq
Sunday, Sept. 8, 2002

The whine of the trucks filled Fatima's ears even as the pungent odor of their exhaust filled her nostrils. The vehicles were close by, on the dune ridge just above her, silhouetted against the luminous night sky. She raised herself to get a better look at them. Sanctions–busters, she thought. Laden with appliances, clothing, foodstuffs, the necessities for daily life— even a few luxuries, like cosmetics. Their destination: the souks of southern Iraq. Probably Najaf too.

She stood now, fully roused, as the caravan sped away over the horizon. Suddenly the desert was as empty as before—and silent except for Khalid's murmuring in his sleep. It was like the old days. Before Baghdad. Even before Najaf. Those simple days when she felt the desert to be her real home. Even as the nomadic Bedouin did.

She heard a rasp as Khalid, fidgeting in his sleep, scraped his sandal over the shaled wall of the wadi. She wished that she could have slept as soundly. She felt sore and exhausted from their punishing ride in Khalid's dilapidated Fiat, a sputtering survivor of innumerable crashes, all the way from Baghdad to Najaf, 100 miles to the south, then off the highway on to a remote outpost where they took food and water. Exactly as Khalid had assured her, they had found there an aged herder who brought them on horseback to a point where they could now proceed on foot. "It's unwise," he counseled, "to get too close to the border with animals, as helicopters do sometimes pass overhead on patrol. It's a lot easier for you or me to hide behind a rock someplace than an uncooperative horse. And when you approach the border, you should lay low during the day and travel only at night." They still had a long trek ahead of them on foot through the southern Iraqi desert.

She needed more sleep, but it was out of the question. She quietly edged down the wadi's creased and crevassed center, strewn with rocks and occasional boulders, where waters from rare desert rainstorms coursed during other seasons. After a short distance, rivulets of sand ran from the wadi into the scrub brush that stretched into the darkness. All the way to the Saudi border, she thought. Toward Omar. Toward freedom and her new life. She climbed the gentle slope of shale to get a better view of the terrain around them.

Once atop the crest of the sandy escarpment, she turned toward the east, where the blue–pink blush of dawn had already begun to backlight the night sky. On the fine line of the horizon, she could barely make out the dark vortex of the dust and diesel exhaust of the trucks as they raced northeast. She let her eyes roam the entire reach of the night sky, the boundless desert sky that she so loved and that she would so miss in her new life in the West. For a while, she stood, erect and alone, on the escarpment, letting the swelling glow of dawn sweep over her, engulfing the somber sea of darkness and making way for the new day. She waited until the first flash of sunlight broke the horizon, then turned to descend back into the wadi. If Khalid had awakened, he would be worried about her.

She stopped as she heard a faint drone in the silence of the desert. At first, she thought it might be the strident whine of the trucks reverberating across the kilometers of vacant desert, but the hum of these machines seemed lower in pitch. Then she saw them. Two black specks in the distance, in the roseate sky north of the sun.

Fatima scrambled down the incline, scraping the back of her sandaled foot on the shale. She ran down the center of the wadi, now suffused by dawn light, until she saw the spot where they had slept. A few meters away, Khalid knelt in his dawn prayers, his head bowed, forehead pressed against the sandy shale.

"Khalid . . . Khalid. Quickly, come. We've got to go—we have to hide somewhere. They're following us. Two helicopters. They're coming this way."

Khalid slowly raised his head and looked at her. "No, it's impossible. It's just your imagination, Fatima. It's playing tricks on you. I was careful to make sure we were not followed from Baghdad."

"If they came to pick me up yesterday, they could guess pretty easily that I'd try to get out through Najaf and head across the desert."

"You are right." Khalid cocked his head in the direction of the sound. "I think I hear something too."

"*Inshallah*, they'll never see us in this terrain. But they might suspect that we'd try to hide in a wadi like this one."

"Farther along the wadi narrows. It's only a few meters across. We're too exposed here."

Khalid pulled himself up, and they began to run up the streambed. After only a few meters, the raspy *clack-clack* of a helicopter assailed their eardrums as it swooped over the wadi's opposite end. They moved quickly, Fatima in the lead, careful not to stumble in the rock-strewn terrain. The wadi turned a degree away from the sun, and suddenly they were in shadow.

"Make yourself look like a boulder," Fatima said, pushing Khalid onto his knees. It was a trick she had learned from her childhood games. She pulled his upper garment over his head, drew her abayah from her shoulders, and spread it over the rest of his body. She spotted a darker depression in the wadi's sloped wall and backed herself into it, her head beside an outcropping of shale, her black dress spread out so as to conceal the form of her body, her right arm aligned along the shadow cast by the shale, her left arm angled across her face, with the sleeve covering most of it, leaving one eye free to look out.

She watched the mechanical beast slowly proceed up the streambed. The pilot was taking his time, picking his way, knowing that any shadow made by the rising sun might well hide the traitors he was assigned to capture and, if necessary, kill. When the helicopter reached the bend in the wadi, it hesitated for an instant. She saw the uniformed pilot peer into the muted landscape, his eyes adjusting to the changing light. The incessant, reverberating din from the twirling blades pounded in her ears, frightening her. A man clothed in a dark suit and sitting in the co-pilot seat gestured in her direction, and the chopper edged forward, meter by meter, stopping once or twice as the pilot studied a particular shape or shadow.

When the thundering craft reached their hiding place, it halted directly opposite them, then swerved slightly as the pilot glanced farther up the wadi toward the other helicopter, which had suddenly appeared in the sky above the ridge where the trucks had passed. She saw the man in the dark suit motion to the pilot and mouth a few words to him. Then, turning his head toward her, the man seemed to rest his eyes on her. He had a Saddam-style mustache and dark eyes. His one distinguishing feature was an odd wrinkle—the flesh was mangled as if he had once been struck with a crude weapon like a scythe or an ax—which dominated the center of his forehead. His bulky frame seemed oddly out of place, almost filling the cockpit of the small craft.

She froze, not even letting herself blink, for fear she would attract the attention of this man. Her eyes were riveted on his, almost of their own accord. The gaze of a woman, she thought. "A woman's gaze can destroy a man," Majid always used to say. "With it she can annihilate his spirit." She concentrated on keeping still, making herself look like a shadow, merging into the wadi's crumbling wall. She took a shallow breath and held it.

She should have cautioned Khalid not to budge. Anyway, he would have to know. He was nobody's fool. She felt a tickle in her right ear. A beetle, she surmised, searching for a warm refuge from the coolness still left from the desert night. It nuzzled her with its pincers, and she repressed an insane demand from her body to scratch at it. She let her breath out slowly, praying that the insect would leave to seek sanctuary elsewhere.

After seconds that seemed minutes, the man's eyes moved along to other shadows in the wadi, obviously hunting for anything that moved in the stillness of the scene. Finally the chopper lumbered onward, farther up along the streambed, finally joining its partner on the horizon. In a flash, they were gone from sight.

Fatima stood, shaking the insect from its sweet repose in the hollow of her ear. She stretched and looked across the rock-strewn center of the wadi.

"Khalid, it's okay. They've gone."

"Don't be so sure," he retorted, readjusting his garments and handing the abayah back to her. "I think they *did* suspect we were here. We'll have to wait until dark to go on. It's too dangerous in the open desert."

They walked farther up the streambed where it narrowed, then sat down under a ledge, where they were sheltered from the rays of the sun and any more prying eyes in the sky.

"Praise Allah, they won't come back," Fatima said.

"I have seen Mukhabarat work this way before. They never give up. They know the consequences if they disappoint those who sent them."

"You probably know them pretty well. How long have you been in the opposition movement?"

"Not so very long. I had a brother who was killed by Uday. It was for no reason. Sport, really. My brother was a tanner. He wasn't political, if you know what I mean."

"I do," she said wistfully. "I wasn't either, at first. But then I became infuriated by where our country was going, where Saddam was taking it. And like so many others, at first I tried to ignore it. Never to speak of it. Not even to think of it. Finally, I could no longer remain silent."

"I read your articles in *Babel*. When you first started writing, you were among the few to allude to social problems that the rest of us knew about but didn't discuss, even within our own families. Why did you stop?"

"It was too hard for me . . . , just too hard," she added shaking her head. "I had to stop writing that type of article although I continued to protest in other ways. I had to . . . ." Her bloodshot eyes, sunken in weariness and strain, suddenly locked on his. "Look, Khalid, I am no hero. No hero. Do you understand?" He nodded mutely. "I have a daughter," she went on. "I have a daughter, dearer to me than anything . . . even life itself. And with all my love, with every bone in my body, I just want her to have a better life than the one I've had. That's all." Her eyes now brimming with tears, she paused, looking across the rock-strewn floor of the wadi as the sun, now rising in the sky, caused heat waves to shimmer off the sand. Khalid knew well enough to remain silent.

"I'll send for her when I get to Canada," she said, to no one in particular. She closed her eyes abruptly, ending their conversation.

They remained in the shadow of the ledge, dozing intermittently and guarding their strength for what challenges lay ahead. Around midday, Khalid drew from his satchel a large round of bread he had purchased in Najaf, a few dates he had carried from Baghdad, and a small flagon of water.

"We've come a long way already," Khalid said, breaking the silence that had settled over them.

"That's true," Fatima replied, grateful for the relief of conversation. "I was glad to see Najaf yesterday, if even for a short time. It's somehow fitting that I'd leave for the West from such a holy place. But I was surprised to see many fewer pilgrims than I remember. When I was a child, there were throngs of pilgrims, thousands and thousands of them, day after day, gathered around Holy Ali's mausoleum. Naturally we all thought that since he was the son-in-law and cousin of the Prophet, we were all a lot more devout than the Sunnis in Baghdad."

"Najaf is no different from the rest of Iraq, though," Khalid countered. "Even in traditional Najaf, things have changed. Where I come from, Mosul, some of us don't keep the fast of Ramadan. At least not during the heat of summer. Then others, like my friend Jamshied Mussli, won't own anything green, out of respect for the Holy Prophet's favorite color."

"He sounds like my brother Majid. He studied at Al Hawza al 'Ilmiya. Believe me, when he was admitted to the institute, my father thrust out his chest more proudly than I'd ever seen. Of course, I studied the Holy Koran too, although not as intensely as Majid. I guess we were all a lot more conscientious in those days."

"Oh, before I forget," Khalid interrupted. "I have something for you. I hope you like it." He reached into his satchel and drew out a small, official-looking pamphlet. "It's your new passport."

She took it, turning it over several times in her hands before she opened it. "We made it specially for you," Khalid went on.

"And how did you do that?" she asked.

"It's a simple process," he answered. "An Iraqi who had already been granted citizenship in another country, shall we say South Africa, Canada or France, is asked to 'lose' his new passport. For the local immigration authorities, whether the passport was actually 'lost' is always a question of proof. Who's to say whether the passport is really lost or not? And once it's—shall I say—'lost,' it can easily be manipulated by one skilled in these matters—a photo easily substituted, a single numerical character subtly altered, a name slightly adjusted—just enough to escape detection by any but the keenest eyes."

"You have done your work well," she said appreciatively, as she studied the slightly worn Canadian passport, bearing her new name "Aisha Qureshi" and her photo.

"It should be enough to get you past the immigration authorities in Saudi Arabia and onto the plane to Munich. After that, it's simply a matter of getting through Munich to Montreal. And getting into Canada isn't that hard. We've done this same trick a few times before," he reassured her, his face breaking into a generous grin. "By the way, I'll be traveling with you as far as Munich as your brother, since the Saudi regulations don't allow women to travel alone. And here are a few American dollars in case you need them." He handed her a small sheaf of green banknotes. "Most shopkeepers will take them, even if they prefer local currency."

"I shall never forget what you're doing for me," she said earnestly.

Toward late afternoon they walked back down the wadi, their eyes scanning the horizon. Once Fatima thought that she heard the helicopters again, but she couldn't be sure. They hurried back to their refuge under the ledge, waiting and watching, the glint of sunlight abating. Then, all at once, the desert night descended upon them, as if the wind had carried it on its wings. Khalid barely had time to kneel toward the southwest in the direction of Mecca.

After a few minutes, he stood and strode to the center of the wadi. "Praise Allah. It's after eight o'clock. Let's go. At once. We must reach the Saudi border before dawn. Now, hurry."

They moved quickly up the shale wall of the wadi and on out into the scrub brush of the desert. Toward a new day, she thought. The start of the rest of her life.

SIX

It was a full three hours before her flight when Fatima Shihabi strode confidently into the lobby of Riyadh's King Khalid International Airport. In the crook of her right arm, she carried the small satchel she had brought from Baghdad, into which she had placed her tickets, her money and her doctored Canadian passport. She was dressed conservatively, in a navy silk suit she had found in a shop near the airport, her black headscarf drawn taut around her face. The model of a Muslim businesswoman or professional from Canada, she thought. From all appearances—his dark suit, his quiet demeanor and his self-assured bearing, her male companion could have been either her husband or her brother. If they didn't look like refugees, nobody would challenge them. With the typically casual style of Arab functionaries, Saudi immigration officials wouldn't ask questions.

The two travelers secured their boarding cards and, after a respectable wait in the lounge, approached the immigration counter. Fatima, having decided that any slight hesitancy in her manner could be suspect, affected an almost brazen hauteur. Her eyes, locking with those of the immigration official, dared him to say something. He blinked before she did and handed back her Canadian passport. After an instant, he waved them on. They strode out of the cinder block building onto the tarmac, into a sun so strong it seemed to pierce their clothes. The stink of the baking tarmac filled her nostrils. They took their positions in the queue waiting to board the plane.

Surely it wouldn't be the last time that the featureless face of officialdom would eye her on her long journey, she thought. She had seen those
eyes before, ogling her father, who had stared back at them in mulish
defiance. It was a few years after her family had moved to Najaf, when
she was all of fifteen years old. Her father was suffering from a long and
terrible lung illness. Their mullah, Ayatollah al Khoel, in a flourish of
Muslim generosity, had paid for her father to travel from Najaf to London for the necessary treatment. She accompanied her father, half pushing and pulling him through Gatwick Airport and its formalities. The
British immigration officer practically spat on the two of them, then
disdainfully asked her father: "Why you no speak English?" Believing that
her father had not understood, she drew on the little English she had
learned in middle school and tried to translate for him. He weighed her
words a few moments. Then he roused himself, his eyes glinting. With
exquisite timing, and with a credible imitation of an upper-crust English
accent she assumed he had picked up from his customers, he practically
shouted at the officer: "And you, sir"—fixing him with a fierce expression—"why you no speak Arabic?" She stifled a smile as the pompous
Brit harrumphed, then shoved their papers back at them. She would never
forget how her father had found the reserves of strength within him to
make the gesture. "Be strong as your father," she would tell herself, when
times became difficult for her. Only later would she come to understand
how much she needed his Bedouin toughness and tenacity.

Fatima glanced down at the passport Khalid had given her, with her
new identity. Turning toward him, she sent him the hint of a smile. So far,
things had gone well in her journey to the West. Perhaps a bit too well,
she mused. Even though they had barely evaded their pursuers, it had
been wise of SCIRI to have her flee to the border through the southern
part of the country. If they had simply driven west from Baghdad to
Amman, they might never have reached the border, with all the spying
eyes on the busy highway. Besides, the south was her land, her one true
home, the country of the desert Shiites. And once again the desert had
bestowed its beneficence on her.

As she stood in the hellacious sun on the oozing tar, with the plane to Munich, her passage to freedom, just meters away, she took a long, deep breath. She told herself not to worry. She soon would have a new life—in a new country. She would soon be free of Saddamland, extricated from Saddam's web of fear, out of the suffocating life as a writer in Iraq, stepping off the plane in Montreal into a fresh existence. She would call Omar when she got to the airport. He'd be surprised to hear her voice on the phone. How pleased he would be to know that she had finally left Iraq! Surely he would come at once from New York, greet her with his warm, caring smile, and help her get settled in her new life in Canada.

A gentle tug at her arm drew her from her reverie. Khalid whispered, "Fatima, I'll be right back. I have a little urgency."

"No problem," she said without hesitation. Men were like that, she thought. Khalid scurried off in the direction of the waiting room, where she had seen a sign for a toilet.

A young family was just ahead of her in the queue, mother enveloped by her chador, husband attired in a beige *thobe* matched by the black-roped *ghutra* atop his head. It was a traditional mode of attire that even in the modern age seemed majestic . . . and intimidating. The man held the hands of two small children, fussing in the heat. The unruly boy, lost in a tantrum, just would not stand up. As the line edged forward, the mother turned and muttered to the child in a language Fatima thought might be Farsi. While their mode of dress looked Saudi, they must be Iranians, she surmised, Shiites like herself, escaping death too. She had barely finished the thought when two Saudi security guards, wielding semiautomatic weapons, were upon them. "Give us your papers," the one said. After a moment, he motioned the family back to the reception area. It was the officer she had bested earlier. As they passed, he glanced at her. This time, she quickly averted her eyes, studying her boarding card as if to check her seat location.

"You—you come too," he said to her without emotion.

The soldiers led the group back toward the waiting room. As they went in, they passed Khalid hurrying back to the queue. Catching his eye, she shook her head as if to warn him to ignore them. There was nothing that he could do. Perhaps they wouldn't bother him. The soldiers led her and the Iranian family through the waiting room, through the lobby of the airport, and out the main entrance. There a bus was waiting. The soldiers shoved them onto it, then got on board. Almost at once, it departed, taking them to a low-lying, cinder block building well away from the main airport terminal. A sentry stood at its heavy metal gate, brandishing an automatic weapon, which he employed to wave them through. When they arrived inside, Fatima saw a long corridor in front of her, down the spine of the building, with nondescript doors running its length, each door mounted with a small glass window through which those inside could be observed. Her escorts opened the third door, pushed her into the room, then slammed the door shut with a finality that made her shiver. The room, whose whitewashed walls had long ago corroded to a dingy gray, was bare except for a wooden chair at its center and a naked bulb hanging from a black cable above it. The stink of urine permeated the air, and she noticed a bucket in a corner by the door.

Hours went by without any contact with the soldiers, although she would occasionally hear the thud of their boots in the corridor. Once she even entertained the notion that they had forgotten about her, but then she felt sure that someone, in some office in some ministry, or even a higher authority, had been called upon to decide what to do with her. In the meantime she waited, expectantly, not daring to surmise what was about to happen to her.

Finally, the soldiers returned. She stood almost automatically, more out of desire to affirm her dignity than from any sort of respect. "Sit down," the senior officer said, forcing her into the latticed back of the chair. He drew a pair of handcuffs from his belt, roughly pulled her arms behind the chair, and locked the cuffs so tightly that they seemed to cut into her wrists. She closed her eyes and imagined she was dreaming.

The back of a bony hand sporting a heavy metal ring smashed against her face. The brutal crunch of the ring against her cheekbone stunned her. Still, her eyes glinted fiercely as they fell on the sneering face of the soldier standing over her.

"Pay attention, Madame Qureshi, if that is your name. We know you are Iraqi," he said in a menacing whisper. "Tell us why you were going to Montreal."

"I am a writer, nothing more. I am simply trying to leave Iraq to live in Canada."

The second soldier rushed at her. "Madame Qureshi or should I say, Madame Shihabi, you're not a Canadian citizen. Do you think we are stupid?" This time it was a shout of rage. He brought the back of his hand again across her face, lower this time, and she felt blood trickle from her lip down her chin. "We already know that you have left Iraq. But we also know that you have certain information you are bringing to the Americans. You know what we are talking about. Admit it, and we will let you go. You can go where you want."

"I am a writer. I write poetry. I am not political." She was proud, un-intimidated. She had faced worse before. From somewhere outside the room, down the corridor, she heard a door slam shut—or the muffled thud of a gunshot, she wasn't sure.

A third soldier came into the room. He was apparently the supervisor of the others. With a flick of his wrist, he motioned them away. He pulled a pack of Camels from his vest pocket and lit one. He paused to take a few puffs. "We're going to send you back to Iraq anyway. They'll know how to deal with you."

"They will kill me." She glared at him.

"Why would they want to kill you if you are just a writer? Do you know something that they wouldn't want you to know? Tell us. Tell us, Madame Shihabi." He suddenly struck her forehead with a wooden baton. Blood streamed over her eye, down her cheek.

"I know nothing." She tasted blood at the corner of her mouth.

"They will find out just what you know," he said, a cruel smile curving his lips. "You will feel Saddam's strength. Someday he will unite all of us. In the brotherhood of Arabs."

He raised the cuff of his uniform pants, revealing a prosthesis. "You see, Madame Shihabi, I am Saudi, and proud to serve my God and my king in the Kingdom's army"—he paused to glance at his subordinates—"but like many other Sunnis whose families came from Iraq, I went back and fought for our homeland, for Iraq, in our Great War with Iran—under our fearless and resolute commander Saddam Hussein." The soldier hoisted his shoulders high, as if to show off the medals he undoubtedly had won on the battlefield. "And you"—he squinted at her—"you vile scum, have betrayed our country. Madame, it will be my personal pleasure to send you back to Baghdad in the morning. You thought that by leaving Iraq, you would escape Saddam's vengeance. How fortunate that you were wrong. So very, very wrong." He puffed a few times on his cigarette. "And so, by the way, was your friend. He tried to evade us, you know, so we were forced to deal with him. Unfortunately, he won't be able to accompany you back to your homeland. He has already embarked, shall we say, on another long voyage."

A rush of guilt overcame her, and she dropped her eyes to the floor. Khalid, the poor man, good and pious Khalid, had paid the ultimate price. Her willful, selfish wish to go to the West had been most certainly responsible. She looked up, and her eyes met those of the supervisor. "May I make one last request?" she said.

"Go ahead."

"Since I certainly will die tomorrow, I would like to say goodbye to my family. May I make one telephone call? I would like to call my brother." Her plight was hopeless. She wanted to call Latifa, but knew that the shock of the call would forever pollute her daughter's spirit.

The supervisor began to shake his head, then paused to drag on his cigarette.

"He's a computer science professor . . . in the United States," she said quickly. Intuitively she felt that a conversation with an American professor, however brief, might be of more than passing interest to one sympathetic to the Iraqi regime and desirous of tracking down its enemies. It was a risk she would have to take.

"All right. You may have one minute—no more." He turned away and opened the door to the room. As he left, she heard him mutter to the guard, "Bring her to the office and let her use the phone. I'll be listening to what she has to say."

SEVEN

King Khalid International Airport
Riyadh, Saudi Arabia
Early morning, Wednesday
Sept. 11, 2002

Fatima awoke to the strains of a zither. The melody was sad, dirgelike, a bit haunting. A guard was playing the radio. Alone in the cell, she sat erect on the hard wooden chair. The interrogation had ended after she called Omar, before midnight she thought. They had not beaten her this time. Simply the cattle prod. Threats, words. Nothing her years of dealing with fear couldn't handle.

The call to Omar had upset her. He seemed flustered when she greeted him, and she discerned a note of anxiety in his voice. Maybe he realized the call was being monitored. He couldn't help her, she thought, even if he wanted to. There was no hope of being saved. Too little time. Too many risks. She mulled the conversation over in her mind.

"Fatima dearest, where are you calling from?" had been his first words to her.

"I've tried to get out of Iraq and escape to Canada. I'm calling from Saudi Arabia. The Saudis found out that my passport was counterfeit. They've arrested me, but the guards gave me the chance to call you. Tomorrow morning I'll be sent back to Iraq."

"No, no. They can't do that. There must be some way to stop them."

"Omar, there's nothing you can do. It's too late. I just wanted to tell you that I love you, Omar."

"I love you too, dearest Fatima. I'm so, so sorry for you." She heard a muffled sob. He knew what it meant for her to go back to Iraq.

"Take care of Latifa for me, will you promise? Will you promise me, Omar?"

"I promise."

A promise that he probably could never keep, she thought. "You are wonderful, my dear Omar."

"Why won't the Saudis let you go?" he asked.

She had been prepared for his question. She broke into the playful Arabic singsong that was their secret code in childhood. Now she had nothing to lose about disclosing what she had learned about Saddam's research facility in Baghdad. It would take those monitoring the call at least a few moments to catch the import of her words.

"I found out that Saddam has been researching how to make a bomb using radioactive material. It's called a 'dirty . . . .'" A burst of static came on the line. "It's at a laboratory under . . . ." The phone clicked off. "Omar, Omar?" she cried into the receiver, but it was dead. The silence seemed final.

In a few hours she would be deported back to Iraq. She tried to block out all thoughts of what would happen. Latifa would miss her, surely. But she would never know what had happened to her mother. Fatima Shihabi would just disappear, like all the others.

She began to prepare herself for what was to come. Finally she would get to meet her fate, embrace it, if not with joy, certainly with dignity. Iraqi intelligence would try to get her to talk. About the people in the opposition who had helped her. About why she had tried to escape. About why she had used such–and–such words in a journal years ago. She would remain silent as long as her body would allow her to. If she were fortunate, they would shoot her, in the back of the head, as was their style. More likely, though, she would suffer a much more prolonged and painful death. Perhaps today. Perhaps tomorrow. Death would come as a relief.

She thought of Latifa. Her slender figure. Her darting eyes, dark as a tarn at midnight, offsetting her olive complexion. Wise beyond her years. The two of them had bonded to a degree rare for even a mother and child. She had made her daughter into her alter ego, both emotional and intellectual—almost even physical, for sometimes she would feel a pain in a finger or a rib or in her head seconds after Latifa complained about one in hers. Often Latifa knew what she was about to say, well before she said it.

She then thought of Omar. She would never see him again. She had waited too long to get his help. Maybe he could have saved her. He certainly would have believed her. About the drawings. She had tried to memorize the location of the plant and the list of technical equipment. Nobody else would have listened to her. She had heard that the Americans never do. They would have dismissed her as a malcontent, or simply another Iraqi trying to save her skin by claiming knowledge of Saddam's weapons.

She drew her abayah from her shoulders and draped it over the chair. Then she stood, her legs wobbly and her bones aching. She hobbled over to the bucket in the corner. She raised her skirt to her waist, lowered her undergarments, bent down, and relieved herself. She couldn't tell if anyone was looking in the window. She went back to the chair.

She then heard the thud of boots in the corridor. Military boots, many of them. *Thud, thud, thud, thump, thud, thud, thump.* The drumbeat of boots was set off by an intermittent thump she thought might be the supervisor's prosthesis, his vaunted vestige of Saddam's Great War. She also heard the scrape of sandals. Another prisoner. They walked past her cell and then stopped abruptly. She heard the supervisor curse. One, two cells away. She made out a groan as a prisoner was shoved into the cell. Then the boots again as the men went away. After a few minutes, she heard the plaintive wail of the mullah calling believers to morning prayers at the mosque. "There is no God but one God, Allah, and Mohammad is his prophet," he cried, the attenuated strains echoing through the prison. She turned toward the door of the room, knelt on the cement floor, and began to pray. She prayed that her passage from this life would be brief, that *inshallah* Latifa would be safe, and that one day in Paradise they would be reunited, mother and child. When she finished, she touched the floor lightly with her forehead, then rose and sat again in the lone chair in the center of the room.

An hour passed before she heard the boots again in the corridor. The same pounding of boots. The key clanked in the old lock, once, twice. Before her stood the supervisor, two guards at his side. Fatima knew that he could have been harder on her. After all, he had let her make the call to Omar. Afterward, she had heard him tell the guards, "Don't waste your effort. Let our brothers in Iraq deal with her."

He looked at her with disdain. "We will return you to the airport at noon for the midday plane to Amman and then to Baghdad. You will go back to your own country. No one can help you now. May Allah go with you." He frowned, shook his head, and left as he had come, not waiting for her to speak. As the metal door slammed shut, she heard him say, "Make sure that one of you goes with her on the flight to Amman. I want no mistakes on this one."

Fatima leaned forward and put her head in her hands. Never before had she felt absolute despair. For sure, there had been moments when she sensed herself at the outermost limit of life, that place which is beyond caring, when it is pointless to go on. Nonetheless, she had always been driven by some mad compulsion to survive. Now she knew that they had won. There was nothing more she could do. Her dear child was lost to her forever. She would accept what Fate had decided for her.

EIGHT

23 Wall Street
Late afternoon, Tuesday
Sept. 10, 2002

"Sarah's on one. Mr. Witherspoon on two. And a guy who says he's a professor from Columbia is on three."

"Got it. Hello, . . . Mr. Witherspoon? Damnation. Hello . . . . Hello?"

"Yes, hello. This is Professor Omar Shihabi."

Hand on the receiver, Charles Sherman shouted to his secretary, "Metta, you gave me the wrong line again." She replied with wordless murmuring as he spoke into the phone. "Yes, Professor. Just hold on a second. I'll be right back."

"No, I need to talk with you. Now."

"Sorry. I picked up this line by mistake. I've got a client holding."

"I need your help." The voice was barely audible.

"I told you, I'll be right back." Charles's voice was edged with irritation.

"No, give me ten seconds. Your partner Mr. Hauck told me to call you." The voice was accented. Probably Middle Eastern.

"Art Hauck? Art did?" Hardly pausing, Charles went on. "Okay, go for it. But make it quick."

"An hour ago, I received a call from my sister. Her name is Fatima Shihabi. She's been arrested by border guards in Saudi Arabia. Tomorrow morning she'll be deported back to Iraq. She will be tortured and killed there. Can you help me?"

"Who are you?"

"A professor of computer science. I teach at Columbia. Here in New York." The caller's voice was articulated. Guttural Arabic rounded by years of English.

"Why did Art refer you to me?"

Of all the partners of Lloyd & Forster, Art Hauck had long been Charles's professional lodestar. Ten years Charles's senior, Art was brilliant—as one partner called him, "a certifiable genius," with the kind of wide-ranging but intensely focused mind that would have made him successful in any field. Art was known for his ability to match deals to competencies—even at the cost of marriages, careers and, some said, the much-revered "fabric" of the firm. And now he was at it again.

"He just said you had good contacts in Saudi."

True, Charles reflected. Well, maybe only partly true. Almost twenty years had passed since he worked as a lawyer for the newly rich Kingdom of Saudi Arabia. It was toward the end of the heydays of the Saudis' munificence, when they could well afford to pay Wall Street firms to sit at their elbow during contract negotiations with international vendors. He was a freshly minted corporation lawyer, at the beginning of his career with Lloyd & Forster, one of the reigning "beauty queens" in a bevy of those firms aspiring to profit from the legal work. He became the first L&F partner to base his practice on work for Middle East clients. But that work had long since dried up, as the Saudi oil revenues stagnated.

Charles flicked on his speakerphone. "I do have a few good contacts in the kingdom—at least I used to."

Charles crossed his tasseled Guccis over a corner of his mahogany desk, as was his habit, and settled back into the soft leathery grip of his chair. His gaze fell on the reticular replica of an oil tanker on his credenza. A deal memento from his Saudi days, the vessel bore on its side the legend "Drayton LNG 1983." The deal that had made his career at Lloyd & Forster.

He remembered Sarah and Witherspoon. "Look, Professor, I agree to talk with you, but just hold on one sec, will you? I do promise to come right back. Okay?"

"Okay."

Charles hit the hold button on his phone and shouted out his office door, "Metta, tell Sarah I'll call her back in a few minutes. Tell Witherspoon I've got the president of AT&T on the line and can I call him back in five minutes. Unless it's an emergency, in which case tell me."

As Charles reached to click off the hold button and get back to the professor, he paused out of instinct. Why, he asked himself, had Art done this? With his known prowess for staffing projects with the right people, he should've realized it just wouldn't work. To refer an immigration case—an Arab woman, an Iraqi, no less—to Charles now, while he was trying to bring home the Goldstar deal—was just out of line. The case should have gone to one of L&F's immigration lawyers. Still, Art always had his reasons. Maybe somebody on Columbia's Board of Trustees was trying to placate an Arab professor on the faculty. Maybe Art felt that at least Charles could get a fix on the issues raised by Fatima Shihabi's case.

And Fatima Shihabi? She had to be one of thousands of Iraqis trying to get out of the country. Spooked by war rumors. Bush against Saddam. Hubrism against Sadism. Mounting clamor for war to rid a schizo of his lethal playthings. Disaster again visits a luckless land. It was not too surprising that an Iraqi might want to get out. Fatima was no different from all the others trying to escape Saddam's horror show. But why, then, would the Saudis want to send her back? What had she done to deserve to be sent back to a certain death? It was a little puzzling.

And then suppose by some miracle he managed to help her? What then? He thought of the two Saudi girls he had once helped at the request of Jameel Zawawi. The Saudi Minister of Telecommunications had come to Jameel, saying that his nieces wanted to go to college in America. Initially Charles had been a little skeptical that two Saudi girls from a desert commune had somehow gotten it into their heads to study in America, but Sarah, whom he had only just started dating, had urged him to do what he could. So, after strenuous efforts, including two calls by Art Hauck to Wellesley's Director of Admissions, the girls were admitted to the college, tuition-free, under what the director called "exceptional circumstances." Charles even met them at the airport, later hosted them several times in New York and, as they had gotten off the plane from Riyadh apparently penniless, financed them for four long years. But his disappointment was keen when he found out, much later, that after graduation they had rushed back to Saudi Arabia, to their village, wedded locals whom Art referred to, with caustic chagrin, as "those camel drivers" in arranged marriages and settled into quite traditional lives behind the veil. He always wondered what had happened to them.

Charles pursed his lips. Where in God's name could he find time to bill to "Shihabi, F.–Pro Bono Matter"? Not as he was about to close the Goldstar deal, an inordinately complex and high-profile transaction that the whole firm—even the Street—was admiring. And it had been years since he had had the Kingdom of Saudi Arabia as a client. He hardly knew anyone in power there, and anyone in power would hardly remember him. Even Jameel seemed a face that had long faded into the past. It would take him hours, days, to reconnect the dots.

Still, he had never let Art down before, and he wouldn't now, no matter how busy he was.

He reached for his phone, cradling it in the crook of his neck. "Where's your sister now?" Charles asked the professor, mustering the last of his patience.

"Somewhere in Saudi Arabia, I—I think she said," the professor stammered.

"And how did she reach you?" Charles asked skeptically.

"By telephone here at my office. About an hour ago. The guards let her call me. She was lucky that I was here."

"Can you call her back?"

"I don't know where she is." This is getting absurd, Charles thought. "You don't know where she is . . . , you don't . . . know . . . where she is," Charles said slowly. Why, why did Art sic him with this—in the midst of the Goldstar deal?

"Excuse me, Mr. Sherman. I didn't hear you."

"Sorry, Professor, I'm just surprised that you don't have more to go on, that's all."

"Maybe you can find out."

"Maybe. Look, hold on another moment, will you? I'll put you on hold, but I'll be right back."

It was already four-thirty in the afternoon. A bad day all around. Witherspoon probably had the offering price. The board knew it was put–up–or–shut–up time. He would have to get the pricing information into the Offer to Purchase, then get the OP to the printer for distribution in the morning. With any luck the SEC staff would have no more comments, and they could go effective at the market opening at 9:00 a.m.

He pushed the intercom for his secretary. "Metta, call Hansen, tell him to drop what he's doing and call Witherspoon. Witherspoon will give him the price for the Goldstar deal. He should tell Witherspoon that we'll all meet at the printer around six tonight."

Frank Hansen. Lloyd & Forster senior associate. A solid, steady straw boss for the Sherman M&A Team . . . maybe a little too sincere. Harvard too, just as he himself was. Hansen's only lack was the seasoning of age. It explained why he sometimes was too fast on the draw, a step ahead of himself.

"Oh, and Metta, tell Hansen to stick the price in the OP. And remind him to get the printer to order dinner for us. Steaks and a decent wine. The usual. It's going to be another long night." He'd have to clear the decks. "Oh, and another thing, cancel my kendo practice. I'd never make it now anyway. Tell Master Kamiura I'll be tied up for the next week or so. And you'd better call Dr. Chambers's office. Tell them I'll call back to reschedule tomorrow's appointment. It's in the morning, first thing."

"Well, now I know you're really swamped, Charles," Metta chastised him. "I thought you promised Sarah you'd never cancel out on your therapist."

"Metta, just get off it," he said with irritation. "I said I'd go when I could. That's all."

Without waiting for her reply, Charles pressed his speakerphone. "Professor, why have the Saudis detained your sister?"

"They caught her going through Riyadh airport on a forged Canadian passport." The voice over the speakerphone was getting stronger.

"And why will she be killed if she is deported back to Iraq?"

"She's a writer, a poet, Shiite like me from Najaf . . . pretty well known in Iraq . . . but a kind of dissident, you might say. She's always been high-spirited . . . independent." He paused. "Oh, and one more thing. She may know a lot about what's going on over there. She hasn't told me anything specific—I mean, she couldn't—although I think she was about to tell me something about a bomb when we were cut off. She has some good connections, that's for sure. She works for *Babel*, Baghdad's daily newspaper. If she went back to Iraq, she'd be killed—tortured first. She was tortured before, by Saddam's interrogators. They suspected that she knew too much about the regime, and that she couldn't be trusted to keep her mouth shut. Actually she does know a lot. And I'd bet that she even knows a lot about Saddam's weapons. She's tough and fearless, but the Iraqis have ways to make you talk."

"And she's your sister," Charles repeated, partly to himself, wrapping his mind around the facts. He would never, ever forgive Art. He didn't need this. "And you say that she's being held by the Saudi authorities?"

"Yes. I think she may have gotten to the airport, but there was a problem with her passport. She had very little time to speak to me. She tried to whisper, but I could tell somebody at her end was listening. She definitely said there was a problem with her passport, that it was fake or something. The Saudis have thrown her into prison until she's sent back to Iraq in the morning."

"Professor, hold for a minute, my secretary needs me." Charles pressed the mute button on his phone.

Metta stood at the door to his office, shaking her head disapprovingly. "Charles, Witherspoon is mad. Uh, um. Yes sir, he is really mad. He said you were supposed to take his call. Then he hung up on me."

"Damnation." Charles drew out the word, syllable by syllable. "Were you able to get Hansen?"

"He's in Houston. Won't get back until the morning. He'll come straight to the office off the redeye."

"Oh, that's just great." For years Lloyd & Forster, more particularly Charles, had competed with two or three other major law firms on the Street for the chance to do deals for Morgan Capital Markets Group, the investment-banking arm of J. P. Morgan Chase. Tenuous in the best of times, the client relationship hung on the personal rapport between the lawyers and the two or three senior dealmakers at Morgan. And now Witherspoon, their senior vice president, was mad. Damn Art. He could've referred this thing to somebody else.

Witherspoon, of course, would camouflage his anger. Except to Metta. His nickname "The Silver Fox" was apt, Charles thought. His vulpine agility, his canny posturing, and his seamless demeanor in deals were the stuff of legend on Wall Street and its insular community of New York investment bankers, corporation lawyers, and financial types. And any time the Street needed one of its own to do a deal—a complex financial restructuring like Chrysler, a hostile tender offer like Grand Met, or a multi–mega–merger like Hewlett Packard and Compaq—Witherspoon's name would invariably surface. While titularly the senior vice president of Capital Markets at Morgan, he actually marched at the head of his own parade with a host of minions, including some of the Street's best-known investment bankers, lawyers, and dealmakers, in tow. And with its offices in the same building five floors below Morgan's, Lloyd & Forster often found itself leading the phalanx of Witherspoon's retained advisers.

From the beginning, when Charles as a young L&F associate had first worked for Witherspoon, he called him "Mr. Witherspoon" to his face. It was a mark of respect the man demanded, even answering his phone "Mr. Witherspoon here." And the mode of address marked the man. He was the sole character in the ever-changing cinema of thriller deals, and Charles held him in a conflicted mix of awe and envy. As a young partner, Charles had set himself two goals. By the age of fifty-five, he would be the most highly paid lawyer on the Street. And, when Witherspoon left the scene, Charles would become the "Silver Fox" of his generation. Now, at the age of forty-six, he was well on his way toward both goals.

"Professor, where can I call you?"

"Here, at my office at Columbia. Your secretary has the number."

"Be back to you in ten minutes." Charles placed his hand gently on the speakerphone and clicked it off.

Charles gingerly lifted his long legs, numb from having fallen asleep on his desk. He gazed out the large window a few feet from his desk, which afforded a view across Wall Street to Federal Hall. At its helm, the patinaed figure of George Washington stood erect at his post. A solitary dove swooped low around the statue, finally alighting on its shoulder.

Charles leaned forward and tried to rub away the soreness in his legs. Witherspoon was not accustomed to being put on hold. Charles would have to make amends. He clicked on his intercom. "Metta, get Witherspoon for me, would you?"

He pushed his large frame from his chair and stood gazing distractedly out the window across Wall Street. The creased but serene visage of his father floated into his mind. His father would have been proud of him, to have merited his own perch on some of the best real estate in America, in the world—so far removed from the penury of his father's time. Charles recalled how his father would go on about the Great Depression, about those days of deprivation, desperation, and despair. "We used to sell the lead from a printing press in our cellar just to buy bread," he would say. "And my own dear mother was never certain in the morning whether she could put meat on the table in the evening." No, his father could never have conceived how Charles's quest for success had earned him such a bountiful payback. And all along the way his deals had only gotten bigger, his office more capacious, his view more enviable. His eyes led him to the edge of his leather-topped desk, to a stack of Lucite blocks, into which miniaturized prospectuses had been embedded. If one were to look carefully, one could read the fine print—words that he himself had cobbled together. Beside the pile lay a few brass plates engraved with tombstone notices of past deals. And, front and center before him, a pen–and–pencil set, with his name embedded in marble, for the Chrysler financial workout in 1980. Trophies of years and years of tender offers, mega–mergers, bond offerings, aircraft financings, loan syndications, asset securitizations. The iconography of power in a white-shoe New York law firm.

The intercom buzzed, breaking his reverie. Sitting down again, he swiveled his chair toward his speaker phone and pressed the button.

"Mr. Witherspoon says he can't talk to you now but asked that you call him back in five minutes. Now don't forget to call him, Charles, *toot day sweet*." Metta stretched French like saltwater taffy. Just as her Haitian forebears probably would have, Charles thought. She delighted in hammering him with it.

"All right, Metta. All right, try him again in a few minutes, would you?" His request for a callback, Charles reflected, was a not-too-subtle reminder that he had his preoccupations too. Charles randomly thumbed through the latest print of the OP. He had to stay focused. After twenty years of law practice, he knew how to keep many balls in the air at the same time. Besides, the sister's predicament sounded hopeless. He would come back to Mrs. Shihabi.

After what seemed longer than five minutes, Metta's voice again came over the intercom. "Okay, I've got him. He's on line three."

Charles clicked the line button and reached for the telephone. "Oh, Mr. Witherspoon, it's Charles. Sorry I couldn't pick up earlier. Had an overseas call. President of a client, on an airplane," he fibbed. "It may have deal potential. You just never know." It was Charles's style, to manufacture the aura that the client was special, even unique. It was why he was the executive committee's fair-haired boy, versed in the subtleties of "client relations."

In years of day-by-day dealings with Charles, Witherspoon never acknowledged his client-relations gambits, although Charles was sure he was wise to them. "Well, that's okay, Charles, I know you're busy," he replied, true to form. "I just wanted to let you know that there's been a delay. The offering price, I mean. Viatech had to convene a board meeting about the change. It's tonight. I'll call you after the meeting. It'll be late."

Charles would not betray his relief. The delay would buy him a few hours to deal with the Shihabi situation, maybe longer.

"We'll have to get to the SEC before the market opens," he reminded Witherspoon. Had to keep pushing, grinding forward. It would mean most of the night at the printer. Sarah would be disappointed.

Shit. Sarah. He had forgotten her call. "I'll wait for your call at my office," Charles told Witherspoon, more deferentially than he had intended. Get Donnelley to bring in the steaks. Better yet, take a break and get over to Delmonico's. Back to the printer to wrap up, and then limo home to Sarah. He would tell her not to expect him for dinner.

"Okay, I'll talk to you later," Witherspoon replied. Charles clicked off his speakerphone. It would buy him some time. Did Art actually expect him to get somebody released from a Saudi prison by morning? Eight thousand miles away? *Hocus pocus habeas corpus?* This was not going to be easy.

"Metta, get Sarah for me. She's at home, in her studio."

NINE

Sarah knew Witherspoon and hated him, Charles mused as he waited for her to come on the line. She associated Witherspoon with his nights at the printer, his days on the road, her evenings alone àt the opera, birthdays missed—and all the other things she felt were wrong with their life together. She ignited at the mere mention of his name, branding him with her private epithet "Witherbottom."

By the fourth ring, she hadn't answered. If she was really concentrating on painting, he knew, it sometimes took Sarah a while to pick up. And if she didn't want to be interrupted at all, she sometimes turned off the phone, as well as the machine. Unlike most people, she didn't feel a need to be attached to the world by a phone line. He held on for a few more rings in the hope she would answer. Well, he could always leave a message on their home voicemail, he thought. As he was about to hang up, her voice came on the line.

He decided to take the direct approach. "Hi, Sarah. Sorry I couldn't take your call earlier. Things got a little crazy here. Look, Witherspoon wants me to wait for his call. I'm going to be late. We'll hit the printer at some point in the evening."

"Well, that's just dandy. So I won't see you until tomorrow, then?" He was taken aback by the chill in her voice, a tone he hadn't heard in a very long time. And it was starting again—the slow, gritty grinding in the pit of his stomach. After a long pause, she added, "I guess you forgot we were going to *Rigoletto*." Damn, he thought. He had forgotten again. Ever since they had gotten back together five years ago—having broken up when a Witherspoon deal interrupted their long-planned holiday in Japan—he had tried to be more considerate, attempting to get home for dinner, going away with her on weekend trips to upstate New York, to Long Island, and to Massachusetts. It seemed as if Sarah too had tried to makes things go more smoothly. She rarely complained about his working late as long as he didn't break engagements with her.

But in the past year he had disappointed her more than once. The worst was when he had had to miss one of her gallery openings. He had been looking forward to attending it for weeks. The morning of the opening Art Hauck called Charles into his office. "Listen, Charles, I hate to hit you with this at the last minute, but Goldman Sachs needs you in Houston again this afternoon for that asset deal with their oil and gas client."

Charles tried to beg off. "Sorry, Art, but tonight Sarah opens at Valentin—a one-woman show. It's that new gallery in the East Village. Very prestigious."

"I saw it in the *Times* a few days ago."

"I promised Sarah I'd be there. It's a big deal for her. And Houston is a cookie-cutter. Hansen can handle it—he's been shadowing me on those Goldman deals."

Art had seemed a little surprised by his response. "I'm sorry, Charles, but it's not really a choice. Goldman's people are already down there." There was no more discussing it. Goldman had to have Charles. Immediately.

He raced home to pack for the overnight trip, dreading the confrontation with Sarah. She had been upset when he told her but had kept her anger under control. "Not tonight of all nights," she said, her disappointment almost palpable. "I've been trying really hard to be understanding about your job, your hours. But this is *my* career. Is it too much to ask you to support what *I* do, just for one evening?" She had been right, of course, and he had felt guilty for days after that. He almost would have preferred if she had yelled at him.

And now, once again, as he might have said in his Paris days, *encore un autre noyau dans la confiture*, "another pit in the marmalade." He'd have to beg for forgiveness. "Oh, Sarah, I am so sorry. I completely blanked on it. But there's nothing I could do anyway. It's that Goldstar deal again. We almost have it wired. I promise I'll make it up to you."

"Promises, promises," she said. He heard her sigh. "Well, I can always ask Anne Hauck if she'd like to use the ticket. She and I always enjoy the opera together," Sarah added with sweet sarcasm. "*Rigoletto* has just enough melody to sooth her to sleep and to keep me awake. It'll be fine." She was simply being good to him. The grinding in his stomach was getting worse.

"There's something else. Some guy—a professor at Columbia—wants me to try to get his sister out of a prison in Saudi Arabia. By tomorrow morning. Can you believe it? I doubt that I'll be able to do anything, but Art asked if I wouldn't mind making a few calls, that's all. It won't take long."

Sarah's voice echoed over the speakerphone. "Charles, you don't need this on top of everything else. I feel sorry for the woman, but can't Art get somebody else to help her?

"Look, Art asked *me* to do it. Probably thinks I still have connections with the Saudis. Anyway, I'll be home as soon as I can. It'll be late—but not an all-nighter."

"Alright, Charles, go ahead, do your deals, save the world, do whatever you damn well want to do. And then maybe after you've been whacked by a cardiac, you'll slow down"—she paused—"if you live that long."

"I don't know what to say . . . except that I'm truly—." Charles didn't complete the sentence. He heard a click as Sarah hung up the phone.

Charles pressed the palms of his hands against his forehead. He could hear Metta packing up for the day. Art rushed by his office, holding a sheaf of documents, on his way to a meeting.

Charles ran out of his office and caught up with Art midway down the corridor. "Hey, Art, Sarah's probably going to call Anne about the opera tonight. I'm under the gun. Witherspoon has me up to my ears in the Goldstar deal. What's the story about this Arab woman?"

"I thought that you'd find it interesting, that's all," Art responded, staring at him blankly. "You're just the ticket for this one, Charles. Don't forget how those Saudis—and I don't mean just Hajir—fell all over themselves for you. Hajir never forgot, you know, how you fasted during Ramadan—and that you never wore green ties. He brought it up every time I saw him."

"Yeah, okay, but, Art, that was ages ago," Charles said, visibly annoyed. "I already served my time out there—in the desert. And you know anybody could have done what I did back then." He paused, glaring at his mentor. Then, raising his voice so loudly that Metta stuck her head into the corridor to investigate, he added, "And you know as well as I do, there are other lawyers in this firm who are *far* better equipped—in terms of time and expertise—to take on this Arab woman." A disgruntled expression on his face, he crossed his arms and glared at Art.

Art placed his hand firmly on Charles's shoulder. "Calm down, Charles. Take it easy, fellow. Look, this firm made a lot of money off the deals you did for the Saudis. And I should know. I had to approve every billing statement we sent to them. But I also know how well you adapted to their culture. Why, there were times in those days when I actually expected you to go native."

"Yeah, okay." Charles nodded warily. He was all too aware of the older man's powers of persuasion.

Art flashed a little smile at him, then went on, "When I got the call about this woman needing help, I knew you were the right guy. I knew it right away. And don't think I'm not aware of how busy you are. And Witherspoon's as pleased as can be with what you're doing for him. I chatted with him earlier today. Listen, my partner"—he paused, keeping his hand on Charles's shoulder—"you'll be able to do something for Mrs. Shihabi. I'm absolutely confident of that. And I don't expect you to spend much time on this. Just make a call or two to your Saudi friends, maybe Jameel or somebody. That's it."

"I'll see what I can do, Art."

"And I'll let Anne know about Sarah."

On his way back to his office, Charles passed Metta's workstation. "Now, Charles—." She held back for an instant. He readied himself for a sermonette. She had overheard Art's little speech and no doubt perceived Sarah's pique as well. Metta put on her smile that let him know that her words were only hinting at what she was really thinking and that if he really listened carefully enough, he just might find out exactly what that hidden meaning might be. "Don't you go spending half the night on the project for that Arab woman. You've got a full plate, you know." She had been his secretary for nine years, and they had fought the wars together. She knew it all.

"Okay, okay, thanks, Metta. I appreciate it. Have a good night."

"*Bone wee*," she replied, grinning at him. He rolled his eyes even as he smiled back.

Charles returned to his desk, stretched his legs out across a corner of it, and thought about what Art had said about his relationship with the Saudis. Even today, he thought, he never wore green ties—and, of course, never had in the Kingdom. "It's just out of my deepest regard for the Prophet Mohammad ," he had told Suliman Hajir, "since that was the Prophet's favorite color." Charles remembered Hajir's rotund figure and fleshy face. Not the appearance of a man accustomed to long fasting, he mused. Until Art mentioned it, Charles had forgotten how he himself had fasted in the midst of negotiations over a telecommunications system in Riyadh. "It's out of my sincerest respect for Islam during these holy days," he had told Hajir. His client had seemed surprised, even flattered, that this Lloyd & Forster lawyer, this paragon of Wall Street capitalism, would show such deference to Muslim culture, in spite of the rigor of fasting during the sizzling Saudi summer.

Charles knew that his respect for Arab ways and traditions had won him the hearts of his Arab clients. It rose to some level bordering on absolute trust. Thus, it wasn't really surprising that Art had fingered him to make a few calls for Mrs. Shihabi. But in the time-compressed world of mega–merger deals, every nanosecond counted, and Charles couldn't help wishing that Art could have asked Fred Berger, with his years of immigration experience, to help the poor woman. Why did he have to be the one? And why when he was in the middle of one of the biggest and most complex deals in the history of the Street? But to be fair, Charles thought, Fred was out of town. And Art probably hadn't had enough time to find anyone else.

Feeling tense, Charles stood and walked over to the window. He stood staring out across Wall Street, thinking. He crossed his arms against a rivulet of damp cold that seemed to pass through the window glass. It had started to rain. George looked cold, his uniform slick from the wet. A military man's plight, Charles thought. He stretched out his muscled arms and assumed the basic posture for *kamae*, or engagement. It had been three weeks at least since his last kendo practice, and his limbs felt stiff and sluggish. He lunged with his imaginary sword and whispered a muffled *ki–ai*, or cry of attack. When he torqued his body around the imaginary weapon and into the turn, he saw Metta standing by his office door.

"Charles, I'm sorry to disturb you, but it's Professor Shihabi again."

"I thought you'd gone home."

"Your overtime secretary hasn't arrived, so I thought that I'd stay a few more minutes." She flashed her big white teeth at him.

"Oh thanks, Metta. Put him through." Charles sat down at his desk.

"Yes, professor," he said into the phone. "I've been working on some ideas." If nothing else, ideas yielded hope, and from hope sprang action. He would have to do something. "First"—he was getting refocused—"I have a good friend in the State Department. She served three years in Jeddah. She'll know somebody in the government there. Then"—he felt himself on a roll—"we should contact the international humanitarian agencies—Carnegie Endowment, International Human Rights Commission, that sort of thing." He was making it up. Barely credible. But enough. "Of course, then there's the United Nations High Commission on Refugees. Your sister is obviously a candidate for some type of humanitarian intervention. But it's already five forty-five. I don't know if any of these people will still be around."

"Please try," the professor pleaded, anguish in his voice.

"I'll call you back within the hour," Charles replied, then hung up.

He would pick an easy way out, he thought, the United States Department of State. He quickly thumbed through his old, beat-up Rolodex, even as he realized that the ever-efficient Metta probably had also patched her number into his Blackberry. Jacobs, Ann . . . Ann Jacobs. She would be surprised to hear from him. It had been almost eight years. Scarily smart, startlingly suave in a dozen cultures, she had held, over a twenty-three year career at State, a succession of embassy posts in Europe and the Middle East—most recently in France, where she served as consul general in Bordeaux. Early on, she had been assistant commercial attaché in Jeddah, before the Saudis decided to move all embassies to the capital, Riyadh. When he had known her then, she possessed an earth–mother beauty—by now, he reflected, most likely encased in corpulence acquired from countless representational functions during her years in diplomatic service. There had been a time, before Sarah, when Charles had tried to imagine himself married to Ann. He knew that he couldn't have lived the life of a State Department spouse, nor she as a Wall Street widow.

He reached her secretary. "Ann's on a boat. In Chesapeake Bay. A State Department conference," she added hastily. "Can't be reached. She'll be back Monday."

"You mean there's no way I can contact her? What if her mother died? There must be some way." He was aware his frustration was showing.

"She's checking her voicemail. Daily. I can put you through so that you can leave a message."

"Thanks."

Charles left a cheery but pointed message. At the end, he added, "This is probably pretty routine stuff to you"—Charles could visualize her nodding in agreement—"but I thought that at least you could give me the name of somebody at our embassy in Riyadh. I can take it from there."

It would all be over before she got the message. Strike one. Okay then, he'd finesse this with another solution closer to home.

Charles clicked on his speakerphone, then swiftly tapped in the number of the UNHCR's New York office. The grainy resonance of the message machine echoed around the room. "This is the UNHCR. All of our staff have gone for the day, but in case of an emergency, you can leave a message and someone will respond. Have a nice day."

He left a succinct message asking for assistance on a matter of "grave humanitarian concern." It wouldn't be until morning, he thought, before he'd receive a reply. And by then it would be too late.

It was too funny. Human rights operating only from nine to five. Damn. Strike two.

Carnegie Endowment's office in Washington had the same message. Maybe all humanitarians were at the same conference? On a boat somewhere? On Chesapeake Bay, no less?

He had to make one or two more calls. Art surely would want him to do that, at least. Besides, time was running out for Fatima Shihabi.

TEN

23 Wall Street
6:00 p.m., Tuesday
Sept. 10, 2002

Charles glanced at his Rolex. It was already 6:00 p.m. in New York. He had a fleeting impression that nobody, except for himself, was at work on the whole East Coast of the United States, not even humanitarians. Anybody who could save Fatima Shihabi had gone home for the evening or was sipping an apéritif on a boat somewhere. In Saudi it would be 2:00 a.m. Fatima would leave the prison "in the morning," the professor had said. Six, at most nine, hours from now.

For his whole professional life, Charles had made his clients believe in him. Often he had said this or that deal was "doable." He had built his practice on the dreams of his clients. It was always a matter of confidence, to be able to see the deal through, to inspire the belief that one could get there from here. But Fatima Shihabi was not your average $30 million bond offering. Nor was it just a matter of saving her life. There was also the sheer challenge of it. Here was a little conundrum of its own, a Rubik's cube where the seamless squares of Fatima's individual persona, her personal circumstances, and her current plight had to be reconfigured and she—an activist Muslim writer—matched with freedom, with life itself. He suddenly recalled the faceless shadows of veiled women he had watched in the Riyadh souk. He felt a swell of energy pass through him. There was still at least one more call he could make.

"Metta, get me Jameel Zawawi," he shouted out the door. "His number is on my Rolodex, my old one."

"Metta's gone home, but I'll do it." It was the unfamiliar voice of an overtime secretary. Maybe okay. Maybe not. Metta finally had to go home. He remembered her words not to work through the night. Like hell he wouldn't. He felt a twinge of chagrin about kendo practice; Master Kamiura surely would take him to task for canceling it again. But *Rigoletto* would have interfered anyway. If he had remembered. If.

"Hold it, hold it, um . . . Miss . . ."

The woman appeared in the doorway. "It's Michele." She sported the sort of warming, winsome smile that told him he could go to bed with her that very minute if he wanted, a smile that made him regret every one of his years past thirty.

"Michele, yes, well, it's in the middle of the night over there. I'll have to send a fax."

Swiftly he dictated a letter with the details and handed the tape to Michele, who went back to her desk. Jameel would have to find the prison. Then pay off the right minister. Impossible task. Nobody else could do it. He asked Jameel to call him in the morning. Saudi time. No matter what hour in New York. He just had to do it.

The intercom broke into his thoughts. "It's a Mr. Witherspoon." Michele with the marvelous smile was taking no chances.

"Put him through." With nothing else to do, he could at least talk to Witherspoon.

"Charles, we won't have a deal until tomorrow. I'll call you when I have more information. We probably won't know anything until first thing in the morning." Scratch the printer's. More time for Mrs. Shihabi. He might even make it home. He thought of Sarah and *Rigoletto*, but decided that it was too late. She would have already called Anne.

"Okay, but I'll be in the office for a while if anything changes," Charles said magnanimously. "Call me at home if you need to reach me tonight."

There was silence at the other end of the line, as Witherspoon must have hung up.

Charles immediately called the professor and got through right away. "I've contacted a well-connected friend of mine in Saudi," Charles said. One probably would not be enough. But it was something, anything to give Fatima Shihabi a chance.

"Thank you, oh thank you, Mr. Sherman," the professor gushed. "My family will never forget you, what you have done for us is so wonderful. You are a great man. I cannot believe your kindness."

"Now don't let your hopes run away with you. It's really unlikely that we'll be able to save her. We won't know until morning Saudi time. My friend will call me," he added reassuringly, even though he knew that Jameel might not even be in the country. Might be at his chalet in St. Moritz or on his yacht in Majorca. Might never receive the fax. Might not know the right minister.

"I'll call you at home tonight when I am contacted." Charles's voice projected determination. Confidence. Twenty years of law practice does that for you, he thought. "In the morning we'll talk with the High Commission for Refugees and the other groups we contacted earlier." By morning it would be too late.

"What about my congressman?" The professor was resourceful. "I am a U.S. citizen, you know. My sister, of course, is not."

"Who is he?"

"Littleford, I think."

"Sure, Bob Littleford. I know him, although not well," Charles said. "But one of my partners chaired his congressional campaign two years ago. We certainly can try the congressman. He's probably home by now. Let me get back to you later."

Charles slowly clicked off the speakerphone. He rolled back in his chair and crossed his feet on the side of the desk toward the window. Across the street the remnants of the rush hour crowd trundled past Federal Hall, as George surveyed them dispassionately. Some don't–hold–dinner–I'll–be–late secretaries, floor clerks and back office workers. A few I'll–catch–the–early–train–and–be–home–for–dinner lawyers and accountants. Pouring themselves down the Broad Street entrance for the

E train, massing up to the Port Authority terminal. Bus to the New Jersey burbs. East Orange. Paterson. Maplewood.

Charles found a number for "R. Littleford – home" in the L&F client phone directory. It had a Washington, D.C. area code. Charles dialed the number, and after a few rings the congressman came on the line.

Their conversation was anything but brief as the congressman went on effusively about the contributions of Charles's partner to the campaign, about the valuable role that "the private sector," Charles's firm being a case in point, had played in the democratic process, about the summers the congressman had spent with Art at his cottage on Nantucket, and about the ups–and–downs of redevelopment of the financial district in the aftermath of 9/11.

"I can't believe it's been a year already. Are you coping all right?—I mean, with the after-effects of September eleventh and all?" the congressman asked.

"I still don't get a decent night's sleep. Our firm was thwacked pretty hard, you know. As you probably heard, we lost two partners who were at Cantor."

"Yeah, I know. And Art called me just afterward to let me know about his daughter. I only met her once, but I understand she was absolutely terrific. Bright as hell. Took after her father."

"Yeah, he and she were close. And I mean real close. He was just about smashed to smithereens when he got the news."

"Art told me you were there, at Windows on the World, that morning. How did you get out?"

"My lucky star must have been shining. But that's a story I'd like to tell you over a drink some time. If that's okay with you."

"Sure. No problem. I understand."

"Listen, I need to run something by you, something a little off the wall, you might say."

"Story of my life, Charles. *Diga-me*, my friend."

Charles embellished the story related by Fatima's brother with what Charles sensed would interest a U.S. congressman in the post-9/11 world.

He described Fatima as a leader of the growing human rights movement in Iraq, a freedom-fighter in a land where "feminist" wasn't in the dictionary. And he noted that she might have information of interest to the CIA or the Pentagon. When he finished, he felt sure he had Congressman Littleford on board.

"For a guy who took it on the chin from those Arab bastards, you're pretty darn decent to take up the cause of this woman." When Charles made no comment, the congressman added, "Let me write a few letters, make a few calls," the congressman said. "I've gotten to know the Saudi ambassador, and I'd have no problem communicating with him. I'll ask him to have his government release the poor woman. But I can't do anything until tomorrow morning."

"That will be too late, I'm afraid," Charles said.

"I'm sorry, Charles. I'd like to help you, but I've got an engagement and need to be on my way."

"I understand," Charles said. "We're exploring some other avenues too. If they don't work out, we'll come back to you."

"Good luck," the congressman said, manifestly pleased that no one expected him to do anything. "Give my best to your partners."

Charles put down the phone. He glanced at his watch, which blinked ten after seven. It had been a long conversation for naught. He quickly clicked open his briefcase, threw in that evening's proof of the OP for the Goldstar deal, then rushed for the elevator. As he strode past Michele's workstation, he cheerily mouthed across her air space, "*Au revoir.*"

With no hesitation a voice behind the stanchion chirped in respectable French, "*Bonne nuit et à bientôt.*"

Now there's an accent, Charles mused. He would have to speak with Metta. He'd pay for her lessons. When he got to the elevator, Art was standing there, briefcase in hand, a copy of *The Wall Street Journal* nestled under his arm.

Art threw him a feisty smile and twitched a few fingers toward him. "Witherspoon tells me you've got the Goldstar deal wired."

"Actually, it is a bit of a high-wire act. If anybody can pull it off, it'll be Witherspoon."

"He's got complete confidence in you, Charles, you know that."

"Yeah, I know, although sometimes I wonder. He's a clever guy."

"That he is," Art replied, his eyes flashing. "That he is," he repeated. I'm on my way up to see him right now. By the way, how's Mrs. Shihabi?"

"I'll know tomorrow morning. I got Jameel cranked up. I've asked him to call me. I hit up Bob Littleford too, and he said to say hello."

"Sounds as if you've covered all the bases," Art replied. The up elevator arrived, its doors swung open noiselessly, and he entered. Alone, he said from the back, "Give Jameel my regards. Good luck with Mrs. Shihabi." As the doors closed, Charles nodded his farewell, sensing at some profound level of his being that somewhere between the Goldstar deal and Fatima Shihabi and Sarah Steinmann, he was going to need more than his share of luck.

After another minute the down elevator came, fully loaded with professional types in suits, their briefcases and laptop bags at their sides, looking very much homeward-bound. They gazed at him with studied vacantness, as if arrested in the midst of an intense discussion. Rehashing an end–of–day meeting, he thought. Perhaps upstairs at Morgan, and possibly with Witherspoon, who seemed to have deals running all the time. Toward the rear was Christopher St. George, one of Millstone Tweed's thundering herd of M&A lawyers, who averted his eyes, pretending not to see him. For all of ten seconds, while the elevator coped with having been called but not boarded, the gallery of duded dealmakers stared at him, and he at them, wordlessly, hardly flexing a facial muscle, as if straining to pose for a photo.

They were like the faces that awful morning, he thought, faces pressed against the panes of those gaping windows. Faces peering out in mute incredulity. Faces frozen in fear and hopelessness. Faces haunting and haunted. Each of them at its own window on the world. He imagined his own face among them, as it easily could have been—as it had been only moments before it happened.

He stood paralyzed. The elevator door hesitated, then closed abruptly. The faces suddenly vanished. His eyes filled with tears, and a profound sadness clutched at his heart. Those poor people, he thought. He would take his time going home.

ELEVEN

43 Central Park West
11:15 p.m., Tuesday
Sept. 10, 2002

Charles heard the clicking of keys at the front door. He tossed onto the coffee table the draft of the Goldstar OP he had been reviewing all evening. He was glad he had eaten dinner earlier, that he hadn't waited for Sarah to come home. He took a quick sip from the wine he had been nursing, their favorite Châteauneuf du Pape.

The door swung open, and Sarah came in. She was wearing her opera clothes, a straight black skirt topped by a gray suede jacket, over which she had draped an Hermès scarf Charles had bought her. Her dressy clothes gave her an air of cool sophistication he had always found intriguing—such a change from her jeans and paint-spattered smock. She gave him a sharp glance, then turned and fumbled with the locks. He could tell she was flustered.

"Welcome home. How'd it go?" he asked, walking down the hallway to meet her.

She turned to him. "You're impossible. I thought of you all through the opera."

"What do you mean?" She was still angry with him, he assumed, for having failed to remember his date with her.

But to his surprise, she was apologetic. "Look, I'm sorry about getting upset with you earlier. I guess I flipped out because I was thinking about the effects of all this stress on you, on your health. Charles, face it, you just can't be all things to all people. It won't work. You can't save all of humanity and be a slave to your pal—Witherbottom—too."

"Oh, you mean the Shihabi matter. Well, Art asked me to do it. That's all."

She walked over to the sofa and sat down. "Oh Art fart. I wouldn't trust him any more than I would . . . Witherbottom."

"Listen, don't worry about me, Sarah. I'm doing fine. Dr. Chambers told me that in general I'm making good progress. As he says, the important thing is to keep my mind occupied. My deals help, naturally. Even kendo keeps my mind on track."

"I prefer kendo. At least it gets you out of the office." She looked up at him. "Did you go to the club today?"

"No way. Not with Goldstar cooking." He didn't dare mention that he'd canceled his appointment with the good Doctor Chambers.

"It's a shame you can't do your kendo at home."

He shook his head. "Not nearly enough room—at least I've never thought so." Then he checked himself, cast a mischievous grin at her, and hurried out of the room. He came back carrying the kitchen broom, which, in his catcher's-mitt hands, looked lethal. Planting himself foursquare in the middle of the living room, he flexed the broom at her as if it were a *jō*, the hard white oak stave he used in his kendo practice. Then, with a ferocious, almost comical look in his eyes, he glared at her, his eyebrows levitating, his facial muscles contorting.

She smiled at his Kabuki-like self-mockery. It was a drill she had seen many times before, in warm-ups for his kendo matches. "Careful, Charles. This is *not* your club, you know."

Slowly at first, then with lightning speed, he began to execute the sixty-four tactics of traditional *jōdō*, the purest form of kendo, each time ticking off in his mind the prescribed order of drill. Thrust. Parry. Block. Deflect. Cover. Throw off. Hold. As he whirled again and again in place to face the imaginary enemy, the whir of the weapon filled the room like the wings of a hundred geese rising from a lake. As he completed the final round of moves and the broomstick whirred one last time, there was an earsplitting crash and a splintering of glass. A strong odor of Châteauneuf du Pape permeated the air.

Charles closed his eyes, dropped the baton and stood, stock still, in the middle of the room. For an instant he was no longer there. He was standing beside Witherspoon. They were looking up as window glass careened down from a hundred stories skyward. Glass that shimmered in the sunlight like fairy dust as it fell earthward. Sheets of glass that shattered on the cement sidewalks girding the towers. Shards of glass that struck like so many stilettos.

Sarah gasped and covered her face with her hands.

"Oh, my gosh. I'm sorry, Sarah. I got carried away." Charles rushed over to the sofa and knelt before her. "Are you okay?"

She raised her head and looked around the wine-splattered room. "Sure, just a perfectly good piece of Baccarat smashed to pieces . . . smashed . . . just like—" She paused, looking at him, her gray–green eyes dwelling on his features. "Just like our lives, Charles, splintered into a zillion tiny slivers . . . that sometimes I feel nothing—not a year, not a lifetime—will ever be able to put back together again." Her eyes reddened, and she began to cry.

"I'm so sorry, Sarah. I'm so sorry." He sat down beside her, took her in his arms, and held her tightly.

She rested her head against his chest. "I know you are. It's okay. It's just that this life is getting to me again. Tonight, as the lights went down and Anne fell into her usual 'opera siesta,' all of a sudden I felt totally alone—in the theater sure, but also in the world, my world. Then, as the night went on, I found myself identifying with Rigoletto, with his pathetic loneliness, everything dear to him corrupted, ruined. It's just so . . . so awful." Then she pulled away and gazed into his eyes. "That's the real reason I blew up at you. I wanted you with me this evening. You realize that a year ago I thought I had lost you. And tonight I just didn't . . . didn't want to be alone."

Charles felt a tightening around his chest and a choke rising in his throat. Then he replied, "You're right what you said—about this past year, that is. September eleventh did change things."

"Yes, it did, although not as much as it did for those whose loved ones didn't make it."

"That's certainly true."

"The anniversary tomorrow is just making things worse." She gently placed her hand on his, and laid her head on his shoulder.

He tightened his embrace. "I had the vision thing again today—I saw those faces, I mean."

"When?"

"It was while I was leaving the office."

She turned her face to look at him. "You poor dear." She placed her soft hand on his stubbled cheek. "It weighs on you, doesn't it?"

"It's always with me. I just can't shake it. And of course whenever I see Witherspoon, he reminds me of those last few minutes."

"That twit. He doesn't have a heart."

"Don't be so hard on him, Sarah. I know that he seems pretty cool about it, about the fact that we made it out. Still, I get the sense that the memories always clutch at him—just as they do at me."

"I know," she added sympathetically. She gently placed her hand on his. "But ever since I've known you, you've always been so . . . centered."

"Yeah, I guess," he said and sighed. "Until this last year, I've always just gone along, same as always, same old Charles, always focused on my deals, always looking after my clients, . . . and, now, I'm just not sure." He paused, glancing down at the wine-spotted rug. An image of blood-spattered pavement crept into his thoughts. He quickly averted his eyes from the rug, forced his mind back to their conversation, and went on. "I'm just not sure. This old master of the universe is beginning to question what sort of universe he's dealing with—whether it's the sort of universe he really wants to be master of."

"What do you mean?" She raised her tear-streaked face and looked into his eyes.

Charles gently ran a fingertip along her jawline. "Well, I've been doing some thinking. It's not that I don't believe in what I do, or have done in my life, it's just that recently, mostly this past year, a part of me feels . . . , well, out of the groove . . . disconnected, somehow."

"Why haven't you said something then?"

"It hasn't been anything I've wanted to talk about. And I haven't really sorted it out for myself. Lately, I feel as if I'm playing some sort of role—a role I can't get out of. I get up in the morning, brush my teeth, put on my pin-stripes and my persona, and go play in the sand box with Witherspoon. I don't know quite what to make of it."

"Have you talked to Dr. Chambers about it?"

"Not yet, but I will. Mostly, I keep rehashing what happened on 9/11. Why did I live? Why did the guys I knew from Morgan who were at the breakfast die? There's not a day I go downtown that I don't think about what happened. Even now, a year later, I just can't let it go." Charles's eyes misted over. "And at night, no matter how late I go to bed, I still wake up with those cursed specks in front of my eyes, like floaters, drifting down and down, one after another. I try not to think about it, but I can't put them out of my head. I just can't . . . ."

The phone rang, startling both of them. Charles glanced at the mantel clock. It read 11:52 p.m. "Who could that be, so late?" Sarah asked.

"I think I know," Charles said and dashed out of the living room and into the kitchen.

He picked up the cordless phone. Jameel's voice, at once recognizable even after many years, came over the line. "Charles, it's Jameel. Jameel Zawawi. I received your fax."

Charles's brain quickly shifted gears. "Jameel, thank you for whatever you can do. I'm sorry to trouble you. I wasn't sure if you were in the Kingdom."

"I'm not. I'm calling from my yacht, just off Malta. My office gave me your message."

The same old Jameel, Charles reflected. As a lawyer–turned–entrepreneur, he had profited enormously from construction projects in the Kingdom in the 1970s and '80s. The Saudi royal family had sent him to Yale, Georgetown Law School, and then Harvard Business School, in the 1960s. After a stint at Citibank in New York, he returned to Saudi Arabia to form a small fiefdom of civil engineering, construction, and manufacturing firms. When oil revenues began to pour into the Kingdom in the mid-1970s, Jameel was first in a long caravan of Saudi contractors to enjoy the new beneficence of the Saudi government. Charles had met him through Art in the early 1980s when Lloyd & Forster had advised the Kingdom on the terms of contracts for the Riyadh airport.

"I can't give you any promises about Fatima Shihabi since I don't know why they put her in prison. With all that's going on in Iraq and your government looking over their shoulders, my government probably doesn't want to appear too lenient toward Iraqis, especially if they could be terrorists."

"This woman's no terrorist, Jameel. She's just a writer. She's written some stuff that's gotten her into trouble with Saddam and his people."

"I understand, Charles, and you may not want to discuss it over the phone. You never know, and maybe my government is suspicious of her. Still, like you, I can't understand why they would want to send an Iraqi, a woman no less, back to her country. It does seem a little strange. But you don't even know where she is. I will see what I can do, anyhow."

"Jameel, I'm sorry to put you through this effort."

"Not at all. It's a pleasure for me. How's Art Hauck? I haven't talked to him in a while."

"He appreciated your note of condolence. He misses his daughter, as you can imagine."

"He's had his share of fighting the good fight. And he's got a big heart. Give him my best, will you?"

"I will," Charles said.

"I'll call you back later this morning."

By the time Charles hung up the phone, Sarah had retired for the night. She had left the door open a crack so that he could come in without disturbing her. She was probably waiting for him, but his mind was now racing. There was no way that he could go to bed. He stretched out on the living room couch and put his hands behind his head. It was starting again: The faces at the windows. The bodies slowly drifting down. The shrieks of terror. The thunk of flesh against concrete. The sirens of emergency vehicles. He fought to get his mind under control. He had a deal to do. He should be bringing all his energies to bear on Goldstar. Witherspoon, Art Hauck, Lloyd & Forster, the Street—they all depended on him to do just that. And then there was Fatima Shihabi.

Sarah was right. He was taking on too much. She always knew things before he did. It disturbed him, her dissatisfaction with their lives. But he was beginning to feel it too. And until this evening, he had never before admitted it, even to himself. He didn't understand exactly why, but it was as if the colossal scale of the World Trade Center bombings had rocked the very foundation of his faith in his settled existence. Ironically now, when he was so close to attaining the goals he had set for himself in his youth, he felt the need to reframe the core question of his life—whether material success alone should dictate the terms of his life. Certainly not the terms of his life with Sarah, he reflected. Eventually he was going to have to make some choices. Perhaps one day he'd even tell Harold Witherspoon to take a hike, he thought and smiled. But that would be a long time coming. In the meantime he had a deal to close.

Witherspoon. Witherspoon. He'd probably called by now. Charles decided to wait until the morning to check his voicemail. It could wait. He shifted his body again on the uncomfortable couch. No question of sleep. The clock on the mantelpiece showed just before 1:00 a.m. He should have called Professor Shihabi. Not much to report, though. It too could wait, he decided, until morning.

Despite himself, he couldn't rid the thought of Fatima Shihabi from his mind. Who was she? he wondered. He tried to visualize her. Soft curves of the Arab face, like the undulating sands of the desert. Dark eyes, with bottomless, brown–black wells at their cores. He thought of the few Arab women he had encountered, how their mystery had beguiled him. Once in Saudi Arabia, he had seen a woman in the souk, standing alone, beneath the veil. She seemed to be looking at him, almost curiously, as if she wanted to tell him something. He had tried to discern her features. Nothing but opaque black cloth. No suggestion of the gentle contours of her face. Jameel once said that Arabs kept their women that way because they were so bewitching. At night, in bed, Jameel had remarked coarsely, they were all the same anyway.

How the veil separated women from the world at large, Charles reflected. He recalled a dinner at Sheik Razan's home in Jeddah. The guests, all men, were served by one of the Sheik's three wives, Allison Murray. A Smith graduate, she had met her husband at U.S.C. when they were graduate students there. As she set the meal on the carpet before them, Charles was tempted to ask impishly, "So how's it going, Allison?" But any acknowledgment of her presence would have been unthinkable. She was a nonperson, a patent nonentity.

He wondered whether Fatima even wore a veil. It seemed somehow antithetical to her identity. Her brother had said that she was a writer, a poet. As an educated woman, a journalist, she probably speaks English, he thought. Writes in Arabic, by all accounts the most expressive language in the world. The most poetic. Sometimes erotic. She must write it well. Too well. Enough to anger Iraqi officialdom.

As he lay on the couch, his eyes began to close. Almost immediately after he fell asleep he began to dream. He was soaring out over the desert, flying like an eagle. Alone. Far below, he could see glistening sand, a vast and undulating expanse, spread out under a blue sky of such intensity it hurt his eyes. A speck of black broke the unmitigated sameness of the scene, far on the horizon. The closer he got, the more it receded. He knew what it was, but, try as he might, he could not remember its name. Without warning it vanished as if it never existed. He tried to call it back but couldn't find the words.

TWELVE

43 Central Park West
Early morning, Wednesday
Sept. 11, 2002

Charles awoke as the first hints of dawn came in the east window from behind the coops on the other side of Central Park. The same sun, Charles imagined, that was shining over Saudi Arabia, over Fatima Shihabi, now probably on her way to Iraq.

He had slept fitfully. It was the same as almost every other night. His mind had wandered in spite of his strenuous efforts to relax, to focus on the task of sleeping. He had tried pills, mind–relaxation exercises, the services of Dr. Raymond Chambers, the firm's hired therapist, all to no avail. The images of 9/11 would force their way back into his brain. Then last night there was the added stimulus of Jameel's call. He had forgotten to tell Jameel that Fatima was from Najaf, probably Shiite. Maybe it made no difference. It was a nit.

And today it would be a year. It was hard to believe, the memory burned so vividly into his mind. And he worried that Al Qaeda would be tempted to celebrate the occasion with another horrific disaster, a reminder in case anybody could forget for half a second. The whole city was on edge, expecting it, murmuring about it in a million communications. Hansen had forwarded an email sent by a contact at Citigroup to a hundred addressees, reporting that a dirty bomb would be detonated somewhere around midtown. Sometime early afternoon, it said. If it came, he'd hop the ferry to Staten Island. Make his way to New Jersey to avoid the prevailing winds, then north. He had told Sarah to make her way north too. They were to meet at Mohonk Mountain House in the Catskills. Somehow they would make it.

He could hear Sarah's rhythmical breathing from the bedroom. Cars were swooshing along Central Park West six stories below. He couldn't think clearly. His conversation with Sarah about the effects of 9/11 troubled him. He had to do something to free up their lives. First, he lectured himself, tell Witherspoon he was going to back off on his time on the Goldstar deal—to give Hansen a larger role, he would explain, then tell Art to find a human rights lawyer—a real one—to handle the Shihabi case. Fred Berger would be the logical choice. And so what if Witherspoon threatened to use a different firm on his next deal? Only a few days ago he had hinted as much to Charles, saying half seriously, "I have to keep you guys honest."

And then last night Sarah seemed to be obsessing about their lives again. She had every right to be upset. September eleventh had taken its toll on both of them. Ever since they had gotten back together, after their disastrous trip to Japan, she had treated him more kindly than he deserved. And how strong, how solicitous she had been toward him in the days and weeks and months after 9/11. He loved her for it, for her steadfastness, but most of all for her depths of understanding.

She had known he was to have breakfast at Windows on the World in the North Tower of the World Trade Center, that morning. Just after the first plane hit, his mother called the apartment from Palm Beach. Sarah had already gone into her studio but picked up the phone anyhow, out of some instinct. "There's been some kind of accident," his mother said, with her usual indirection. "Turn on the TV. I'll stay on the line." The two of them then watched in horror as the events of 9/11 unfolded. Soon it became apparent that he must be trapped high in the North Tower, above the floors engulfed in the fires from the crash. The two women began to weep, first one and then the other, on and on.

After they saw the second plane strike, this time the South Tower, Sarah became hysterical. "I should get off the phone in case he's tried to call me," she cried frantically. But there was no message. And when the towers fell, first the South Tower and then the North, Sarah couldn't stand it any longer. She turned off the TV and sat in the living room of their apartment, staring into space, numbed by the shock of it all. For two hours she had no word from him, since the network for his cell phone had shut down. She seemed practically crazy with joy when he finally appeared at the door of their apartment.

On Dr. Chambers's advice, he had tried to be more solicitous toward her this past year, in spite of all the normal pressures on their lives. He thought of the weekend he had spent with her recently at Art's place on Nantucket. For Charles, most of it had been on the phone with Witherspoon as the Goldstar deal was breaking. For her, it hadn't exactly been thrilling. On the ferry back to Cape Cod she had stood beside him at the rail, her slate-green eyes leveled on the horizon. Then, turning to him, she let her eyes lock on his. It was a look of complete understanding and unswerving commitment He would never forget it.

What a difference she had made in his life. Before he met her, he had filled up his time outside the office with what L&F lawyers recorded in their time sheets as "client entertainment"—evenings at restaurants or the theater, weekend afternoons at Jets or Yankees games, sometimes a sporting event at the firm's skybox at the Garden. The only contact he had had with anybody besides lawyers, accountants or clients was his weekly kendo workout. Nights—after he arrived home, which would always be late—he'd watch some mindless TV and then crash. He rarely attended concerts or art exhibits, although he liked them. He could cook well enough for his few good friends, mostly other lawyers or accountants, to welcome his infrequent invitations to dinner at his Park Avenue apartment. He usually managed to join his brother or sister and their families for Sunday dinner every few months. He would visit his mother in Palm Beach on holidays and birthdays. But except for weekend splurges to Aspen or Paris, he never took vacations. It was an ordered life, he thought, although, admittedly, a bit lonely. Everything given its proper due, in its proper place. Not an unhappy existence, he reflected. But not thrilling either. Sarah had changed all that.

He had never thought seriously about a committed relationship until he met her. Sharing his life with someone was in the realm of "perhaps," or "sometime in the future," "when the right girl comes along." And, he was the first to admit, he had had his share of women—mostly a lot younger and very attractive. He would date them for a few months—until he became bored or they became annoyed by his long work hours. So it was until he met Sarah. Somewhere along the line, he must have done something good to deserve her.

Enough daydreaming. He had to get to the office. He raised himself from the tufted sofa and slowly opened the door to the bedroom. It creaked, and a voice emerged from the semi-darkness.

"It was a long night without you," Sarah said with mock chagrin. She was in good humor.

"Sorry," he replied, picking up her playfulness. "I can't say I had a better offer in the living room."

"Actually I confess I was so tired I hardly realized you weren't beside me."

"I figured as much." He leaned over and kissed her on the lips. She moved over to give him room to get in beside her. "*Je regrette, mon amour,* but I've got to get into the office. I need to get back to Witherspoon. Then there's that little Saudi project—you know, what Jameel called me about last night."

"Yeah. I remember. Look, tell Art to hire himself a human rights lawyer for that Arab woman. I do feel sorry for her, but with all you have going on, she shouldn't be your responsibility. Did you have breakfast?"

"I'll grab a bagel at the corner." Charles threw off the clothes he had slept in, then quickly shaved and showered. Sarah sat at the edge of the bed, her flannel bathrobe wrapped around her, watching him as he dressed.

"Last night I forgot to tell you." she said. "In the second act Domingo fell apart. Somebody said he had the flu."

"Sounds as if the evening was a disaster all around."

"I did get to talk with Anne during the intermission. I do like her—even though, as usual, she slept through half of the opera."

Charles laughed. "I'm really sorry I couldn't go with you." He bent down and kissed her on the forehead. "I love you, you know."

"I know, Charles." Sarah stood. A shadow of concern crept over her face. "Charles, I hate to see you go—I mean, downtown. Especially today."

Instantly he knew what was on her mind—those hours a year ago when he couldn't reach her, couldn't tell her that he'd survived. He sighed, studying the worried look on her face. "You know where to reach me if anything happens." He gave her a lingering kiss, then quickly left the apartment.

The subway was nearly empty at 7:20 a.m. The cold, harsh glare of the subway lights annoyed him. He carefully folded *The New York Times* in longitudinal quarters so he could read them. He quickly scanned the top stories: Saddam shown to have extensive ties to Al Qaeda. Invasion needed posthaste to preempt his attack with murderous weapons. Chirac making a plea to put the UN inspectors back without conditions. Bush claiming that he had no choice but to act. Glancing up, Charles noticed, across the aisle, two brown eyes gazing at him from a Middle Eastern face encircled by a headscarf. Thoughts of Fatima Shihabi raced through his mind.

When the train reached the 23rd Street Station, there was a long delay. He felt anxiety rise in his gorge, and then suppressed it, mentally working through his kendo moves as Dr. Chambers had suggested. After a seemingly interminable wait, static came over the loudspeaker, then a scratchy voice announcing the car was out of service. He hurried across the platform and switched to the local.

It was going to be a rough day.

THIRTEEN

23 Wall Street
Early morning, Wednesday
Sept. 11, 2002

The phone was ringing as he came into his office. Metta hadn't yet arrived.

"Charles, it's Jameel. I'm calling from Valletta, in Malta. I have good news for you. We've got your girl. We docked so I could call you on a landline. You know you can't talk on those cell phones any more. You never know if they're secure."

"How did you do it?"

"We were lucky. This morning she was on a bus at the airport to go to the plane when she was found. It wasn't easy. She had been traveling under . . . a counterfeit passport. Nobody knew where she was in prison. My brother who works for the Ministry of the Interior did it."

"Where is she now?"

"She's on her way to Lebanon. She'll be given a Saudi visa in Beirut and then brought back to the Kingdom, where she'll be able to stay for ninety days."

"Why did the Saudis want to send her back to Iraq?"

"My brother thinks that the prison warden could be an Iraqi sympathizer. Maybe paid by the Iraqis to watch for certain people fleeing Iraq, people who have fallen out of favor with Saddam, people who know too much about what's going on there, people who have been targeted for assassination. You know the story, Charles. I can't be more specific than that. The Iraqis have their supporters throughout the Muslim world."

"I thought that she was just a dissident writer."

"She may be that too. Have you ever heard of Mukhabarat?"

"Saddam's secret police?"

"Right. They are what you might call Saddam's foreign service. Mostly in Arab countries. But many of them are in Western Europe. Some in the States too. I don't want to go into specifics."

"I well understand," Charles replied, pausing before he went on. "Look, Jameel, how can I ever repay you?"

"Forget it. Just buy me dinner the next time I'm in New York. Don't worry about anything. I've asked Mrs. Shihabi to call her brother when she gets back to the Kingdom."

"Thanks again, my friend."

"Oh, and by the way, give my sincerest condolences again to Art. Hard to believe that a year has gone by."

"Thanks, Jameel. I will. Say a prayer we all make it through today."

"*Inshallah*, Charles. Take good care of yourself."

A few more pleasantries, and Charles put down the phone. He opened the bottom drawer of his desk and raised the lid of an elaborately carved humidor he once had received as a deal memento. He selected a Davidoff, one of a dozen Art had given him—after spiriting them through customs at the Canadian border. Methodically he pressed the blade of the coupe-cigar and discarded the cigar end. Then he hit the floor button for the automatic door-closer, and his office door swung shut. In spite of Lloyd & Forster's going smoke-free years ago, Charles and his mentor were widely known to indulge their passion for Cuban cigars if the occasion was right. That this was such an occasion there could be no doubt, he thought.

He had saved the life of Fatima Shihabi. One woman's life. With a phone call, a simple phone call. He felt a curious mix of awe and shame. He drew a few puffs from the cigar, suffused with the pleasure of the moment, and launched voluminous clouds of cigar smoke into the smoke-free air.

He had to call the professor. The phone was picked up before the first ring had finished.

"Your sister is safe. They got her as she was going off to the airport."

Charles heard a gasp, then the sound of crying. It triggered something deep inside him. He tried to speak, then caught himself. He felt tears well in his eyes. The two men, each surprised and embarrassed by the strength of the other's feelings, valiantly strained to muffle their emotions. After a long pause, Charles composed himself and choked out, "She's coming back to Riyadh tonight . . . might be there already. She'll have ninety days to leave Saudi Arabia. At least she'll be able to move freely around the country."

"Can she come to America?" Crying without reserve, the professor pulsed out the words. Charles heard a knock at his door, then caught a glimpse of Hansen in the doorway and quickly took out a linen handkerchief. Dabbing at his tear-filled eyes, he motioned to Hansen to get out and shut the door behind him.

"Of course. We'll get her in as a refugee or maybe asylum, since she's a writer. I'm not an immigration lawyer, but with all that she's been through, I'd think that our government would allow her to live with you here in America."

Professor Shihabi was silent a few seconds. Then, he said, "I've heard it's very difficult."

Charles backpedaled. "Well, if not America, Canada could be possible. Maybe South America. But we'll get her to a safe place."

"It must be away from the Middle East. Too many Iraqi spies."

"What do you mean?"

"Well, Saddam's worldwide network for one thing. His secret police, Mukhabarat. But he also has sympathizers. He's paid off many, many people to be informers."

"But there must be many Iraqis who know about Saddam's weapons and oppose his regime. Why would Mukhabarat want to target your sister in particular?"

"Saddam would have some special reasons for targeting her, I believe. First, she knows far more than the ordinary Iraqi—too much—about what's going on in Iraq. She always did, you know, because as a journalist she was in touch with so many people. And then, who knows how much she actually knows about Saddam's military arsenal, his weapons? Since the UN arms inspectors can't get to Saddam's presidential palaces, who knows what he may be cooking up? But there's another thing. Fatima's writing has always had a uniquely compelling quality. It's the sort of writing that makes people want to act, to storm the barricades, to spit in the face of the tyrant. Mr. Sherman, you'll see. Some of her poetry has been translated into English. Naturally in the original Arabic the poems are more, shall I say, expressive. But at least you'll feel their sting. I'll send them to you."

"Thanks, Professor. I'm beginning to understand why Saddam would want to go after her."

"Well, there's something else as well. What really galls Saddam is that in a country of fear, that is to say modern-day Iraq, my sister gives the impression that she is utterly without fear. People think of her as being courageous beyond reason, maybe a little crazy even. The problem is that she is also beautiful, and so she attracts attention wherever she goes. I haven't seen her in a long time, but as a child, she had huge, soulful eyes, darker than a moonless sky at midnight. She's sent me a few photographs over the years, and she still has what you might call classic Arab beauty—but of the sort that would be admired—or envied—in any country. People feel challenged by her, and you would too if you were to meet her. So you see why I am so worried about her."

"Don't be concerned, Professor Shihabi. I have some friends in the State Department. We'll also get a good immigration lawyer. My partner Fred Berger is first-class . . . in fact world-class, tops in the city. He's a real miracle-worker. I'll talk to him. We'll have your sister apply for some sort of asylum."

"That's wonderful. You are so wonderful. I . . . my family . . . we will never forget you." The professor began to choke up again. He paused, then added, "When can I speak with my sister?"

"She's supposed to call you when she gets back to Saudi later today."

"I'll let you know when she does. Thank you, thank you, Mr. Sherman, for all you've done. You have saved the life of my sister. I . . . we . . . will never forget you . . . never, . . . ever. You are so wonderful, . . . so . . . wonderful." The professor's voice trailed off as the dial tone clicked on.

Charles hung up his phone and pushed back his chair. He didn't know why, but he had the unsettling feeling that the story of Fatima Shihabi was far from over.

FOURTEEN

King Khalid International Airport
Riyadh, Saudi Arabia
Late morning, Wednesday
Sept. 11, 2002

When the bus arrived back at the airport, a soldier with a gun was waiting. He motioned Fatima off. She knew she had no choice. If she ran, he would kill her. Slowly she stepped to the ground. Then, approaching her, the soldier muttered, "Get in the car—over there." He pointed in the direction of a shiny black sedan, its windows tinted, stationed at the curb. "You are going back to the detention center. Your plane does not leave for an hour." Puzzled, she kept silent. Within minutes she was back in her cell.

Something had changed, she sensed. And all at once, there rose in her heart the faintest hope that somehow, some way, as had happened once before, Abdeljelil had learned of her plight, had come to her rescue. But how? And at what price? She took her place in the same straight-backed chair as the preceding day, getting up after a while to pace around the room. A good hour passed. Then she heard the staccato thump of boots coming down the corridor. She could discern the half-beat of the supervisor's step. The cell door clanked open, and the three Saudi soldiers came in.

The supervisor's expression was grim. "You will go to Beirut this afternoon with my subordinates," he muttered. "You will receive a visa to come back to Saudi Arabia. I will wait for you at this airport. You may stay in the Kingdom for ninety days. That's all. Do you understand?" He parroted the words at her as if he had been instructed to deliver these words and no more, no less.

She nodded, not daring to speak.

"We will come get you when the plane is ready." He paused, then beyond his mandate, he added, "You are lucky this time, Madame Qureshi." He stood over her, glowering. "The next time, do not imagine, even for one instant, that your friends will save you. The next time it will be too late. You will be food for the dogs." With that, he turned on his heel and, beckoning the two other soldiers to follow him, hobbled out the door, which banged shut behind them.

Dazed and confused, Fatima released her body against the laddered ribs of the wooden chair. It had been a trying four days, and she had been surprised at having to confront so many challenges so early in her journey. Truly, as the supervisor reminded her, she had been lucky. She had been lucky to escape Iraq, and now lucky to escape Saddam's clutches. But as welcome as the word of her release might be, her relief was muted by a new and sobering concern about what might lie ahead of her. Her thoughts turned to Latifa, and she prayed that if her luck ever did turn, regardless of whatever might happen, she would be able to insulate Latifa from the consequences.

An hour later, the supervisor's subordinates came to get her. They carried pistols equipped with silencers. She sensed that if she were to run, they would kill her instantly. Besides, she thought, she had no passport, no papers. After September eleventh—after all that had happened since then—no airport in the world would let her on a plane without documentation. There could be no thought of escape. One on each side of her, stonily silent and watching her every move, the soldiers escorted her onto the bus back to the airport, walked her to the plane, and then accompanied her on the flight to Lebanon.

In Beirut the authorities processed her visa quickly. Before she could even think about it, her escorts had put her on a flight returning to Saudi Arabia, and she found herself back in the Riyadh airport. At the arrival gate the supervisor greeted her, even a little warmly. He handed her back her satchel with her belongings. Then he invited her to a shop in the airport lobby for coffee, asking her with a wry inquisitiveness about her family.

"Now, tell me, Madame Qureshi, how many children did you say you have?" His rough hands were folded before him. He managed a twinkle in his eye.

"Just one," she said warily.

"Is she a good student?" The conversation was becoming more absurd with each passing moment.

"Yes, she is a star pupil."

"She must take after her mother." The supervisor was pathetic. She was becoming delirious. "You must miss her."

She could not continue this charade. "Why are you so kind to me so suddenly?" she asked, adding, "What has happened?"

"I have received instructions. From someone in the Royal Family," he said, a little defensively. "To take care of you. You must be very important. We are supposed to do anything we can for you. My name is Ali Akbar," he said, handing her his card. "You may call me Ali," he added, his insincere smile flashing two prominent gold fillings. It almost made her shiver.

That evening the supervisor brought her to a two-story villa he had found for her at the edge of the city, in the district of Nasriyyah, near Wadi Hanifah, on the northern outskirts of Riyadh. The house was fronted by a small courtyard and beyond by a stone wall, topped with bottle shards, facing onto the street. It had an enclosed garden in the rear. Once he was assured that she would be comfortable, he handed her a stack of Saudi riyals, saying, "There's a souk a little farther up the road where you can buy food and other necessities. I'll call you in a day or two, Madame Qureshi, just to make sure everything is satisfactory."

Exhausted from the events of the day, she dragged herself up the stairs to a bedroom on the second floor. She threw herself onto the plush bed and almost at once fell into a fitful sleep. She dreamt that she was wearing a shimmering gossamer gown, embroidered with the finest gold thread. She stood proudly atop a high stone altar before a throng of a thousand men, in a vast amphitheater. Naked except for loincloths, their bodies glistened with sweat. In a guttural cacophony they chanted vicious blood curses, primeval utterances, taunting her. "Fatima, Hell Maiden Art Thou. Fatima, Thou Unholy One. Fatima, Bride of the Devil." She felt herself tumbling down the stone stairs, her limp corpse now falling into a bottomless chasm, the chanting men on its rim far above. Out of the west, above a glorious sun, a winged stallion swooped toward her, riderless. At the last possible instant the steed snatched her from the abyss, lifted her body into the heavens, on and on through a luminous sky, finally settling on a vast plain of velvet grass. As it flew off, it beckoned her to follow, but try as she might, she could not raise her head.

FIFTEEN

23 Wall Street
Late morning, Wednesday
Sept. 11, 2002

Charles heard the rap of knuckles on his office door, and before he could speak, Metta had inserted her smiling face through the opening. "Your old *patty aimy* Ann Jacobs is on line one." One more of Metta's fractured French utterances that he would choose to ignore, as even a small price to pay for a first-class legal secretary. "She said she's calling from a boat."

"Okay, thanks Metta, I'll take it."

Charles picked up the phone. "Hey, Ann. Thanks for getting back to me. Where are you?"

"Actually I'm calling from a yacht on Chesapeake Bay—at the State Department's Senior Seminar. I'm learning to bond with my fellow State Department officers."

He caught the irony in her voice and visualized Ann's pert, round face. "I'm sorry to bother you about this. I trust you got my message."

"Sure. I just got it. I was on my way to a meeting on board a few minutes ago and checked my voicemail. It's been awhile, Charles, but I'm always pleased to hear from you."

He quickly got to the point. "Ann, look, I don't want to keep you from your meeting. But the Saudis have agreed to let this woman stay in Saudi Arabia for ninety days. I just need to get her a visa or asylum or something to get her into the U.S."

"Charles, you know I'd do anything to try to help you, but I'm afraid you're on your own with this one. Our government can't stop to help every poor schmuck around the world who decides he'd like to live in the States."

"This one is different. She is a writer, a poet. She also seems to know something about Saddam's weapons. She'll be killed if she has to go back to Iraq."

"Charles, you're wonderful. But unfortunately you're also a little naive. This dissident, as you've described her, is tough. She will fend for herself. And there are hundreds of Iraqis now who claim they know something about the weapons. It's all over the papers that Saddam has them. The refugees say they know exactly where and what, just so somebody will pay attention to them, give them refugee status in the West. Then when we interview them, it turns out they're not credible. It's a total waste of time. Charles, honestly, why don't you go back to your deals?"

Ann was right. He had no business playing in this high-stakes game of life and death. He made a final parry, repeating the request he had made on her voice mail. "Can't you give me the name of someone at our embassy in Riyadh whom I might just talk with?"

"Sure, you can call Rita Lane. She's the consular official on duty there. But don't mention my name."

"Thanks, I won't." The hell he wouldn't. They signed off, with Charles promising to buy Ann lunch the next time he was in Washington.

He lifted himself out of his leather chair and walked toward the window. As he passed his credenza, his eyes fell upon the Drayton tanker model. He lifted it off its stand and admired its fine detail. The hardest deal he had ever done, Jameel had saved him on that one too. He gently placed the nautical model back on its pedestal, paced a few times back and forth across the carpet, and returned to his desk. He had started to read the Goldstar prospectus one more time when Metta buzzed him on the intercom.

"It's Mr. Witherspoon."

Witherspoon. Charles knew the call had to come. He should have called him back earlier.

"We're to meet at one-thirty at Citibank," Witherspoon said commandingly. "The board gave its approval last night. It was just after midnight. I tried to reach you on your home phone, but I couldn't get through. I thought you said you'd be at home."

Damnation. With all the excitement he had forgotten to check his messages. The call must have come when he was speaking with Jameel.

"No, actually I was on the phone. I'm in the early stages of another deal . . . international—which is why the line was tied up. Sorry about that, Mr. Witherspoon." Well, hell yes, Charles thought, he had only saved somebody's life a million miles away. Witherspoon wouldn't want to know.

Witherspoon continued as if Charles hadn't spoken. "They want to make the announcement by the end of September, before the end of the quarter. I'll need a term sheet for the meeting this afternoon. The usual kind. Just for me to use. Can you put one together?"

"Yeah, sure, I'll have it for you." He would have to clear the decks. Fatima Shihabi could wait.

"I'll see you at one-thirty sharp this afternoon in the lobby."

Citibank's main conference room was on the thirty-third floor of Citicorp Center. It ran the entire width of the building, halfway down Fifty-third Street between Lexington and Third. After many Wall Street brokerage houses moved their offices to midtown in the late 1970's, the banks, law firms, and accounting firms followed their customers and clients to spacious digs on Park and Lexington. And Citibank had had the foresight to ensconce in its corporate offices a room like no other. The conference table alone seemed to stretch to the vanishing point of infinity. The room had seen some of the biggest and most fabled deals in the history of New York's financial community. And after 9/11, it had taken its place as the largest and best-appointed conference room in the entire New York metropolitan area. For a deal to be scheduled there meant that it had achieved a special scale and importance.

Charles arrived at the art-bedecked lobby of the thirty-third floor a few minutes early. Moments later, Witherspoon—tall, distinguished, with silver hair chevroned over his ears into a wavelet at the nape of his neck, his Saville Row suit immaculately tailored—fairly glided off the elevator and into the lobby, in the same suave way he moved through the world of mergers and acquisitions, a shark through deep water. Charles approached him almost reverentially.

"Remember where we were a year ago?" Witherspoon asked.

"How could I forget? Hard to believe it's been a year already."

"It was pure luck to have gotten out of there. Thank God you had to get back to your office."

"It was fate, you know. We were lucky," Charles replied, hoping his offhand take on that morning's events would cap the subject. If Charles let him, Witherspoon would rehash it all again, as he regularly did. It was too upsetting. Charles remained silent.

"Well, Charles, are you ready for this?" Witherspoon asked finally. The question would have been ridiculous if it had not been perfunctory.

"Naturally, Mr. Witherspoon. It won't be easy, but none of them are, of course."

"Right you are, Charles, but this one is a little different. In many ways, it's the first of a new sort of deal we're going to see a lot of in the future. And the Street is going to remember this one for a long time."

A phalanx of pinstripes marched out of the elevator and headed toward the conference room. "Perhaps we should go in, Mr. Witherspoon," Charles suggested. "They can't have the party without us."

Charles Sherman and his client Harold Witherspoon took their places at the precise middle of the long conference table. This was their deal, and there was no mistaking it. The assembled attorneys, investment bankers and industry mucky-mucks, resplendent in their corporate couture of worsted wools, designer ties, and tasseled loafers, now swarmed into the vast chamber and sat in formation up and down each side of the table.

Witherspoon welcomed the many familiar faces around the table and then called the meeting to order. "Charles Sherman, would you do us the favor of presenting our position to Viatech?" It was a mark of Witherspoon's regard for Charles. And in the chivalry of investment bankers in Manhattan, it was the equivalent of a laying–on–of–hands as a Knight of the Order. At least for this deal.

"Of course, but I'd suggest that you not hesitate to let me know if I miss anything," Charles said, smiling at Witherspoon. Charles wouldn't miss anything. The room knew it and appreciated his nonchalance.

"All right," Witherspoon said, relaxed and confident. "I'll do just that." He smiled back. It was patter playing almost as if it had been rehearsed.

The meeting was over minutes after it had begun. It had gone well. "Almost too cozy, I thought," Charles told Witherspoon afterward. He had positioned Goldstar's offer so that if the $74.20 a share approved by Viatech's board proved unacceptable to the dissident shareholders, they would have an alternative: either a higher cash price or a partial stock and cash deal equating to $82.00. After a brief discussion, they took the cash and agreed to proceed—subject, in the usual course, to a written agreement. The closing was scheduled for Monday, September 30, with a pre-closing, to iron out any remaining nits, to be held the Friday before. Attorneys to work out the details, with Charles picked to draft the deal papers within the week. Then there would be an all-hands meeting at Lloyd & Forster to resolve any drafting issues. Witherspoon was pleased.

Charles and Witherspoon exited the conference room together, striding back into the thirty-third floor lobby, the two of them practically arm in arm.

"Charles, you and your girl, what's her name? Sarah? You should join Helen and me for a quiet dinner. Just the four of us. Early next week. We'd be delighted to see both of you." It was a rare offer, as Witherspoon's private life had always been a matter of some conjecture among the partners of Lloyd & Forster.

"This has been a busy time for me, Mr. Witherspoon," Charles said, recalling Sarah's undisguised antipathy toward his most important client. He doubted that Sarah would ever agree to spend an evening with Witherspoon, but he would ask her. The image of an Arab woman's eyes flashed through his mind. "This deal is on a pretty short fuse. Perhaps the week after would work better for me. Can I get back to you?"

Witherspoon pursed his lips and nodded. "Why certainly, Charles, my friend," he said, placing his arm over Charles's left shoulder.

When the elevator arrived and its doors silently slid open, the two men stepped forward to go in, but just before their feet crossed the threshold, Witherspoon stepped back. "You go on ahead, why don't you, Charles. I'll catch up with you later. There are a few calls I'd like to make from here."

Witherspoon was like that, Charles thought. A man of multiple agendas. "Sure, okay, Mr. Witherspoon. No problem. Talk to you later." As Charles entered the elevator, which was empty, he turned to give Witherspoon a final nod. But he had already sped off. The doors swooshed shut, and Charles felt his body lighten as the elevator began its earthward acceleration.

Maybe the day was going to turn out all right after all, he thought. His most important client seemed satisfied, even magnanimous in his appreciation for Charles's handiwork. The Shihabi matter was wired, at least enough to get it on track. And by this time, mid-afternoon of the first anniversary of 9/11, no terrorist had seen fit to bomb the bejesus out of mid-town Manhattan. No, it wasn't such a bad day after all.

And yet, he reflected, his deals rarely unfolded in quite the way he would have expected. In fact they occasionally took directions he would have least expected. He sighed, wondering what surprises lay ahead in his current projects. The anxiety he had felt earlier in the day began to come back. He sighed again, then took in a deep breath and held it for a few seconds, a palliative Dr. Chambers had suggested.

When the elevator landed, he barely felt it. The doors opened soundlessly, and he went out, crossed the lobby, and headed back to his office.

SIXTEEN

Riyadh, Saudi Arabia
Thursday–Sunday
Sept. 12–15, 2002

The morning after Fatima was installed in the villa, the supervisor Ali Akbar called to check on her. After that, he did not call again. She was unconcerned since she was now quite self-sufficient. Ali had handed her enough riyal banknotes to last several months. She was just three blocks away from a small souk and could go back and forth easily. She was careful to drape her abayah over her head, covering her face, since an unveiled woman alone in the Nasriyyah souk, unlike in the city's central souk, certainly would be a curiosity. The religious police could beat her, possibly even arrest her. Because she would have to go to the souk alone, she would also risk harassment for not being accompanied by a male relative, but she had no choice.

When she went out, which was seldom, she walked slowly, imitating the neighborhood women, so as not to attract attention. Once or twice, she sensed that someone had followed her from the souk, but she could not be sure. Unaccustomed to wearing the full veil over her eyes, she was bothered that beneath it she could only identify shapes of objects and shades of gray. Dusk was a particularly hard time. On her way to the souk one evening for bread, she hit her head on a pole in the street. After that, she decided to go out only in full sunlight.

Two days after she moved into the house, she concluded that the beggar on the corner opposite her villa was watching her come and go. The next day, Saturday, around noon, she quietly left her house, carefully locking the door to the courtyard. She walked in her usual deliberate manner to the souk, where she found a stall with rugs hanging in the back. She shoved them aside, then entered the adjoining stall, and quickly left the souk. On her return, the beggar was not at his usual post.

That the Saudis would monitor her activities did not surprise her. However the arrangements for her release from prison had been made, she knew that someone high in the Saudi government had secured her release and would protect her. Of greater concern, she thought, was the chance that someone—either the supervisor Ali Akbar or another Iraqi sympathizer or a paid informer—had alerted the Iraqi authorities that she was in Riyadh. She had heard reports that the Iraqi secret police tracked down and assassinated Iraqi opponents of the regime long after they had left Iraq. In the Islamic world, Iraq did not find it difficult to find sources throughout the Middle East, even in key government ministries, who were willing to serve as informants for a price. And Mukhabarat moved swiftly and ruthlessly. Hundreds of dissidents, writers, professors, intellectuals, and others who opposed the Iraqi regime had been hunted down and killed in their countries of exile.

Once again a sense of foreboding crept into her heart. She would have to take precautions. She decided to stop going to the souk. She planned what to do if they came for her during the day: she would flee by the back door if she heard their rap on the front door. That night, she carefully bolted the front door and moved a table against it so she could hear them if they came. Then, leaving the back door open, she slept in a corner of the garden, her veil wrapped around her. She would not let them take her without a fight.

SEVENTEEN

23 Wall Street
Thursday–Saturday
Sept. 12–14, 2002

As he worked feverishly to complete the Goldstar contract, Charles decided to put Fatima Shihabi out of his head, at least for a few days. He tried to fire up the old Charles, the workaholic he had been years before, before he and Sarah had gone to Japan, before their split-up. He barely communicated with the world at large, except to make small talk with the limo chauffer each night, respond to Sarah's concerned calls and react to Metta's mildly irritating wisecracking. As he once had done, he even asked Sarah to leave his dinner warming in the oven. Then he would collapse into bed beside her still body, only to rise after a few hours of restless sleep, reappear at his desk, and continue the march. It was inordinately complex work, demanding his total concentration. But try as he might, he couldn't stop the vision of a veiled woman from invading his thoughts. All too often, even in the midst of drafting the most convoluted contract terms, the proportionate stock redemption provisions that would apply if Goldstar were ever to buy back their shares, his mind would begin to wander and he would find himself wondering how Fatima Shihabi would get on if she came to the States and why she had to leave Iraq and whether she had ever read the poet Rumi.

Friday afternoon, more as a distraction than anything else, Charles went to his kendo class. It got him out of the office, and he was grateful for the respite. He turned off his cell phone, donned his padded cotton uniform with its "International Sanjuriu Martial Arts" logo, and dug out his polished oak baton from the back of his locker. In spite of his long absence, he was greeted warmly by Master Kamiura, although he allowed Charles no quarter in the intense give–and–take of the workout. After a good twenty minutes of feints and strikes and intercepts, Charles let his mind wander for a split-second as it dawned on him that Canada just might have an open-door policy for political refugees. Just then, the master thwacked Charles resoundingly on his helmet, a match point to be sure, but also a blow that would surely have been fatal if it had been administered to a poorly padded adversary in actual combat. At that, his head aching slightly, Charles decided to demur and ceremonially bowed, presenting his weapon in a gesture of surrender. Then he quickly showered, donned his suit and tie, and retreated to his office.

Toward the end of the third day, late on Saturday afternoon, Professor Shihabi called. He hadn't spoken with his sister since she came back to Saudi Arabia from Beirut. His voice was edged with tension. It was becoming clear to him that in fewer than ninety days, she would have to seek refuge in some other country. Preferably the United States or Canada, but any country would do.

"We are working against time. The ninety days will expire before we know it. My sister cannot return to Iraq. With an invasion by the Americans likely, Saddam will be even more repressive than before. I've heard that he's slaughtering anybody who doesn't do his bidding, who he thinks has betrayed him, his family, or the country. Then he wipes out their families."

Charles tried to be reassuring. "Don't worry, Professor, don't worry. I should've contacted my immigration partner Fred Berger before this, but I've been swamped by a big project. I'll see him right now. I will. He's usually in the office on Saturdays. I'll do it as soon as we hang up. As I've told you, he's a superb immigration attorney. It's just a matter of getting the right paperwork. If anyone qualifies for asylum in the States, it's your sister."

The professor seemed relieved. "Thanks be to Allah that my family has you to help us."

"Hold your thanks until Fatima is safely in the United States."

"May Allah bless you anyway for all you have done."

As soon as he clicked off his speakerphone, Charles strode out of his office. "Michele, hold my calls. I'll be with Fred Berger a little while." She beamed him her I–am–always–available–for–you smile. He found himself wishing that Metta worked on Saturdays.

Fred Berger was not so reassuring. In fact, he held out little hope. "Charles, people like Fatima Shihabi just can't get on an airplane, fly to the United States and, when they get here, ask for asylum. Especially after 9/11. It would take a minor miracle for an Arab from Iraq to get asylum in this country. For one thing, the airlines won't even let them on a plane unless they have a visa. If someone like Ms. Shihabi managed to get on a plane, which itself is unlikely, our Immigration and Naturalization Service would fine the airline thousands of dollars. INS makes no exceptions. Ms. Shihabi doesn't stand a chance of flying here on a commercial airline."

"Okay then, why don't we just have her apply for asylum from Saudi Arabia, have her get a visa, and come here legally?"

"It could take a year," Berger said. "The INS is terribly slow in processing asylum applications—especially now after 9/11, most particularly from Iraq. You're going to have to bag this one, Charles."

"What if she knows something about Saddam's weapons?"

"Yeah, right. I've tried this with one client already. The problem is that there are too many Iraqis who claim they know about the weapons. Give me asylum, they say, and I'll tell you what and where. But our government won't buy it. You've got to have documents, maps, plans—that sort of thing. Unless this girl has the goods on Saddam, they'll say she doesn't have . . ."

". . . credibility," Charles added, finishing the thought. "I doubt she's got any documents, Fred. Even if she had any, the Saudis probably took them away."

"Charles, you say that she has less than ninety days?"

"I could try to get that extended, but I suspect that the Saudi government would not be excited about harboring a prominent Iraqi dissident for a whole year. And besides, the Iraqis will be looking for her if they think she knows too much."

"I do understand that," Berger responded, his tone sympathetic.

"In other words, you're telling me that even if Fatima has a good asylum case, there's no way that she can get to the front door of the United States to submit it?"

"That's right. It's a Catch–Twenty-two you don't find in your prissy corporate practice," Fred answered, smirking.

"Fred Berger, if you weren't one of my favorite partners I'd do a kendo move on you—right now." Charles assumed the classic kendo "frontal entrance" stance. "*Ni . . . ku . . . te*," he grunted, pretending to work through the tactics of initial engagement. Then he laid down his imaginary weapon, and hands on hips, faced the other man. "Okay, Fred, listen," his tone suddenly serious. "I know that we don't have a lot of life-or-death cases in corporate, but one thing we do have is contacts, lots of them, ones that you immigration guys could only dream about. There're plenty of ways to get around the airlines. I'll just buy her a ticket on a freighter from Jeddah. Or have one of my corporate clients, like P&G or Siemens, fly her to the States on the corporate jet from Saudi. You guys just don't get it. You're off in your rarified area of the practice. You really don't know how the world works." Charles glared at him.

"Okay, okay, Charlie, calm down. First I think you'll find that your corporate clients won't risk the fines. Not to mention the bad publicity. Even for you. But then there's another thing. You may remember from law school that, as an attorney, you're an 'officer of the court' as they put it? Do you remember that?"

"I do, naturally." Charles was fuming now.

"Well, I'll put it to you straight. The rules of ethics prohibit you from helping Fatima to get to the United States illegally."

"You mean that I can't help her get here, to Uncle Sam's front door, to deliver an asylum application that would almost certainly be granted?"

"Correct."

"God damn it. Maybe I should become a—what do they call those people who help the Mexican wetbacks across the Rio Grande?"

"A mule. Or a coyote."

"Yeah, a mule."

"Mules are illegal too. You could risk disbarment. It'd be professional *hara-kiri.*"

"Okay, Fred, I get the point."

"You could always marry her . . . for real, I mean."

"No, thanks. I've never even met her."

"I suggest that you'd be better off trying one of the international agencies, like the International Refugee Committee. The IRC is supposed to handle cases like this one."

"Where will they send her?"

"They'll decide. Normally you've got no control over where she'll go."

"At least she'll be outside Saudi Arabia. So what do I tell my client?"

"You already said it. Contacts . . . contacts, Charles."

"What do you mean?"

"You really want to save the life of this woman?"

"Most certainly," Charles replied, a little indignant.

"You've got the contacts. Use 'em, Charles. Now, get the hell out of here so I can go back to practicing law. At some point I'd like to get out of this nightclub so I can start my weekend."

On his way back to his office, Charles was passed by Hansen sprinting down the corridor to a meeting. Hansen turned, raced back to Charles and, out of breath, said, "I'm late . . . for a meeting but I just want to congratu . . . late you . . . on the Goldstar deal. A buddy of mine at NationsBank . . . the whole Street . . . is talking about how you and Witherspoon pulled it off and got the shareholders to agree. Sorry, got to run." He took off.

Charles mouthed into the now empty hallway, "Thanks, Hansen."

Back in his office, Charles got Professor Shihabi on the line and told him what Fred Berger had said.

"Well, at least we know my sister is safe in Saudi Arabia, under the protection of your friends there. I can always visit her in another country that is willing to take her in."

Charles tried to be solicitous. "Why sure. She might even approach the IRC office in Saudi, to see where they'd suggest relocating her. It'd make more sense for her to reach them herself. Besides, she probably has contacts."

"That's what it's all about, isn't it? Isn't that what your partner said?"

"How so?"

"Contacts. Whom you know. That sort of thing." Whether because of Charles's blithe self-assurance or the professor's own growing faith that his sister somehow would be rescued, a hint of bonhomie now tinged the professor's voice.

"Law practice is a people business, sure. But as you no doubt find in academia, contacts only help row the boat—you've got to set the compass."

"And find the port in the storm."

"Yeah." It was late-Saturday-afternoon banter, Charles reflected, and he wanted to go home. "Professor, your sister should be okay for a few days. Get some rest. I'll be back to you as soon as I hear anything."

After he signed off, Charles threw a few papers into his briefcase and left his office. As he hustled down the corridor, he passed Fred Berger's office. Fred was still at his post, on his phone. He nodded at him as he went by.

Contacts, Fred had counseled him, use them. Contacts. He would have to find some.

EIGHTEEN

43 Central Park West
Evening, Monday
Sept. 16, 2002

It had been another day of drafting the Goldstar documents, back and forth with Witherspoon on the phone, intermittent e-mails of contract terms, a deli sandwich and a Coke at his desk for lunch, and a long meeting with Hansen about legal issues to be researched. When Charles arrived home around 8:30 p.m., Sarah was seated at the kitchen counter, glancing at *The New York Times* and drinking a glass of wine.

She raised her head and smiled. "Hi. I wasn't sure when you'd be home, so I've already eaten."

Charles inhaled deeply. "Chicken cassoulet—smells terrific," he said.

"Help yourself," she said. "It's probably still warm."

"I will, thanks, but I'm going to have a glass of wine first." He gave Sarah a quick hug, then filled a wineglass from the bottle of Châteauneuf du Pape that was on the counter. "That smell makes me nostalgic for my days in Paris."

"You were so lucky to be able to live there. I wish I had known you then. I guess we'll never be able to say—what was that line from *Casablanca?*—'We'll always have Paris'?"

"We'll always have New York then. It's better," he said, nodding in agreement with himself as he sat down on the stool beside her.

"Better for whom?" she asked. "*I've* always had New York," she said, smiling. Sarah had been born and grown up in Manhattan, in the very apartment they were living in now, which she had inherited after her parents died.

Charles returned her smile. "Lucky you," he said. While Sarah had grown up in the City, the only child of wealthy parents, he had been raised in Hoboken, New Jersey, with a sister and brother. His father worked as a conductor on the Erie Lackawanna train line that ran west into the metropolitan suburbs.

She didn't respond. After taking a long draw of her wine, she gazed at him. "I've been thinking about the conversation we had last week about September eleventh—also about the effect it's had on us."

"I really worried about the first anniversary, Sarah. Thank God we got through the day without an incident. I've been so busy, I forgot to tell you—actually I think I might have repressed it—but that afternoon, when Witherspoon and I had our big meeting on Goldstar, do you know what he did? I was with him two minutes, and he brings up how we got out, how I somehow saved his life. Sarah, I just don't want to think about it any more. I've had enough. I've got to get on with my life."

Sarah took another long sip of wine. "Well, I have an idea of how you can get on with your life—how *we* can get on with *our* life together."

He grinned. Trying to tease her out of her sudden seriousness, he asked, "What's that, O Wise One?"

"I'm being serious. You're going to think I'm loony, but here it is: Let's leave New York and move to Paris."

"What?" He stared at her.

"Let's move to Paris," she repeated, her voice animated. "We'll sell the coop, you take early retirement, and we get ourselves out of here."

"Sarah, have you had too much vino? That's a crazy idea. I'm only forty-six—I'm not ready to retire. There's just no way."

"Why not?"

"Well, for one thing, I've got too much invested. I've worked too hard to get where I am."

"Oh nonsense. You even said the other night that you're questioning it all."

"Yeah, but that's a hell of a long way from saying that I'd give it all up." He was beginning to feel anger rising in his throat. "Sarah, you know how hard I've worked to get here."

"Yes, Charles, if anyone knows that, I do. You hardly have time for anything else."

The old arguments were starting up again. He needed to diffuse them. "Look, I've been doing some thinking too. The other night, after our talk, I couldn't sleep. I started thinking about making some changes—maybe cutting back on my hours, getting Hansen to take on some of Witherspoon's scut work—after Goldstar, of course. Just let me come out the other end of this deal, and I'll be okay. I know it probably sounds contradictory, but right now, my work is my escape. It helps keep the demons at bay."

"So 9/11 made you want to change your life, but because of 9/11 you can't change?"

"Not exactly. But work does make you free, in a certain sense."

"Tell me about it," Sarah sighed. "Okay, I can understand that you're not ready to run away to Paris, and I didn't truly believe you would. What I really want is to spend more time with you—poke around art galleries, go to the theater, take a *real* vacation. Lately, I feel like we're moving backward. You're working longer and longer hours, we don't eat dinner together, and you can't even manage to go to the opera with me. I won't go back to the way we were before—I simply won't!"

Charles had an unsettling sense of déjà vu. "Don't think I don't want to spend more time with you, too." As soon as the words were out of his mouth, he realized how inadequate they sounded.

"Don't humor me, Charles."

"I'm not," he said. "Once this deal is over, how about we fly to Paris for a long weekend and have dinner at Taillevent?"

She slammed the counter with her palm, startling him. "Charles Sherman, haven't you learned anything in all the years we've lived to-gether? It's not about spending money. We've been there, done that. I'd be happy to spend an afternoon with you at the Metropolitan Museum and eat in the cafeteria."

"Deal," Charles said, hoping to cajole her out of her anger. "You always were a cheap date."

She rolled her eyes, but he could tell that her mood was softening. "I *just* want to spend more time with you," she reiterated.

He took her chin in his hand and looked into her eyes. "And *I* want to spend more time with *you*. And I promise I will, once the Goldstar deal is over and I've helped Art with Mrs. Shihabi—the Iraqi woman." He leaned back in his chair and took a sip of wine.

Sarah leaned over and briefly put her head on his shoulder. "I can get so angry at you when you spend all those hours with Witherbottom, but you're really such a good person. I'm sorry about sounding so angry when you told me you were helping this—Mrs. Shihabi?" He nodded. "You're running yourself ragged with work—and now this. I worry about you, but I also understand that you want to help this poor woman. At heart I think you're a do-gooder."

"Oh, you mean I'm capable of thinking of something besides making money?" He grinned.

She gave him a playful punch on the arm. "You know what I mean. It's not the first time you've helped someone get out of prison, which is pretty amazing, now that I think about it. I remember when you organized that group of downtown lawyers to petition for the release of that human rights lawyer Pavel Popovich from the prison in Dubrovnik? And you've helped other people too, like those Saudi girls. You got them through Wellesley."

Charles shook his head at the thought. "Yeah, and then they both went straight back to Saudi Arabia and got married to guys they never met before."

"But still, you were there for them. Just like you've been there for Mrs. Shihabi."

"The situation's a little different, though; it's a lot more serious. She's still not out of the woods—or should I say the desert? We still don't have a place for her to live. It could be years before Saddam is overthrown, taken out or whatever. She has less than ninety days left to stay in Saudi."

"And until Art assigns another lawyer to her case—or *if* he does—I know you're not going to let the case drop—it's like finding a stray dog on the street; you just can't walk away."

"You know me too well," he said.

She pushed herself away from the counter and stood. "But it's all too much for you, Charles—Goldstar . . . Witherbottom . . . Mrs. Shihabi . . . your 9/11 nightmares . . . all of it. I worry about you. I really do But right now, I'm tired, I'm a little buzzed, and I'm going to bed. Don't forget to eat."

"I won't. Good night, Sarah dear."

While he was eating the chicken cassoulet, he paged through the Goldstar OP one last time, then decided to go to bed. Tomorrow was going to be a big day.

NINETEEN

Riyadh, Saudi Arabia
Monday, Sept. 16, 2002

As another day passed and she weakened from hunger and fatigue, Fatima realized that she could no longer remain sequestered in the villa. She wondered whether her mind was playing tricks on her—perhaps she was becoming unduly fearful or even paranoid because of being detained. She decided to observe her observer more closely. At first she watched the beggar furtively from a corner of the window, then once when he left for a short while, she cut a small hole in her bedroom's drapery. She studied him as he solicited alms, raising his palms upward to each intended benefactor and bowing his shoulders each time a donation was made. From time to time, she noticed him glancing, ever so casually, over to her villa. And then late one afternoon, two men in dark business suits stopped before him as if to give alms. They began talking animatedly. The older man, whose forehead was disfigured by an odd fold of skin, appeared severe, even hard-bitten. When he motioned in the direction of her villa, the other man nodded vigorously. She sensed that they were discussing her.

Once again her heart began to pound with fear. They *had* to be discussing her! But she had come too far to let herself be taken by them in the night to some wadi out beyond the city, stabbed, and left to die alone in some forsaken place. As she had done before, she would take charge of her own destiny. She would run.

When darkness fell, she put into her brown cloth sack the few provisions she had, left the villa through the rear, and quietly let herself out the back gate of the garden. Lowering her veil around her shoulders so she could pick out obstacles in her path, she kept to the shadows and gradually made her way across the city. Except for a few merchants returning from the souk and the occasional car or taxi, the streets were deserted. When she reached Diriyyah Street, she could see in the distance the lights of ornate palaces that wealthy Saudi princes had built for themselves years before. She found a small depression, fronted by scruffy brush that hid her from the street. She pulled her veil over her head, wrapped it firmly around her, and drew her legs to her chest. The night was cold, and she would soon be uncomfortable. Sleep would not come, and after a while she pulled her veil away from her head and raised her eyes to a moonlit sky radiant with stars. She thought of Latifa and wondered what would become of her. At least Abdeljelil would be able to protect her until she was able to get her out of Iraq. She thought of Omar and the love he had shown her. He had saved her life.

Tomorrow she would figure out a way to call Omar and ask him what to do. She would find some way to survive, no matter what.

TWENTY

23 Wall Street
Afternoon, Tuesday
Sept. 17, 2002

I thought that we had full agreement when we met at Citibank last week." Charles's eyes flashed anger. Witherspoon nodded vigorously, his bushy eyebrows levitating.

The cold, almost disembodied voice of Christopher St. George, Millstone Tweed's senior partner and counsel for the dissident shareholders, reverberated up and down Lloyd & Forster's longest conference table. "That was when the dissidents had no continuing product liability after the sale. Since then, we looked at your draft of the agreement. You evidently expect our side to pick up the liability. We never agreed to that."

Charles glanced around the firm's cavernous conference room, elaborately framed portraits of Messrs. Lloyd and Forster commanding the walls at each end. Up and down the long table, row after row of gray stripes. Protective coloration of the species. Two-toned striped shirts framing animal-theme silk ties. A few women in less-muted mufti. Lawyers from Cravath, Sullivan and his own firm, Lloyd & Forster. Accountants from the big–three–or–four CPA firms. Investment bankers from Salomon, from CS First Boston. Chief financial officers. The two company presidents. New York power personified, he thought. If a deal were to be done, this would be the group to do it.

"Okay, why don't we think of a way to compromise the issue?" Charles's trademark response. Never give up. Maybe the pig will fly, as they said at the Law School. "How about putting a limit of five percent of the acquisition price on your side's exposure?" Charles asked. He knew instinctively that Witherspoon would agree. They had expected resistance on the product liability issue, and Witherspoon had told him privately that he'd be willing to concede the issue if necessary. "Bring it up if you feel we should, although it's not a big issue for me," he had said.

"That's ridiculous," St. George countered. "We could never agree to any proposal that forces the selling shareholders to pay anything after the closing." A murmur of assent moved up the table.

"Suppose the shareholders were seriously negligent or even deliberately concealed information?" Charles felt a bead of perspiration run down the curve of his armpit. He had to salvage something from the point. He had to win. Something.

Witherspoon seemed a little edgy. He caught Charles's eye.

Suddenly Charles saw Metta Jenkins at the conference room door. Oh no, he thought. No, no. Not now, Metta. Not now.

All eyes turned to her as she surveyed the room and zeroed in on Charles. She motioned to him, then bustled officiously down his side of the conference table and placed the pink slip facedown on the table before him. As she stepped back away from the table, she gave him her you'd–better–get–right–on–this, Buster look. After glancing at Witherspoon, who appeared distressed, Charles flipped the note over. It read, "Call Professor Shihabi immediately. Most urgent. It's his sister."

God damn it, Charles thought. For a split second, he wavered. He looked at Witherspoon, at the purple veins swelling on the side of his head. He looked at Christopher St. George pumping out his chest, glaring at him, across the conference table. He looked up and down the assembled ranks of bespoke suits and handmade ties. Here was one of the largest, most important deals on the Street, one of the most important deals of his career, and on behalf of his firm's most important client. If he stepped away from the table, the other side could consider it a sign of hesitation, of weakness. How could a telephone call from another client ever take precedence over this discussion of a deal-breaker issue? Not on this deal.

Charles looked again at the note and then raised his eyes back to the conference table. "Ladies and gentlemen. This is obviously a key point for both sides. I would suggest that we caucus for five minutes to give each side a chance to think about our respective positions."

"You can caucus all you want, but we are definitely not going to accept any ongoing liability," Christopher St. George trumpeted. Like backbenchers in a Parliamentary debate, the assemblage across the table erupted in a chorus of harrumphs and harangues.

"Well, I have to consult with my client," Charles said stiffly. He pushed his chair back from the table and leaned over to Witherspoon. "Let me talk with you outside." Witherspoon now seemed exasperated.

In the lobby outside the conference room, Witherspoon, striving to keep his voice low, groused. "Charles, what the hell is going on?"

"I have to make a call."

"It must be pretty damned important."

"Mr. Witherspoon, it's a matter of life or death." Charles eyeballed Witherspoon. "Mother. Heart attack," he mumbled. "I'll be back in just a minute."

Witherspoon shrugged his shoulders as if to say, "Do whatever you need to do. Abandon me, you bastard."

Charles averted his eyes. He lowered his head. In apparent mortification. But he had to do it. Had to get to the professor. Had to save Fatima Shihabi.

He headed down the corridor and went into the first empty office he could find. Hastily he dialed the professor's number.

Professor Shihabi's voice was thin with stress and exhaustion. "My God," he wailed, "after getting her out of prison, we have now lost her. I had not heard from her since the day she was released. She could not reach a phone. Then, a few minutes ago she called, with a cell phone she bought. She had to leave her villa because she was being tracked by Mukhabarat—the Iraqi Secret Police. She slept out of doors last night. Wandered around Riyadh during the day. She's too worried to eat, and feels sick and very tired. Oh, Charles, I just don't know what to do. . . ."

"Did you suggest that she talk with the International Rescue Committee?"

"Yes, but she had heard from an Iraqi woman she met in the souk that someone in the IRC in Riyadh serves as an informer to the Iraqi authorities. They've paid him off. A few weeks ago a group of twenty Iraqi dissidents were deported from Saudi to Iraq after they turned themselves in to the IRC office in Riyadh. Fatima is worried that the same thing could happen to her."

"Do you have her cell phone number?"

"Sure, I asked her to keep the phone on until I could talk with you. That's why I asked your secretary to interrupt you at your meeting."

"That's okay, professor. Look, call her back and tell her to go see Jameel Zawawi. He's a lawyer. Very powerful and a good friend of mine. His office is on King Saud Boulevard. I think the number is 223, but your sister will find it. It's a circular building in downtown Riyadh. Very distinctive. Tell her to go there right away. I'll let him know she's coming."

"But I'm sure he is too busy to help someone like my sister. There must be thousands like her who are outside Iraq and cannot go back."

"True, but Jameel will help if I ask him."

"I hope so. Thank you."

As the professor hung up, there was a knock on the office door. Witherspoon appeared in the doorway. "Charles, may I see you *now?*"

"Sure, but we'd better get back to the meeting."

"There is no meeting. They walked."

Charles felt a knot in his stomach.

"Their lawyer has accused us, specifically you, of acting in bad faith in inserting the product liability clause into the contract you drafted. They walked out a few minutes ago."

"No way."

"And they say that they are reconsidering the entire deal. Their lawyer—that St. George character—is a complete asshole. It's a delaying tactic really. They want to keep us off guard."

At least Witherspoon seemed a little detached about it. That offered a little consolation, Charles thought. But Witherspoon would make him pay.

Goddamn Professor Shihabi. Goddamn Fatima Shihabi. Ann Jacobs had been right. He should never have gotten involved. These individual client cases were too emotional. Out of his league. He should stick to his deals.

"I'll call them," Charles said, abashed. "We should have conceded the point anyway."

"You might wait until later today. To give them time to settle down a bit."

"I'll do that. Sorry about having to leave the conference room. There was something I just had to do." Charles rolled his eyes significantly. He prayed that Witherspoon wouldn't ask him about his mother.

Witherspoon was too smart by leagues for that. "Don't worry," he said, reassuringly. "If there is a deal to be done, it will get done. If you hadn't put the product liability language in the contract, there would've been something else."

"Right," Charles said, a bit too emphatically, he decided, after the word left his lips. Witherspoon gave him a long look, then turned on his heels, and left the office, leaving the door open. Charles lingered for a while, assessing the sudden turn of events, then slowly walked back to his office.

As he passed Metta's cubicle, her voice came from over the partition. "Charles, while you've been gone, the professor called back. He was able to reach his sister. Oh, and he said something about going to see Jameel." She stood and beamed him a broad smile, her big white teeth flashing.

"Thanks, Metta. Thanks a lot. I'll take it from here."

Within Charles there rose a visceral collision of feelings. The momentary gladness he felt about aiding Fatima Shihabi was now offset, measure for measure, by a deeper remorse at missing by a few degrees the deal of his career. Witherspoon was wrong. Goldstar was gone, cratered. They'd never get it back. His partners at Lloyd & Foster, Art Hauck, the Street—

everyone—would hear about it. Witherspoon wasn't known for his *delicatesse*. Charles put his head in his hands and let himself succumb to an overpowering sense of chagrin. He hadn't had to raise the liability issue in the contract or try to defend the point at the meeting. Witherspoon hadn't even needed it to do the deal. He could have sidestepped the issue, maybe raising it tentatively, expecting it to be shot down or traded for one of scores of other deal points. But far worse was to have left the meeting just at the crucial juncture when everything could have been settled. Right then and there, magnanimously, he should have caved. Witherspoon would never forgive him. He would never forgive himself.

Yet, in the middle of the meeting, his heart had sent him a sign, and for a rare moment in his life he had heeded it. And whatever the consequences were, he would accept them. He suddenly felt an irresistible need to talk to Sarah. As he picked up the phone to call her, Metta buzzed on the intercom.

"Mr. Witherspoon on two. You be nice to him now. He seems pissed."

"I think I know why. Thanks, Metta." As Charles picked up the receiver, he hesitated for an instant, then punched line two.

Witherspoon wasted no time getting to the point. "Charles, I just got off the phone with the board. They would like Lloyd & Foster to prepare a new set of terms, this time without your liability language, to Viatech by tomorrow morning." Witherspoon was not subtle. "Of course, if you're not in a position to do it, I could ask one of your partners."

"No, no, Mr. Witherspoon. Not to worry. I'll have a new draft for you first thing in the morning. I will. No problem."

"Charles, just remember who pays to keep the lights burning down there."

"I hear you, Mr. Witherspoon. No problem, we'll have the terms for you. Nice and early. Call me at the office here when you get in." Charles thought he heard Witherspoon mutter something under his breath as he hung up.

All thoughts of Fatima Shihabi forgotten, Charles pushed back his chair. It was not a reprieve. Only expediency. He pulled the draft of Goldstar's documentation from his briefcase and thumbed through it. He then pushed the intercom button. "Metta, get me overtime for tonight. It's going to be a long one."

TWENTY-ONE

223 King Saud Blvd., Riyadh, Saudi Arabia
Morning, Wednesday
Sept. 18, 2002

Fatima Shihabi sat comfortably in a leather, overstuffed chair as Jameel Zawawi spoke softly but authoritatively into the phone. A handsome man with a disarming smile, he was, she surmised, in his early sixties. He wore the traditional long white thobe and, on his head, a matching ghutra with its black cords. A dark blue cape edged in gold braid covered his broad shoulders. He appeared majestic, godlike, seated in a huge thronelike chair behind a modernistic glass-topped desk in the center of a large room looking west over the city of Riyadh. Fingering his worry beads, he spoke in a dulcet voice—punctuated by the gutturals of his native Arabic and, to her surprise, sprinkled with English words and phrases. Probably educated in England, she thought. No, America. He seemed possessed of a gentility that cleverly veneered his intelligence and power.

"Tell the king that Robert Drayton wants to see him tomorrow morning. No, make that early tomorrow afternoon. That's right. Then, we'll come to see Prince Sultan sometime Friday. It's about the new American defense procurement package. Yes, I know we have to deal with him. I have someone in my office now." He beamed a smile at Fatima, his brown eyes crinkling at the corners. "But I will call the prince later today. No, I will."

Jameel Zawawi hung up the phone and stood before his desk. He extended his hand in greeting. "Charlie told me you would come to see me.

Welcome to Saudi Arabia." His pure white teeth, amazingly even, she thought, glistened behind a warm, gracious smile.

After two nights of sleeping in the open, dodging the religious police, and walking, walking, walking through the streets of Riyadh, Fatima could contain her feelings no longer. She began to cry, then spoke through her tears. "I don't know why I am so fortunate. Somebody seems to be looking out for me."

"Charlie and I have known each other for many years. He is a good man. You are lucky to know him. How can I help you?"

Secure in the belief that Jameel would understand, Fatima recounted her harassment by the Iraqi government, how she had escaped from Iraq, and her experiences in the Riyadh airport, in the Saudi prison. She left nothing out. She even spoke of her love for her daughter.

"You may have difficulty getting her out of Iraq. They will try to use her as bait, to pressure you to come back."

"Yes, I know, but at this point I have no choice. I must save myself so I can save her."

"You certainly are a brave woman."

"No, I am only a survivor. There are many others like me. I am only one of the lucky ones."

"Life is not only about choosing options. It is also about identifying them. You have managed to find an option where, for many others, there are none."

"I am not sure where this will all lead."

"That is your fate, of course."

She smiled. "You are a wise man."

He returned her smile. "You must come from a wonderful family. They must have helped you a lot, given what you have accomplished . . . to become a respected writer and journalist, I mean."

"Actually, things were a bit challenging for me, at first in Kassim, my village, and then in Najaf . . . , especially in a family with four sons. My father gave me a lot of support."

"And your brothers?"

"I always had to deal with them on their terms—not mine. And each of my brothers was different and special: When the soldiers at the airport stopped me, I was on my way to meet my oldest brother Omar. He lives in New York, where he's a professor of computer science. He's even become an American citizen. He writes to me often and, I must confess, always has been my favorite. He's supposed to meet me in Montreal—if I ever get there." She felt a sudden swell of emotion and as quickly quieted it. "I hope that I'm not taking too much of your time," she added respectfully.

"Not at all. Not at all, Mrs. Shihabi. I have a cousin who lives in Najaf, and it's nice to hear about your family there."

"Actually only my older brother Majid still lives there. I don't see much of him these days. He's quite serious and hard working, he has absolutely no sense of humor, and he always has his head buried in the Holy Koran. You may know from your cousin that a lot of people from Najaf are just that way —very conservative. We aren't close, as you can imagine. I really don't know him very well. Another brother died during the war with Iran."

Jameel's secretary brought in a tray with small glass cups of Arab tea. He handed her one of the cups. Jameel took one, and said, "Please go on, Mrs. Shihabi."

"Thank you," she said and took a sip of tea before continuing, "Finally there's my brother Abdeljelil, the most extroverted and my 'protector,' you might say. He's a high-level bureaucrat in the Ministry of Interior. Very, very political, very well connected with Saddam's family. He's saved me once from being imprisoned for subjects I wrote about in *Babel.* My daughter Latifa lives with him and will stay there until I can arrange for her to leave Iraq."

"Did you go to school in Najaf?"

"Yes. Living in Najaf in the 1970's, I was in that first wave of girls who saw the benefits of the Baathe Party's revolution in 1968 and the changes made by Saddam. Like all children in Najaf in those days, I was required to go to school. I even went to secondary school there. Can you imagine, Mr. Zawawi? Even in ultraconservative Najaf, I was able to have the same schooling as my brothers. And, Praise Allah, I was especially privileged to learn the Holy Koran, which was a large part of my studies. Even Majid complimented me on my recitations."

"Well, you're a marvelous woman to have come so far. And I'm pleased to be able to help you while you are in the Kingdom. My office will help you find an apartment—shall I say—out of sight, until Charlie can make his arrangements to get you to the United States."

"He's a good man, this Charles."

"He certainly is. And he has a soft spot for the Arab people, you know. Charlie and I go back a long time. He even worked here in the Kingdom with me for a few years. His partner Art Hauck sold the Saudi royal family on the idea of hiring Lloyd & Forster to be their lawyers in the first place. Oh, we worked together on all sorts of projects—airports, refineries, pipelines, and port complexes. In those days we had big plans to modernize our small country—even though our traditions and culture haven't changed very much since the Middle Ages."

"It's changed a lot, I'd imagine, over the last twenty years."

"Actually, Madame Shihabi, not all that much, except of course for the many new palaces and other structures you see all over Riyadh and Jiddah. At the time when Charlie was coming here, the country was flooded with petrodollars—the dollars earned from the sale of oil. You in Iraq had some of those too, of course, at least in Saddam's early days. As you can imagine, Saudi ministers and their subordinates profited wondrously. Sometimes it was from legitimate subcontracts with foreign suppliers." He paused momentarily. "And sometimes it was from *baksheesh*," he continued, rubbing the tips of his fingers together. "I think that in Iraq maybe you know about these things."

"Yes, Mr. Zawawi, we have that too," Fatima replied, smiling. "People are the same everywhere you know." Fatima was by now captivated by the charm of the man.

Jameel took a sip of tea, then said, "Well, in this country princes and sheiks built sumptuous palaces whose grandeur was limited only by the imaginations of their builders. Vast stores of wealth accumulated, as simple but clever men like Suliman Hajir came out of nowhere—from the desert even—to bring the workers to the oil fields. First in their taxis, then in their buses and, after a while, through airports and airlines they helped construct and finance. Ultimately they would transport the oil itself to foreign markets in their fleets of tankers. From outside the King dom, those supplying equipment, building refineries, selling goods and services of every description, siphoned off yet more of the petrodollar cascade. Every major international engineering or construction firm the Bechtels, Draytons and Fluors of the world, maybe you've heard of them—set up offices in Jiddah or Riyadh or Al Khobar and jostled with one another for the huge deals that flowed almost as freely as the oil that financed them. We here in the Kingdom wanted new industrial cities to rise out of the desert sands, and Charles Sherman and his colleagues at Lloyd & Forster helped us do it—for a price, I might add."

"How very interesting, all of this. I would love to hear more about Mr. Sherman."

"Well, at that time, of course, Charlie was just a young lawyer, but his firm's senior partner Art Hauck, a man I know very well, picked him to work for the Kingdom. Yes, Charles Sherman made quite an impression on all of us. Our client Hajir especially loved him. He just seemed different from all the others who came here to make money."

"What do you mean?"

"When I first met Charlie, he naturally seemed thrilled at what Mr. Hauck used to call 'carrying the money bags' to the deal. We all felt the power of working for the royal family here. It was a wonderful time, I must say." Jameel took a long sip of tea. "Then, after a time, Charlie found that he excelled in the art of negotiating contracts, of making deals. You know, Mrs. Shihabi"—Jameel again paused, clicking his worry beads—"we Arabs are skilled negotiators. It's part of our culture, the culture of the souk, you might say. But Charles perfected this art to a level I have never seen even in the members of my own family—and I am from an old mercantile family from Jiddah." Jameel clicked his worry beads faster now. "Charlie loved the high drama of contract negotiations. And, as a negotiator, he proved highly effective. Partly it was due to the greed of suppliers to the Kingdom, but mostly it was due to his own determination to win—occasionally, it seemed to me at least—at any cost, even to his own client."

"How is it that he is so different from other Americans, then? My brother in New York tells me that a lot of them are just that way—brash, maybe a bit arrogant, more interested in winning, making money, that sort of thing. But the vast majority of them know nothing about Arab culture."

"Well, in Charlie's case, we eventually learned that beneath all that bravura, he was actually a very sensitive fellow. Sometimes I find that if you can overlook that impetuous, overconfident manner of Americans, that high–and–mighty superiority they all seem to give off, some of them—like Charlie—are actually very kind and feeling people. And some are intrigued by Arab culture. I know, for most Arabs, that *is* difficult to comprehend."

"That's certainly not the impression you get from the media. Americans seem interested in us only enough to get our business."

"True, but I must say that Charlie's own sensitivity to Saudi mores and morals went well beyond the superficialities of business etiquette. True, he didn't wear the thobe and ghutra." Jameel raised his arms slightly to display the full reach of his gold-edged cape. "He generally wore a dark suit and a silk tie. There were times when I'd feel sorry for him in the sweltering Saudi summers. But in many other respects he observed the customs of the Kingdom. He studied the history and doctrine of Islam. He read large parts of the Koran and learned how, during his negotiations for the royal family, to invoke the *shari'a*, the Koranic law. And, both in public and in private, he remained ever respectful of our traditions and culture. He was somebody who tried to understand us. His sincerity impressed us all and, as I look back on those days, I think he really got inside our skin. He really felt our pain but also our joy." Jameel paused to arrange his flowing cape around his shoulders. "And our humor, Mrs. Shihabi," he added, grinning at her. For the first time in many days, Fatima felt relaxed, her eyes twinkling, as she basked in the warmth of his smile.

"Let me tell you about my last dinner with Charlie, just before he left the Kingdom for good. It was during Ramadan, and there was a farewell feast for him in a large tent in the desert, spread with luxurious carpets, beautiful silk rugs from Persia of intricate design, I'll never forget them. Our host that evening was a certain Prince Abdullah, nephew of our king, and it being Ramadan, the meal was *mechoui* and the traditional Ramadan dishes I'm sure you know. Here in Riyadh we break our fast in the old Bedouin way: at the exact moment at dusk when our mullah can no longer distinguish between a black and a white thread, he gives the signal for a cannon in the center of the city to go off. Then, as I'm sure you do in Baghdad, the fasting for the day officially ends and, you might say, we begin to sip our *chorba*. Well, at this particular dinner, I was on one side of Charlie and the prince was on the other. We watched him carefully to see whether he would wait for the boom of the cannon, and sure enough, he waited patiently with us. When we began to take the food from the dishes, the prince wasn't sure Charlie was so excited about eating with his hands. You know Americans are so . . . fastidious sometimes. So, first the prince would reach for the *mechoui*, tear off a piece of mutton, put it on Charlie's plate and then I would do the same—to make sure Charlie had enough to eat. Well then, after a while, since the dinner was really in honor of Char-lie, the prince presented him the eyeball of the sheep, as is our custom. Mrs. Shihabi, you may have the same custom in Iraq, especially in the desert. Here it's a delicacy reserved for only the most esteemed guests."

Fatima nodded affirmatively, and Jameel went on. "Well, Charlie didn't hesitate. He smiled at the prince, smiled at me, and then swallowed the eyeball without even hesitating for an instant. I think the prince was quite impressed because we Saudis know the Americans, and this is cer-tainly not their tradition. So, the dinner went on for a while, and I'm afraid the prince and I became a little . . . shall we say, mischievous." Jameel's eyes were sparkling now as he gazed at her. "Speaking a local

Najd dialect between us so Charlie wouldn't understand, the prince and I . . . ,well, we decided to see how far Charlie would go with all this. So, I reached deep into the carcass of the animal and drew out the testicles and deposited them nicely on Charlie's plate. Then the prince said to him warmly in English, 'You are our brother.' Now, in those days, I knew Charlie really well, and I could tell that he hesitated just for a second. Actually I think he was about to ask what they were, but all of a sudden he reached for the two mushy pieces, cradled them in the curve of his fingers, and, smiling gamely at both of us 'conspirators,' if you will, he just gulped them down, one after the other. He never did ask me what they were, although I always suspected he knew. It's no big deal for us, of course, but the Americans are different. He's an amazing guy, really."

"I look forward to meeting this man."

"I hope that you will have the chance." Jameel rose majestically from his chair. "Well, Mrs. Shihabi, I have kept you too long with my stories. We have to get you a secure place, away from our friends in the Ministry of Defense, until Charlie figures out what to do with you." Jameel pressed a button on his desk, and moments later his secretary came in. "Mr. Mir, I want you to find a good, safe apartment for Mrs. Shihabi. Perhaps near the rug souk so that she can come and go with no one noticing. And give her anything she needs."

Fatima stood, and Jameel came over to her. "It has been truly a delight to meet you, Mrs. Shihabi. Do not worry about anything. You are in good hands. *Inshallah*, you will be here just a short time. I know that Charles will be working to get you into the States. You may see him before I do, so by all means give my best regards to him and his partner Art Hauck. In the meantime, while you are in the Kingdom, let me know if you need anything." Jameel reached out and took her hand and kissed it. It must have been a gesture he had learned abroad, Fatima thought. She felt a frisson of bliss pass through her.

Her euphoria remained in her heart for the next hour as Mr. Mir made various telephone calls on her behalf, twice went into to Jameel's office to consult with him, and finally escorted her to a furnished apartment in the center of Riyadh, close to the rug market. She would be safe there, Mr. Mir assured her, provided, of course, she did nothing to draw the attention of the police who regularly patrolled the area. Any difficulties whatsoever she was to report to Mr. Mir, who would look in on her every other day.

For the first time since she left Iraq, she experienced a profound sense of security. Powerful forces, generous and beneficent, she could see, now had taken up her case. Everything was working out—not quite in the way she had expected but certainly to a degree that justified some confidence in the future. There would be obstacles and setbacks, sure, but Charles Sherman, his connections, and his associates would come through for her. They would open the doors through which she had to pass to reach her goal. Thus freed from anxiety about her own survival, her mind once again began to entertain hopes of going to the West, of seeing Omar again, of gaining her freedom. She began to think about the next chapter in her life.

And she began to worry about her daughter.

TWENTY-TWO

23 Wall Street
Wednesday–Saturday
Sept. 18–21, 2002

True to his word, Charles worked well into the night, revising the Goldstar documents to address the deal point in contention, and early the following morning he personally dropped the revised drafts at Mr. Witherspoon's door, although with a strong premonition that the deal was forever lost. And when he came back to his office later that morning, he cleared his desk, made arrangements to put his other client projects on hold, and turned his full attention to Shihabi, F.–Pro Bono Matter.

For the next three days, from morning until close of business, he made call after call, striving to interest foreign embassies and international relief agencies in Fatima's case. All expressed sympathy. At no cost to them, Charles thought. Some offered to compose letters of support. Others offered to make phone calls. But not one would agree to extend her a visa to enter their country. And without a visa, Fatima Shihabi could not get on a plane to go anywhere.

In all, Charles tried no fewer than twenty-eight different countries. Each time the routine was the same. First, the challenge of reaching an actual human being willing to talk. Then, the formulaic words of support for the proposition that political refugees were granted visas, even welcomed, to the particular country. But for an Iraqi dissident writer living in Saudi Arabia? "No, I don't think so" was the universal response. "You might try Canada." It was as if all the visa officials were reading the same script.

But he *had* tried Canada; he had tried their consulate first. But after two days of busy signals, he reached the touch-tone-activated phone system of the Visa Section of the Canadian Consulate in Manhattan. It had been cleverly designed to thwart any outsider's effort to speak with an actual human being. He left a message, one that he knew would never be returned. And it never was.

Friday, the end of the normal workweek, came and went, still with no result. No one was interested in giving a visa to an Iraqi intellectual. Not after 9/11. Better to draw the skein of governmental bureaucracy over the whole idea. Charles was holding the U.S. Embassy in Riyadh as a trump card. But first he would have to speak with Fatima directly. She would have just one chance to sway U.S. officialdom, and she would have to make the best of it.

First thing on Saturday morning he called Professor Shihabi. He got right to the point. "Omar, I must speak with your sister. She needs to prepare herself to go to the American embassy and meet with the consul in charge of visas and asylum petitions. It's our last resort. I'll set it up, but I need to speak with your sister first."

Professor Shihabi responded with enthusiasm, "Of course, Mr. Sherman."

Charles interjected, "You may call me Charles."

"Oh, thank you Mr. Sherman—I mean Charles. We can call her right now. It's late afternoon in Riyadh."

Charles patched in the number the professor gave him, then as the phone was ringing, added it to his Blackberry. A woman's voice, barely audible, answered in Arabic. The professor began the conversation, and Charles recognized his name repeated several times during the exchanges. After a few minutes, the woman switched to speaking English. Her voice was pleasant, confident, surprisingly modulated, even if accented, as if she had spoken English for years.

"Mr. Sherman, before we begin, allow me to thank you in all sincerity for what you have done for me. Truly you have saved my life. I shall be forever grateful to you."

"Not at all . . . not at all. It's a privilege for me to be able to help you. Your brother has told me much about you. You are an amazing woman to have done what you did. As for me, I didn't do anything at all. I just called a friend of mine. I trust that you have met him, Jameel Zawawi."

"Oh, yes. He is a very kind man. He has found me a safe apartment in Riyadh, where I am now staying."

"Very good. I'm very pleased about that. Your brother and I are working to get you asylum in the U.S. I have connections with our embassy in Riyadh, and we'll get you a meeting there so that they can tell you what you have to do in order to qualify for asylum. It may take awhile, but you seem to have a good case based upon the persecution you have endured because of your political and humanitarian activities."

"After all your government's threats and demands toward my country, I can't believe that they'd take up my case even if I were the Queen of Sheba," she retorted firmly. Fatima was no idiot, Charles reflected.

"Why shouldn't they?" Charles replied. "You're an individual, not the Iraqi government. Your brother is a U.S. citizen, you have a reasonable fear of persecution for your political views in Iraq, and I understand that you have important information about Saddam's weapons to give to the Americans. And a friend of mine in the U.S. State Department gave me a contact at the embassy." He paused. "Okay, maybe they won't grant you asylum on the spot, but at least they'll talk to you. You might get some idea about what to do," he added. "I'll call them to set up the meeting for you. You'll be meeting with an embassy official in order to discuss your case. We'll call you back at this time tomorrow to give you more information about where to go, what to say, and that sort of thing."

"If that is what you think I should do, I'll do it. You are a very kind man, Mr. Sherman."

Ignoring the compliment, he went on. "Mrs. Shihabi, it would help me when I speak with the embassy if you could tell me what you know about Saddam's weapons."

Fatima began hesitatingly but then told Charles how she had been approached by the wife of a physics professor whom Saddam Hussein had charged with building a nuclear-enriched weapon at a secret research facility in Baghdad. She omitted nothing, although several times Omar had to translate certain technical Arabic words and phrases for her. It was a good ten minutes before she finished telling him all she knew.

"And now where are the documents, the ones that the researcher's wife gave you?"

"I had to destroy them."

"What? . . . . Why?"

"I had no choice really. If Saddam's people had found them on me, they would have killed me—and my daughter. Will there be any problem if I don't have them?"

"Well, it might have made things easier. But a problem? No, not really. It'll be fine. Just tell the American government what you know. You're an inspiration to us all. I look forward to meeting you in person."

"*Inshallah*, we shall have that chance. I am deeply indebted to you. You have given me hope."

"Take care of yourself, Mrs. Shihabi. I'll speak with you again just as soon as I find out the time and place for your meeting at the embassy."

He put down the receiver and immediately picked it back up. As he dialed the number for Rita Lane, the U.S. consul in Riyadh, he thought how fortunate it was that Saturday was a workday in the Arab world. It took several minutes of routing through the embassy switchboard, and several secretaries before he reached her. He introduced himself as a New York lawyer with long experience in working in Saudi Arabia, then added that a "mutual friend at State," had suggested that he call about a "delicate problem" he had regarding a client. In a tone as respectful as it was deferential, he said that his call was on behalf of "a distinguished writer and poet who has been persecuted for her political views in Iraq and who is planning to seek asylum in the United States." He paused and then continued, "She recently escaped from Iraq and now is being tracked by Saddam Hussein's secret police. In a word, her life is in danger." For a few moments, silence reigned on the other end of the line. Charles added, "I was only wondering if you might spend a few minutes with Ms. Shihabi—just to meet with her, of course, to give her any advice you might have about securing asylum in the States." More silence. Now a bit edgy, he went on, "By the way, Ann Jacobs thought you might be able to help on this one."

Rita Lane was coldly polite. "Congress enacted a law some years ago that prohibits me from helping your client," she said without a trace of warmth. "By law, I cannot even meet with her since she is not a U.S. citizen. After September eleventh we're even stricter about observing this rule than before. And now with the prospect of a war with Iraq in front of us, I just can't allocate any of my staff's time to the plight of one Iraqi no matter who she is—not even if her life is in danger."

"You mean that you can't take ten minutes just to hear her story and give her some friendly advice?" He couldn't help it—he knew that he sounded exasperated.

"The answer is no. Not even ten seconds. Now, Mr. Sherwood, if you'll excuse me, I must leave for a representational function."

"I think she knows where Saddam keeps his weapons." Charles added quickly, waiting for the words to sink in.

"Oh yeah, like every other Iraqi who wants asylum. Even if she did know something, she's probably not credible. And she can't add anything to what we already know."

His heart sank. So that was the way it was going to be. Even if you spoke the truth, you weren't credible if you didn't have the papers to prove it. And Fatima didn't have them and never would. "So you don't even want to talk with her?" he finally asked, suspecting what the answer would be.

"That's right. You've got it, Mr. Sherwood. I am sorry, but I must go. Nice talking with you, though." She hung up abruptly. Charles fumed. Nice talking with you too. He stood, paced angrily several times around his office, and then tapped his speakerphone. He could barely bring himself to report to the professor but forced himself to place the call.

"Omar, maybe I'm a little naive about all this," Charles said, "but if distinguished people from around the world are treated this shabbily, a lot of people out there must think we Americans are pretty heartless."

"Welcome to the wonderful world of visa bureaucracy," the professor replied. Then he said lightly, "Perhaps we should try other countries, like Ireland."

"Actually, I tried it two days ago. No dice. If you've got family connections there, sure they'll take you in. But not an Arab woman who might cause trouble. It's ironic, isn't it? Ireland would make even Tony Galente a citizen if he had a grandparent born there, but they won't give the time of day to an Arab refugee fleeing persecution. Actually, my own mother's from Ireland. She met my dad in London while he was stationed there during World War II. So, as soon as Congress decided to allow Americans to hold dual nationality, seven or eight years ago, I was able to get an Irish passport. These days, when I travel overseas, I carry both my U.S. and Irish passports with me. So, when Al Qaeda takes over my plane and demands all the Americans come up front . . . , well, I'll just put on an Irish accent, I guess. Just kidding, of course."

"If only Fatima were so lucky," the professor said. "I'm afraid that she only has Iraqi blood in her veins. Arabs certainly are getting short shrift by America too these days, after September eleventh."

"Oh no," Charles said, his tone sarcastic. "Not at all. Our country grants visas to Arabs. Sure it does. But to get one, you have to climb towering cliffs of administration, cross mountain ranges of paperwork, and endure enormous challenges to human patience and affronts to human dignity. And yet, after all that, the terrorists who brought down the World Trade Center came in on legitimate visas. Figure that one out." Charles could always feel when he was becoming histrionic, and now was one of those times. "And the shame of it all is that a remarkable person like your sister is left out in the cold."

"Thank you, Charles. You're a kind man."

"We should call her—your sister I mean. I'll explain it to her. And tell her not to worry and all that. We'll find a way, I'm sure of it."

Fatima answered the phone on the first ring. Charles played back the conversation with Rita, soft-pedaling her coldness. Almost as he ended his account, Fatima interjected, her voice rising in anger, "It's true what a lot of Muslims say, isn't it?"

"What do you mean?" Charles replied.

"That your democracy, your international laws, your so-called 'concern' for human rights—they're all a sham. They really are. Our imam in Baghdad says you're all morally empty—beneath your shining symbols of freedom and hope. Of course I shouldn't have expected anything from you—I mean, of course, America—anyway." As she caught her breath, Charles tried to interrupt, but Fatima began again, now fairly shouting, "Mr. Sherman, Mr. Sherman, I know earlier I questioned whether your embassy would take up my case, not even if I were some famous person, but I truly cannot—*cannot*—believe that your embassy, flying the flag of the United States of America, wouldn't even talk with me. How do you think I feel, Mr. Sherman? How do you think I feel? I feel like a nonperson, like a nobody, just as all Muslims do when we think about your government today. And some day, not too far in the future, the Holy Koran and its regard for the value of every human life—that's what going to prevail in the world, that's what's going to triumph. Islam doesn't treat even its worst enemies this way."

"Calm down, Mrs. Shihabi. Calm down, will you?" Charles said, anger swelling in his voice.

Omar, who had been listening quietly until this moment, added, "Fatima, please. Please. Charles is just trying to help you. You've been under a lot of stress, with all the trouble you've had. Just listen to what he has to say." Omar himself sounded strained, his guttural accent more pronounced than usual.

In a dispassionate, professional voice, Charles continued, "Look, Ms. Lane was just one official. They aren't all like that, believe me. There are some very understanding officials in our government. Ms. Lane was just having a bad day. So, don't give up at this point, Mrs. Shihabi. You've come too far already. We're going to get you out of there somehow. I know we will. I've just had another idea I'd like to investigate for you. It may take a few days, though. Omar and I will call you back as soon as I know something."

Across the phone lines Fatima's ire seemed almost palpable. Not hearing a response, Charles pressed the receiver tightly against his ear. "Mrs. Shihabi? Fatima? Hello, hello?"

Finally Fatima answered, her voice now restrained yet still firm. "Mr. Sherman, I'm sorry to be so angry. I don't have anything against you. It's just that like so many people, I have such high expectations for America even as I hear so many bad things about it from so many people around me. I really don't know what to think, to be honest."

"Keep the faith," Charles replied, taken by surprise at Fatima's resilience. "America needs people like you, with your courage and determination. And we're going to find the right door for you to come into the country. Just sit tight for a while and let Omar and me work on this new angle. We'll call you back about it in a few days. I'm going to sign off now, but you and Omar can stay on this telephone line. You both probably will want to talk. Good luck to you, Mrs. Shihabi."

As he was about to put back the receiver, he heard an odd click and then a brief whir. He was about to ask Fatima if she had been cut off when he heard her voice again, speaking Arabic with her brother. Must have been the international connection, he told himself, and placed the receiver back, punching the hold button so that the outside lines could remain connected. Sighing, he shook his head in vexation and stood up from his desk. He strode out of his office.

"Hold my calls, Michele. I'll be with Arthur Hauck awhile."

"Not even if Mr. Witherspoon calls?" Michele with the marvelous smile was not above teasing him.

"Not even," Charles replied.

Art usually spent Saturday in his office, catching up on billing and other administrative matters. Charles found him alone, twisting a paper clip in his fingers, lost in thought. He seemed a little startled to see Charles, almost as if he had just that moment been thinking about him.

As Charles laid out his request to his mentor, Art seemed agreeable, even pleased. "I would ask you to do this only because you were the one to pull me in on this little project," Charles said, smiling good-naturedly. Art had always understood him. Probably more than he knew, thought Charles.

Art grinned. "I thought that you'd find this one intriguing," he said with characteristic understatement. "I knew that I could place it in your capable hands. I was even half-tempted to handle it myself, you know. It's the sort of case that makes a lawyer grow, stretches him a little, gives him the rare chance to spread his wings, and yet forces him to keep his feet planted on the ground, in touch with what makes us all, well, a bit more human." Art smiled at Charles paternally. "You know you've handled a lot of deals for my clients over the years, Charles, and I'd say that by and large you've performed better than anyone might have expected, in some cases better than even I could have done myself. It's been my privilege to give you a little guidance now and then, to serve as your rudder to help you, well, stay the course at the firm, you might say." Art stood up from his desk and ambled over to the window. Then he suddenly turned and, his voice assuming a somber tone, said, "I'd like you to do everything you can for this Iraqi woman. And, trust me, I'm only too pleased to do what I can to help you see this one through." He came around his desk and sat back in his chair, smiling at Charles. "Let me see what I can do over the weekend. I'll make a few calls. You see, I still have a few chums from my old days at the Paris office." Art always downplayed his ability to finesse things. "I was there a long time before you were . . . back when friends stayed friends for their whole lives," Art mused.

"And to think I thought doing deals was gut-wrenching," Charles rejoined, rolling his eyes.

"I knew that if anyone in this firm could save the girl, it would be you." Art always knew how to be encouraging. "And who knows? Maybe this deal will be one that'll open up some new directions for you."

"You mean as a human rights lawyer?" Charles laughed.

"You never know, do you?" Art grinned.

"Thanks, but no thanks, Art. I don't know that I could stand the pressure. Besides, doing deals is my game." Charles rose from his chair to leave.

"Oh, that reminds me, I was terribly sorry to hear that your Goldstar deal cratered. The subject even came up at yesterday's meeting of the executive committee. It could've been a real feather in your cap. Viatech's lawyer must've been a real jerk."

"It may be the last deal we do for Witherspoon for a while. He had already been threatening to jump ship."

"Charles, I know. He's pretty upset. I spoke with him at lunch yesterday. He hinted that he could have another deal in the works. It probably would be modeled on Goldstar." Art looked at Charles as if expecting a response.

Charles shook his head. "Something made me lose my stride on Goldstar. I don't know what it was. I just don't know." He paused and looked Art in the eyes. "Anyway, Art, I need to get back to work. I'll look forward to any help your Parisian friends can offer Mrs. Shihabi." He turned and headed back to his office, leaving Art to his thoughts.

By the time he got back to his office, Michele had left for the day. Saturday afternoon was the hardest for overtime secretaries. It cut too far into the precious weekend. It was probably why Metta wouldn't work weekends.

Charles ambled into his office and closed the door. His mind was muddled and his heart troubled. His talk with Art had resolved nothing. He felt that his world was becoming unglued. First Goldstar tanked. Then Sarah seemed more troubled about their lives than he had seen her for a long time. Now this Arab woman whose life he was trying to save **had** badmouthed the U.S., and maybe with good reason. His eyes wandered around the room, then out the window to Federal Hall. Out at George's stolid figure, decked in his colonial best, atop the staircase. His patinaed face seemed poised, floating almost as a thing apart, in the dusky air. His eyes, forever riveted across Wall Street, seemed both benign yet oddly exigent. They were resolute eyes, eyes bereft of expression, eyes that seemed to meet his own.

TWENTY-THREE

43 Central Park West
Late morning, Sunday
Sept. 22, 2002

Oh, Charles, it's your client on the phone—Professor Shihabi," Sarah shouted from the kitchen. She raced into the living room and held out the cordless phone.

Tossing aside the business section of the Sunday *Times*, Charles took the phone and put it to his ear. "Good morning, Omar," he said cheerily and relaxed into the comfort of the sofa cushions.

The professor's voice sounded as if he were at the bottom of a well. As he began to speak, he coughed several times and then choked out his words. "Charles, I'm sorry to call you at home on a Sunday morning, but I had to speak with you."

"You sound terrible, Omar. Are you sick?"

"I know I sound terrible. I must have caught bronchitis or something. The pressure of the past weeks has gotten to me, I'm afraid. I haven't slept in days, and I have no appetite. I had to reach you right away, though."

"Omar, you need to take care of yourself. It's going to be a long and difficult road for all of us, you know. You've got to stay strong for your sister. What's going on?"

"Well, bad news. Fatima has decided to go back to Iraq. She won't give me the reason. I begged her not to go, but she's adamant. I think it might have something to do with our family, maybe even her daughter, I don't know. It's the only thing I can think of. Charles, I don't know what to do. I'm really worried about her. She plans to leave Riyadh and go to the Iraqi border tomorrow morning."

Charles shouted into the phone, "No, no, no! That's crazy. The Iraqis will torture and kill her."

"She's obstinate. She says that she's lost hope of ever leaving Saudi Arabia for America. She doesn't believe that she will ever get a visa to come here. But I think that something else is bothering her. Otherwise, she would have nothing to lose in waiting for a visa in Saudi."

"Omar, we have to talk with her right now."

"Maybe you can get her to change her mind."

"I'll put through the call. I can conference her in with this phone." Charles swiftly thumbed through his Blackberry's phone list, pulled up Fatima's cell phone number, and dialed it on the apartment phone. Fatima's phone rang and rang interminably, and then her voice, barely audible, came on the line.

"Mrs. Shihabi, this is Charles Sherman calling. I have your brother Omar on the line with me. We understand that you plan to go back to Iraq in the morning. Is this true?"

"Yes."

"Can you tell us why?"

"I would rather not."

"You certainly understand that if you return, Saddam Hussein's soldiers will arrest you, probably torture you, and almost certainly kill you?"

"I don't care."

Charles paced to the kitchen and back, then bellowed into the phone, "Mrs. Shihabi, listen. Your brother Omar, your favorite brother whom you love dearly, and I have worked very, very hard to keep the Saudis from sending you back to Iraq. Your poor brother is sick with worry about you. At least give us the courtesy of telling us why you feel you must return to Iraq. After all, if you are killed, whatever you tell us won't matter anyway. And we promise that we will tell no one."

"First, Mr. Sherman, I am sorry to have caused you and my brother such trouble. I am not worth any of your fine efforts. But I must do what I have to do. It's about my daughter."

"Is she sick?"

"No, it's not that at all. It's just that I feel as if I've abandoned her. It was wrong of me in the first place to leave my only child in order to save myself. That is not our way."

Charles heard Omar sigh.

"Mrs. Shihabi, too many people have worked too hard for you to give up now. Besides, if you can save yourself, you can save your daughter too. You can't do anything for her now. But you can send for her after you get to America."

"But that's the other thing. I am losing my hope of ever getting to America."

"Because of our conversation yesterday?" Charles asked.

"Naturally. Your own embassy won't even talk with me. How can I begin to think that they'll ever grant me asylum? Of course I'm quite aware of your work for me, Mr. Sherman, and naturally I appreciate it very much. By the grace of Allah, you have done so much for me."

"Look, Mrs. Shihabi, please stay in Saudi Arabia, just a little while longer . . . just for Omar and me, will you? We're working on some very promising ideas for you. We'll know in the next few days. It won't be long."

"Well, . . . all right, Mr. Sherman," she said weakly. "All right, I will."

"I'm going to sign off, but you'll stay connected with your brother. I'm sure he'll want to speak with you some more."

"Thank you. Thank you again, Mr. Sherman."

Charles put down the receiver, letting the outside lines stay connected. It was another ten minutes before he saw the lighted button on the phone finally blink off. He picked up the newspaper again, but he couldn't keep his mind focused. Fatima was strong to be sure. But she could also be fragile and sensitive. He would do everything he could for her.

TWENTY-FOUR

23 Wall Street
Late morning, Monday
Sept. 23, 2002

Charles, a call for you on line three." Metta stood in the doorway of
his office. "Somebody who says he's from the French embassy in Washington. Daubin or Douban or something like that. *Com si . . . com sa.*"
Thrusting out her hips, Metta waved her open palms side to side. He
would have to have a talk with her. It was becoming a bit much. Not in
keeping with professional decorum.

"Put him through," he replied a bit roughly. Art had worked fast.

The First Secretary was direct. "We've agreed to give your client a
visa. On the condition that she not engage in any political activities while
she is in France. She may remain in France indefinitely, but we must have
your word that she will be invisible—at least as far as the government of
Iraq is concerned—especially during these troublesome times. As you
may know, our government has worked hard for many years to build
good relations with the Arab world. We have succeeded only because we
have not countenanced any anti-Arab propaganda on our soil. I'm sure
you can understand that."

"Thank you, Your Excellency. I can give you my word that our client
has no desire to, and indeed will not, engage in any political activity in
France. You will not know she is there."

"Ask your client to report to the French embassy in Riyadh tomorrow
morning. We will see that she gets the proper papers to enter France. Oh,
and one more thing. Our ambassador has asked me to give his best regards to your partner Arthur Hauck. Although they haven't seen each

other in a while, Ambassador de Rochefort told me to tell Monsieur Hauck that he misses the very fine Armagnac that Monsieur Hauck used to keep in his wine cellar in Paris."

"I'll be sure to tell him," Charles replied. "And please thank the ambassador for us."

Even as he hung up the receiver, Charles felt an intense wave of satisfaction sweep over him. He let out a whoop of exultation and pumped his fists in the air. He bounded up from his desk as Metta, who had been all ears outside the open door of his office, bustled in. Charles stood in the middle of his office and jumped up and down like a school kid on the last day of the school year.

"Charles, I've never seen you act like this," Metta said. "You'd better call the professor right away."

When Charles gave him the news, he heard the professor gasp and then there was silence. Charles finally had to say, "Professor, are you okay?"

His voice clenched by bronchitis and emotion, the professor rasped into the phone. "Charles, this is the most wonderful day of my life. My sister able to escape her life lived in fear. And go to France. To Paris. You have given life back to her. I cannot believe it. I just cannot believe it. She will be free, she will finally be free."

Charles put his head in his hands, overcome by feelings so intense that, try as he might, he couldn't control. He had not felt this way since the death of his father. He had wept uncontrollably then, and now he sensed that his emotions were about to let loose again. "Omar, I'll have to call you back," he managed to choke out before clicking off his speaker-phone.

As he hung up, Hansen, who apparently had been watching the buttons on Metta's phone, knocked perfunctorily on Charles's office door and opened it. He was halfway across the room when he spotted Charles's tear-soaked eyes. As Charles took out his linen handkerchief, Hansen did a double-take, seemed about to ask a question, then excused himself, turned on his heel and went back out the door, muttering, "My question can wait . . . . I didn't believe it the first time . . . and I don't believe it now."

After a few minutes, Charles again punched the professor's number on the speakerphone. Though still a little choked up, the professor, too, had composed himself.

"Omar, the French said that her papers would be waiting for her tomorrow at their embassy in Riyadh. She should be able to leave Saudi Arabia for France any time after that."

"I'll have to buy her ticket since she has no money," the professor replied. "Tentatively why don't I make her a reservation for next Monday, September 30? That will give me time to book a hotel and make other arrangements; she'll arrive in Paris at the beginning of the work week."

"Why don't you go over and meet her?" Charles asked. "You could rendezvous in Paris and make sure that she gets settled."

"And what about you—why don't you come too?" the professor asked with a sudden ebullience.

"Actually I *am* between deals," Charles lied. He thought of Witherspoon. Of the Goldstar deal, now all but dead. Of his conversation with Art. "The problem is that around here you're required to announce your vacation months in advance so other lawyers can be lined up to handle your clients' deals while you're out of the office. Taking off on the spur of the moment is not considered good form. And you never know, my last deal may not be entirely over."

"But can't your assistant—what's his name?—Hansen? Can't he handle things if more work has to be done on it?"

"No, it's not the same. Somebody like our client Mr. Witherspoon would take it as a personal affront if I weren't around. That happened to me once before." The memory of his aborted vacation with Sarah in Japan still gnawed at him.

"Well, if you change your mind, let me know. You have a few days."

"No, Omar. No chance. Several days ago I heard a rumor that Mr. Witherspoon has another deal in the works. It would essentially be 'Son of Goldstar.' I need to be here in case it takes off."

"We'll miss you," the professor said.

"After what you and Fatima have been through, you'll be relieved to be in the City of Lights. Let Metta know if you need help with arrangements, and we'll have our Paris office make them. I spent three years there some years ago and know Paris better than I know most parts of New York."

"Thanks, Charles, we'll do that. I'll call my sister now and let her know the good news."

"Do that, do that. Please give her my best wishes. Tell her that her long saga is finally coming to an end. Once she gets settled in Paris, we'll get her daughter out of Iraq too."

"I will tell her. Thank you, Charles. You're truly a miracle worker."

"No, Omar, I just have a few good connections."

As soon as he hung up with Omar, Charles phoned Sarah. "Well, you're not going to believe this, . . . but we got Fatima into France."

"Charles, that's absolutely wonderful. It really is. I'm really happy for you. I don't know why, but somehow this whole immigration case has become more important to you than one of your merger deals. I'm really excited for you."

"Thanks, Sarah. It actually was Art's doing. He called one of his old cronies at the French embassy. Fatima's going to leave Saudi next Monday and go up to Paris. Omar will go over to meet her there. He wanted me to go too, but I begged off. I'm worried that if I'm not around when Son of Goldstar comes down the pike, Witherspoon's going to abandon ship."

"You mean hire a different firm?"

"He's been threatening to do just that for a long time."

"Oh, rats. That little twit. Just let him."

"God dammit, Sarah." Charles whispered into the phone. "Not now, not over the phone." He tried to be circumspect about phone conversations, always assuming that Metta or even the firm's switchboard surreptitiously could cut in on a call.

Sarah paused. Then in a voice full of urging, she said, "Charles, you should go to Paris. You have to go. This isn't just another one of your crummy big deals. This is . . . too important to you. You've got to meet this woman. . . . It's not every day you've saved someone's life."

He was taken aback by the force of her reply and at first was speechless. Then he said, "There's no way. I've got a full plate. You think that Witherspoon's going to understand? I can't just drop everything, zip off to Paris like that, on the spot."

"You have a week, almost," she replied, then stayed silent.

"I have an idea. You've said you want to go off to Paris. Let's both go."

"Forget it. This is your deal."

"Well, I'll think about it," he murmured finally. Even so, he had to admit, there was a part of him that wanted to go.

TWENTY-FIVE

Air France Flight 007
Sunday–Monday
Sept. 29–30, 2002

Two hours into the flight to Paris momentary turbulence awakened Charles. He opened his eyes and saw that the professor was sleeping fitfully. He got up and stood in the aisle, shaking out his long legs. He then ambled to the back of first-class, got a flight attendant to give him a glass of water, which he downed in a gulp, and returned to his seat. Omar had awakened and was straightening himself in his seat. Charles sat down beside him.

"So what convinced you to come along?" the professor asked.

"Sarah."

"You haven't told me much about her, but she sounds like a wonderful person."

"She is. And she's a better negotiator than I am, I guess. She roughed me up pretty bad," Charles said ruefully. "I didn't have a prayer in hell. I called her just after we got word from the French, just after I spoke with you, and she started right in with the idea that I had to go to Paris to meet your sister. Then, that evening, when I got back to the apartment—late as usual, she had whipped up some French bouillabaisse. It's very aromatic, at least the way she makes it—my *numero uno*, all-time favorite. And it was ready to go, bubbling on the stove when I came in the front door. Even before I hung up my coat, she started in, asking me when I'd be going to Paris. It was as if she'd made up her mind that I was going. It was a little tense. I must admit that things have been a little dicey, you might say, between Sarah and me recently. At first I told her nothing doing, out of the question, no way was I going to Paris while our client Mr. Witherspoon might be about to do another of his deals.

"Then, after a glass or two of wine, she finally said to me, for the umpteenth time, 'Charles, why don't you go? Just go. It will be just for a few days. It will do you good.'"

"What did she mean by that?"

"Oh, I suppose to get away. Between my deals. Something like that. She's always been after me to take vacations."

"She sounds like a very nice woman, . . . and you are a man blessed by Allah."

Whether because of Omar's response, his accent, or his dark complexion, Charles suddenly had the thought that Omar was very much a Muslim, and continued, "Well, it wasn't only Sarah. . . ." Charles paused and took a sip of fruit juice. "There was something about going to Paris to meet your sister—whose life I helped save . . . well, frankly, there was something about it that stirred my imagination. It sounds a little corny, sure, but somehow this little adventure . . . , well, it came at the right time for me. I was just intrigued to meet this woman, your sister, whom on some level I deeply admire and—oh hell, Omar, if you want to know the truth, I don't know what came over me."

Omar laughed. "Well, I'm glad you've come," he said. "And it was good of Sarah to have encouraged you."

"Of course, she knew full well what you and I have gone through these past few weeks. She was there. All the time." Charles flicked on the light over his seat. "She just made up her mind that I was going to do it, that's all."

"She must care a lot about you. How long have you known her?"

"Eleven years or so. Not that we've been together all that time. A short time after we met, we started living together. That lasted about four years. Then we split up. And I'll be the first to admit that it was on account of my work habits. We stayed apart for almost two years."

"That's a long time to be separated."

"I agree," Charles said. "Too long. And I hated being without Sarah. I had always been able to lose myself in my work, but in those two years, I worked so hard I felt like a first-year lawyer again—eighty, ninety-hour weeks. The few times when I forced myself out to a concert or a gallery, all I could think about was Sarah. I kept wondering what she was doing at almost every damn moment."

"Was it really your fault that you split up?"

"Oh sure, she was right to kick me out. I really was impossible. Beyond impossible. I've never been much for self-analysis or that sort of thing, but to tell you the truth, I behaved pretty badly. What ended it all was when Witherspoon called me back to New York from Japan, at the beginning of a big vacation Sarah had planned for some time. I kept the client, but I lost Sarah. After that, I just felt tremendously lonely, that's all. I missed her angled take on the world. Her stupid, crazy intellectual ju-jitsu. A light had fizzled out in my life."

"So how did you get back together?"

Charles smiled as he thought about it. "It was on one beautiful Saturday afternoon in the fall of 1997. As I often do on Saturdays, I spent most of the day in my office—something I've tried to do a little less of since we've gotten back together. When I left the office, instead of going home, I took the subway up to the Metropolitan Museum, which was mounting a special exhibit on Frida Kahlo and Diego Rivera." Charles paused. Into his mind flickered the image of that dazzling day in New York—sunlight glinting out of the Delft-blue sky and radiating from the City's steel and glass like fire from the points of a sapphire. "It was one of those beautiful New York days. It seemed like half of New York was on Fifth Avenue, taking advantage of the exceptional weather.

"And, as one might expect, everybody and his brother had converged on the exhibit. The crowd was suffocating, and after just a few minutes I decided to leave. On my way out, I spotted Sarah. My heart stopped for a split second. She was on the far side of the room, headphones on and totally absorbed in a small portrait. At first I thought that I just might leave her alone, but then she turned toward me. Her face lit up, and she pulled off the headset. She started walking toward me. Instinctively, I reached out and took her hand. I felt this incredible surge of affection for her and realized just how much I had missed her.

"We went out a few times after that, and then suddenly one day it seemed only natural for me to move into her apartment on Central Park West. By then she had inherited it from her folks, who made a bundle in the diamond business in midtown. After a year I sold my apartment on Park Avenue, since I was rarely there. Once we got together again, it was as if we had never separated. Since then, I've really tried to get home by eight. Not every night. But most. And she doesn't complain about my long hours unless it affects our life together—like when I forget we have opera tickets. We've both compromised, I guess, although I think she's had to do more of the compromising than I have." He paused. "Still, she's extremely independent. She has her career and is very successful. Every year she takes one long trip, but after Japan she's never again asked me to go with her." He smiled ruefully.

"She does seem independent—a little like my sister." Omar paused, then asked, "Do you think that you'll get married?" It was the sort of question that only a computer science professor sitting in the forced intimacy of an airplane cabin at 32,000 feet could pose without seeming nosy.

"I'd marry her in a minute if that was what she wanted. But she was married once before, and it was a very bad marriage. The guy was abusive, and she had to work to support both of them. So, she's happy with the status quo." Charles smiled, a hint of chagrin crossing his features. Then he added, half-kiddingly, "Although I think she might consider marrying me if she didn't believe I was already married to my job."

"She *is* a very independent woman."

"Yes. And she's always been that way. Her parents were Auschwitz survivors, and they taught her what it is to be strong and independent and fearless. But recently there's been an insecurity about her I've never seen before, and she's been going after me again about my hours, my work-load, my clients."

"Why do you think that is?"

"Well, without going into the whole long story, I was at the World Trade Center the morning of the bombings and got out of the North Tower just before the first plane hit. I was at a breakfast meeting at Windows on the World. I left early, but several of my good business buddies weren't so lucky."

"How terrible!"

Charles nodded "I was in shock and by the time I thought to call Sarah, I couldn't get through. The whole communications network downtown had gone down. I didn't go back to the office, and I had to walk home from the World Trade Center to our building on Sixty-first and Central Park West, which took a couple of hours. By the time I got there Sarah was beside herself. She knew I was at that breakfast meeting, and she didn't know if I was alive or dead. It's taken us a while to settle back to normal. I'm no psychologist, but I think she's had a delayed reaction to what happened. She wants to spend more time with me, she wants me to cut back on my hours."

"That's natural, don't you think?"

"I suppose. But she seems to need me more now than even a year ago. Recently she even suggested that I quit my job, that we sell our coop and move to Paris. And even though she said later that she didn't *really* expect it to happen, I think there was a part of her that truly wanted it."

"Expect you to give up all that, your life? Well, I have no idea if that's a reaction to 9/11, but she *does* sound as if she's under stress, if you ask me." Omar paused for a few minutes, then added, "Charles, listen, take my advice." Omar put his hand on Charles's shoulder. "Go find a nice Arab girl and marry her. You'll never have a problem." Charles stifled a guffaw. "No, seriously. They know their place, and won't give you any trouble. You'll never go wrong with them." He smiled, then quipped, "Of course, then there are women like my sister. I guess you might say that she's an exception!" His eyes began to droop from sleepiness. Their conversation was as good as over.

Charles, too, was feeling sleepy. He put on his sleep mask, closed his eyes, and curled into the familiar arc of the first-class seat. In keeping with habit, he had skipped the dinner meal and drunk only an Armagnac as a nightcap and a little juice during the flight. As he dosed off, he thought of the years he had been posted at Lloyd & Forster's Paris office, when he'd shuttled back and forth to New York for client meetings, conferences with colleagues, and even, once, the firm's holiday party. He would joke, to impress clients, that his spine had permanently curved to the shape of the Concorde seat.

He had barely fallen back to sleep when he was awakened again by turbulence. He found himself thinking about Sarah again and the first time they met. It was in 1991, at an elegant party at an East Side gallery for the opening of an exhibit of French watercolors. Normally, he would have ignored the invitation since the next day he had to close the refinancing of an oil refinery located in Dubai. But when Michael Meyer, a Citigroup vice president and a productive source of client referrals, said that his sister was mounting the exhibition, Charles decided to go. Arriving ten minutes before the reception was to end, he raced through the exhibit, slowing once to scan a Mallarmé poem tableaued over a pastel fleur-de-lys. On his way out and back to his office, he gave his compliments to the sister, who was chatting with a petite, animated woman, wearing a green cashmere coat, her wispy, russet hair streaked with gray and tied back from her temples. "Oh, Charles, this is Sarah Steinmann. A great friend and a wonderful painter. We were at City College together. That was ye . . . e . . . a . . . rs ago," the sister said, winking at Sarah.

Idling in the gallery foyer, he and Sarah stumbled into a conversation about impressionism. When, surprise to them, they were told that the gallery was closing for the night, they left together. It had begun to drizzle. A New York drizzle. Rain just enough to irritate the umbrella-less. After their coats had been thoroughly misted, Sarah unfurled a fold-up from her purse. They wedged themselves beneath it for a few minutes before Charles spotted an empty taxi. He suggested that they take it together, and he'd drop her off. Just before they arrived at her apartment, he asked her to dinner the following Tuesday. It was the beginning of their relationship.

She was very different from any other woman he had ever known. She knew a lot about literature. She had a deep appreciation of music. But she was absolutely passionate about the visual arts. In that arena, he himself was a sort of self-made cognoscente who, without a smidgen of priggishness, was confident in his own good taste. But the keenness of her aesthetic insight sometimes would startle him. She hardly fit the stereotype of what his friends teasingly termed the typical "Charlie's angel." She was a few years younger than he, and her loveliness lay in the special harmony her mind enjoyed with her body, with her manner, and with her character: even to those who hardly knew her, she seemed comfortable in her skin. And when she enthused about a painting, something would strum deep inside him.

Sarah did not equate success with working long hours and earning bundles of money. Thus she failed to understand—a failing she shared with him all too frequently—how he—"who obviously loves the same things I do"—could be so "addicted"—her word—to his work. It nagged at her, and as her emotions were never fully constrained by the skeins of her personality, it followed that she nagged at him. After each of their tangles on the subject of work and money, his nerves would entreat him to leave her. But, after a few hours of separation, the allure of her spirit and the appeal of her intellect would always draw him back.

He was also attracted by her self-reliance. He had never come across a woman so determinedly independent. Even on those occasions—when the check arrived at a restaurant, or when the taxi driver reached back for his fare, or at the box office before a show—when convention would allow, yea demand, the American male to fork over his credit card, she would be the first on the draw and pay her own way and then some. And with a few notable exceptions, among them a trip to Paris on the Concorde, she adamantly refused to indulge him his lapses into extravagance, which had been considerable before he met her. Once, she returned a pearl necklace from Tiffany's he had given her. "It's just too costly," she said, adding "Besides, you can't tell natural pearls from cultured ones."

The plane again hit a stretch of turbulence, which interrupted his thoughts. He switched on the overhead light, then took out of his briefcase two back issues of *Martial Arts* and restlessly flipped through the magazines, stopping at an article entitled "Kendo Tactic No. 3: Centering the Spirit Against the Adversary." As he began to read, Omar turned in his seat, finally awakening.

"I hope the light didn't wake you," Charles apologized.

"Not at all. Rough flight," Omar said, shaking his head. "I see you're interested in martial arts."

"It's just a way of getting my mind off my practice. Pretty effective actually. I've been working out with kendo for years. It's the Japanese sport of fencing with bamboo staves. Very fast. It takes concentration."

"I've never heard of it."

"It's been around a long time. For the last two years of high school, I went to a military academy. There, I took kendo and got pretty good at it. I actually earned a black belt with three bars."

Omar regarded Charles. "You're so tall, you must make a pretty good target."

"That's true," Charles said, laughing. "But I've always had fast reflexes. I still keep up my technique, although of course my reflexes aren't what they used to be." As Charles talked about kendo, twisting in his seat to demonstrate the thrust and parry of *nikute*, he noticed Omar's eyelids once again descend to half-mast, flutter a few times, and then come down entirely. He held his tongue as the professor slowly drifted back into slumber. Charles again picked up *Martial Arts* magazine and began to page through it randomly, stopping at an article on the *ki–ai*, the exaggerated cry uttered by a kendoist at the moment the opponent is confronted. The article's author stressed the need to combine *ki–ai* with appropriate eye contact with the opponent as well as the customary flourishes of the kendo stave itself. It was, the author argued, a mode of intimidation more telling than even the first strikes of the baton. Charles switched off the overhead light. In the darkness he began to mug the fierce goggling of the eyes, the showy motions of the eyebrows, and the elaborate contortions of the facial muscles that comprise the kendoist's art. After just a few minutes he too fell back to sleep.

It was almost two hours later, as the plane jolted roughly on landing, when he awoke. Looking over, he saw that Omar was also awake and beginning to check his email.

"So you have a Blackberry too."

"Can't be a computer science professor without being equipped with the latest and greatest. But it's actually *not* a Blackberry. It looks the same, and has a lot of the same features," Omar said, displaying the device to Charles. "Obviously a phone, which you can adjust for use in Europe. And naturally it has email. I've even programmed an Arabic dictionary into it in case I need it. What's different is that it also has a Global Position System or GPS. I've never actually used it, but it's supposed to tell me where I am if I'm lost in the woods."

"Or in Central Park," Charles joked. "Pretty neat! Where'd you get it?"

"It's a prototype GPS phone. Every cell phone maker in the world is working on one. That's one of the perks of being a tech prof at a school like Columbia, you know, to get to test out these toys. The manufacturer—a big Silicon Valley firm, though I can't say which one— wants to release it next year. It's project name is 'XzPhone.'"

"Well, your 'XzPhone' is a lot more sophisticated than mine," Charles retorted, pulling his Blackberry from his shirt pocket. "I certainly don't have the GPS option, though it *is* configured for Europe." He shook the stiffness from his arms.

"You're a sound sleeper," Omar said, changing the tone.

"I actually enjoy sleeping on planes. Lots of experience. I normally like airplane food too—although I rarely eat it on long flights."

"You New York lawyers are a strange breed, I'll say that."

"You're probably right." Charles laughed. He was about to go on when the plane stopped abruptly at the landing gate, again jostling the passengers. "This pilot must be in a pretty foul humor. He's certainly taking it out on us."

"It's all this worry about terrorism on these international flights, I'll bet," Omar said. "It puts everybody a little off kilter."

A few minutes later, the pilot announced that because of an "equipment failure," disembarkment would be delayed for at least twenty minutes. Meanwhile, all passengers were to remain in their seats. Charles gazed out the window. The skies over Paris appeared grim and gray, as if it were about to rain.

Omar had become quiet. He fidgeted with his prized XzPhone, but now and then looked up, his eyes darting around the plane. He seemed out of sorts, strangely moody after their jovial repartee during the flight. Charles tried to pick up the thread of their earlier conversation. "You play that thing like a piano. Do you play?"

"No."

"Well, I do . . . at least I did. Don't get much time to practice, though."

"I'm not surprised." Omar's response was nothing but perfunctory.

"My mother was what you might call a 'would–be–concert–pianist–turned–music–teacher,' so I came by it naturally. I hardly ever practiced, but I do . . . did . . . have an ear. In high school, I could pound out pretty good jazz. And I even whacked away at a few warhorse classical pieces that my mother taught me. I really liked it—especially how you could lose yourself in it." Charles observed a steward in the first-class galley take a particular interest in his virtual monologue.

Omar looked hard at Charles, as if surprised that he—or anyone—could be so cheerful after such a night flight. Charles ignored the look and rolled blithely on. "Harvard really gave me the chance to deepen my interest in music. A lot of mornings I'd commandeer a piano on the second floor of the Union dining hall. That's where all the freshmen have their meals. You have the same deal at Columbia, I think."

Still looking around the plane, Omar seemed distracted, and Charles went on, "For an hour or so before classes, I'd play my heart out, and get my classmates all revved up for the day's jousts with academia." Noticing that the steward's interest seemed to have intensified, Charles wondered whether the man might be studying Charles's Arab companion. "The trouble was, you see, the damn thing was never in tune, and I had to practically jackhammer the keys with my fingers to get any sound to come out." Charles paused to see the effect of his resolute cheerfulness. Omar obliged with a smile, which, albeit wan, was the first since he had fallen into his mood. Charles continued, "Actually, I only pursued music for amusement and never took it seriously enough to study it formally, and of course I gave it up a long time ago. I did have a lot of fun with it then, though. In my junior year, I wrote the tunes—and I might add, most of the lyrics—to our annual Hasty Pudding Show. You know, that's the one that the Harvard undergrads put on, mostly in drag. It's always a little scurrilous if not even scandalous. I don't know if Columbia has anything like it." Charles paused long enough to force a response. The steward came down the aisle, stopped at the seat across from Charles's, and began to fiddle with the overhead luggage compartment.

"We don't," Omar said glumly.

"Well, the year I did it, we called the show 'A Goose for the Holidays.'" Charles waited for a reaction, and Omar brightened, then chuckled bemusedly.

"They're all the same—Ivy League undergrads I mean," Omar said dolefully. "Sex and grades. But the techies like me always put them in reverse order." Omar gave a self-deprecating chuckle.

"Well, the show had some sex too," Charles persisted. "The star my year was Eunice the Eunuch—played by yours truly, of course. She had what we called 'the largest female parts in the show'—or, as the French say, "*il y a du monde au balcon*—too many people on the balcony." Charles cupped his hands beneath his sternum, then guffawed and let his body convulse with merriment. Omar chuckled again and gave Charles a broad smile. The steward, who must have been overhearing their conversation, abruptly turned to them, caught Charles's eye, and whispered, in a strong

French accent, "I couldn't help but notice you two fellows off on a business trip together. Will you be in Paris for a few days?"

"Yes," Charles responded a little warily. He decided that the man had to be an air marshal or other security official.

"Well, I just thought you might be," the man said in a low voice. "I don't know whether you two gentlemen would be interested, but a friend of mine operates an elegant *boîte de nuit*, a nightclub, you know, near Pigalle. It's called the 'Boom Boom Room.' The girls are very, very nice, I tell you. Shows every two hours." He twisted his hips for effect, glanced around to see whether any other passengers were watching, flashed a wry smile at one of them, and then handed Charles a business card. "Tell them Louie sent you, will you?"

Charles blanched. Then, mugging a droll gape at Omar, he begged off politely but firmly, saying, "No, no, no. But thanks. Not this time . . . maybe next." The steward winked nevertheless and continued on down the aisle. Charles rolled his eyes and shook his head in amusement. Omar laughed a little nervously. Charles grasped Omar's arm and said, "You know you're in Paris, right?" A good-natured smile crossed Omar's face. But Charles wondered whether Omar harbored the same suspicion he had about the steward's motives.

After several more minutes, the pilot announced that the technical problem had been resolved. En masse, the passengers stood up from their seats and took up their positions in the aisles. But it was another ten minutes before the doors of the plane finally creaked open. There had been a problem with the docking platform, the steward reported over the sound system.

At Charles' insistence, he and Omar had traveled light, with only carry-on bags. "We're only in Paris for three nights," Charles had said, "and the queue for luggage at Charles de Gaulle can be humongous." When their turn came, they headed down the aisle, Charles holding a large, soft leather bag, Omar with a garment bag slung over his shoulder. As they approached the cabin exit, the captain thanked the departing passengers just ahead of them, but when it came their turn, he simply nodded to Charles and looked at Omar stonily, as if sizing him up. Charles wondered whether his Arab companion might have fallen into the wrong profile. He hardly looked the part of a terrorist, yet the French immigration authorities probably had screened the passenger manifest for Arabs arriving from New York.

"There was more of a story to that 'technical problem' than we'd care to know, I'd say," Charles murmured to his companion when they emerged into the cool morning air. Already a little on edge, perhaps, Charles thought, out of concern about his sister, Omar simply gave Charles a blank stare. The two men silently trundled onto the airport bus that was to take them to immigration and customs. After passing through the formalities without complications, they headed for the taxi stand.

"Do the airline people always treat you like that?" Charles asked Omar matter-of-factly.

"They give Arabs a hard time—even me, with an American passport," Omar replied. "That's always been the case but even more so after September eleventh."

"It must be tough. I mean . . . to be stereotyped like that."

"It used to bother me. Not now, though. I've nothing to fear." Omar extracted a pack of cigarillos from his suit jacket as he looked Charles in the eye.

"I didn't know you smoked," Charles said, consciously changing the subject.

"Only when I get nervous. And only these brown babies. I actually like them. They're Gauloises."

"So I noticed," Charles responded, curling his index finger around his nose. "As the French say, '*Chacun à son goût.*' It means that everyone has their own taste."

"It's my only vice," replied the professor.

It took them only a few minutes to reach the head of the queue. A brown Citroën taxi pulled up to the curb, and a tall man wearing a beret, with a distinguished, almost aristocratic, mien, and sporting a thin mustache flecked with gray, got out. He asked for their destination, first in

French and then, when he caught Charles's accent, in passable English. His manner reminded Charles that, in some quarters in Paris at least, driving a taxi was still thought an honorable calling in itself, not merely a *pied dans la porte*, the foot in the door it had long ago become for *immigrés* from France's former colonies. The man smiled at Charles genially and offered to take their bags.

As Omar leaned down to pick up his bag, the entire packet of Gauloises slipped from his vest pocket and its contents tumbled helter-skelter onto the sidewalk, a few cigarillos even rolling into the street. Almost in unison, the taxi driver and his passengers squatted down to pick them up. When they were back securely in his pocket, Omar apologized. "Sorry, I wasn't thinking. I've always have had my head in the clouds, I guess." Dismissing Omar's chagrin with a toss of his head and a wave of his hand, the driver picked up their bags and placed them in the immaculate trunk of his car. Then, with Gallic gallantry, he opened the doors for his two passengers, and they got in. Charles sat by the curbside window. Glancing out, he noticed that Omar had overlooked a few cigarillos that still lay in the street.

As the taxi sped off in the direction of Paris, Charles wondered whether the professor's absentmindedness—a classic feature of the species—had ever led him astray.

All too soon, he would have his answer.

TWENTY-SIX

Paris
Morning, Monday
Sept. 30, 2002

Approximately an hour before her brother and Charles arrived in Paris, Fatima Shihabi had stepped off Air France flight 905 arriving from Riyadh at Charles de Gaulle airport in Paris. The French Embassy in Riyadh had issued her temporary travel documentation since the Saudi immigration authorities had retained her forged Canadian passport. The French consular official had assured her that the documents would be adequate for her to stay in France indefinitely. "Do not try to travel outside France on these papers," he cautioned. "You will fail and may have to return to Iraq."

Now she would know whether her travel documents would work. As she presented them to the French immigration officer, she flashed a smile at the young man. Sternly he took the papers and studied them intensely. He spoke to her in French. She thought of her father's passage through Gatwick many years before. In English, she addressed him deferentially, "I'm sorry, I did not understand your question." The official looked at her sharply, then said, this time in English, "Did you enjoy your brief holiday abroad, Mrs. Shihabi?" She smiled, nodded, and silently left the immigration stall, then proceeded past a few desultory customs officials and out the swinging doors into a throng of people waiting for arriving passengers.

She could hardly believe it. Until that moment she had harbored doubts as to whether or not she would ever be free. Free from the torture. Free from all the uncertainty. Free to write her poetry. Even as she had arrived back at the airport in Riyadh, to take the plane to Paris, she had fretted that once again she would be called back. She had worried that perhaps she was a little too conspicuous in the blue silk suit the shopkeeper in Riyadh had assured her would be stylish enough in a Western city. It had surely drawn Ali's eyes to her in the Riyadh airport as he hobbled through the lobby, suspiciously eying the departing passengers. He had seen her, and of course remembered her. It was only the presence of Jameel's associate with her that had made him back off. How Ali had glared at her, as he stood by helplessly, as the associate took her arm and escorted her onto the plane. Her last vision of Ali had been as he frantically thumbed his cell phone, about to upbraid his superiors, no doubt, that one more dangerous criminal had been let go.

Now, as Fatima strode proudly along through the Charles de Gaulle Airport lobby, her sack casually across her shoulder, her head high, and her spirits ebullient as they never had been before, her thoughts turned to Latifa. How she missed her. Her bright smile, her elfin frame, her enthusiasm for the drawings she made in her copybook. How she would all too quickly tire of Fatima's embrace, begin to fidget, and then steal away. She must get Latifa out of Iraq. She would find a way.

The line for taxis seemed endless, and Fatima could hardly contain her impatience. At long last, as her taxi emerged from the chaotic bustle of the airport onto a feeder road marked for Paris, Fatima sighed with relief. Another stage on her journey was complete. It would only be a half-hour ride by taxi to the center of Paris, her brother had said. On the airport road there were just a few vehicles—their taxi and, as she saw glancing out the back window, a dirty white delivery truck that left the airport soon after they did and, well behind that, a black sedan with tinted windows.

As the taxi circled a roundabout, she spotted a panel marked "A6 (Paris)." The driver took the turn, headed down the artery, and eased the car into the heavy, Monday morning traffic on the A6. Fatima tried to remember her telephone conversation with her brother. "Go to Hotel Duc de Saint-Simon," he had told her. "On the Left Bank. Rue Saint-

Simon. Tell the driver. We'll meet you in the lobby." He had been very specific. She would do exactly as he had said.

She sat back, pulling toward her the cloth sack in which she carried her possessions, including her travel papers, a black cotton sweater, and the abayah and other things she had brought from Baghdad. She looked out the window of the taxi. The sky was gray, nondescript and sodden, as if it might rain at any moment. Yet, a strange euphoria pervaded her spirits, and happiness suffused her entire being. She was no longer Fatima Shihabi; she was somebody with her skin, her face, her persona, a facsimile of herself. Even the stylish suit she wore, so as not to seem different in the West, wasn't hers. She was living somebody else's dream.

Why had she been so lucky? To have reached her brother by telephone from the prison. To have found Charles Sherman. To know Jameel Zawawi.

Once before, she had almost come to Paris. It was about two years after she had begun working for *Babel*, and she had been invited to attend a PEN conference in Paris. She couldn't participate because of the interdiction on unaccompanied women under the age of 45 leaving the country. How ironic, she thought, that the prohibition against women traveling alone actually had had the opposite effect from the one intended: it was resulting in an increase in divorces. A woman whose husband had already fled the country to live in exile would divorce him and then marry a willing accomplice on a temporary basis so as to be able to leave the country together, only to divorce again and remarry the first husband as soon as she had gotten out of Iraq.

Fatima shut her eyes and tried to visualize Charles Sherman. She would soon meet him. Jameel had described a sensitive man, unusually well attuned to the nuances of Arab culture. Yet a man of the world, with influential friends. A partner of a big New York law firm. A busy man, for sure. And yet giving of his time. She could never repay him for what he had done for her. Why then had he helped her? Why would he even come to Paris to see her? She was deeply curious.

Mile after mile of drab apartment buildings passed before her. She had imagined that Paris would be more beautiful. It seemed tattered, like a beggar, arms out for alms in the souk. Traffic slowed, then slowed again, finally coming to an abrupt stop. Omar would worry if she were not at the hotel when he arrived. She told herself to keep calm and closed her eyes again for a few minutes. When she opened them, she caught the driver gazing at her in the rear-view mirror. "Circulation on the Périphérique is slow at this hour," he interjected quickly in heavily accented English, adding, "because many people go to work late these days, I think. Like me, they don't want to work too hard," he said amiably. Her reverie fractured, she again looked at the passing scene. In the distance, she saw a mosquelike church with a rounded dome, glistening white in a sudden parting of the clouds, surrounded by a vast mosaic of structures stretching to the horizon.

"What's that?" she asked, a concession to the driver that she had never been in Paris before.

"*C'est le Sacré-Cœur, Madame*. A beeeg church. *Chrétienne*, you know."

She caught the reference. Christian. She was determined to take in everything even if it meant that a Parisian taxi driver might overcharge her. The traffic began to flow again. As she looked around her, she glimpsed a black sedan in a merging lane of traffic, several cars back. It seemed identical to one that had been behind them when they left the airport. She followed its reflection in the wing mirror on the taxi's right side. The windows were tinted, and she could see only the shapes of the driver and his passenger. As they turned off the Périphérique, the sedan turned off too but stayed well behind. Many black sedans like that one in Paris, she told herself. She must set her concerns aside. This was not Iraq, after all.

But as their taxi threaded its way through the narrow streets, the thought that it might be the same sedan nagged at her. When they turned off onto a wide tree-lined boulevard, the sedan turned too, and a sudden frisson of fear passed through her. She leaned forward and addressed the driver in a tremulous voice. "How far to the hotel?"

"This Boulevard St. Germain. Hotel not far. Maybe two minutes."

The taxi stopped for a light at a busy intersection. Noticing a sign with a blue "M," she asked the driver, "Is that the Paris Metro—the subway?"

"Yes, Madame, there . . . down those stairs."

"Good, stop there. Quickly. Drop me over there." She pointed to a busy intersection. "I'll walk the rest of the way." She would take no chances. She hoisted her satchel over her shoulder in readiness.

"Yes, here, right here. Stop. Stop." She handed the driver a sheaf of large-denomination Euros, and when he took them all without comment, she bolted from the taxi and raced down the steps, jostling a man carrying a heavy valise. She had no idea where to go but ran as fast as she could down a long underground corridor. When she saw a ticket booth, she joined the queue, bought a Metro ticket, and took the first subway that came into the station. She went two stops and got out, then darted up the stairs. Joining the melee of the lunchtime crowd, she walked several blocks in no particular direction. Once or twice, from a distance, she saw a man dressed in a dark suit and wearing a fedora look toward her, but when he raised his arm to hail a taxi, it was apparent that he was not following her. Not long after that, she came upon a taxi that had just discharged its passengers, got in, and gave the driver the name of the hotel Saint-Simon.

The hotel was on a quiet street, well removed from the congested thoroughfares taken by the driver. At the hotel, she got out and entered the small courtyard that lay before the hotel's entrance. The courtyard's walls seemed to whirl around her, and she felt dizzy. With what seemed her last bit of energy, she pushed through the revolving doors of the entrance and entered the small lobby. She smiled at the receptionist and took a seat on a low banquette across the room. She picked up a copy of *Elle* from a glass-topped table before her and began to page through it as if she could read it. But she was overcome by a mixture of confusion and resignation. And the elation she had felt on arriving in Paris was now supplanted by a numbing fear. Where was Omar? Where was Charles Sherman?

TWENTY-SEVEN

Paris
Morning, Monday
Sept. 30, 2002

On the A6 to Paris, Omar, sitting beside Charles, nervously chain-smoked one Gauloise after another. Feeling himself practically asphyxiated, Charles opened the rear window and gulped the cool, flat air of the Paris suburbs. Several times he tried to coax Omar out of his anxiety. Each time the effort fell flat, and a deadening silence would enshroud them. Finally, Charles gave up and looked out the window at the passing apartment buildings, commercial establishments, and warehouses. He loved Paris, was happy to be back, but his happiness was tempered by Omar's mood.

It was Omar who finally broke the silence. "I can't believe, after all these years, I'm about to see my dear sister," Omar said. "You've done a wonderful thing for my family. And you and I, we make a great team."

"Yes, we *are* quite a team, aren't we? I'm very much looking forward to seeing Fatima too. It will be fantastic, just fantastic. . . . I know it will." But echoing beneath Charles's bonhomie were the mordant strains of the professor's late moodiness, which had touched Charles's heart and sobered him.

Silence descended again. Charles noticed the minaret-like spires of Montmartre swing into view. How the beauties of Paris can banish even the deepest melancholy, he mused. Paris the siren who makes men delirious with her perfumed extravagances. Over the coming days its soaring spires would surely lift Omar's deflated spirits.

Indeed, Charles reflected, their choice of hotel, the Duc de Saint-Simon, was perfectly designed to let them access all the distractions of *le tout Paris*. Inconspicuous but elegant, it occupied a corner of the Left Bank where a person could remain out of sight for a few weeks, or longer if necessary. Fatima could wait there until the arrangements for her long-term stay in France could be settled. They were to meet her in the lobby in case the flight from Saudi Arabia was late as, Charles could well remember, it often was.

Their taxi stopped across the street from the hotel entrance. As he paid the driver, Charles leaned over to the professor and said, "I must confess that I'm actually a little nervous. Does she know that I am with you?"

"Of course she knows, and she very much looks forward to meeting you. She puts you in the same category as Jesus Christ." It was a cute frivolity, particularly for a Muslim, Charles thought, but it typified the friendly tone that had evolved over the preceding weeks between the two men.

Charles smiled good-naturedly and glanced over the professor's shoulder toward the hotel entrance. Talking to the doorman was a short, stocky man, probably of Middle Eastern origin, wearing a brown fedora. Their conversation was intense, and Charles glimpsed the man reach into his pocket and then give the doorman the "golden handshake" well known to doormen everywhere.

"Does anyone else know that your sister is in Paris?" Charles murmured as he lifted his bag from the taxi's trunk.

"I can't imagine it," said the professor. "I'd think that she'd be pretty careful to avoid being seen as she left Saudi. Of course, you can never be sure."

Charles paid the taxi driver, who bowed genteelly as he took the fare. Charles then glanced back at the hotel door. Both men had disappeared.

"Paris weather sure hasn't changed," Charles said lightly. "At least from the time I lived here. We're in for rain today, I think."

"We'll have to remember our umbrellas," the professor responded.

As they entered the little courtyard before the entrance to the hotel, Charles noticed a striking, dark-haired woman in a navy suit, seated on a banquette on the other side of the lobby. They pushed through the glass doors, and she rose gracefully, bent to put down the magazine she had been reading, then glided toward them.

Fatima would have recognized her brother immediately even if he hadn't sent her many photos over the years. Omar was followed by a tall, broad-shouldered man with an athletic bearing, a pronounced jaw, and a face chiseled with lines of humor and kindness, Charles Sherman.

Omar rushed across the lobby. "Praise be to Allah. Praise to Allah, the merciful one. He is so bountiful—so good to us." He took his sister in his arms, his embrace almost suffocating her. Fatima drew back her face and looked into his sparkling eyes, awash with tears.

"Hello, my dear brother. I thought that I'd never see you again." Scarcely able to contain her joy, she buried her face in his neck, drawing him toward her. "It was the thought of you during those hard times . . . that kept me going, kept me alive," she sobbed.

"I know, Fatima, I know. . . . I often thought of you too over these many years. We have a lot to talk about. But first"—he pulled back from the embrace and turned—"let me introduce Charles . . . or, I should say, Mr. Sherman. He is our brother—just the same as if he had been born in the same bed as you and I. Praise Allah, who has given us the gift of his aid." Fatima and Omar reached for him, drawing him into their centrifuge of emotion, their faces flush with tears, their sobs merging as one. Charles felt Fatima's lean frame flattened against his bulky one. The dry, dusty smell of the desert invaded his nostrils. He found himself falling into the bottomless depths of the most wondrous eyes he had ever seen. Dark eyes scintillating with a remarkable brilliance, a chiaroscuro lit by some mysterious light, like a smoldering campfire in a Rembrandt nightscape he had once seen at the Frick. Her olive complexion was offset by a black mole on her left cheek.

After a few minutes, they pulled away from one another, but Fatima's hand rested on her brother's shoulder. She turned to Charles, cocked her head slightly, and said, "You saved my life."

"You saved yourself."

"I'll be forever in your debt."

"If all my debtors were like you, I'd be a lucky guy," Charles quipped.

She caught the humor and laughed lightly. "Really, Mr. Sherman, I can't thank you enough for what you've done for me."

"It's not over."

"I know." She wasn't sure whether to tell him that she had been followed from the airport.

"We should get out of here," Charles murmured, looking at the doorman watching them. "Go to a café or something. We should check in first, of course."

"No, I think that maybe I shouldn't stay here."

"Oh, there shouldn't be any problem at this hotel. It's quiet, and it's convenient for exploring the city. Nobody's going to bother you here. You're free now, you know, . . . free from your persecutors in Iraq."

Fatima bit her lip, then replied, "But I should say . . . they know I'm in Paris. I think they saw me get on the flight from Riyadh." She told Charles how she had evaded her pursuers from the airport.

Charles frowned as she spoke, and he thought of the man he had seen talking to the doorman.

"No problem," he said. "We'll give them the slip. Walk over there as if the two of you are checking in." Charles pointed to the front desk at the rear of the lobby. "Then stop for a moment as if to discuss your room, but keep going out the back door. You'll be on a little street, rue Courier, that leads out to rue de Grenelle. Take the first taxi you can find to the Bristol. It's a small hotel on Faubourg St. Honoré. Ask for Jacques, Jacques Weil, the manager. Tell him I sent you. He'll give you a room. Send me an email when you've checked in." Charles shifted his gaze to the professor. "I'll pick up your message off my Blackberry. In the meantime, I'll distract our friendly doorman over there."

Charles ambled casually over to the doorman and asked in badly fractured French, "Monsieur, can you give me directions to le Café Deux Magots?"

"*Mais oui,*" responded the doorman, who though ebullient, seemed a bit nervous. At first Charles pretended not to understand, then asked if they might step outside so that the doorman could direct him more easily toward the place.

As they passed through the revolving glass doors, Charles glanced back at the front desk. Fatima and the professor were gone. He spent a few minutes with the doorman in front of the hotel, repeating the directions slowly as if to be sure to understand them and gesticulating as if he were being so directed, for the benefit of anyone watching the front entrance. Finally, he thanked the man, and, like any tourist bent on a walking tour of Paris, he shuffled along, satchel in hand, admiring the fine points of the Left Bank's architectural gems. When he reached the newspaper kiosk at Boulevard St. Germain, he stopped as if to make a purchase. As he took his place in the queue, he casually looked behind him. The doorman was gesturing in his direction to a man in a dark suit.

Heart racing, Charles began running down St. Germain toward rue du Bac. When he reached the Metro stop at the corner, he threw himself down the stairs two at a time. The line for Metro tickets was long. Oh for the days when one could vault over the turnstiles, he thought. Just as he began to head out the other side of the Metro stop, the guard opened a gate to allow a young couple to bring two large cardboard boxes and their luggage into the Metro. Charles quickly pushed through with them, handing the Metro official a 50 Euro note. He ran down the platform and waited in an alcove for the next train. It came almost immediately, and he took it three stops to Place de la Concorde and then switched to the Neuilly line. He exited the train at the avenue Franklin Roosevelt stop, at the corner of the Champs-Elysées. Leaving the station, he put his head down and moved quickly but deliberately along, merging into the usual Parisian mêlée of tourists, shoppers, street musicians, panhandlers and an assortment of *les âmes perdues,* lost souls in search of someone or something that only Paris could deliver. He went one block up the Champs and strode into a Pizza Pino on the corner. He sat several rows back, where he could watch the street.

After about ten minutes, he saw the man in the black suit. The man was ambling along, looking around, as if he were an ordinary business-man from the Middle East with a few holiday hours to spare in Paris. Struck by the shrewdness of the man, by his ability to stay on the trail of his pursuit for so long, Charles experienced a sudden panic. He had underestimated the danger that Fatima, and now her brother and indeed he himself, faced in Paris. He took a good look at his pursuer. His dark suit was well pressed, and his head was bald as if he had shaved it. Charles noticed an odd wrinkle in the skin of his forehead, like a birthmark or a scar. The cast of his face was brutishly intelligent. It was the face of a killer, Charles thought.

As he began to turn in Charles's direction, Charles leaned over in his chair as if to tie his shoe. After ten seconds, he looked up, and the man was gone. Charles waited another ten minutes. He then paid for the espresso and left the café.

He walked hurriedly in the opposite direction from his pursuer up the Champs Elysées toward avenue George V, where Lloyd & Forster used to have their Paris office and where he had spent three years of his life. And now, in his old neighborhood, he was on the run from the Iraqi secret service. They would kill him if they had the chance. And just as easily, they would kill Fatima.

Still fresh in his memory were her wondrous eyes. Dark and lustrous, they were widely spaced, intelligent and inquisitive, lighting her fine-boned face. She was far more beautiful than he had imagined. The mole in the center of her left cheek only served to enhance her fine features. He had felt her taut, sinewy body press against his. It was *un coup de foudre*, he thought, a "clap of thunder" that reverberated to the depths of his being.

Slow down, Charles Sherman, he told himself. Slow, slow down. It's just infatuation. You hardly know this woman. It's ridiculous. A Muslim.

An Iraqi no less. But smart. And unquestionably beautiful. Forget it, Charles. Just forget it. You'll make a fool of yourself. Just get on with it. Do what you have to do.

First he had to find her—and her brother. By now they should be settled at the Bristol, he thought. He'd have to assume that they had evaded their pursuers. Things would have happened too quickly for anyone following them to react, Charles surmised. It was the advantage of surprise.

As he walked along the Champs Elysées, it began to rain lightly. A September cold spell in Paris, he thought. Rare but possible almost any month of the year. The sort of penetrating, bone-chilling cold that had made Mimi burn her poetry. Or was it Marcello? He spotted a telephone kiosk a short distance down George V. It would give him a wide vista up and down the sidewalk. After entering it, he stood for several minutes, looking out, making sure he was not being watched. He took out his Blackberry and pulled up his email. The first one, from Omar, was abrupt.

"Hotel de la Paix on Vavin. Meet you in the lobby at 4:00 p.m. Be sure you are not followed."

Charles fingered back the words, "CU then and there."

Charles worried why they were not at the Bristol. A small hotel, perhaps it had no room for them. He checked his watch. It was 2:40 p.m. As he left the kiosk, it was raining heavily. He drew an umbrella from his bag and raised it. As he strode along, he decided that he would have to get Fatima out of Paris. It was the only way. He'd have to find a sanctuary where she could hole up, isolated, safe, maybe even for months, until he could figure out how to get her into the States. But where? Where could a person stay out of sight, walled away from the world? Where? It was going to take some doing.

TWENTY-EIGHT

Paris
Early afternoon, Monday
Sept. 30, 2002

Fatima Shihabi sat at the edge of a plush settee and looked out at the passing traffic on rue Vavin. Her brother lay on the only bed in the room, fingering his XzPhone. Restless, she got up and stood by him. "Have we heard anything from Mr. Sherman yet?" she asked.

"Yes, Fatima, and he'll meet us here at four p.m. I was just checking my email, mostly from my students. They're a little confused since I had to reschedule my classes so I could come to Paris. The university sent me a couple of messages too. My department head just informed me that I'm to receive an increase in my salary."

"Congratulations, Omar. You've made a wonderful success for yourself in the United States. Father would have been very proud of you, you know."

"And you too, dear Fatima. You were always so close to him." Omar sat up on the side of the bed, took his sister's hand, and gently pressed it.

"I only hope that Latifa inherits the same spirit."

"How is she these days?"

"I worry a lot about her, especially about her reaction to my departure. After all my problems at *Babel*, I had told her that one day it might be necessary for me to leave Iraq. When I actually left Baghdad, I wanted to say goodbye to her, to give her one final embrace, but she was sleeping and, anyway, I didn't know how she would have reacted. Honestly, Omar, I think that if she had been terribly upset, I just would have stayed with her. I'm sure Majid would have liked that."

"Did he know you were planning to leave?"

"This past summer he came up to Baghdad to visit Abdeljelil, to plead for more money for the Institute. He overheard something I said about leaving Iraq. Well, he made a terrible scene. He paced back and forth in the courtyard before my villa, shouting at me. You know how he is. And it was all in front of Latifa. He accused me of abandoning my family and my daughter, of breaking faith with the Holy Koran. It was deeply upsetting. Latifa will never forget it, I'm afraid. So, you see, Omar," she said sighing, "I've shame on my soul." She waited for a reaction.

"No, not at all, Fatima. You most certainly did the right thing, both for you and Latifa." He stood and embraced her. "Good acts are never wasted in this world. Some great good will come from your courage, from the pain you have suffered. I feel sure of that."

"We're so lucky to have Mr. Sherman helping us," she interjected. "I don't know how we could endure, otherwise."

"That's true. He's a great man."

Leaning against Omar's shoulder, she thought of Charles's broad, craggy face, the gaze of his keen steely-blue eyes, and how they had locked onto hers. Tall and strapping, he had struck a commanding presence in the hotel lobby. As he left them, he had seemed anxious, troubled to know that she had been followed. Why was he doing all this? He had saved her life at least once already, and now, risking his own life, he was doing it again. Maybe even he didn't know what was motivating him. He never could have imagined that a simple phone call on a Tuesday less than three weeks ago could have enmeshed him in her web of troubles. Surely, he must have friends, his work, his life. A wife and children even. He had left all that just to meet her, to meet her here in Paris.

Perhaps it was his fate as well as hers, Fatima reflected. The will of Allah in his merciful bounty, inexorably and ultimately to be accepted. And yet, in spite of her faith, and indeed rather because of the strength it gave her, she was resolved to do what she believed she had to do. And she recognized in Charles the same strength, the same determination that she herself possessed. But there was something else too: he had gazed at her with an intensity she had never seen in a man before.

Fatima drew herself away from her brother's embrace. She retreated back to her post at the window and pensively looked out. The conversation with her brother had stirred her concerns about her daughter.

"Omar, it's going to be Latifa's turn one of these days, you know— I've tried to be a separate voice—not really to oppose the traditions of our culture, but rather to nourish its finest values. And honestly," she said, crooking her head at him, "It's been difficult. I don't know that she's going to be prepared for it . . . for the struggle to raise herself up. Right now, she's like a desert rose pleading for water. Without me, she's going to dry up, I'm sure of it." She sighed deeply. "Oh, Omar, I wish I could speak with her."

"You could try to call her, of course. It should be safe from here."

"Yes," Fatima agreed, "I will do that. Not today but perhaps in a day or two." Better to wait until she could melt into the anonymity of immigrant life in Paris.

The ring of Omar's XzPhone startled them, jerking them back to the here and now.

TWENTY-NINE

Paris
Afternoon, September 30, 2002

The sun had chased away the rain just before Charles arrived at Hotel de la Paix, a good hour before he was supposed to meet Fatima and her brother. To give them a chance to rest after the excitement of the morning but more important to give himself time to call Sarah, he told the taxi driver to drop him at rue Vaugiraud, a half-block from the hotel. Sauntering down rue Vavin, he eyed a quiet café across the boulevard. Café des Errants. How appropriate, he thought. The wanderers. Like Fatima. Maybe himself too.

He plunked his body, sapped of energy, at a table inside. The sole customer, he waited impatiently for the waiter to arrive, then asked for a café au lait.

"Slow down, slow down, Charles," he lectured himself. Must focus. Must focus.

He was, after all, a dealmaker. Whose highest ambition was to structure reality, not interpolate it. The Street prized him precisely because of his ability to apply raw intelligence and dealmaking prowess to find the way forward. While his skill at satisfying clients was mythic at Lloyd & Forster, and he would sometimes find glory in seeing his deals on the front page of *The Wall Street Journal*, he drew his greatest pleasure from the negotiations themselves—from the thrill of the chase of the deal. And now he found himself at a café in Paris, after having been tracked all morning by Iraqi intelligence, a demon more monstrous than any he had slain in his corporate deals. Even as the Goldstar deal was in *extremis*, Charles thought and chuckled, Witherspoon had never threatened his life—as much as he might have liked to. At bottom, Charles conceded to himself, saving Fatima Shihabi was the grandest, gutsiest deal of his life.

He must get Fatima out of Paris. Sooner or later, the Iraqis would find her, and then it would be a simple matter of one more Arab dissident disappearing in Paris. But an Arab woman, especially one of her striking beauty and literary renown, hiding out alone in France would be like an albino in a camel auction. The Arab community in France, large and concentrated in major cities, had its "street" too, and a Muslim woman living alone would eventually draw attention to herself. No, he had to find a more secluded refuge for her, perhaps in a village in the mountains. Suddenly he smiled. He had an idea.

He extracted his Blackberry from his vest pocket and thumbed through his address book. Malone, David Malone. The name pulled up immediately. Metta Caldwell had earned her stripes again. When the firm gave him his Blackberry, Metta had spent days patching in an assortment of numbers from his Rolodex. The call connected at once.

"David, is that you? This is Charles Sherman. . . . Yes, it's been ages. How are things at Coudert?" Pause. "You are very kind. I was just lucky, I guess. . . . No, I'm still not hitched, officially that is. . . . I do live with a wonderful woman in New York." Another pause. "You never know."

"Listen, David, I'm calling to ask a favor. Do you still have your summer place in Talloires?" Pause. "It would just be for a week or two. I have a client who needs to disappear for a while." A longer pause.

"No, it would be easier for us to get the key from your neighbors. Okay, the Lamirands. We'll get ourselves over there sometime tomorrow."

Charles grinned. "I can't explain now, but if you knew what I'm up against, you would wish me luck. Thanks, David. See you soon, I hope."

As he hung up, Charles recalled the first time he had met David Malone. It had been on a Société Générale financing when Charles worked at Lloyd & Forster's Paris office and David, as a partner of Coudert Brothers, had represented the borrower, a Houston oil company with a pipeline in Guatemala. Some fifteen years Charles's senior and a long-time resident of Paris, David always had treated him as a son, and more than once Charles had joined the Malone family at their capacious *maison des vacances* on Lac d'Annecy in the tiny village of Talloires in the eastern part of France. Tucked against the foothills of the French Alps, it was the perfect place, Charles thought, where Fatima would be safe until they figured out what to do next.

Charles glanced at his watch: 3:45 p.m. Time to make one more call.

Sarah was in her studio. "Sarah, it's me," he said. "I'm in Paris. Just wanted to say hello. I'm going to be delayed for a few days. I hope to get back by the weekend."

"Charles, I miss you, I really do. I'm awfully glad that you went to see Mrs. Shihabi in Paris. Aren't you glad you went?"

"Well, it remains to be seen." It was his way of being cagey. His way of not communicating. "Things are not going quite as well here as I had hoped." First prize for understatement, Charles told himself.

"Your life isn't in danger, is it?"

"Not really. At least . . . ." He never was a credible liar. "Hold on a second, Sarah." His eyes lit on a sedan that had just pulled up in front of the café, not twenty feet from where he sat. The two men inside turned and looked across the boulevard, one looking at his watch and the other staring intently toward the hotel. Charles recognized the second man—he was the man who had tried to follow him a few hours before.

It was too coincidental. He was the only one who knew that Fatima and her brother were at Hotel de la Paix. Or was he? Mukhabarat must have followed Fatima and her brother from the Hotel St. Simon, just as they had tracked Fatima to the St. Simon in the first place. There must be more than a few of Saddam's minions in Paris interested in intercepting her.

"Sarah, sorry but I have to go," he said and hung up abruptly. He moved to the back of the café and quickly dialed the number for Omar's phone.

"Hello," Omar answered.

"It's Charles. Sorry to tell you this, but there's a welcoming committee waiting for me in front of the hotel."

Charles heard a gasp at the other end of the line.

"They must have followed you from the Duc de Simon."

"Wow, these guys are pros. I really thought we weren't followed. Fatima knows how to evade pursuers. Once we got near this hotel, we separated. First Fatima waited and then I did. They surely couldn't have been on our trail."

"What about the email you sent me? Could they have hacked into your email?"

"Not likely, it's too difficult—although the Iraqis are known to have a pretty high level of techno wizardry."

"Okay, Omar, the next time you'd better be careful with your email. At least don't reveal where you are or where you're going."

"Sorry, Charles, I guess that should've occurred to me. I'll just turn this thing off."

"Look, I don't care what you do, but you'd better get out of there fast. You're going to have to do your hotel–back–door trick again. By now you must be getting good at it," Charles wisecracked. He sometimes astounded himself at his ability to keep cool under pressure. "We still have a little time before they realize we know. Leave the hotel by the back door. Get a taxi to Gare de Lyon. Take the first train you can get to Annecy in eastern France. Annecy, that's right." Charles spelled it for him. "I'll try to meet you at the train, but if I don't get there, take the boat at the lake to the village of Talloires. It's on the other side of the lake. Talloires. Go to 31 rue du Lac. The neighbors, the Lamirands, are expecting you tomorrow. Just tell them you arrived early."

"Will you be okay?"

"I'll be fine. Just take care of your sister and don't wait to pay your bill. Take Fatima and go now." He paused. "Oh, and do be careful with your email." He heard a click. He wasn't sure that Omar had heard him.

Charles waited a few minutes in the shadows of the cafe, studying the faces of the two men. Elegance and distinction marked the taller man.

Diplomat, Charles surmised. Probably at the Iraqi embassy. The other man's thick, dark features and boxer nose gave him a brutish air; his stocky build was masked by an oversize, though well-tailored, black suit. His fedora, which he tipped nervously from time to time, almost hid the odd wrinkle of skin on his forehead. Once he shifted his gaze about the car, and Charles drew himself farther back in the shadows. Just before 4:00 p.m., Charles peered at the waiting car one last time, paid his bill, and let himself out into the alley at the rear of the café.

The alley opened out on a narrow, sinuous street typical of the Left Bank. Charles took the street, crossing several intersections before he was confident that he was well away from the hotel. It had begun to drizzle again and he raised his umbrella. As he strode along, a well of anger began to rise in his throat, almost stifling him. Anger against the two-bit assassins assigned to kill one Fatima Shihabi, a person he now knew to be one courageous human being, one great humanitarian, one marvelous woman whose only crime was that she wanted to write the truth in her journalism and in her poetry. But then there was another kind of anger, of a different sort, one directed at the monolithic mausoleums of power and arrogance in the West, at the Rita Lanes and all the other petty functionaries of this world, at their rank indifference to the plight of émigrés even as they parroted the platitudes of democracy, freedom, and self-fulfillment. It all seemed quite clear to him, he reflected as he hurried along the wet pavement. If only Fatima had been granted asylum in America in the first place, as well she had earned it, he wouldn't be schlepping through the back streets of Paris in the rain. And Fatima and her brother wouldn't be running for their lives.

He walked a few more blocks and then hailed a taxi for the Gare de Lyon.

THIRTY

Gare de Lyon, Paris
Late afternoon, Monday
Sept. 30, 2002

Charles arrived at the station just minutes before a train for Annecy
was to depart. The quay and the train itself were nearly empty, probably
because late on this Monday afternoon most Parisians had long come
back from their extended weekend in the mountains. He entered the train
by the first car and methodically moved through the train, checking each
compartment, striding down the long aisles of banquette seats, the vacant
corridors, compartment after compartment, until suddenly to his surprise
he came upon the head of the train. Surely, he thought, in his haste he
had passed by Fatima and Omar. He ran back through the train, inspect-
ing each cabin, each row of seats, more carefully this time, again to no
avail. He tried to call Omar's phone, but when there was no answer, he
remembered Omar had turned it off. Charles had to find his clients.

But, as he completed his second pass through the train, it was dawning on him that Fatima and Omar had, for reasons Charles dreaded to
imagine, missed the train. By the time he returned to the first car, the
train's electric motors had begun to whine and a portly trainman on the
quay was announcing the train's imminent departure. As Charles left the
train and stepped down onto the quay, he asked the official how much
time he had. "*Une minute, Monsieur,*" the man replied brusquely. Charles
pulled his wallet from his inside jacket pocket, opened it, gave the man
the first paper money he found, a fifty Euro note, flashed his New York
driver's license and, vaulting back up the steps, added in his worst American accent, "*le Service Secret Americain. Je cherche des Arabes dans le train. Je*

reviens dans deux minutes." Looking for Arabs. Right. Wins every time, he lamented. He had two minutes. Once again he raced up and down the long corridors, checking every seat and cabin. He was a man possessed, praying to God, beseeching the deities, anyone who would listen, until, faint with effort, he caught a glimpse of blue silk in the corridor window of a compartment whose occupants had diligently drawn the shade against uninvited guests and were pressing themselves into the corners on either side of the cabin door.

"We were worried about you," Omar said, relieved, as Charles bolted into the compartment.

"For a minute there, I thought I had lost you," Charles replied. "Whoa. I'm glad I had my Wheaties this morning." Catching his breath, he forced a wan smile at Fatima. Omar moved to Fatima's side, and Charles sat on the banquette opposite them.

Fatima softened her features at him. "Welcome, Mr. Sherman."

"You may call me Charles."

"Charles then." She paused for an instant. "And you may call me Fatima," she half-whispered, smiling. He felt a thrill pass through him no less intense than if she had kissed him.

After another minute the train lurched back and forth a few times, a signal it was departing the station. Then, it began to roll forward, picked up steam, and sped away from Paris to the east. Apart from the exigencies of the moment, Charles thought, they could have been three ordinary tourists, setting out on an early fall excursion to the mountains, disposing themselves comfortably in a compartment made for six. Their trials in Paris and jet lag had exhausted them, and, once having settled themselves in the car, the three weary travelers almost as one fell asleep as the train's steady *clack–clack* coerced them into slumber. It was broken only when the cabin door jarred open and the conductor, eyeing the *agent americain* and his two Arab charges with suspicion, demanded to see their tickets. Charles nodded solemnly, gave the man a conspiratorial wink, and handed him the fare for their trip to Annecy.

Soon after, Fatima and Omar again closed their eyes, and Charles, half-awake, looked out the cabin window. The setting sun had dramatized the passing countryside, the long shadows of dusk bracketing the intermittent expanses of sunlit fields, cozied against the occasional village or town. He lay stretched out on the brown vinyl seat, his feet propped against the compartment door. Across from him, his charges slept, Omar with his long legs extended across the narrow space between the banquettes and Fatima with her head on her brother's lap. Charles took in the full beauty of Fatima's face, a face now in repose, pure of skin, refined in all its features save one, the curious mole on her cheek, which Charles now realized was a scar.

Even as he gazed at Fatima, a vision of Sarah floated across Charles's mind. He closed his eyes and thought of her. Practical, self-reliant, but always loving Sarah. He would have given anything to recount to her the day's events. She would have known what to do long before he did. She would have been upset with him too, to put his life at risk. She sometimes twitted him about his willingness to do anything for a client. But Fatima Shihabi was no ordinary client, hardly a case of business before pleasure.

As the express train rumbled through a station in a commune well to the east of Paris, Charles blinked open his eyes, straining against the glare of the station lights. He stretched his arms before him. Across the narrow space of the compartment, Fatima was curled on the faded brown seat, her dark eyes fixed on him.

"My brother has told me that you are famous—a famous American lawyer, he said."

"Not as famous as you are a poet." Charles managed a grin.

"You are very kind. We will never forget what you have done for us."

"I really have done nothing. You've done it all." His mind was rousing itself. "I walk in your shadow." His intent was poetic, but it came out sounding strange.

"I am so small, I do not cast a shadow," she replied coyly.

He grinned again. She had bested him. She knew it too. They both laughed, waking up her brother.

A few stations later, Omar dozed off again, and Charles and Fatima were left to explore that alluring land that lies between a man and a woman of different worlds. They communicated guilelessly—he in the measured, cultivated cadences of a New York lawyer, she in a sweet, lacy voice embellished with Arab accents. They spoke of their lives, their families, their work, and their interests. Charles enthused about martial arts, even miming a few kendo moves for her from his banquette, while she talked about her poetry and the ecstasy she felt in composing it. Like misbegotten children, they faltered forward, one recounting to the other the myriad details of experience that made up their separate existences. In the end, though, their thoughts turned back to more immediate concerns.

"I thank you for introducing me to Jameel Zawawi. He was most helpful."

"Sure, don't mention it. He's a good guy."

"He likes you too, a lot. He told me very much about you. He asked me to say hello to you and also to your partner, . . . Art, I believe he said."

"Art Hauck? That's nice, I'll tell him."

"Mr. Zawawi told me that you spent much time in Saudi Arabia."

"I did. It was over many trips. My firm, like many others, worked for the Saudis in the late 1970's and early 1980's. I became a virtual commuter to Saudi Arabia from Lloyd & Forster's Paris office."

"You are very popular in Saudi Arabia, Charles. They still remember how you became so close to the Arab people. Mr. Zawawi told me all about you, even how you ate something very unusual for Americans the last meal you had with him. Unfortunately I don't know the word in English for them. My brothers used to eat them all the time in our village." She reached over and shook Omar, who groggily opened his eyes. She spoke to him in Arabic, seeming to repeat the same word or phrase over and over.

"Testicles," Omar finally said, a little vaguely.

"That's what those things were?" Charles exclaimed. "Well, I always wondered, I have to say. I'll never forget them. They were pretty disgusting. I've never forgiven Jameel for that, you know," Charles said, laughing.

"In my village, Kassim, in the Iraqi desert, we eat them when we kill a sheep."

"Remind me not to go there, thank you," he said, grinning at her. "In spite of that, I did, and do, find Arabic culture fascinating—something mysterious and wonderful." Charles gazed into her deep, dark eyes. He thought at first she might be wearing eye makeup but concluded that it had to be her long, naturally dark eyelashes. "Your brother tells me that you're a feminist," said Charles. "I suppose there are not too many of you in Iraq."

"We don't use that word in my country. In fact, for us it has a negative meaning because of the bad effects feminism has on the family—which we hold sacred. But it's true that I am interested in the problems of women," she said, smiling graciously, "in my country and in other countries as well."

"It a subject that interests me too." Even as he spoke, he realized that his desire to connect with this exotic creature before him, as well as his propensity for bravura, had enticed him into foreign terrain. Feminism was not in his regular diet of topics of casual conversation. Sarah was so strongly self-reliant that, for her, feminism as such almost seemed beside the point. And to discuss feminism with Hansen? Or Witherspoon? Better to talk about the molecular structure of moon rocks.

"Why are you interested in women's problems?" Fatima asked.

Uncharacteristically, Charles found himself foundering for lack of a response. "I suppose it began in my student days, at Harvard. I've always been interested in social science, history, the Middle Ages, that sort of thing. I suppose it represents the other side of me, I guess you might say."

"You *are* most unusual, Charles. You are amazing!"

Chuckling bemusedly, Charles went on, "Sometimes I have the feeling that Islamic women are stuck in their own Middle Ages." It was now becoming swampy, treacherous terrain, but he forged valiantly on. "Actually, you know, women in Western Europe in the twelve hundreds had exactly the problems you in the Islamic world have today," he said. "Lack of education. Oppression by a culture that exalted men. They couldn't even own property. Couldn't divorce their husbands. When they were young, they belonged to their fathers. And when they were married, they belonged to their husbands. And the marriages were arranged just as they are for Islamic women today. Often to much older men."

Fatima listened intently but said nothing. Charles blithely stumbled on.

"Western women in the Middle Ages were not much different from slaves. And it's taken them almost a thousand years to free themselves." Charles smiled, a little embarrassed by his sermonette. Deprecating his own preachiness with a bemused, I–know–better–than–that air, he added, "And of course women in the West still have their problems. Even my friend Sarah had trouble with her former husband, who abused her."

"My brother has told me a little about her. I think I would like her."

"Well, maybe someday you will have the chance to meet her."

Changing the subject, Fatima said, "As a journalist, I've always admired your ability to obtain information in the West. You probably read a lot of books, I'd imagine."

"When I was a kid, my idea of a good time was to settle into my father's lounge chair in our living room and spend summer afternoons working through the classics—*Bleak House*, *Crime and Punishment* or *War and Peace*. I also loved the Arthurian legends, Greek and Roman myths, absolutely anything about ancient peoples. When I was eighteen or so, I read about a hundred books a year."

"That *is* amazing!"

"Oh, I used to be excited about books. In fact, I'd find words . . . just plain, ordinary words . . . interesting, downright satisfying. As a kid, I'd always be curious about where they came from and what their exact meaning was. I was totally taken in by them—by how authors would put them together into stories. I was the only kid I knew who *liked* using the dictionary. Sometimes I'd look up one word, then I'd see another, look that one up, and I'd actually get lost reading the dictionary! Strange, huh?"

"Not at all. People in my culture love books and poetry and admire the beauty of words too." She paused and then asked, "Have you read any authors from the Middle East—perhaps Mahfouz, Djebar, or El Saadawi? Any of the poetry of Rumi?"

"Funny you should ask. I *have* read some Rumi—a long time ago. I really liked it. Can't say I've read the others, though I'd like to. Nowadays I barely have time to read anything. I barely have time to read the newspaper."

"I'm sorry to hear that."

It was a conversational cul-de-sac, and he decided to retreat to an earlier topic, one he knew interested the woman before him. "Fatima, earlier we were talking about the condition of women in your culture. Do *you* think that Muslim women are oppressed?" he asked.

"Yes and no. That is not a simple question to answer," she replied, taking him more seriously than he had intended. "It's a very complicated subject. Every country in the Arab world is different." Fatima fixed her eyes on him, her bottomless black eyes drawing him in. Now, she pulled herself back and inclined her face almost warily.

"First of all, Charles, I must tell you a little history. Islam is not—how can I put it?—anti-woman. The Prophet Mohammad was good—very good—for women. He stopped the slavery of women and the killing of baby girls, and he gave women the right to get property from their parents. How do you say that in English?"

"You mean inherit?"

"Yes, inherit." She mimicked his pronunciation precisely.

"In those days, women had more rights under Islam than even under Christianity or Judaism."

"So why do women wear the veil?"

"The veil is part of our culture. For most Muslim women, it is not a wall we feel between us and the world, it is part of the lives we lead. Muslim women wear the veil—or don't wear the veil—for many different reasons. For some of us, it is a way of keeping our identity, for others a way of expressing it, of—how do you say that?—making a statement?

What you Americans don't realize, it's often a question of choice for us." She paused as the noisy swoosh of a passing Paris-bound train interrupted her.

"For other Muslim women, though, the veil is really not a choice. It is a symbol of how the fundamental rights given to Muslim women under Islam have been taken away from them for so many years. There are many reasons why this is so. But it was *not* Mohammad who made women take the veil or who took away their rights. What has happened is that the Holy Koran has been badly interpreted for many centuries. So, conservative traditions have been built up—based upon these bad interpretations. This is all more complicated because of the poverty of our people. And because they lack education. So, now we have the Islamic fundamentalists who again are using the Holy Koran in the wrong way, just in order to get power for themselves."

"Even the devil can quote scripture," Charles interjected.

"What does that mean?"

"Well, ever since the Bible and the Koran were put down on paper, people have misinterpreted them for their own ends."

"I see. But for Muslim women, these misinterpretations of the Holy Koran have been disastrous. The very religion that first liberated women—Islam—is now being used to oppress them. Women are being forced to obey the dictates of fundamentalism—either by the men in their families or by the threat of personal violence from their *ummas*, their communities. And the great progress that Muslim women made in the 1950s through the 1970s is now being taken away by totalitarian regimes."

"So, why don't women take more of a stand?"

"Actually, the majority of women these days are just struggling to survive." She shook her head dejectedly and rubbed her forehead. "Even for me and my family, it has been difficult . . . very, very difficult . . . although not as bad as for many other families." She then tossed her head, turning as if to look out at lights in a village station as the train rumbled by it.

She seemed on edge, Charles thought, perhaps concerned about her own loved ones in Iraq, surely about her daughter. She remained silent a long time, and he respected her need to be alone with her thoughts. Meanwhile, Omar slept on, budging only when the train's rhythm was syncopated by the occasional roads, bridges and stations. Finally, to break her mood, Charles said, "Your brother is a sound sleeper." When she didn't respond, he added, "He slept on the plane last night but probably not very well."

"I know," she said. "For me, last night seems a very long time away."

Charles sighed, memories of the day's events still fresh.

"How long will I stay in Talloires?" she asked him after a few minutes.

"Not very long, I hope. Perhaps several weeks . . . a month. We've got to get you out of France. It's too dangerous here."

"Where will I go?"

"The States, of course."

"But I have no visa. As you told my brother, asylum from outside America takes a year or more. By then, Mukhabarat will find me."

"There's the refugee program."

"I am not sure about that. There are millions of refugees around the world. And America each year takes only very few—fewer even now after September eleventh. Do you think I can count on that?"

"Maybe we can get you to America another way."

"Swim?" She laughed dryly. "Do you think that any airline or ship will take me when they know that they might have to pay a big fine?"

Omar roused himself. Eyes shut, he had been listening to their conversation. "It's a Catch–Twenty-two situation," he interjected, repeating verbatim what Charles had previously told him. "America will give refugees asylum, but they have to make it to the front door first. America then erects barriers to prevent them from getting to the front door. But then again, if the refugees don't get there, they might be killed, so America won't have to worry about them because they'll be dead."

"Or worse," she added. "In my case sent back to Iraq, where I'll be tortured first and *then* killed."

"Don't think that way, Fatima. Something *will* come along."

"It's hopeless really." She lowered her head.

"Don't underestimate me," Charles said.

"I won't. I have already learned to be confident in you." She paused. "Like all your other clients." She was needling him. He loved it.

"Thanks. That helps." He smiled ruefully.

The train had reached the gentle hills of eastern France, now silhouetted in the moonlit sky. It steamed south for a time, tracing the cuts between the forested slopes and enveloped by the darkness. It was with some relief that Charles heard the trainmaster announce that Annecy would be the next stop.

Except for the lone trainman holding a lantern on the quay, the station was deserted when they stepped off the train. The ferry had berthed for the night, so they hired a taxi to take them around the curve of the lake to its eastern shore and the small village of Talloires. As they sped along the shore road, Charles reached for his wallet but instead found Fatima's hand, which he squeezed once and then held firmly until they reached the village.

About thirteen hundred inhabitants lived permanently in Talloires— mostly villagers who had passed their entire lives in the region, with some *pensionnaires* from elsewhere in France, and the rest a scattering of artisans and writers, hotel and restaurant personnel, and vagabonds of every ilk. But the village drew its vitality from its summer crowd—mainly French, Swiss, and German vacationers. And now, in late September, its sepulcher-like seclusion made it the ideal place, Charles reflected, to keep Fatima out of harm's way until he could figure out how to get her out of France and into a safer haven.

David Malone's house was located on a hill above the village, well removed from lakeside bustle and sheltered from the prying eyes of visitors to the village. The Lamirands, David's neighbors, came to the door only after Charles rapped on it repeatedly. The two villagers eyed the two Middle Easterners with suspicion, but, after some reassurance from Charles, they opened David's house for the fatigued travelers.

Charles remembered the house from times past. It had been constructed in a *grand luxe* style mirroring the extravagant tastes of its owner.

A wide verandah, running the full length of the house, allowed one to take in the lovely lake, the verdant foothills in the west, and the sloped roofs of the village. In good weather, from the house's raised portico one could see the famous "Teeth of the Dragon" on a forested ridge that towered behind the house, and higher still, the soaring heights of the French Alps, already dusted with snow. The house sat in the middle of a large property abundant with Alpine firs. And it was well stocked with all the necessities· food and wine and, as Fatima was pleased to see, a surprisingly wide assortment of books.

When he spotted a computer in a corner, Charles was reminded of Mukhabarat's technical prowess. "Don't forget that the Iraqis may have hacked into your email," he said. The remark brought them out of their bewilderment over finding themselves, after the day's travails, in such a pleasant place.

"I'll be careful," Omar replied.

Charles looked at his watch. "Well, it's now 9:15 p.m. I suggest that we just leave our things here and, to celebrate our safe arrival in what's going to be Fatima's new home for the coming weeks, why don't we walk down to an auberge I know on the shore of the lake? It's not far, and the restaurant is really quite good."

Omar, who had borne up well all day, but who now seemed exhausted, said, "Charles, I'm sorry, but I just need to unwind. It's been quite a day. Would anyone mind if I just stayed back for once?" He glanced at his sister but did not wait for a reply. "All I want is to eat some soup and get to bed."

"I will be happy to go with you, Charles," said Fatima quickly.

He had to admit to himself that he relished the thought of a quiet dinner alone with such a lovely companion at a romantic restaurant in the French Alps. It would be an evening unlike any other.

"Let's go then, just you and I," he responded, a little lilt in his voice.

THIRTY-ONE

Talloires, France
Late Evening, Monday
Sept. 30, 2002

As they left the house, a brisk wind gusting from the lake buffeted the couple, causing them to quicken their steps. There was just enough moonlight glinting through the trees to let them make out the narrow road to the village. In the half-light Fatima stumbled, and Charles grasped her upper arm, his thick fingers encircling her thin arm. She had found a black shawl in a closet and now pulled it tightly around her. She seemed pensive.

"Are you worried about something?" Charles asked.

"Yes. I am. My daughter."

"You must miss her very much."

"She is more precious to me than my own life, really."

"You'll be able to help her only if you can save yourself."

"Sometimes I wish I never left Baghdad."

"You'd be dead by now."

"It doesn't matter."

"It matters to a lot of people, *especially* to your daughter."

They sank into the same eloquent silence they had had on the train.

When they arrived at the restaurant, the owner, Madame Chambert, was prepared to turn them away. It was too late. "*Désolée, monsieur,*" she said. She was sorry. Officiously she showed them to the door. As she opened it, letting in a blast of cold air, Charles, in his best French, dropped the name of David Malone. At once, she let down her imperious facade and welcomed them in. "A friend of David's? Why, of course. You should have said so."

The restaurant seemed warm and festive. Twenty or so guests, grouped in little clusters of conviviality around the large room, were well into their cheese and dessert courses. As Charles and Fatima stood in the foyer, waiting for their table, he caught her eye. She smiled at him. It was a smile that quickened his pulse and radiated deeply, in a hidden and vulnerable domain inside him.

Madame Chambert escorted them to a table in a small recess off the main room, with a view of the moonlit lake. "*Bon appétit,*" she said with surprising warmth and an amused glance. As they took up their menus, Charles said, "Madame Shihabi, I think that I should let you know that you are proving to be the most fascinating client I have had for a very long time." Fatima beamed, then broke into a laugh. A throaty, soulful laugh. Her dark eyes flashed merrily. It was as if every part of her face reveled in the pleasure of her laugh. Even her diminutive nostrils trembled slightly. Such a depth of feeling, Charles thought, that it was easy to understand why she was a poet. It was truly the most beautiful laugh he had ever encountered.

Because of the lateness of the hour, they placed their orders posthaste, Charles selecting his favorite *homble de chevalier*, a fish found in the shadowy depths of the deep lake, and Fatima, the *suprême de volaille*, a house specialty that Madame Chambert urged upon her. Their meals arrived quickly, served by Madame Chambert herself, and were as soon devoured by the ravenous couple.

Whether it was the gleam of lights from Annecy on the lake, the Châteauneuf du Pape wine, the relief they felt from having eluded their pursuers, or simply the sense of being cosseted by a caring establishment—it loosened their tongues from the constraints of culture and of propriety. It was as if anything either of them might think of would be an appropriate subject of conversation.

"You might think this is strange," Charles said, "but, back in New York, when I was trying to imagine what you might look like, I wondered whether you might be wearing a veil."

"It's a shame, you know—that picture of a Muslim woman you get in your country. Somebody kept like a slave, whipped three times a day. Hidden under a veil. Without any rights. Not even educated."

"Except for you, of course." He cracked a smile, but she remained serious.

"Well, that's true. In Baghdad I did go to university. I studied journalism."

"You must have taken a lot of English classes too, judging from your command of the language."

"Eight years. I get by, although I do have gaps in my vocabulary, as you know."

He smiled, thinking of the word she had missed on the train. "I'll bet the university really changed *your* life."

"Yes, it was very liberating for me—as for many Iraqi women. But"—she paused and studied his face, then added with more than a trace of bitterness—"the fact is, *I* practically suffocated from the lack of intellectual freedom. A few years ago, I wrote an article for *Babel*, a piece that really got me in trouble with Uday Hussein—you know, Saddam's son. It was about the terrible conditions in my country. I was careful not to criticize Saddam; I even praised him. Yet, because of that article, I was put in prison and tortured so badly I thought I would die."

He couldn't imagine this beautiful, graceful, intelligence woman being tortured, yet he knew it had happened. "Your brother told me a bit about that," he said softly. "That must have been so terrible for you."

"I survived," she said. "After I got out, I avoided controversial subjects for a while, but then I couldn't resist. My writings began to appear, not under my name of course, in other countries. But then someone in power found out, and I was warned by a member of the underground that I had to get out of Iraq immediately. And that is a very short story of how I ended up here. Thanks to you."

Charles waved his hand dismissively. "Not just me. Thanks to your brother and to a lot of other people."

"Yes, that *is* true," she said.

Charles leaned forward. "Tell me," he said, "did you ever get to read Western books and magazines?"

"Everything is censored," she said, "but Omar managed, through a friend, to smuggle American books to me. Also, I had other friends who received books and magazines from the West. We passed them from hand to hand. I even saw a few videos of your TV shows."

"Which shows?"

"Oh, soap operas mainly, but also a show that seems very successful in your country—*Sex and the City.*"

Charles cringed. "Not the best examples of our culture."

"I hope not. I absolutely hated them—all that violence, teenagers out of control, families falling apart or full of conflict, everyone sleeping with everyone, rich people who, no matter how much money they have, never think they have enough. I thought soap operas were positively disgusting! In my world, the core of our culture *is* the family, and wealth is *not* an end in itself. No, like most people in my country, I detest Western values. I want nothing to do with your American lifestyle." She paused for a sip of wine. "Are you understanding me okay?"

"You're coming in loud and clear," he replied, steadying his eyes on hers. "I guess there are misconceptions on both sides—both Iraqi and American."

She nodded. "I don't think people in your country know much about the Arab world and our way of life."

"Whereas Arabs generally get a pretty heavy dose of American culture—movies, popular music, fast food chains, all of it. It's a good thing you know as much about us as you do."

"Oh. Actually not. There's a big difference between educating Muslims about the West and subjecting them to its bad influences. Education doesn't mean broadcasting your decadent TV programs into every Muslim home every night or putting a McDonald's on every street corner in

Cairo. It's more about letting people understand the motivations of others, building respect for each other's point of view. That's where Arabs need to be educated."

"And I presume you'd include women in that."

"That's right. Education has *really* helped women in the Arab world. For one thing, it lets women interpret the Holy Koran for themselves. Then they don't have to accept on faith what they are told by the fundamentalists."

"Who are mainly men."

"Right. And you know, for the most part it's the men who make the rules in Muslim society . . . as they did with our law, the *shari'a*, . . . and then they reserve for themselves the right to interpret them. The women almost always accept their decisions—like the claim that the veil is part of our religion, that the Holy Koran requires it. Education changes all that. It makes men and women equal."

"It's certainly worked that way in the West. But it seems that as Arabs have become better educated, Islamic fundamentalism has actually been growing."

"Sure, but that's as a reaction to Westernization and repressive governments in the Arab world, but not to education. After all, scholars, thinkers, and writers have always been admired in Islamic society." She paused for another sip of wine.

"They'd do well to help educate us in the West about Arab culture. Perhaps through your writing and your poetry *you* can do that."

"Perhaps."

He found himself wanting to know everything about her. "Your brother mentioned that you had been married. What did your husband think of your poetry?"

"He didn't know."

Charles frowned. "What do you mean, 'he didn't know'?"

"My former husband was much older. Like most men his age, he thought of educated women as the *enemy*." Charles raised an eyebrow. "He actually did," she said. "Sometimes, he would beat me if I even opened a book or a newspaper at home. And when women would participate in any activity of public life, he would become crazy. Once he threw an ashtray through our TV screen when two Iraqi women on the TV were interviewed about their children. About their *children*! 'Look at those women. *Rajlha zahqa*,' he shouted. *Prostitutes*. Well, after that, when we would go to family parties—when I didn't have to wear my face veil—I could not wear cosmetics. He just forbid it."

"Forbade." She glared at him. "Sorry."

"Forbade, then," she replied. It was obvious she didn't like being corrected on minor points of English grammar.

"So, he never knew about your writing then?"

She shook her head. "I had to keep my poetry hidden from him. I could write and read only for short periods while he was at work. The rest of the time, I would have to take care of the house and prepare his meals. He always came home around noon, when the offices closed, and went back to work in the late afternoon for a few hours."

"What would have happened if he had found out?"

Leaning over her plate, Fatima whispered in a conspiratorial tone, "He was in the police force and later in Mukhabarat. He would have been furious if he had known that I was writing about the problems of women while we were married—more so, if he had learned I was writing about *him*. He might have arranged for me to . . . to . . . just disappear—even after he divorced me."

"What? Have you killed?" Charles exclaimed.

"Yes. I was really quite worried about it. After our divorce, I thought he might be spying on me—even in Baghdad."

Madame Chambert appeared before their table almost out of nowhere. Charles wondered whether she might have been listening to their conversation. "It's getting late," she said kindly, "and the restaurant will close soon. But I see that you two have a lot to discuss. I will make you a little proposal. If you would like, you may stay here, continue your conversation, enjoy your wine, and when you are finished, you may simply close that door behind you," she said, pointing to a door on the lakeside verandah. "It will lock automatically."

Charles looked to Fatima for a response, and she nodded. She seemed to have come alive in the course of their conversation, losing her initial reserve, and neither of them wanted the evening to end. "That will be fine with us," Charles said. "*C'est gentil, Madame Chambert.*" It was indeed kind of her. He noticed for the first time that they were the only remaining guests.

"Anything for friends of David Malone," she said, smiling as she departed.

Charles picked up a thread of their earlier exchange. "You mentioned that your husband made you wear a face veil. Otherwise, did you wear it?"

He remembered what Omar had told him about Fatima's independent spirit.

"Charles, you are such a typical American—so fascinated with the veil," she responded with exasperation. "But, to answer your question, yes, I did wear the veil—for a while. I started wearing what we call the abayah at the age of twelve. I come from a very conservative region, and it is the custom that all women be fully covered from head to foot. Where I lived, respectable women—even if they wore their abayah—could not be seen on the street alone. A woman on the street alone was trespassing on male territory. So, when I married my husband, who was very religious, he forced me to wear the abayah whenever we went out. As I said, he made me cover my face with it, except for my eyes. But once he divorced me and I moved to Baghdad, I did wear Western-style clothes, sometimes with a simple headscarf around my face. As you can see, I still dress conservatively. As a Muslim woman, I still feel more comfortable doing that."

Charles realized he had struck a nerve. "Listen, Fatima. I've got to apologize for any preconceived ideas I may have. When I worked in Saudi Arabia, I *never* had the chance to talk with any Muslim women. And you *do* seem so—so Western. I mean, you're sitting here drinking wine."

"In principle drinking alcohol *is* against our religion. But my brother Abdeljelil had his ways of getting good French wine and champagne. He would often serve it to guests at parties." She gave a tiny shrug. "I guess I got a taste for it."

"So you're really not all that strict."

"It's true, what you say. I guess I'm not—at least not exactly. And to be honest, I'm not even that devout, although I am proud to be a Muslim. But, Charles, please"—she shook her head at him—"despite what you might think, I'm not one of your so-called 'feminists' either. As I told you on the train, for Muslims that word is loaded with bad meanings. It reminds us of all the worst aspects of Western culture. But I will admit, I'm probably more—how would you say it?—individualis? . . . ."

"Individualistic. In other words, you're your own person."

"Yes, that's it. I am more *in–di–vi–du–al–is–tic*"—she beamed him a triumphant smile—"than many other Muslim women because I haven't remarried. But, for as long as I can remember, my whole life has been my family—my brothers, my father and mother when they were alive, and naturally, for the past twelve years, Latifa. I love them all, and there is nothing that I wouldn't do for them. I hold them all above myself. And I am not unusual. There are many, many Muslim women who believe what I believe."

She had fully warmed to their conversation, and raising the wineglass to her lips, she again smiled at him. Even a little seductively, he imagined.

"But I should admit something to you."

"Okay." He wondered what she was going to say.

"Well, a few years ago, I started wearing the abayah again. I put it back on after my first arrest. At that time, it was becoming more common again—with the rise of fundamentalism and the economic effects of the UN sanctions. But the reason I wore it was because I wanted to avoid attention."—she paused for a sip of water—"and disappear into the crowd. The veil helped to hide my comings and goings. Still, believe it or not, people usually can tell who a woman is just by the way she walks in her abayah. So, I often walked with a slight limp."

"Ah," Charles said. "So the veil is your disguise."

"For me, yes," Fatima said. "It allows me to move more freely, without being recognized. But, don't forget, its origin is from the Holy Koran, which says that 'women shall be modest.' Those are the exact words— naturally in English. That's been interpreted—by men, of course—to mean that women should have no public identity—therefore the veil. But a few lines earlier in the Holy Koran it says, 'Men shall be modest.' But what Muslim man would ever agree to put on the veil?"

"Not just Muslim men," Charles said. "I don't think any man would agree to wear a veil."

She just stared at him and then shook her head. "For a Harvard guy, you're pretty dense." She seemed almost gleeful.

Nobody had ever called him "dense" before, he thought. Not even Sarah in her most exasperated moments. He was about to respond when she placed her napkin on the table. "Excuse me a moment," she said. "Don't go away." She gave him a luminous smile.

"I wouldn't think of it," he said, rising to help her from the chair. At that moment there was nowhere he would rather be. He watched her walk toward the back of the restaurant, her body slender and strong, yet soft and feminine. He had never met a woman quite like her.

After several minutes, she glided back to her seat. She cocked her head at him, her dark eyes smoldering. Like a desert campfire at night, Charles thought.

"Now it is my turn to ask the questions," she said.

"Okay," he replied. "What would you like to know?" He took a sip of his water.

"Why have you never married?"

He almost choked on his water. "How do you know I'm *not* married?"

She cocked her head at him again and smiled. "I said that *I* am asking the questions now. Omar said that you live with someone but that you are not married."

"Yes, that's true." He paused. He wondered what else Omar had told her. "I live with a wonderful woman, Sarah Steinmann. She's an artist—a painter—and exhibits her work in a very prestigious gallery in Manhattan. Before I met her—and I've known her eleven years—there was no one I ever dated seriously. I worked really long hours, and I wasn't looking for any kind of serious relationship."

"But if you've been with Sarah eleven years, why haven't the two of you married?"

"We've talked about it, but Sarah was married once before. As I've told you, she had problems with her ex-husband too. He didn't beat her up, but he mentally abused her and, in general, made her life miserable. She's never had a great interest in getting married again."

"She's lucky to have you."

Charles looked rueful. "I'm not sure she'd agree with that—at least not when I'm working nights and weekends."

"Didn't you ever want to have children? They *are* a great joy, you know. My daughter certainly is."

"I'm forty-six, and she's forty-three. It's too late for us."

"But what about before? You've been together so long."

"Well, Sarah was establishing herself as an artist, and I was building my career. Children just didn't seem to fit into our lifestyle."

"Ah, lifestyle. That is such an American phrase. It's so toxic to the family." She leaned across the table and stared at him sternly. "And, Charles, I'm sorry to say this, but you yourself are proof of that."

"I hadn't thought of it that way before."

"Well, it's all because in your country and mine, it's *men* who make the rules."

"In spite of what you say, you certainly sound like a feminist to me."

"No, not at all. I just think that Muslim women understand better than anybody the different roles of men and women—both in your culture and in mine. You might say it's our special perspective."

"What do you mean?"

"Well, first I have to ask you a question."

"Go for it."

"What's the best-known symbol of freedom and democracy in your country?"

"Well, the Statue of Liberty, of course."

"Man or woman?"

"Okay. I get your point."

"Well, do you? What does the Statue of Liberty—what does *she*—stand for? *The moral conscience of your country.* It always works that way. Women protect—how shall I put it?—moral standards, the code of morality. They *are* the nation. You've seen her picture: Britannia in England, Germania in Germany."

"Marianne in France," he added. Go with the flow, he told himself.

"That's it. But, what you should know, it's the same way in the Muslim world. Men put us women on our—what do you call them in English?—those things where they put statues?"

"You mean pedestals?"

"Yes, exactly, pedestals—until of course we fall off. But who sets the agenda? Who decides what the moral code is? Simple. It's the men—in my country and yours. *The code is fixed by men.* They're the cocks whose breasts puff out when a country goes to war."

"Okay, but why then do women buy into the code, as you say?"

"It's all about the greater power men have in our cultures—yours and mine. Take matters of sex, for example."

Charles had the uncanny feeling that she had never before talked about such subjects with a man, and surely not with an American man. Vaguely uneasy, he took a long sip of wine. He wasn't exactly ready for this. "Okay," he said gamely.

"Well, first of all, Islam takes from women the control over their own bodies. Your body does not belong to you. It belongs to nobody but Allah. So, even if a woman is afraid of becoming poor, she cannot decide to stop having children. She must trust that Allah, in his wisdom, will take care of her and her family. Now, doesn't this all seem familiar to you?" She looked across the table at him but didn't wait for his answer. "In your country, aren't Western women faced with the same issue of control over their bodies? In your society too, it's mostly men who make the rules. So they are the ones who decide when human life begins and ends."

"So, no birth control then?" Charles wondered how far she would go.

Fatima, nonplused, locked her eyes on his. "Well, to be honest, many Muslim women"—she began to smile—"insist on condoms. A lot of us believe that if you can control the number of children you have, the entire *umma*—the Muslim community—will become stronger. But it's not clear, I must tell you."

"They help women avoid diseases like AIDS," he added.

"Yes, they help a little, though AIDS is not as much a problem in Muslim countries as it is in America. Most Muslim women don't have sex if they are not married. Many traditional marriages are arranged. Like mine was."

"Things are sure different in my neighborhood," he said and grinned.

"Seriously, Charles, in the world of Islam, just as in your culture, women are waking up. It's going to be a slow process, but it's happening all over this world. And this is true even though there are forces—again, all over—who, as you say, would like to send women back to the Middle Ages. Before I left Baghdad, I wrote a short poem about this. I wrote it in Arabic, but I haven't yet translated it. I have a dictionary in my things, but my English may not be up to the task."

"I'd love to read it. Why don't you get your brother to help you translate it?"

"Why not? We'll do it together. It will be our joint gift to you. You'll see."

Charles glanced at his watch. "My God, it's almost one-thirty. Funny, even though I know I'm exhausted, I'm not a bit sleepy. Even after all that's happened today."

"I could talk with you all the night," Fatima replied.

"You're very persuasive. I think you would've made a good lawyer."

Fatima laughed. "That's what my brother Abdeljelil always says. But we have many more interesting subjects to cover. We should save a few for the next time. Perhaps we should head back."

Leaving the restaurant, they were greeted by gusts of frosty air sweeping off the lake. Stars shone coldly in the velvety sky. The moon, astride the hills on the lake's other shore, beamed across the water a ribbon of light that trailed them as they climbed the hill. They walked in silence, each preoccupied. Once Fatima shivered visibly, and Charles gently placed his arm across her shoulders.

"When do you have to go?" she asked.

"Tomorrow. Twelve-thirty. I have to meet with an old friend in Paris. To see what he can do to help you—us. For a few days I'll work out of our Paris office, and then I'll come back to check on you."

"Don't do anything difficult for you. I'm not worth it."

"Fatima, the problems of most of my clients aren't worth the time of day. It's exhilarating to do something that I believe in."

"But you are a famous American lawyer. You have a life of your own."

"I know that."

"But why me?"

He paused as they came to a bend in the road. As she gazed at him, moonlight flickered across her face. She took his arm.

"To be honest, when your case first came in the door, I was a little put out. Actually I was pretty angry about it," he said, laughing into the woods as Art Hauck's face flashed into his mind, "about the interruption from my work, about the intrusion into my life, you might say. But at the same time, almost from the beginning, your case intrigued me. It kept drawing me on . . . like one of those searches for the Holy Grail I used to love to read about. I couldn't stop myself. I may even have blown one of my biggest deals because of it."

"Is that what you think of me? Your 'case'?" She was teasing him now. "That still doesn't explain why you tried to help me."

"I just don't know," he said, shaking his head. "I really don't know. It simply seemed the right thing to do." With a little nudge from Art, he thought. And some prodding by Sarah.

Fatima suddenly squeezed his arm. "You are my very special lawyer," she said warmly. He had the feeling that somehow she understood.

Charles was silent for a while. At the next bend in the road, they could see the house, brightly lit up thanks to Omar, who evidently had left on all the lights when he retired. The surrounding woods were suffused with a glow from their blaze and from the shine of the moon, now high in the sky.

Drained by the physical and psychic demands of the day, Charles and Fatima stumbled the last few yards through the property to the house. They found the door locked and had to rouse Omar from his sleep. Beyond exhaustion, Fatima fell onto a large bed in a room off the verandah, while Charles extinguished the lights and checked the doors and windows through the house. When he was finished, he passed by Fatima's room. She was already asleep. He whispered to the motionless shape on the bed, "Good night, Fatima. You really are my favorite client, you know. We'll get through all this. Everything will work out. I just know it will."

THIRTY-TWO

Talloires, France
Morning and afternoon, Tuesday
Oct. 1, 2002

It was mid-morning by the time Charles awoke. Someone had opened the shutters, and bands of sunlight streamed through the window. A pot clattered from the kitchen, and the faintest aroma of coffee scented the air. He could see the lake in the distance, shimmering through gaps in the trees. He dressed quickly, then made his way out into the spacious atrium, to the doorway of the kitchen.

Fatima and Omar sat at a large wooden table in the middle of the kitchen. Charles knew at once that he had interrupted a strained conversation. "Is everything all right?" he asked.

"No problem," Omar quickly replied, drawing on the cigarillo between his lips. "It's just a family matter." Fatima looked up at Charles, blinked away a tear, and smiled at him wanly, her cheeks drained of color.

Charles nodded as if he understood. "Yesterday was pretty intense," he said. "I hope that the two of you can rest here for a while. I'll go back to Paris this afternoon, but I'll check in with you later. Maybe I'll have some news for you after my meeting."

"Charles, before you go I have a little something for you," said Fatima, getting up. "I awoke early this morning, . . . couldn't sleep. I was thinking about our conversation last evening. Let's sit out on the verandah."

"Why don't the two of you go ahead?" said the professor, now standing. "I'll take care of preparing breakfast. I, too, woke up early and walked to the village for some provisions. I found a *boulangerie* open and bought some of their specialties for us."

Charles reached for Fatima's arm, and the two of them walked outside. They sat together on a wicker bench facing the lake and the hills beyond. Fatima raised her hand against the bright sun and then directed her dark eyes at him. "Charles, first I have a little gift for you. Actually it's from Omar *and* me. We put it together while you were sleeping." She handed him a sheet of paper on which was a poem, written in long, flowing script. For a second he thought it was Arabic.

"It was the last poem I wrote before I left Baghdad. Omar helped me translate it for you."

While he admired the beauty of the handwriting, he could scarcely make out the words. Fatima must have sensed his difficulty for she interjected, "Here, give it back to me for a minute. Let me read it for you. It's called 'The End of the World.' I've dedicated it to a Guatemalan writer, Ana Lucretia Maldonado, who has fought a long time for human rights for her people—the indigenous people of the north. She impressed me with her great strength of character—in spite of her many adversities—as well as the power of her poetry. You know they've had a lot of social problems in her country. Lots of innocent people killed . . . by the army."

Charles nodded, remembering having read about it.

"So then, Charles, 'The End of the World.'" Fatima began to recite in a strong, modulated voice.

"From the table the guttural murmur of men
Fatigues sweat-soaked, sick of night,
Contending, now agreed, as one,
The strike at dawn
The village of Panjot.

And I, I am bent
Listening, arms akimbo,
Over yesterday's wash,
The bread rising

And my dear child in her bower,
Fidgeting
Nervously.

So has it always been, Solanya,
Men must have their fate
And do the work of men,
While we draw our veils more firmly,
Around our limned lives.

Who are we to say, my child,
Daughters of this sad history,
Women of this weary world,
Witnesses to such crimes,
Accessories before the fact

When the world ends
In that tenebrous vale,
Between the two rivers,
I will hear your lament, my sisters,
The ululation's of your torment,
Feel his scabrous hands on my breasts
And know the knife's kind cut,
Its sweet invitation
To death.

And so it will be, my Solanya,
When the world ends
In the village
Of Panjot.

But this is no women's work
Of rack and rape
Through endless night.
The drumbeat of soldiers,
The echoing waves of tanks
Through the villages.

I hear you fussing now—
Brave Solanya,
Your rage mounting
As you awake from aching somnolence
Into the dawn of this new day
Of your making."

As she finished, Fatima slowly raised her eyes to Charles, then handed the paper back to him.

"It's extraordinary!" Charles exclaimed. "Not only as a poem but also as a call to action for women." He felt deeply touched that she had given the poem to him. It was a gift unlike any other.

"This is how I like to write. For me, poetry is a sharp dagger in a silver sheath. Like the Bedouins, I keep my weapons out of sight." Fatima reddened, casting her glistening eyes out at the lake.

"Not *too* much out of sight, I hope. Have you published any of your poetry in the States?"

"Not yet. I've published one book of poetry through an Egyptian company, and I plan to translate it into English—if I ever get to America."

"Don't worry, you will," he said reassuringly. And when she got to the States, he'd talk with the firm's intellectual property lawyers about getting a client to publish her work. "Has Latifa inherited your love for poetry?"

"Certainly. She carries a little notebook with her wherever she goes. When she has an idea, she writes it down. When I have time, I ask her to read me her compositions. They are often quite good. They're about nature, family, friends—that sort of thing."

"Not about politics then?" He grinned at her.

"Not *yet*," Fatima replied, smiling back at him.

"Is all your poetry about politics?" His eyes fell upon the paper in his hands.

"That—and social problems, women, children, . . . humanitarian concerns in general. I pick up rocks in the desert, you might say, and expose the scorpions underneath."

"It's a great way for you to express yourself too."

"You could say it's a way for me to shed my veils—metaphorically speaking—I guess."

"Muslim women certainly have a lot of them." He knew instantly that he had said the wrong thing. He braced himself, as she glared at him.

"Well, don't think we're the only ones who wear them. You in the West have your *own* veils. They're so second nature to you, you don't even know you're wearing them."

Chagrined at having slighted her, he had no choice but to let her go on. "What are you thinking of, exactly?"

"What better example than my own predicament? Last night you said your Statue of Liberty was the symbol of freedom in your country. Sure. In the inscription on her statue, she boasts to the world, 'Give me your huddled masses, yearning to break free.' Yet, you won't give me a visa—at least for enough time so I can survive until Saddam is deposed or assassinated. *You* won't even give me the chance to speak to someone at your embassy. Ha! *You* won't even give me the time of day. Veiled beneath your smug self-satisfaction, you don't, and maybe can't, look yourself in the mirror." Fatima shook her head in frustration.

"Oh—kay," he responded, a bit cagily. He straightened his back. Bring it on, he thought. Bring it all on. He had asked for it. "What are you saying?"

"It's that beneath your veils of empty promises and platitudes, America is a withered old woman who still thinks she's the beautiful bride.

Sometime in the past you lost your virginity, and now you are losing your soul. We in the Muslim world *know* about veils and what evils they can conceal. And some of us *do* get to read your newspapers—and others of us observe your country on CNN or over the Internet. Just look at the violence in America directed at women and children, the number of your citizens in jails, and the hunger and poverty in your country. The worst is how you discriminate against your black people. It's just disgraceful." She shook her head again.

"Sure we have our challenges in America. Every country does. But we in America at least can control our own destiny. Most of the Arab countries are dictatorships, you know."

"That is so much drivel, Charles. Who gets elected in America? It's only the rich. Who else can afford the billions of dollars it takes to run for your Presidency or Congress? No, your elections are only contests of money, where whoever carries the most moneybags into the match wins. Your candidates manufacture the same lies, distortions and falsehoods that our leaders in the Arab world do—the difference of course is that we know we're going to be fooled and we expect it. The truth is that for the vast majority of Muslims, who's in power makes very little difference to them in their ordinary lives. Many Muslims actually like the idea of a strong, benevolent autocrat. It makes life simpler, you know."

"Right, life under Saddam Hussein is simple. Sure."

"That's not what I'm saying, and you know it."

"Sorry, my cynicism creeps out every so often. Why are you trying to go to America anyway—if things are as bad there as you say?"

"To be honest with you, I'd never have thought of leaving my country if it hadn't been for Saddam. And when he's gone, I plan to go back, go home. And if by some miracle, Latifa escapes Saddam's cruelty and comes to Europe or America, I hope that one day she goes back home too, to our culture and our people."

"I have to say, I'm surprised. How can you think about going back to Iraq after all you've done to escape?"

"You don't seem to understand," she said, glowering at him. "Iraq is *my* country, Islam is *my* religion, and Arab culture is *my* culture. I just hope that I have a country to go back to."

"Saddam is certainly making a mess of things over there."

"*And* he seems to be provoking the Americans to attack him. I'm worried that—how do you say it?—the cure may be worse than the disease. The last time America went to war to save a country—Vietnam—it was totally devastated. The Gulf War absolutely ruined my country. I simply don't trust the American army in a country with such a different culture like Iraq. Maybe if it had a stronger commitment to human rights, but America has a long way to go just to clean up its own record."

"What exactly do you mean?" he asked, trying not to seem indignant. "Of course we have a strong commitment to human rights."

"You may be right, but what the Muslim world thinks, is that America doesn't take human rights seriously—if you even believed in them in the first place. You use these words only when it's convenient, to get your way." Fatima rose and walked to the railing around the verandah. Then she turned suddenly and looked at Charles.

"Isn't it true that since the World Trade Center bombings, the majority of Americans—not all, but most—believe that we Muslims somehow have lost the right to be treated with dignity and respect? Don't you all suspect every last one of us of being a terrorist?"

Fatima's questions *had* to be rhetorical, he thought. He shrugged his shoulders. Yet, he remembered the delay he and Omar had experienced in leaving the plane in Paris.

Fatima paused and then went on, "You don't break bread with us. You don't even invite us to the table."

"Muslims have hardly welcomed us with open arms either."

Fatima took a deep breath, obviously composing herself. Finally, she said, "Sure, today relations are strained, mostly over Palestine, but historically Muslims have lived peacefully with people of other faiths in many countries around the world. We are *not* at heart exclusionary. We embrace the 'Others' every bit as much as you do." She stood before him, her arms out as if to embrace *him*, her voice decibels higher than when they began their conversation.

All of a sudden Omar emerged onto the verandah. With a flourish, he presented the delicacies he had found in the village. Charles met Fatima's glance, and silently they resolved to defer their discussion. They sat at a table on the verandah, and the three feasted on fresh croissants with café au lait. The mountain air, the dazzling sun, and the splendid view lifted their spirits.

It was Omar who stirred the embers of Charles and Fatima's fiery exchange. "I hope you found enough to talk about last night at the restaurant and this morning," he teased his sister.

"Your friend here," Fatima flashed a devilish glance toward Charles, "never expected such a lecture from me. But quite honestly I've never before had any man—much less an American man—lend me his ear like this."

"Thanks, Fatima. You did seem to have a lot bottled up inside you." Charles smiled good-naturedly. "But you shouldn't forget that America is a great country. And as an American, I'm proud of what we've been able to accomplish in our country and in the world." He paused and straightened his shoulders. "Of course, like any great country, it may have a few shortcomings. But the vast majority of my countrymen *are* kind and generous people—trying to raise their kids, hold down their jobs, find a little time for leisure, maybe enjoy the good life . . . ."

"I understand," she replied. "I do."

"My sister has always been passionate about what she believes. I'm afraid she does go on a bit, though," Omar said, smiling at Fatima and then turning back to Charles. "I hope you don't send us a bill for listening," Omar added. "After all"—he looked at Fatima again—"let's not forget that Charles is one of those high-priced corporation lawyers you find in those tall buildings you see everywhere in New York City."

Charles's grin erupted in a laugh. "No, no. Don't worry. It's all pro bono—you'll never get a bill from me." His office seemed worlds away. "Speaking of time . . . ." He glanced at his watch. It was 11:52 a.m. "Oh, no," he groaned and looked up. "We've lost track of it. If I don't hurry, I'll miss the 12:30 train to Paris."

They hastily said their farewells. Charles politely thanked Fatima for educating him on what he delicately termed "the Arab perspective." Then, gazing into her dark eyes, which seemed somber and distant, he said firmly, "You'll be safe here. There's nothing to worry about. I've left a jacket and some other things in my room. I'll be back in a few days . . . after I talk to a few friends in Paris about what we can do. And I'll call you when I have some news."

"Thank you, Charles. We can never thank you enough. . . . *I* can never thank you enough. May Allah in his bountiful mercy guide you. We shall wait for you." Fatima then solemnly bowed her head toward him. He resisted an impulse to give her a hug—not a gesture respectful of Arab culture, he decided. Then, suddenly thinking the better of it—it was France, after all—he glanced at Omar, who gave him a warm smile, and he put his arms around Fatima's slender frame and squeezed her gently. "You are dear, dear people," he said, holding her lightly. "Everything's going to work out for you, you'll see."

He then released her and, without looking back, ran to their neighbors' house. After several minutes of pleasantries, he prevailed on Monsieur Lamirand to drive him into Annecy. He boarded the train seconds before it left the station.

As the train pulled away and slowly rounded the shores of Lac d'Annecy, Charles stood by a door in the entryway and looked out. On the other side of the water, barely visible through the mist rising off the lake, appeared the village of Talloires, tiny in the distance, sequestered below the conifer-covered hills and the towering mounts of the French Alps. It was the perfect sanctuary for his charges, he told himself. But, at the same time, he had grave misgivings about leaving Fatima and her brother alone. He recalled his surprise at the persistence of the two men who had been following them in Paris. He prayed that their dogged pursuers had long since lost the scent of their trail.

When the train entered a wooded valley, Charles left his post at the window. He strode through several cars before he found an open section filled with empty faux-leather banquettes. As he took a seat by a window, he muttered to himself, "Okay, Charles Sherman, let's get going. The case of Fatima Shihabi is far from over." He would have to figure out a way to get Fatima out of France. It seemed clear that, as isolated as they might now be, they could not stay out of harm's way forever. He would have to find a failsafe solution for Fatima, some corner of the world that would take her in and give her the chance to live free, liberated from her hellhole of fear and repression.

And why shouldn't somebody take up her cause? Fatima was a remarkable woman. Fascinating, in fact. He called up the image of her pure face, her bewitching eyes, the slight quiver of her nostrils when she laughed or cried, the sweep of her elegant neck, and her glorious smile. She's brilliant too, he reflected. Articulate in English. Writes exquisite poetry. Strong character, boundless courage. Survived torture and hardship. Endless capacity to endure. Stop. Stop it, he told himself.

One thing was clear. Her capacity for sacrifice was limitless. She made him feel small and selfish. Sure, once he had helped a sorry soul escape prison in Dubrovnik. Okay, he paid for some kids from Saudi to go to school in the US. But lay down his life for a principle? For some abstract idea of freedom? The vast majority of *his* days he had spent on his madcap quest for power, fame, and a fat paycheck.

It had almost cost him his relationship with Sarah. The torment of that time had seared his memory like a branding iron.

It was in 1995 at a five-star resort hotel in Tokyo. Every year, Sarah planned a trip abroad, but unlike her previous trips to what she called her "world heritage destinations"—the ruins of Tikal, the pyramids at Cheops, the temple of Borobudur—which she had taken by herself, she had planned the trip to Japan for the two of them. And she planned it months in advance so that he would be able to build the time into his schedule. They were to spend three weeks in Japan, and she had organized the trip with him in mind. They would spend five days in the old city of Kyoto, in its museums and galleries, tour Lake Hakone and its region, where they would climb Fujiyama, and visit the grave of the kendo master Takeo Matsui in Hokaido. And, Charles recalled, he actually had looked forward to it. Except for two weeks in Hawaii several years before, it was the first time he had been away from the office for such a long period. He had just closed a complicated restructuring of Olicon International's debt on behalf of a consortium of L&F banking clients so he anticipated no trouble getting away for the full three weeks.

Just after they had checked into their hotel in Tokyo, the phone in their room rang. He was not too surprised. It was Witherspoon.

"Charles, you know the Olicon deal better than anyone else in New York. Well, Deltech Equipment will file for bankruptcy next Monday if we don't restructure their debt. Ten thousand people out of work. A two-billion-dollar company will bite the dust. A huge hole in the U.S. auto industry. And the Deltech deal will be modeled on your Olicon deal. Same structure, same documents. Piece of cake. We need you, Charles. You're our man. I'm sorry to do this to you, but if you value our relationship, you'll get yourself back here pronto."

"What about Kowalski?" Jack Kowalski, then an associate and now a partner in L&F's Tax Department, had preceded Hansen as Charles's "turtle."

"He's in Alaska. Denali. On his honeymoon. Anyway, we can't reach him. You're in the batter's box, Charles."

He looked across the room at Sarah. She knew what was coming.

"Okay," he told Witherspoon, "I'll get myself back there—yes, yes, next plane. See you late tomorrow."

Sarah could hardly believe it as Charles spoke the words. As he put down the phone, she rushed at him and pushed him so hard that he fell back onto the bed.

"What? What? Charles, you can't do this to me. We are on vacation. *We . . . are . . . on . . . va . . . ca . . . tion.* I have spent so much time—so much time—planning this trip. I have worked so hard to make it special for you. Isn't there anybody—*anybody*—else who can do this deal for you?"

He told her about Kowalski. He also told her that if it had been a client other than Witherspoon, he might have gotten one of his partners to work on the deal, at least until he and Sarah got back to New York. But because of his special relationship with Witherspoon, he had to go back at once.

"Relationship? . . . relationship?" Sarah sputtered. "What about *our* relationship? Doesn't that count for anything?"

"We can go back on vacation when this deal is over. I swear we can."

Her fury was mounting. "Okay, go back to your dear Witherbottom," she said derisively, "but I"—she looked at him with hatred in her eyes— "never want to see you again. By the time I get back, make sure that you are completely out of my apartment—out of it!" she yelled. Half sobbing, head high, she strode to the door, flung it open, and headed into the corridor, the slam of the door booming after her.

After his sixteen-hour flight from Tokyo, he went straight to his office. He worked on the Deltech deal virtually around the clock for the next five days, meeting with the banks, accountants, lawyers, and company executives during the day and drafting the documents at night. Then, during a break for a few hours on Saturday afternoon, he moved his things out of Sarah's place and into a warehouse on the West Side. He checked into the St. Regis, where he stayed for a week before he found a coop in Art's building. His relationship with Sarah was *kaput*. It was the beginning of his barren years, he thought.

His mind raced between Fatima and Sarah. Sarah and Fatima. A Memling portraiture and an Arabian rose. Torah and Kasbah. Child of the city and child of the desert. Both independent, with abiding instincts for survival. Do whatever you can do for Fatima, Art had instructed him. And for the moment he would do whatever he could do. "Don't underestimate me," he had told her. And now he would be put to the test. To do that, though, he was going to have to cash in chits from years ago.

He would first call on Claude. Claude Vergier, formerly Président Directeur Général of l'Éléphant, one of the largest hypermarkets in Europe. Trained as a lawyer, he had ascended to high corporate office by dint of his talent and, Charles always suspected, his contacts in French officialdom. Since his retirement from the business world—easily over ten years ago, he ran a low-profile law practice in Paris, mainly advising wealthy foreign clients on their dealings with government ministries. Charles had known Claude for almost twenty years now, had spent summer holidays with him and his family, had been half in love with his charming, spirited wife Josephine, and doted on their three children, who even in their adult years continued to call him "Cha–cha", their affectionate nickname for him. And so he trusted Claude as he would a brother. What Claude could do wasn't evident, but his old friend surely would try to help. Even in the face of the impossible.

As he was lulled into a half-sleep by the rocking of the car, Charles mulled over the wreckage of the Goldstar deal. His eye had come off the ball. A trifle off the mark. It was just enough to crater the deal. Art had known it too. Witherspoon would have told him. Probably over their lunch, he reflected. Art knew it all, he thought. He always knew, everything, Charles mused as he drifted off.

He awoke as the Annecy train approached the environs of Paris. The day had become dismal, and a gloomy mist blotted out the mottled green of the countryside. For an instant he wondered if it might be an ominous portent.

As the train pulled into the Gare de Lyon, he rose from his seat, and made his way down the aisle toward the exit. He glanced out the window at the crowd milling on the quay. Another train, with cars destined for Dijon, Aix-les-Bains, and Annecy, sat on the adjoining track across the platform. It was the return train, the one that they had caught the preceding day, now ready for its diurnal duty, back to the mountains. He gazed at the passengers as they boarded, thinking that in a few days he too would be among them, on his way back to his charges, back to their alpine refuge.

"*Débarquement immédiat,*" the stationmaster intoned, as the Annecy train was poised to depart for points east. Charles reached overhead to help an elderly woman ahead of him with her suitcase. As he set it in the aisle, he peered out the window of the car and glimpsed a dark-skinned man in a black suit ambling along the quay, carrying a small brown sports bag. Now and then the man glanced around him. Instinctively, Charles turned away for an instant, and when he looked back, he saw the man board the train, which slowly began to depart the station. Charles felt a sudden stab of fright. It was the man with the wrinkled brow who had pursued them through Paris.

Once off the train, Charles quickly pulled out his Blackberry and dialed Omar. Oddly the number was busy. Why would Omar and his sister be using his phone now? Charles asked himself. Was it possible that something had already gone wrong, only four hours after his departure? Had the Iraqis been able to track them down? And so fast? Perhaps it was only his imagination that the man in the black suit was the same man who had trailed him through Paris. Ethnic profiling, he thought. Maybe he was becoming paranoid. Likely, in fact, with all the stress of the past two days. He decided to wait to call again until after he met with Claude Vergier.

He was in luck. Claude picked up on the first ring. Charles came to the point quickly. "Claude, I've got a problem I'd like to discuss with you in private."

"You know, Charles, that I would do anything for you."

"This one is complicated."

"So much the better. Why don't you come see me now? We're still on Avenue Foch. Number 28. I've just come from the office and have a little free time before Josephine and I attend the opera this evening."

Charles tried Omar's cell phone again. It was still busy. For the first time in his life Charles was scared, scared for Fatima and Omar, scared that events were unfolding that, no matter how ingenious he might be, how hard he might try, he could no longer control. His apprehension nearly overwhelmed him, and it was all he could do to hail a taxi to 28 Avenue Foch.

THIRTY-THREE

Talloires, France
Late afternoon, Tuesday
Oct. 1, 2002

"It's your mother. I am alive—in France," Fatima breathed into the cell phone. The clock in the kitchen showed 4:52 p.m.

"Oh, I am so happy, dear mother. They told me you had died in Saudi Arabia."

"They lied."

"This time I was sure it was the end. I was so depressed. I love you so much."

"I love you too—more than anything in the world."

"Mother, how can I reach you?"

"I must go. I'll call you again in a few days." She put down the phone quickly.

Fatima turned to her brother. "I had to do it. I miss her so much," she said, adding, "And Latifa needed to hear the voice of her mother."

"We must be very careful."

We also must keep our faith in Allah . . . and in Charles." She smiled confidently.

Fatima stared pensively out the kitchen's wide window, up at the fir-bedecked foothills, to the silvery ridges of the high Alps beyond. The afternoon sky, cloudless, refracted an intense blue, and the sun sparkled off snow dusting the highest peaks thousands of feet above them.

"I'm restless." She sat down, on a stool across from her brother. "Someday, I'd like not to be on the run, living on the edge."

"I know."

"Charles is an exceptional man."

"He seems fond of you."

Only a brother could say that, she thought, half amused. "I do care for him too, you know—if it's not obvious."

"He'll work hard for us—for you."

"I am not worth it. He may be in danger. You know how ruthless they are. I feel that I must stop it."

"No. You must let him try. Your fates are already crossed."

"He'll die." She put her head in her hands.

"Listen, Fatima, there will be a good end to all of this. I feel it. You must have faith."

Fatima abruptly stepped off the stool, walked into the atrium, then out onto the verandah. She stood at the railing a long time, thinking of Charles. He so closely fit her idea of a perfect man—generous-spirited, sensitive yet strong, self-deprecating in spite of being an American and a Christian. At one level, she barely knew him. Yet, she sensed that, at a deeper level, she understood him. He was like her in a way: one part cloaked with all the accoutrements of culture, but another part imbued with an almost instinctual care about the "Others"—in Omar's sense of that word—a genuine concern far removed from simple voyeuristic curiosity. Charles exuded confidence too, she reflected. Even more than she did. But perhaps the two of them were foolishly overconfident against such relentless adversaries. For the time being, she decided, she would simply let Fate fly in the window, she would climb on its wings of hope, and she would let herself be transported to whatever new realms it was ready to reveal to her.

She walked back and forth along the verandah several times, then sat on the wicker bench, took out a pen and some blank paper from her jacket. For an hour or so, under the porch light, she wrote, in a neat, ordered script.

Shameless

A camel rasps
  In the souk
Silent, I wait
  In your tent.
Mad passion
  Of my past,
Soft zephyr
  Of this wind,
Sweet perfume
  Of my sense.

Shameless,
  I raise my veil,
Guiltless,
  I feel your touch,
Mindless,
  I taste your lips,
Tenderly,
  I merge myself,
One with you.

Then, chilled by the wind coming off the lake, she went inside.

THIRTY-FOUR

28 Avenue Foch, Paris
Late afternoon, Tuesday
Oct. 1, 2002

"Charles, let me make a few calls. I think that I might be able to help."

Charles knew he could count on Claude Vergier. If not to solve a problem, then at least to provide some workable ideas.

"My brother is in the Quai d'Orsay. Head of the Political Section. I will call him. You know, at a certain level these minor immigration issues can be solved very easily." Claude waved his hands as if he were swatting an insect. "It's all a matter of the right word . . . said at the right time." He paused, then added, "If you know what I mean."

"That's why I came to see you."

"Look, call me later this evening. I'm planning to escape from the opera early," he said, winking mischievously.

The scene at the Gare de Lyon surfaced in Charles's mind. "I'm running out of time."

"I know. But I'll have to reach my brother. Give me a few hours. I've never been a big fan of the opera anyway. And tonight it's a revival of *Bomarzo*, . . . the topless opera," Claude said, rolling his eyes. "Call me, Charles. Here at home. About nine-thirty. I'll know more then."

As Charles left Claude's apartment, he had a strange foreboding. Things had almost gone too well with Claude. Sooner or later he would have to face Mukhabarat. He had to reach Fatima and her brother.

He sat on a bench on the avenue Foch outside Claude's apartment building. He drew out his Blackberry and called Omar. This time the call went right through.

"Omar, I must be brief. Did you check your emails with your . . . what's it called . . . ?"

"XzPhone? Absolutely not," Omar replied defensively. "Especially not after what happened yesterday. I stayed away from the Internet completely. I assume that somehow the Iraqis can monitor my email messages. I wouldn't lie to you."

"You're sure you didn't use it? And Fatima didn't either?"

"No, Charles. No. No. No. Why? Is something wrong?"

"I'm not sure, but I think the Iraqis may have figured out where you are. What other contacts have you had with the outside world?"

"As you know, I went into the village to buy our croissants this morning."

"What else?"

"I also was on and off the phone all afternoon. I called my office at Columbia to find out more about my salary increase. Then I talked to a few of my students about grades, that sort of thing. Naturally, I used my XzPhone to make the calls, but I certainly didn't say where I was calling from—you never know when cell phone calls can be monitored."

"That must have been when I tried to reach you earlier, around four-thirty this afternoon, when my train got into Paris."

"Yes. . . . But there's another thing." Omar spoke in a hushed voice so as not to be overheard. "Charles, I must tell you," he whispered. "Fatima decided to call her daughter in Baghdad. I told her not to do it. It's why things were strained between us in the kitchen this morning."

"Damnation," Charles said. Perhaps he had misjudged Fatima. "But she didn't say where she was calling from either?"

"Not at all. I was listening to their conversation."

"What time did she call?"

"I think it was about five."

"Then I doubt that her call was responsible. In fact, it would have been impossible for the Iraqis to trace the call so quickly. Their man was getting on the eastbound train well before five p.m., just as I was arriving in Paris."

"No way. Oh no! I can't believe it," Omar exclaimed.

Charles could hear Fatima cry out in the background. "Somehow they've managed to do it," he said glumly.

"There is something else." Omar seemed to be speaking to himself. "It should have occurred to me earlier. Why, how clever. Of course, that's it. Charles, that's it."

"What do you mean?"

"Well, as I said, I've been using my XzPhone to make calls to New York. It's one of those do–it–all devices, you know."

"Yes, yes I know," Charles said impatiently. "But you didn't use it to get your emails or to connect to the Internet after Paris, right?"

"That's right. I assure you. But, Charles, I'm afraid I've overlooked something. With everything else that's happened to us these last two days, I've had my head in the clouds again." There was a pause on the other end of the line. "It's all now clear. Clear, you see."

"What?" Charles made no effort to conceal his exasperation.

"Well, let me try to keep this simple. Let's suppose your Blackberry is equipped with the Global Positioning System, as my XzPhone is. Well, it's possible for a hacker—a good one—to hack into the email software on your Blackberry and reach the GPS on your phone."

"What? So, what happens then?"

"After that, all the hacker does is to instruct your Blackberry so that each time you use it, it first checks your GPS coordinates—with the satellite system, you know, and then sends those coordinates from your Blackberry by email or phone to the hacker. You don't even know it's happening."

"So every time you check email or make a phone call, your Blackberry, without your knowing it, automatically gives away your location to the hacker?"

"That's right. If you use your Blackberry to call anywhere, you tell the world exactly where you are . . . at least within thirty feet."

"So how did they locate you?"

"Even as I was talking to New York this afternoon, my XzPhone was probably sending my precise location to Mukhabarat."

"It's too incredible. You're a computer science professor. How the hell could you have overlooked this? You knew all along we were being followed by Mukhabarat."

"I'm sorry. I really am." Omar began to cry into the phone. "It's all my fault, my fault. I knew the theory all right, but I just never connected the dots. It was a new product, a prototype. I never imagined they would be capable of . . . . " Omar began to moan mournfully. Charles now could hear Fatima shouting at him.

"Omar, listen to me. Listen to me. Try to pull yourself together. You must get yourself and your sister out of the house. Right now! Don't go toward the train station. Go up the hill behind the house. There is a narrow path up the mountain. Follow it toward the *Dents de Lanfon*, the Teeth of the Dragon, on the mountain's crest. The path leads from the garden in back of the house. On the way up, you'll see a small chapel on a promontory looking over the lake. Wait for me there. Remember to take a flashlight, as it will be pretty dark on the path. But make sure nobody sees you leave. The next train leaves at six-thirty. I have forty-five minutes to make it. It will get me to Annecy just before ten-thirty. I'll meet you at the chapel with a taxi. Be careful."

It was too far to walk to the Gare de Lyon. He took the Metro and ran up to the street level at the stop. He walked quickly around the vicinity of the train station. As he passed a small shop that displayed hunting equipment in its window, he paused for a moment and then went in. The proprietor refused to sell him a gun. He did not have a permit. He bought two hunting knives and a leg strap for one of them. The other he stuck in his belt.

Gare de Lyon was quiet as he arrived. It was still six minutes before the train departed. He strode down three cars of the waiting train and leapt aboard, then sat in an open section. The car was empty except for two youths with Mohawked-hair and silver-studded ears, their knapsacks stashed on the shelf above them; a lone functionary whose satiny windbreaker bore the logo of France Télécom; and three bourgeois businessmen in drab suits, who began to play cards from the moment they sat down, in the seats just ahead of him.

He dialed the number of his office on his Blackberry. No answer. It was nearly 12:30 p.m. in New York. Metta had probably left for lunch, he thought. He left a voicemail. "Metta, it's Charles, still in Paris. Tell everyone, including Witherspoon, that it will still be a few days before I'll get back to New York. I can't tell you where I'll be staying. I'll call you in the next few days. Wish me luck."

Next he called Sarah at her studio. She picked up immediately. "Hi," he said softly into the phone. "Just thought I'd give you a call before I start on the next phase of this project. It's gotten a little more complicated than we first thought." He tried to seem calm but probably overcompensated. Sarah would know.

"Look, Charles, do what you have to do. I know it's terribly important to you. But remember to look after yourself." She seemed to be trying to stay in control of herself too. He wished that he could tell her more, but she would only worry.

"Sarah, I'll call you again in a few days. Everything is fine, just fine." He wanted to seem nonchalant, but he wound up sounding almost professional.

"I know," she said. "But dearest Charles, whatever happens, I want you to know that I love you."

"I love you too, Sarah. I really do. I'm going to need your support on this." The words came out cold as if he were soliciting a donation to a charity. He could only imagine what she must be thinking. He added carefully, "Everything's okay. I'll call you as soon as I can. I have to go." It was enough to let her know that he was okay, thinking of her.

At 6:30 p.m. the scene out the window began to change, and he realized the train was moving. He sat bolt upright in his seat, staring out the window for a long time without seeing. Then he took an issue of *Martial Arts* from his satchel, put it in his lap but didn't open it. He felt a fillet of sweat form in his armpit. Nervously he glanced around him, meeting the poker faces of the cardplayers as they looked up from their game. For an instant, he wished he could escape into their world, their illusion of reality. Then, bucking himself up, he began to repeat to himself, mantra-like, words to appease his fear. Stay focused, Charles. Stay focused.

If only he could reach them in time. If.

THIRTY-FIVE

Talloires, France
Evening, Tuesday
Oct. 1, 2002

Fatima and her brother quickly packed their small bags and left David Malone's summerhouse so hurriedly that they neglected to close the verandah door. They rushed into the garden and through its green steel gate. As Omar clumsily shut the gate, his jacket caught in the latch, tearing it and upending his packet of cigarillos onto the path.

"Oh, I'm sorry," he said, as he bent to pick them up.

"Hurry, Omar. Just leave them. We've no time," she replied, drawing her black shawl around her.

They trudged along in silence, the sinuous trail unwinding before them amid the spectral shadows of the night. At first the path took them through a dense wood. Fatima was glad for the flashlight, which Omar waved back and forth into the trees. After a half-hour of continuous climbing, they found themselves before a rock cliff that towered up into the darkness. Strewn at their feet were old tires, an upturned stove, and a multitude of plastic food containers and broken wine bottles. A fetid smell, like that of rotting newspapers, infused the dank air. The path just seemed to end.

"Oh, no. No. It looks like the village dump," Omar said. "I can't believe it. We must have lost the way."

"We'll have to go back."

It was a good fifteen minutes of descent before they could find the trail again. At the juncture, she whispered, "Omar. Omar, switch off the light." Holding her breath, she tried to pick out the faintest sound from the trail below them. But apart from the rustling of the trees, she heard nothing. They stood in darkness and silence for several minutes before she touched his shoulder and murmured, "Okay. Let's go on."

After another hour and a half of steady ascent, she spotted the faint rooflines of the chapel atop the ridge. Well before they reached it, the flashlight began to flicker. "We're losing our light," Omar said. Moments later it dimmed to the point of uselessness, and he threw it into the bushes bordering the path.

"We'll just go slowly," she replied, "I think I saw the chapel up ahead." They picked their way along in the moonlight, heading ever upward. After a few minutes, the trail broke free of the conifers and passed through a small pasture. "There. Thanks be to Allah, there it is," she said, as they came upon a shadowed structure.

They crossed the graveled road that lay before the chapel. When they reached its portal, they turned and looked back down the hill, down the way they had come. Far below, the lights from farmhouses across the lake and from the town of Annecy glimmered across its blackness, while the full moon cast its beams here and there around the clouded sky, transforming the night world into variegated shades of black.

"It's beautiful, isn't it, Omar? I've never seen such a scene— from the top of a mountain."

"We're a long way from Kassim," he replied. "That's for sure. It's pretty dramatic." He paused for a few moments before adding, "But maybe we'd better wait for Charles inside."

They heaved the chapel door open, then felt their way down the dank nave past a few pews, and sat on a cold stone outcropping in the small sanctuary. The professor lit a match and held it above him. They saw that they were seated on a stone bench at the side of a stone altar. Several wooden kneelers were arrayed before them, and a dark wooden hutch, with its own door, stood against the wall beside them. "It's where the Catholics confess their sins," Omar said. "They tell the priest, and somehow the sins go away."

"It's like going to Mecca then," she responded. "Look—back there," Fatima exclaimed, gesturing toward the rear of the chapel, behind the altar. "It's a painting." Once their eyes adjusted to the light, they could make out a large painting that rose impressively to the ceiling and dominated the chapel's interior. It depicted a desert scene at the center of which a robed figure bearing two engraved tablets pointed to a phantasmal landscape in the distance.

"I think it's from the Bible," Omar said. "Moses on his way to the Promised Land."

"It's an omen," Fatima said to her brother, "Don't you think? . . . the Promised Land, I mean. I hope we get there," she added.

Omar fished out a cigarillo from his vest pocket and lit it. At once, the acrid stench of the burning Gauloise insulted her nostrils.

"Maybe you shouldn't smoke that smelly thing in here," Fatima said. "Out of respect, I mean."

"Maybe you're right," Omar replied, stubbing out the glowing embers on the chapel's stone floor.

Within minutes clouds covered the moon, and the chapel's interior darkened even further than before, to an intense blackness. For about three hours, they sat silently, standing up now and then only to stretch their tired limbs, their ears pricked up, waiting. A brisk wind from the east eased open the chapel door, and they let it be so they could watch the stars blink on, one by one, as the clouds moved on and the moon rose ever higher in the night sky. At one point Fatima produced two croissants, left over from their morning's repast, which they consumed eagerly.

"It's taking him a long time to get here," Omar said. His heart was aching again from guilt over his earlier inadvertence. "I hope he finds the way in the dark," he added wistfully.

"I know he will, Omar. I just know he will." Fatima thought of Charles, his broad shoulders, his kind face, and his keen, earnest expression. She thought of the wonderful evening they had shared at the restaurant in Talloires. It had been many years, she reflected, back to the time when she would stand with her father under the night sky in the desert, since she had felt so completely free to express her thoughts to a man.

About 11:15 p.m. Omar caught a sound outside the chapel door, a barely audible crunch of gravel on the path. It must be Charles, he thought. Then acting on instinct, he touched Fatima's shoulder and half-whispered, "Behind the altar." As she passed by a kneeler next to the altar, her foot struck it heavily. As it began to fall, she trapped it in her arms, and it rasped ever so slightly against the stone floor. It was a sound that surely spoke to whoever was listening on the chapel path. Omar regretted having lit the cigarillo; he was sure the smell lingered.

Omar and Fatima tiptoed to the back of the chapel until they felt its cold stone walls. From behind the altar, they stared at the chapel's open portal. After an eternity, a silhouette appeared, a shadow visible against the moonlit sky. A man of short stature, wearing a fedora. When she saw the shape, Fatima shuddered, then gasped involuntarily.

THIRTY-SIX

Talloires, France
Late evening, Tuesday
Oct. 1, 2002

Charles slouched in his seat, fuming. The connector train between Aix-les-Bains and Annecy was already fifteen minutes behind its departure time. "Damn," he muttered. His watch read 10:05 p.m. "Why doesn't the train start?" he demanded to no one in particular. Frustrated, he got up, looked up and down the vacant aisles, the empty maws of seats staring back at him. He frantically searched for a copy of the train schedule. Then at last the conductor reappeared, crossing the quay with a coffee cup in hand. The French put the important things first, Charles mused. Like coffee before conducting, lunch before loving, dinner before dying. Back in his seat, he told himself to gather his wits. He would first have to find Fatima and her brother. Then he would get them back to Paris, where Claude could hide them. Let them be alive, he prayed. Let them be alive.

The train jolted forward. Thirty-seven minutes later it entered the Annecy station. Charles carefully observed the platform, but at this hour there were only two old bums on the dimly lit quay, neither one questionable. He bounded off the train and raced through the stationhouse. Once outside, he engaged the only taxi, and the driver claiming to know the way, they sped off for the mountain road above Talloires.

It took them almost a half hour to find the road to the Chapel of Ste. Geneviève. Out of caution, Charles had the driver drop him a few hundred yards from the chapel, screened by a bend in the road.

"Wait for me here. No matter how long it takes." Charles handed the driver a roll of banknotes.

"No. Not necessary." The driver seemed insulted. "I will wait right over there." He pointed to a small clearing among trees along the road.

In the night's clear moonlight, Charles could easily discern the paved mountain road, bounded by walled fields stretching up into the darkness. He ran the short distance uphill as quickly as his gasping lungs and rasping throat would allow him. As he rounded the curve, he was able to make out the profile of the chapel ahead. Just as he reached the gravel path to the chapel door, he heard a gunshot—but muffled as if it had been fired into a pillow. A silencer, he thought. Simultaneously there was a moan, followed by Fatima's cry, sharp and shrill.

Holding his body low, so as not to silhouette himself in the portal, he peered through the open door. The interior was devoid of light, even of shadow. He could see nothing. Fatima was still alive, apparently, and would have found some niche, some narrow haven in a recess of the chapel. The gunman was probably feeling his way through the blackness toward her.

Charles drew one of the hunting knives from his leg holster and held it before him. Against a gun in the dark, he knew he barely had a chance. Still, it was better than nothing, and if he could distract the shooter . . . . Charles reached around and picked up a handful of gravel from the path and threw it hard against the stone floor inside the chapel. Then he began to close the heavy wooden door, which creaked as its ancient hinges were set in motion. There was another muffled shot from somewhere in the darkness.

The bullet passed close to his neck. He heard its whir, like a passing insect, and felt a warm rivulet of air. Instantly he heard someone run from the back of the chapel, and out of the darkness he caught the faint outline of an even darker shape. Holding the knife at the height of a short man's throat, Charles threw himself against the emerging shadow. He felt the muscle and sinew of a powerful body as it hit him full force, and heard the man moan in pain. Both men rolled down the gravel path just outside the door. Atop his attacker, Charles tried several times to grab the wrist of the man's gun hand. Finally he caught it and smashed the hand again and again into the gravel. With his free hand the man punched at Charles, at his chest, his head and his neck, hammering him incessantly and with surprising strength. About to lose his grip on the man's wrist, Charles pulled the knife from his belt and, with one last desperate lunge, stabbed at the hand holding the gun. The knife stuck the trigger, causing the weapon to fire into the air, and then pierced the soft flesh of the hand itself. The man roared and, crazed by rage, with a seemingly effortless motion, rolled out from under Charles, who felt sure that a bullet would follow. Instead, there was an unnerving silence.

After a few moments, while Charles awaited another discharge from the silencer, he heard the sound of a man stumbling down the path, then onto the road, out into the darkness. Charles figured that he had aimed the knife too high, that it had done the man's neck some grave harm, without killing him. And most probably the man was also bleeding from the wound to his hand.

Charles dreaded what he would find in the chapel. He raised himself from the path, ran to the door, and in a low voice uttered, "Fatima."

He heard a heart-sob. "Charles, I think my brother is dead."

He felt his way past the pews. As he passed the stone altar, his foot struck something soft. He knelt, touched the professor's forehead, felt a sticky warmth, and then heard Omar groan.

"He's alive, but we'd better get help for him. I have a driver waiting. Not far from here. Don't move him."

Charles bolted out the chapel door and raced through the darkness like a madman. He lunged down the road, heedless of what lay ahead of him. As he turned the bend, he thought he heard sounds in a pasture. Cows or sheep, he thought. Or maybe a man with his hand punctured and his throat partially cut.

The driver had kept his word. Charles could see the glow of the man's cigarette well before he saw the vehicle.

"There's a man injured, in the chapel up the road. Can you take him to a medical clinic?"

"No problem. *Allons–y.*"

When they reached the chapel, the driver urged the car up along the gravel path to the door, then blazed its lights into the chapel's interior. Charles and the driver picked up the unconscious professor and, cradling his body between them, placed him on the car's rear seat. The driver took his seat in front, and Charles and Fatima wedged themselves beside him, Charles placing his arm around Fatima's shoulders. At first, she cried softly into her shawl and then fell silent. As the car swerved around the mountain curves, he felt her strong, supple body leaning into him.

Fatima turned and looked at her brother in the back seat. He was so still he could have been asleep. "They'll stop at nothing, you know," she muttered. "They're like vicious dogs, all of them, maddened at a blood feast."

"Fatima, I'm sorry this has happened."

"It's not your fault. I never should have allowed my brother to convince me not to return to Iraq. I should be back with my family where I belong." She took out her abayah from her sack and dabbed at her eyes.

"You'd be dead."

"Look at my poor brother," she sobbed, holding the abayah to her face.

"Your brother's going to be fine. I'm sure of it."

"I just don't know, Charles. Oh, I just don't know. He is such a good man, . . . such a good man. May Allah in his mercy protect him." She again looked back at the prone figure of her brother, then fell silent.

Charles reached for Fatima's hand and found it, cold and unresponsive. How she had suffered, he thought. Life had dealt her its hardest blows. Exile from her native country. Separation from her family, her daughter. Dashed hopes. And now perhaps even the death of the brother she loved so dearly. How fragile life is, he reflected, how suddenly one can be forced to surrender it. So it must have seemed to those at his table at Windows on the World. In their final moments, they must have been utterly astounded at their predicament, disbelieving that life could be taken from them so unceremoniously, without appeal. And why them, and not him? It was a question he had asked himself a thousand times. He wondered whether Fatima was asking herself the same question now.

The taxi barreled its way down the mountain and then traversed the route along the lakeshore toward Annecy. When they finally reached its lighted outskirts, Fatima glanced over at Charles, her expression softening as their eyes met. "The hospital's in the center of town," he whispered. "We'll be there in a minute or so." Putting her abayah back in her satchel, she nodded but made no response.

THIRTY-SEVEN

Clinique Générale Annecy
Annecy, France
Wednesday–Friday
Oct. 2–4, 2002

"C'est extrêmement sérieux," the surgeon said. "He could die very quickly. The bullet passed two centimeters from the cerebral cortex and lodged in the back of his brain. We couldn't risk removing it in the surgery. He's lost too much blood."

Charles turned toward Fatima and put his arm around her. Tearful, she said, "Why did I put all of you through this? My own brother now dying. I should have allowed them to kill me in Iraq. I'm not worth all this."

"You would have done the same for him."

"The men who did this are inhuman. They are evil."

"I know," Charles said gently. "But you must not give up. Omar would want you to fight."

Around seven in the morning, not long after they saw the doctor, two uniformed gendarmes, summoned by the hospital, arrived from the Annecy police station. At once, Charles presented himself as an American *avocat*, a lawyer from New York. The gendarmes paid scant heed to this information, and in the hospital's waiting room they questioned Charles and Fatima intensively, demanding to know each fact leading to the shooting, and with Charles translating Fatima's account into French. Recalling his earlier assurances to the French government, Charles worried that any investigation could jeopardize Fatima's status in France. He tried to downplay what he referred to as "a little incident," attributing it to an Arab malcontent, of unknown identity, who for some unknown reason had harbored a long-standing grudge against the Shihabi family. "Just another one of those *tempêtes arabiques*," Charles said with the mien of a man of the law, possessing all due respect for French jurisprudence.

The gendarmes were unconvinced. "What proof do you have, Monsieur Sherman, that the victim is indeed Madame Shihabi's brother?" asked the senior gendarme officiously.

"Or that the mysterious assailant even exists?" asked the other. "It is always possible—not that we are accusing anybody, of course—that someone else—someone else, Monsieur—tried to assassinate the victim." The gendarmes eyed him suspiciously.

"That's ridiculous," Charles exclaimed. "Why then would we have tried to get help for Mr. Shihabi?"

"You tell me, Monsieur. Maybe to cover your tracks." Then the gendarmes drew Charles aside, out of earshot of Fatima. "Tell us, Monsieur Sherman, honestly," the senior gendarme muttered. "What was it you were really doing in the company of these two Arabs in the French Alps? *Ce n'est pas normal, Monsieur.* It's not normal."

"We were on vacation. That's all."

"How then did Madame Shihabi secure permission to come to this country?"

"She has all the necessary papers."

"She has given them to us. We think they are forgeries. It's not that difficult, you know."

Fatima rushed over to them. Hysterically, she cried, "My brother is dying in there. Can't we discuss this all later?"

The senior gendarme, failing to understand her accented English, looked at Charles, who translated for him. Then the gendarme looked at her unsympathetically and responded in French, "Madame, you—and your cohort there"—he gestured at Charles—"are prime witnesses to an attempted murder. At this point you are also suspects in the crime. And you'll remain in custody until this case can be fully investigated. Now, you will come with us to the police station for further questioning. You'll be able to come back later, of course."

"Allow me a few moments to translate all this for my client," Charles replied. He drew Fatima aside to a corner of the waiting room. Doing his best to mute the tenor of the gendarme's words, he explained that they had no choice but to cooperate fully and that the gendarmes wanted them both to go to the police station.

"I am *not* leaving my brother," Fatima said. "They can shoot me if they want. I will *not* leave here, I simply will not." Pausing, she looked at him pleadingly, then added, "Charles, there must be something you can do."

Charles was struck by her determination. Never before had he encountered such extraordinary resolve. Suddenly, he had an idea. "Wait here, Fatima. I'll be right back."

Addressing the gendarmes with exaggerated respect, Charles said rather gravely, "Messieurs, unfortunately this case is more complicated than one might think. As you quite correctly have surmised, this is no ordinary matter. It's a matter of international diplomacy. I'd like to call someone in Paris to give you further information about the case. Would that be a problem for you?"

"Not at all, Monsieur Sherman," replied the senior officer, who seemed relieved to know that there could in fact be wider influences on this unusual case.

Charles drew out his Blackberry, dialed David Malone's number, and, after interminable rings, heard David answer in a cheery voice.

"David, it's Charles Sherman. I'm calling from Annecy. We've run into a little problem here. My clients and I are about to be drawn into a police investigation that, I can assure you, is without any foundation whatsoever. It's a case on which Art Hauck and I have been working for a while, to gain asylum in France for an Iraqi writer of some note. Ambassador de Rochefort even helped set it up for us. The investigation could be embarrassing to everyone involved. It's a case of some overly diligent *inspecteurs*, at the local level here in Annecy, who are, shall we say, a bit too curious."

"Sure, Charles, I'm with you. What do you want me to do?"

"I was thinking that you might just talk to your friends at the *Préfecture de police* and get these fellows off our back."

"You say that Guy de Rochefort is working with you?"

"That's right."

"That'll help. And I'm pretty close to the *préfet* too, Raymond Metayer, although I know him less well than Guy, of course. Give me an hour or so, and I'll get back to you if you don't hear anything sooner. Where are you now?"

"At the Annecy hospital, the waiting room."

"Okaaaay. Wait there and we'll call you."

"David, I owe you one on this, . . . can't thank you enough."

"Don't mention it. Come see me when you're in Paris."

"I will."

When Charles signed off, the two gendarmes were eying him coldly, and he worried that they had understood some of his conversation with David. Fatima had revived and was sitting in a chair. She seemed dazed, but he caught her eye. Her face softened, and he shot a half-smile back at her. Turning to the gendarmes, he said respectfully, "You'll be receiving a call from Paris within the hour. It will explain everything."

They gendarmes were skeptical. "In the meantime, you'll come with us to the police station," said the senior officer.

"No." Charles responded firmly, his eyes glinting with anger. "Your superiors would surely want you to talk with Paris first. You'll just have to be patient. You wouldn't want to start a major international incident, now would you?"

The bluff worked. The senior officer looked at his subordinate and then said gruffly, "*Très bien.* Very well, we'll wait. One hour."

Charles and Fatima went in to see Omar, who was in a deep coma. He was exceedingly pale and his breathing labored. They waited by his side for almost an hour. When there was no change in his condition, they returned to the waiting room. The two gendarmes were standing by the door, talking to each other in hushed voices.

When the gendarmes saw Charles and Fatima, they motioned Charles to join them. The senior officer said portentously, "We've received a call a little while ago. We now have our instructions. This case is to be handled by higher departmental authority. We have all the information we need for our report. It will state that this is a case of attempted murder of an Arab tourist, against which the three victims appeared to have quite properly defended themselves." He paused and stared into Charles's eyes for a few seconds, without blinking. "*C'est normal,*" he added finally. It was customary. They shook Charles's hand and nodded politely at Fatima. Then proudly raising their heads, they left.

The next two days passed with excruciating slowness. Two days of waiting, watching Omar in his final hours of life. Charles and Fatima sat on gray swivel chairs beside the bed. On the third night, toward one in the morning, Omar groaned and began to fidget, raising himself from the bed as if some deep need impelled him to get up. Without warning, he opened his eyes wide. For a second he gazed at Charles. Then his eyes fell upon Fatima. His face radiated a flash of recognition, and his mouth turned up as at the start of a smile. At once she reached for his hands and clutched them. Then he closed his eyes and was gone.

"Omar, my dearest brother. Come back. Come back to us. Don't leave us. Don't, don't . . . go." Fatima threw herself on her brother's body. She cried without reserve, without solace, from the innermost part of her heart. Lost in her grief, she embraced the dead body, rocking it to and fro, as if she might be able to force life back into it. She frantically clutched at the lifeless fingers, which grew colder the more tightly she held them.

Charles bowed his head in his hands and wept quietly. Then, he rose and stood beside the bed. He placed his hand on Fatima's shoulder. "Fatima, I am truly sorry. I loved him too. Almost like a brother." Then he added, "You have suffered so much." Tenderly he grasped her arm and drew her up toward him. His arm around her, they stood beside the deathbed, wreathed in sorrow, their tears falling freely on the starched white sheets.

THIRTY-EIGHT

Annecy, France
Friday
Oct. 4, 2002

With the hospital's help, Charles made the necessary arrangements for Omar's burial. In keeping with Muslim custom, he explained to the hospital staff, the body was to be interred the same day as the death. *"C'est impossible, Monsieur, impossible ici en France,"* they remonstrated but directed Charles anyway to the town cemetery just outside Annecy along the shore of the lake. With luck Charles chanced upon an amiable gravedigger, who agreed, with the persuasion of a fifty Euro bill pressed into his hand, to prepare the gravesite. The same man agreed to send a hearse to the hospital to take the body, although Charles practically had to move mountains of bureaucracy to secure its release.

Early in the afternoon Fatima and Charles went back to the cemetery for the interment. Morose, Fatima recited from memory a passage from the Koran. She then placed her hand gently on the cold gray metal of the casket that the gravedigger had secured for them. As she stood in silence, Charles said the Lord's Prayer. He then reached for her other hand, and they bowed their heads as the casket was slowly lowered into the ground.

Even as she grieved, Fatima was seized by an enormous guilt. Guilt raw as the saddle sore of an overpacked camel. She just couldn't rid herself of it. And she knew, if she allowed it, it would easily consume her. Selfish it had been, to wish to escape her destiny. Were it not for her, Omar would even now be in his classroom, surrounded by his students, safe in his treasured realm of computers. And then there was Khalid—dear Khalid—whose sole reason for sacrificing himself had

been to let her escape Iraq and secure her freedom. And now Charles—
who himself had become a target of the villainous Mukhabarat.

How could she have given birth to such tragedy? she wondered. She
should have stayed put in Iraq until that day when she no longer had to
suffer choice in her own life. She should have welcomed death, should
have rejoiced in it. For now, her brother was dead, and her own spirit was
waning. If she were to go on, they would find her anyway. She would
further endanger Charles. And perhaps her daughter too.

Fatima picked up a clod of earth, broke it in her fingers, and let the
lumps drop gently down, down into the awful, mawing hole. Then she
took Charles's arm, pulled him against her, and drew him along the shore
of the lake back to the town. When they reached the first houses, Charles
broke the mournful silence.

"We'll need to stay on our guard. We won't be hearing from your
brother's killer for a while, but of course Mukhabarat has other people in
France. There were others on our tail in Paris, you recall." He thought of
the distinguished diplomat waiting in the car in Paris. "And now they
have an idea of where you are, . . . where we are. I'm a little surprised that
we haven't heard from them already. They may simply be watching the
train station since it's how they'd expect us to go back to Paris. Tonight I
thought that we might hole up in a quiet hotel along the lake. I'll call
Claude this afternoon to see if he's had any luck with your visa to America. But first I'd like to go back to Talloires, to David's chalet, and collect
my things. You can stay in the hotel."

"I'm coming with you," Fatima said. Charles gave her a long look. By
the firmness in her voice, he knew there would be no argument about it.
He kept his silence as they headed for the center of town.

As they came upon Place de la Libération at the center of Annecy,
Charles spotted a *tête de station* with an empty taxi waiting, and soon they
were on their way back along the lake to the village of Talloires. The
vehicle sped along the narrow, windy road, slowing as it drove through
the occasional hamlets and for a hardy band of cyclists braving the cold
and wind. A grayish fog had settled on the lake's wide expanse, and the

wind had whipped it into the leaden sky, obscuring the countryside with a pasty translucence. When at last they reached the chalet, it seemed as gapingly empty as a bone-white skull. It had the air of death about it.

As they left the taxi, Charles asked the driver to wait for them. "We always kept the front door locked," Fatima whispered as they went up the steps to the house. Warily they went around to the verandah door, from which Fatima and Omar had left on their fateful journey up the mountainside. The door was ajar, and the two of them furtively went in, their senses on alert. As they tiptoed into the main room, Charles spied a trail of red–black splotches leading from the door across the polished oak floor. It led to the kitchen, where the counter and phone too were spotted with dried blood.

"He came back here to clean himself up, maybe to call for help," Charles whispered. "He must have been in bad shape. It's a wonder he made it."

"I think he was very strong. A real animal," Fatima replied in a low voice. "I hope we never see him again."

The house had a ghostly, vacant air. Charles sensed that no one had been to it since their bloodied assailant had taken refuge there. He walked into the atrium adjoining the verandah while Fatima went down the hallway to be certain she hadn't left anything. He'd have to ask the Lamirands to get a *femme de ménage*, he thought. Someone to clean up. Then conjure up a story to explain the blood, lest somebody try to bring the police back into the picture. There could be more questions about Fatima's status.

On a low settee in the center of the room lay the professor's GPS phone. Where he had left it in haste. After having been betrayed by his own gadgetry, Charles reflected. He picked it up, fingered its techno features, studying it pensively. He placed it in the vest pocket of his suit, but then thought the better of it; he took it back out and held it in his hand. He opened the door to the verandah and went outside.

Damp gusts nipped at him as he strode to the railing. The conifers lay in their billowy cushion of fog like so many holiday ornaments, and for several minutes, he watched the milky haze swirl in and about them. It was the view that only days ago was so clear and refractive, he recalled. Resting his elbows against the railing, he looked at the phone one more time. Then he cast it with all his strength into the mist.

As he turned to go inside, he saw her. She had been standing there, gazing at him.

Drawing the shawl around her more firmly, Fatima silently came over to him and took his hand. He felt the daintiness of her long fingers against the thickness of his own. Standing at the railing together, they stared into the haze, without seeing, without caring to see, as the breeze rustled through the woods.

"You must be cold," he said after a while.

"I wanted to be with you." He turned and looked into her eyes. Two limpid pools of liquid ebony, beneath which lay more than the usual darkness, clouds of deep gray dissipating into her cheeks. They were eyes that now looked into his soul.

"I love you," he said. He surprised himself even as he spoke the words. So unconscious. Like a breath. He released her hand and gently grasped her upper right arm, as if rooting himself back in reality.

She was silent for a few seconds. Then she nodded. "I love you too, Charles. I knew it here on this spot a few days ago. I even wrote a poem about it."

She leaned up to kiss him, and he wrapped his arms around her shoulders, feeling her fragility and her womanliness. He kissed her deeply. Then twice more.

Abruptly he pulled himself away and looked at her—as if she were something unreal, a museum piece in Madame Tussaud's or a mannequin in a Bergdorf display window. "I can't believe it. I just can't believe it." He was back in the here and now.

"You began to tell me with your eyes on the train," she replied.

"I think your brother probably knew too."

"He did. I'm sure he did. I think that's why he wanted to give us time together at the restaurant."

He drew her close to him and kissed her again. A long, penetrating kiss that reached down to the bedrock of his being.

"It's crazy . . . and wonderful . . . how Fate works her plans." He sighed.

"Ah, then you admit that Fate is a woman," Fatima said, smiling.

His hearty laugh reverberated in the trees as he pulled her even more tightly against him. "Maybe it's in the stars, . . . the constellations," he said, adding, "but of course a lot of them have genders too." They both chuckled. He kissed her gently on the lips. Then they kissed again, long and passionately, embracing each other with fierce desire.

They sat on the wicker bench alongside the railing. Huddling together against the wind and the cold, they fell silent. For the first time in his life, Charles felt the giddiness, the absolute lunacy of loving someone without question, without reserve, and with total abandon. With all the passion he had invested in every other pursuit of his life, he now surrendered himself wholly—submerged in the wonderment of love. He felt himself falling, as in a dream where one cannot speak, yet perceives oneself in descent. At that very moment he was conscious of losing himself in love even as he glimpsed himself carried uncontrollably onward—borne by phantasmal feelings that lay well beyond his capacity to comprehend them. Almost unwittingly, and certainly without premeditation, he had sworn to Fatima the unspoken pact that binds lovers. And, to his infinite surprise and delight, she understood and reciprocated his love.

"You know," she said wistfully, breaking the silence, "in my country there is a saying that autumn love has no future."

"Where I come from," Charles countered, "they say that love conquers all."

"Well, naturally, as your client I have to follow your advice in these matters," she said with mock seriousness. Then, suddenly as the pain of the last several days once again swept over her, her face clouded. She slowly raised her eyes. They were filled with tears.

"I mean it. I really do love you," he said fervently.

"I know. You have a big place in my heart too," she replied.

Then she drew herself away slightly. "Charles, as you know, my whole world is falling to pieces. I've lost those very treasures that are dearest to me. And I don't know what will become of me. But one thing is for sure. I will always remember these moments together, with you. I will always carry your words with me."

"Fatima, it's all going to work out for you. I just know it will. Sure, that old world out there is falling apart. But we're just not going to let the pieces fall on you—or us. Just . . . just keep going. That's all." He kissed her again.

"I will, Charles. I will, I promise you. I will try."

They heard a shout from around the side of the house. Charles recognized the voice of their driver.

"*Zut*," he said, rolling his eyes as he smiled at her. "I forgot about the taxi. We have to go."

They raced around the chalet, checking to be sure that they had left nothing. Then they closed the shutters and hurried out the verandah door. Charles reached for the handle to pull the door closed when he spotted the blood covering it. He shuddered, turned away, and went on down the stairs. One day he would explain it all to David Malone. But he had a sudden premonition that that day would be long coming.

THIRTY-NINE

L'Auberge Bellevue
Annecy, France
Afternoon, Friday
Oct. 4, 2002

It was toward mid-afternoon by the time they arrived back in Annecy.
They checked into l'Auberge Bellevue, a small and unassuming hotel
beside the lake, well removed from the bustle of the town, and of no
particular distinction. It was less likely to draw interest to this unusual
couple—he a fair-haired, well-built American type (or, from a distance,
even a muscled *mec* from the countryside), she a raven-haired beauty of
exotic mien. When the solicitous clerk at the desk asked for their names,
Charles presented themselves as Mr. and Mrs. Webster, medical doctors
newly arrived from Phoenix, barely conversant in French but desirous of
a few nights lodging as they toured the region. They would stay longer,
Charles went on, if their schedule would permit it.

"*Mais nous sommes fermés le premier de novembre,*" the woman replied,
they would be closed the first of November.

"We'll be gone well before then. We'll stay a week at most, . . . just a
short visit this time. But as medical doctors from America"—he shot a
significant glance at Fatima, who had the good sense to remain silent—
"we've come to Annecy in search of privacy."

"*Bien entendu, Monsieur. Pas de question.*" Well-understood. No questions asked. Suddenly she seemed about to ask them something, perhaps
for their passports Charles feared, but then she hesitated. He flashed a
smile. Then she then pursed her lips into a classic French "pouf" and

handed him the key to their room. A romantic at heart she was, he thought bemusedly.

"*Merci beaucoup, Madame.*" She had understood, well and truly, he believed, but to fortify her resolve Charles firmly grasped her hand and, winking ever so slightly, pressed a 100 Euro bill into it.

When they arrived at their room on the second floor of the hotel, they found it shuttered against the afternoon sun. Charles pulled aside the heavy velour drapes, bent back the wooden shutters and anchored them, releasing the light to stream into the large and comfortable chamber. At the far end of the room a narrow door opened onto a tiny foyer with a wooden writing desk. The entire effect was one of tasteful spaciousness and rustic comfort.

"It pays to come to these places during off-season," Charles observed as he stood before the open window. "In summer you'd be lucky to find a room in an alpine chalet like this one. Fatima, just look at this."

She glided over to him, felt for his hand, and the two of them took in the scene before them. Over the lake the sky was swathed in the gauzy brilliance of the afternoon sun. The wind had crept back into its mountain fastness, and spirals of fog swirled like wraiths up into the warming air. Shouts from a few children playing on the little beach carried up to the two lovers as they stood hand in hand at the window. From their vantage point, they could see the whole length of the shimmering blue lake, past the hamlets along the shore, beyond the village of Talloires, then up, up, to the heights of the Col Forclaz, where they could pick out tiny figures of hang-gliders winding down, down, down from the piney mounts to the level of the lake.

Suddenly recoiling from the window, Charles covered his eyes with the palm of his right hand.

"What's wrong, Charles? Are you okay?"

"I just had a passing thought, that's all. Nothing serious."

"No, no, tell me. What is it? I want to know."

"The scene brings back some bad memories—about what happened at the World Trade Center."

"You mean because of the people parachuting over there?"

"Yes, the hang-gliders."

"Oh Charles, I'm so sorry for you. My brother told me that you were there. It must have been *very* bad."

"It was horrible. People were jumping from a hundred stories above us. At first they were only specks—too small and falling too fast to see what they were—even that they were people. But down they plummeted, head over heels, out of the sky. Just before they hit the ground, I caught glimpses of some of them, their arms and legs flailing, their hands clutch ing vainly at the air, as their bodies splattered on streets, sidewalks, every- where, before my eyes. With all the sirens blaring, people yelling, debris crashing down, the noise was absolutely deafening. But through it all, I thought I heard their screams—screams that ended abruptly as each body thudded into a splotch of flesh, clothes, and blood. I will never, ever, get that scene out of my mind." Charles hugged Fatima tightly. He was crying now, and her body shook with his sobs. "It was only the next day, on the Internet, that I saw the photos of those faces at the windows. The faces of people peering out, hardly believing their own eyes. People in their final moments before they broke those windows and threw themselves into the air. People who suddenly felt themselves falling, who saw the street rise to meet them, whose last choice was between jumping or being burned alive. They were people just like me, just like my friends at break- fast that morning, people who didn't make it. The only thing was, I wasn't there with them." He had let himself go completely now. Heartsick, he wept without reserve, weeping until he had no tears left to shed, as all the while Fatima tried to console him.

When he had composed himself somewhat, Fatima said, "Dear, dear Charles, you were so lucky to have escaped. How did you do it?" She stretched her thin arm over his broad, muscled back and gave him a gentle squeeze.

"My client Harold Witherspoon and I had just left the North Tower after a breakfast meeting at a restaurant, Windows on the World, on the top floor. I had to leave early to get to a meeting back at my office, and

Mr. Witherspoon decided to come back with me. We were crossing the street in front of the building when we heard the first plane coming in. We heard a huge explosion, and when we looked up, it was clear that the plane had hit the tower we had just left. Within minutes the higher floors of the tower were engulfed in flames. At that time, of course, we thought it was an accident—a terrible, devastating accident. We took refuge in the entryway of a building across the street from the towers, waited for a while, and then decided to walk back to Wall Street, where we both work. As we were about to leave, the second plane hit, this time the South Tower. After that, there was mass confusion. We waited a little while longer to be sure we could safely leave the overhang and head uptown, away from the area. As we began to run, I turned to look back one more time. It was then that I heard the splintering of glass from broken windows. And then I began to see them, falling earthward—the bodies of people who had jumped."

"Oh, Charles, I'm so sorry. I'm so sorry," she cried, embracing him with all her strength. "When I heard what had happened, I called my brother Abdeljelil at his office. He came home right away, and for an entire day we sat in front of the television. We couldn't move. I cried and cried for days after that. And of course we also were worried about Omar, who lived in the city."

Charles pulled Fatima tightly and began to sob uncontrollably again. "Fatima, each and every one of the other people with whom we had breakfast that morning died when the North Tower fell. If the plane had hit five minutes earlier, I would've been one of those poor bastards. Ever since then, I've felt that I should've gone down with them. What business of mine was it to have gotten off scot-free?"

"That was your fate. It was not yet your time."

"It would've been better if I'd gone down with them. I'm tormented by these images. It's absolutely horrible. I haven't even told Sarah all the details. I try not to think about them, honestly, but I can't help myself."

"I understand. I really do. But you must stand tall and strong, like the towers themselves, lest you become a victim too. You should consider yourself one of the privileged. Fate has reserved another, special role for you. It is up to you to find out what it is. It took me a long time to do that for myself. But in the end, you'll be the better for it. You'll know what you have to do."

Charles dried the tears from his eyes with the sleeve of his shirt. He then leaned down to her and kissed her tenderly on the lips. "You're very wise, dear Fatima. I'm sorry to break down like this." He was silent for a moment. Then he said, "I could stay here forever, with you."

"I know, it's just beautiful," Fatima said. "I never want to leave either." She paused, cocking her head at him and setting her jaw resolutely. "Charles, I do want you to listen to me. This entire world of ours is only a little hamlet in a vast, vast desert. Like that desert, our destinies offer us infinite possibility or total annihilation. It's up to you, me, all of us—all of us who live in our tiny hamlet—to explore that desert, to learn about its goodness and ultimately to find Allah, God, Fate—call it what you will—there. And to do that we must learn to live together—and that means understanding each other a lot better than we do now."

Charles kissed her again, this time with intensity. He could not get enough of her. As he put his arms around her shoulders, he caught a glimpse of his watch. A pang of concern passed through him. "Oh Fatima, excuse me, but I'm a little worried. If I don't call Claude soon, he may be gone for the weekend. I'd like to catch him at the office. Every day counts you know," he said, a note of seriousness in his voice.

"Yes, I understand. I also would like to make a call . . . to my daughter." She looked at her watch. "It would be a good time now."

"Don't use the hotel phone. Even though it doesn't have GPS—like your brother's cell phone," Charles said, alluding to their earlier misadventure, "the hotel probably does get a record of overseas calls. Who knows what prying eyes might like to know whom you're calling? You can use my Blackberry. It doesn't have GPS, thank God." Then he added, "But first let me call Claude."

"You think of everything, Charles," she said. She hugged him fiercely and then sat on the side of the bed. He stood by her and thumbed in the telephone number for Claude Vergier in Paris.

The recorded message kicked in immediately. Mâitre Vergier would be gone for two days, it recited, but then would return and respond to all calls at once. If, in the meantime, the call was urgent, his secretary would return it.

"*Zut*," Charles muttered. "Tell me that French lawyers are not as hedonistic as their countrymen. He's already gone for the weekend, probably at his manor in the Loire Valley. I'll try again to reach his secretary on Monday." He proffered the Blackberry to Fatima. "You're on."

"What does it mean—'you're on'?"

"It means it's your turn."

"Oh. I didn't know that," she said, beaming a brave smile at him. She pressed in the numbers, but she couldn't get through. Her phone in her house in Baghdad didn't ring. There was no sound at the other end of the line.

"The phone must be out of order. I'll try tomorrow." She looked down at the mobile phone. "I'm worried about Latifa," she said, bowing her head. "I would die if anything happens to her."

"I'm sure she's all right," Charles said reassuringly. "She's probably out with her friends. Why don't you call your brother Abdeljelil?"

Fatima hesitated for a moment, then quickly dialed the telephone number of Abdeljelil's villa in Baghdad. No answer. The phone stopped ringing almost as it began. Then there was no sound. "It's odd," she said. "He usually goes to the mosque early Friday morning and then works at home in the afternoon, when it's quiet. There may be a general telephone outage in Baghdad. These days it happens often enough."

"Or the telephone lines to Baghdad may just be tied up," Charles replied, "with the controversy over the weapons inspectors and everything. The talk of war. It'll probably get worse, you know."

"I'm afraid for my family," she said. "We suffered so much during the Gulf War and the sanctions. We barely had enough food. It was frightening. It will be worse if the Americans invade."

"Is there anyone else you can call?"

"There's my brother Majid. He still lives in Najaf. We were close as children, but not in recent years. I'll try to call him tomorrow. He always goes to the mosque on Fridays for the entire day, then spends the night in prayer and fasting at Al Hawza al 'Ilmiya, his old school."

"Don't worry, Fatima, you'll find that Latifa is with her friends. She'll be fine." Charles placed his arms around her, drawing her toward him.

"*Inshallah*, I'll be able to reach them all tomorrow," Fatima said.

Charles placed his hand lightly on Fatima's shoulder. She drew back, stood, and went over to the window, where she seemed to study the hang-gliders in the distance. Then as if speaking to the wind, she said, "Charles, there's something I have to tell you."

"Okay," he said a bit edgily.

"First, you have to understand that I truly love you. It's so ironic that the first man who I feel begins to understand me is a non-Muslim, an American no less! You really listen to what I have to say—like in the restaurant the other night, when I'm afraid I got a little carried away."

"You aren't referring to calling me 'dense,' are you?" he asked, his eyes twinkling. She started to look over her shoulder, but before she could answer, he added quickly, "It's okay. I probably deserved it. I just hope I didn't ask too many questions."

"Not at all. I could talk to you forever—about anything." She turned and looked directly at him, her eyes large and luminous. "I've never felt like this toward any man—of any faith or nationality—before. We've known each other for such a brief time, and yet it's as if we've known each other our whole lives. I have the feeling that we have many, many things in common. It's quite strange, you know. I feel that our love is written in the stars I used to try to read with my father in the desert—when I was a child. We were somehow fated to meet."

"You know that I feel the same way about you."

"I know." Fatima nodded. She came over to him and sat on the bed beside him. "Still, we can't ignore the fact that we belong to two different worlds—and I am not referring just to our different cultures and religions. You're a successful American lawyer. You have the love of a woman who needs you. You have what you've worked for so many years to achieve, and you have your future, with the promise of much happiness. I also have my own life, with my two brothers in Iraq, my beautiful daughter. And I have my writing, which—thanks be to Allah—has enjoyed some modest success, and my concerns for the problems of women in my country. And then there are all the difficulties faced by my fellow citizens while Saddam is in power." She set her jaw and cocked her head, as was her habit when she became serious.

"I understand," he said.

"But there's something else. Almost four weeks ago I set out on this journey determined to improve my life but not really having any clear idea what could happen to me. Well, within the first few days, I almost met my death and became a marked woman, then my brother was killed, and now I am worried about my daughter. After all my efforts, it appears that there is no place safe for me in this world. Charles, honestly I don't know what will become of me. I really don't. And yet I feel I have to settle things in my own mind before I can go on. In other words, at this time I'm just not ready to go farther down the path of love, if you know what I mean. I hope you can understand."

"Fatima, I do understand. I do. You needn't say any more. Don't. I respect your feelings, at the same time that I love you. And, although I'd hardly admit it to anyone else, I feel as if my own life is teetering at the edge of that abyss faced by those folks at Windows on the World. This last year has been trying for me—as you can tell, and I'm only now getting around to sorting out how I feel about it," he said as he wiped away the remaining moisture in his eyes. "So, Fatima, I understand—fully."

"You're wonderful." Fatima touched Charles's face and gently kissed him. Then they hugged each other tightly, each desperately needing the profound comfort offered by the other's love.

FORTY

L'Auberge Bellevue
Annecy, France
Morning, Saturday
Oct. 5, 2002

Charles awoke to the glimmer of dawn light from the lake. Fatima was not in the room. After a pang of concern, he heard papers rustling in the adjoining foyer. The door was open a crack. She's at it, he thought. Her poetry. Probably for hours. What a remarkable woman. He loved her with all his being.

Again a sound from the foyer. Of a pen striking a wooden desk. Whatever it was, it was finished. Then the door creaked open, and her smiling face appeared in the doorway.

"Oh, Charles dearest, I had hoped that you wouldn't hear me. I tried to be quiet."

"Not at all. I way just lying here thinking about how much I love you."

She came over to the side of the bed and sat beside him. "I love you too," she said. "I got up early this morning to write about it. Yesterday, on the verandah in Talloires, I had made up my mind to do it. The poem is called 'The Love of My Life.' I wrote it as I was waiting for you to get up," she teased, laughing lightly. "I hope you like it. My little dictionary didn't have all the words I needed, so I apologize if it isn't quite correct." She handed him a single sheet of hotel stationery on which were written in black ink, in a flowery script, the following words:

The Love of My Life

Autumn love has no future,
So I told my lover, laughing
That I had Cupid's left ear
(The right one I'd reserved for spring)
It only has a past, I said, a memory.
Hold dear these days, I warned,
And well he would.

But I am wiser now,
I've spied the Janus face of love,
Wall-eyed, blind-eyed
Sweetly pie-eyed.

On the Paris metro,
In the Baghdad bazaar,
Eyeing a bagatelle
By the lake in Talloires,
Across the damask
One September eve
Bursting with plenitude
In the mountains.

It's our turn now
To seek those leaf-strewn trails
In love's labyrinth
Its sinuous tendrils
Binding us
Like two fated cicadas,
Cocooned in jasmine lace.

"It's beautiful," Charles said. "You're a wonderful poet."

Fatima smiled at him wryly. "Like any poet, I'm only as good as my inspiration. And that's you, of course." He laughed so loud she worried it could be heard out on the lake.

She smiled, warmed by his response. Then, gloom suddenly fell across her features. "Charles, I'm still worried about Latifa. I've been thinking about her. I'm going to try to call her again." She picked up his Blackberry from the bedside table and dialed the number for her phone in Baghdad, but once again there was only silence on the other end. "I guess I have no alternative but to call Majid."

"Go right ahead."

She dialed again. After many rings a voice answered. It was her brother. He greeted her brusquely, almost rudely. "Oh, haven't you heard?" he said. "Latifa tried to commit suicide. It was two days ago. She said that she missed her mother, . . . that you no longer loved her, and that you had left her never to return. We managed to save her, but she almost died."

"What? I spoke to her only four days ago, and she was fine." At that Fatima could hear her brother shout to someone in the background. She could not make out the words.

"Her schoolmates were hard on her. They said that her mother is a traitor and has become an infidel. Latifa just couldn't stand it any longer, and she's given up on you."

"I've tried to call her yesterday and today. Where, where is she?"

"No. You can't speak to her. She's been hospitalized."

"Where?"

"An asylum for the mentally ill. She's under sedation and can't be disturbed."

"I don't believe you."

"Come home to her, and you'll see. You made a big mistake when you left your family. It is against Islamic tradition, against the sacred precepts of the Holy Koran. You will be punished for this, you know.

Allah, bless him, will scourge your soul. You will be cast down like the demons in hell. You will burn in the fires of eternity. Unless you come back, back to Latifa, back to your only child, back to your family, you are doomed." With that he cursed her several times, then abruptly hung up.

Fatima slowly put down the phone. She began to cry. Long, deep sobs. She threw herself onto the bed.

Charles held her in his arms. He cradled her body, kissing her tears and consoling her with his embraces. She lay with her head on the pillow for a long time, her eyes wide open, staring into the room. First her brother. Now her daughter. What next, she thought. It was all because of her selfishness.

Suddenly raising herself up, she sat at the edge of the bed. She reached for Charles's hand and held it firmly. "I'm going back to Baghdad," she said determinedly. "My daughter needs me. I'm going to get her out of that miserable country."

"No. Impossible. Out of the question," he rejoined. "Too many people have worked to save you. You owe it to Omar to reach freedom in America. Look, try to call your other brother, Abdeljelil, and ask him how Latifa is doing. Maybe she's okay."

"Charles, as much as I'd like to do that, I can't. It was a mistake to try to call Abdeljelil yesterday."

"Why, in heaven's name?"

"Don't you think that Saddam monitors his phone? Shall I implicate Abdeljelil too—in my selfish scheme gone dreadfully wrong? Charles, it doesn't matter, it just doesn't matter any more," Fatima cried, shaking her head. "I need to go to my daughter—and give her a mother's love. Besides, I cannot jeopardize more lives. Including yours. Sooner or later, Mukhabarat will find me again. And they will kill you too."

"Dam . . . na . . . tion." He let the word out syllable by syllable. "Forget me. I've achieved all I have ever wanted in life. Fatima, think only of yourself. If you go back now, you'll lose everything!" He was almost shouting.

"Charles. I must go back. I must. Majid told me that Latifa tried to commit suicide." She was adamant.

"Don't you realize that's just an excuse to get you back to Iraq? It's the *only* thing they have over you—your daughter. Majid must hate you. For what you stand for. His own sister a new voice for women, a challenge to the norms of your culture. There's nothing he'd like more than to force you back. To get his vengeance. And to kill you probably. Fatima, you've got to save yourself so you can save your daughter. Omar would've wanted you to go to America. It's your promised land."

"That all means nothing to me now. Omar is dead, and I must decide what is right for me. And for my daughter. She's just like me. She's capable of anything. I too suspect Majid is lying, especially if the phones have been out in Baghdad the last couple of days. Since he's in Najaf, how could he have known that Latifa tried to take her own life? And Latifa seemed okay to me only four days ago when I spoke with her. Yet, I can't take the risk that she . . . ." Fatima lowered her eyes and wiped the tears from them. "I just can't take the risk. That's all."

Charles held his tongue. He knew when to cave. "All right, all right." He paused. "If that's your decision, . . . I'll go with you."

"No, no. No. You'd attract too much attention. You wouldn't last five minutes in my country. Saddam would be only too happy to hang you as a spy."

"They *don't* know me. They only know you."

"They won't know me after I put on my abayah. Besides, they'd never imagine that I would ever come back. And by the time they do, it'll be too late. I'll take Latifa with me and get out well before they realize what I've done."

He moved next to her on the bed. "Well, I can't wear the abayah, but I can travel as a journalist. There are hundreds of them now in the country—following the inspectors, poking around, reporting on all sorts of things—from the price of bread in the market to the opinions of people in the street."

"But an American journalist would have a high profile. You'd be followed everywhere. There are minders, you know. One would be assigned to you."

"Okay, I'll say that I'm working for a French paper and use my Irish passport. I'm sure that Claude can get me the proper documentation. A day or two for the press credentials, then a walk-up visa at the Iraqi embassy. It shouldn't be that difficult to get into the country. And, as for the minders, surely I'll be able to give them the slip. Getting out of Iraq, though. That could be a different matter."

Fatima looked at him quizzically, her dark eyes searching his for a sign. Some hesitancy. Some reflexive fear. "You really mean this, don't you?"

He nodded. "Fatima, I love you. I'm not going to let you go back to Iraq alone. Where you go, I go. That's very simply the deal."

She was silent for a few moments, then sat up very straight. Charles could tell by her expression that she had come to a decision. "All right," she said, her tone resolute. "I have friends who can get us out. After all, I've done it before. Through the desert . . . to Saudi Arabia. You get into the Southern Region, where the Shiites live. We'd go to the end of the road by car, then down toward the border on horseback. After that it's a day's walk to the border. It's not too bad."

"It would be better if we each traveled alone," Charles cautioned. "Maybe on the same flight, though. We'll join up somewhere in Baghdad. I'll ditch my minder somehow, then pick you up in a taxi. We'll agree on a place. Wherever you want."

"Are you sure that you want to do this? It could be hard for you. And very dangerous."

"Fatima, I'll be with you. For me, that's quite enough. I know that we can do this. I'm sure of it." He encircled her slender shoulders with his strong arms and kissed her passionately.

FORTY-ONE

Baghdad
Mid-morning, Wednesday
Oct. 9, 2002

A few days later, Charles Sherman and Fatima Shihabi, traveling separately on Air France Flight 3265 from Paris to Amman, connecting on Royal Jordanian Airlines, stepped onto the tarmac at Saddam International Airport in Baghdad. Traveling on his Irish passport, Charles had arranged for an Iraqi business visa in Paris; he convinced the consular section of the Iraqi embassy, with the aid of certain employment certifications that Claude had procured for him, that he was a correspondent for *Le Monde*.

He had been a little nervous when he approached the consular window of the Iraqi embassy in Paris. The clerk behind the semicircular grill studied the papers for a long time. Then, something must have stirred his suspicions for he began to query Charles.

"Irish citizen, you say. Now why would your paper hire somebody from Ireland? And then send him to my country?"

"To be perfectly honest, sir, I didn't want to go," Charles lied. "But you know that my paper has criticized Bush—that crazy warmonger—and the Americans at every turn, and actually my French colleagues are now all preoccupied with the next round of anti-American coverage. Well, they didn't trust my British colleague at the paper to report on what's going on in Baghdad . . . for obvious reasons." Charles looked the clerk squarely in the eye and nodded seriously. "So, at the end of the day, they picked me." He sighed audibly. "Ireland's always been a neutral country, you know. A little like Switzerland."

Charles's blather had been just enough. Only just, he thought. And now, as he strode toward the airport building, he composed himself, stretching out his long legs and adjusting his grip on his satchel. He was traveling light, carrying with him a voice recorder clearly labeled in French, "Propriété de *Le Monde*," three legal-sized yellow pads, a few toiletries, and a change of clothing.

For Fatima it was not as easy as they had hoped. Without an Iraqi passport, all she could present were the temporary travel documents that the French embassy in Riyadh had given her. She figured, correctly, that the Iraqi immigration authorities would never expect her to try to reenter Iraq. At least not the officials at the Baghdad airport. "My passport was stolen in Paris," she avowed. "I didn't have enough time to get a new one before my flight." The official then asked why she had gone to Paris in the first place. "For medical treatment," she replied. "A women's problem," she added boldly. The official frowned and hesitated for a moment. He seemed to study the computer screen in front of him. Suddenly he turned, went into an office in the rear, and closed the door behind him. Fatima caught her breath and her heart pounded. She felt faint and wished that Charles had stayed with her. After a few minutes, the official returned, a sardonic smile on his face.

"Welcome back to Iraq, . . . Mrs. Shihabi." His tone of voice was just enough to make her realize that he knew who she was. He had received his instructions. His superiors in the Iraqi constabulary probably thought she might lead them to other treasonous dissidents. When he handed her back her papers, she calmly folded them and put them in her traveling bag and, not dignifying the official with even a glance, stepped away from his booth and headed for the airport lobby. Purposefully, knowing that her every step was being observed, she strode across the lobby and then through the glass doors at the airport's front entrance. She walked over to a line of waiting taxis and got in the queue. It was lamentably long, and after a good ten minutes she found herself at its head. An old Citroën station wagon, whose driver wore a dirty white thobe and red-checkered head covering, labored up to her. As she settled in the rear seat, she told the driver to go to Alywesa Street, and, with a breathy wheeze, the car moved forward.

She knew that the taxi would be followed. "Go quickly, as quickly as you can," she told the driver in a flat voice.

"*Inshallah*, we'll get there," the man said in the thick, guttural accent of her native Najaf. "I will beat this camel all the way to the Gates of Paradise if he doesn't obey me."

In the meantime Charles encountered no difficulties. He had worked his contacts at *Le Monde* well. The visa papers raised no eyebrows, and he easily transited the usual formalities. As he left Iraqi immigration, he was immediately greeted by his minder—Abdul al Naim, a friendly functionary probably pried from a desk in the bowels of the Ministry of Communications to accompany him on his journalistic mission, Charles thought. Not too swift, but no dummy either. He would have to risk it. He had no choice.

"I wonder if we might stop at a cafe for a soda. I'm terribly thirsty after the long flight," Charles said, holding his throat.

"Why not?" Abdul said. "We go. Not far."

The cafe was just outside the airport building, on one side of a large plaza filled with people and automobiles. On the other side was the taxi stand. As they took their seats at a table outside the cafe, he saw Fatima, erect, head held high, taking her place at the end of the queue. She was striking, he thought.

Charles began to engage his minder with pleasant banter, steering the conversation toward subjects of common professional interest, their home lives (Charles professing to be happily married with three "wonderful" children), the views of his historically neutral homeland Ireland as well as those of his adopted country France, which, he noted, had long worked in the interests of Iraq. It was a carefully calculated conversation, long on the trust elements.

Finally he spotted Fatima stepping into her taxi. It puttered off, and then, as expected, another vehicle, a blue Datsun of recent vintage, took off after it. Two men sat in the front seat. Charles could only see the passenger from the side. His neck was wrapped in what appeared to be a thick, white bandage. What Charles could see of the face looked oddly familiar, though out of place, here in Baghdad. Then suddenly he knew. It was the man who had followed him in Paris, likely the man who had killed Omar. Charles would have to work quickly.

"Abdul, you are my friend," Charles said, looking the man straight in the eye, "and, I can see, a true professional colleague. You are a good man. I wouldn't ask you this if I didn't feel I could without embarrassing you. And surely tell me if this gives you any problem at all. It is, shall we say, something man to man. And, as a Muslim man, you can understand what I am about to tell you—it involves a woman." Charles gave him a confidential wink.

Abdul twisted in his chair uncomfortably. He was visibly suspicious.

Charles went on. "You see, I have had a woman friend—the French would call her a *petite amie*—who works for Royal Jordanian Airlines here in Baghdad. She used to work in its Paris office, when I knew her. She was transferred here three years ago. I haven't seen her for almost six months now. She knows that I've come to Baghdad." Charles glanced at Abdul for an early reaction.

"I see," Abdul said, straining to catch the import of his colleague's words. "I see."

"She has asked me to meet her at the airline's office—here at the airport. She must work until lunchtime, but then we'll go to her hotel. It would be just for a few hours—until about five this afternoon. At that time, not one minute later, I will meet you back here, right at this table." Before Abdul had a chance to object, Charles continued. "And because you are my professional colleague and such a good man and, as I can plainly see, with the same needs for your family as my own, I would like to make you a small gift for any inconvenience this all might cause you." Charles reached across the table as if to shake hands. Abdul almost instinctively reached his hand forward, and Charles pressed a thick wad of hundred Euro bills into it. *C'est la vie en Arabie*, he thought. Just like the old days in Saudi. It was that way with *baksheesh*. It would be a hard gift to refuse.

Fingering the bills under the table, Abdul whistled through his teeth. The bargain was struck. "All right, Charles . . . I trust you, you are my brother."

Charles paid the bill, and after the two men took their leave, Charles walked back in the direction of the airport entrance. He glanced back and could see Abdul slowly dawdling along the pavement after him. Once inside the building, Charles headed straight to the Royal Jordanian Airline desk, where a pert, stylishly attired attendant was on duty.

"Hello. I wonder if you might be able to help me. Do you speak English?" He gave her his most engaging smile.

"I speak little. How can I do for you?" she asked, returning his smile.

"Well, I'm from Ireland, and I've been a little lost, you see. I've looked everywhere for your ticket office. I asked many people, and nobody could tell me. But a few minutes ago a very, very nice man showed me." Charles paused for a moment as the woman warmed to his charm. Then he added, "You know, after so many weeks in your country, it is a pleasure for me to speak English once again, especially with such a beautiful representative of Arab culture. But of course, you must have many men tell you that."

The woman beamed, then smiled at him amusedly. She figured he had an angle, Charles thought, but she couldn't guess what it was.

Charles busied himself with some papers at the counter, then spotted Abdul wandering through the airport entrance. Charles pretended to happen to notice him and waved vigorously.

"Why, that's that nice Iraqi who helped me find you," Charles said to the attendant. "Would you mind waving to him for me? He was just such a good man."

The attendant waved a little timidly. "No, no. Really give him a good wave, if you would," Charles urged her. "I really want him to know that Irish visitors like me so much appreciate the help of the local people." She then waved very vigorously. Then Charles waved again. After feigning that he hadn't seen them, the minder gave them a slight down-turned half-wave of his right hand, then glanced around to see whether anyone had seen the gesture. All of a sudden he turned on his heel and went out the way he had come in.

Charles chatted with the woman several more minutes, then thanked her again profusely, excused himself politely, and went back outside. Abdul was nowhere in sight. Charles got in the queue, which now, after a swell of arriving flights, had lengthened to a score of clients. Nevertheless, plenty of taxis had been waiting for just this moment, and he quickly got a taxi and headed off. For a few hours at least, he was free.

FORTY-TWO

Baghdad
Late morning, Wednesday
Oct. 9, 2002

Alywesa Street was a side street in the souk, normally chockablock
with people just before the midday closing. Fatima watched the blue
Datsun behind the taxi, weaving behind it, in and out of the traffic, hardly
making an effort to conceal itself. Well, she would not make it easy for
them, she thought. She would do a little "shopping" before she went
home. Let them try and find her in the souk.

When the taxi pulled into Alywesa Street, she threw a packet of dinars
into the front seat, telling the driver that it would be more than enough
for the fare. She pulled on her abayah, draping it over her head and framing her face in an oval of black. Then she sprang from the taxi and
plunged into the crowd, first weaving through the melee of the market,
then hastening through the souk's covered sections, and finally emerging
into an area of open-air stands, where she squeezed through the narrow
spaces between the stalls. She ignored the strident cries of ever-vigilant
vendors primed, if they saw eyes rest even for an instant on their mer-
chandise, to inveigle a would-be client and to extol the special (even
unique, Madame) merits of their wares. She passed rugs from Turkmeni-
stan (and for you, Madame, a special price, Madame). Washing machines
from China. Wine from the Caucasus. Every product required for the
ordinary life of a person. As she rushed along, she was again astonished
that the Alywesa souk had it all, at exorbitant prices to be sure, in spite of
the sanctions.

As she hurried along, she didn't look back, knowing that, from behind, her draped shape had now merged with the masses of other black shapes surrounding her. She moved as a formless phantom, threading her way in and out, up and down the maze of passages, shifting direction abruptly as old and familiar routes opened before her. Finally, out of breath, she stopped at a stall in the rug souk. Peering behind her, around the edge of her abayah, she saw no sign of her pursuers.

She waited several minutes to be certain. Then, walking at a normal gait, she left the souk by an alley heading toward her old neighborhood. Please Allah, she prayed, let Charles be there.

They were to meet at the corner of Wazeer Street and El Sadik Boulevard, a few blocks from her brother's home. Her home, too, these twelve years. And Latifa's. Would she find her home from school for lunch as she normally was? Or would she find the house hauntingly empty if, as Majid had said, Latifa had been hospitalized? She felt sure Majid was lying. But she had no choice. She would gamble that her daughter would be at home to greet her.

From a distance she could see no one at the intersection. It was empty except for a truck parked near the corner, across the street on El Sadik Boulevard. She gathered her abayah around her and rushed down the waste-strewn footpath along Wazeer Street, stumbling once on a tree root that long ago had spitefully poised itself to menace those in haste. She pressed on, praying that Charles would somehow be waiting for her. When she reached the corner, she heard a whisper from the entryway of a leather goods shop.

"Psst, Fatima, over here." Charles was standing in the shadows of the shop entrance. Arms crossed, he smiled at her mischievously. "What took you so long?"

"Charles, I was so worried about you. How did you get away from your minder?"

"It was a guy thing," he replied. "I'll explain it to you later."

"We must hurry," she said. "There's not much time. Let's go."

They went back down Wazeer Street, past the alley where she had come from the souk, and entered a quiet residential zone, with row houses fronted by rough masonry walls the height of a small man, topped with metal grid barriers. So that she could see more easily, she lowered her abayah around her shoulders, in the style popular among younger Baghdad women. A wisp of raven hair fell across her forehead. He scanned her delicate features, which had taken on a melancholy aspect.

"Many times while I lived in Abdeljelil's villa, I walked this way back and forth from the souk. Along Wazeer Street. Sometimes twice a day, I would come by this way—if my brother's family needed things. I did all the shopping."

"It's a long way from where I come from," Charles replied, smiling. He had lapsed into a detached, devil–may–care frame of mind, practically buoyant. For no reason, he thought. Or rather because, for once, he wasn't tyrannized by the prospect of having to do that which was expected of him. He felt at once freed of all conventionality and in complete control of himself. A vision of Sarah flashed through his mind. At a dinner party on the Upper East Side. The clink of Buccellati against Wedgwood. Witherspoon holding forth across the table.

Fatima peered into his face. "Charles." He looked at the black-draped figure trundling beside him, her shining eyes fixed on him. Fatima seemed real—yet at the same time, dreamlike. "Charles dear, are you sure you're ready for this?"

"At this moment there's nowhere else on this planet I'd rather be," he said. "But get your daughter and then leave. Don't stay for more than a minute."

At the end of a short, dirt alley, they came upon a tree-lined avenue, bordered by two-story villas visible behind walls running the length of the dusty pavement. "That's my street, Zankat al Hudh. In English it means Fortune Street," she said.

"How appropriate." For a second he shuddered. The name gave him the willies.

"Our house is left around this block. Down four houses. If Latifa is okay, she should be home from school by this time. You must stay here. My neighbors are very suspicious."

"Wait," Charles interjected, pulling Fatima back into the alley. "Look who's waiting for you."

It was the same blue Datsun, with two men inside, he had seen take off after her taxi at the airport. It was parked across the cobblestoned street from Fatima's house. Since it was facing away from them, Charles felt fairly confident that the men had not seen him. "You should go in the back door."

"We always keep the garden gate locked from the inside. But don't worry. I'll surprise them," Fatima whispered. "They'd never expect me to arrive so suddenly, and go in the front gate of my house. They'll think I'm not wise to them. I'm only a woman after all."

"Don't underestimate them."

"I know these types. They've been told to keep me under surveillance. Just to see who I meet with. They'll check with the higher-ups one last time before they arrest me. Otherwise, they could've taken me at the airport. I have a few minutes at least."

"Suppose one of them is inside."

"Not likely. They'd know who my brother is and normally would never enter his house without permission. Besides, they'll think that I'll just come back out the front door, and then they'll arrest me. Instead, Latifa and I will go out the garden door on the alleyway. Then back to the souk. And I'll just do my disappearing act again. It's one of the advantages of these clothes, you see. From the back anyway, we all look alike." She flashed her black eyes and beamed a smile at him. "And sometimes women cover their whole head with the abayah, and I can do that too."

She grasped his arm and added, "It's not safe for you to wait here. Go back to Wazeer Street, then back to El Sadik Boulevard and the intersection where I met you. I'll meet you there again in a half-hour."

"Fatima, you must be careful."

"Wish me luck," she said with determination, as she raised her abayah over her head and drew it tightly around her face.

FORTY-THREE

Baghdad
Midday, Wednesday
Oct. 9, 2002

Fatima proceeded deliberately but calmly along Zankat al Hudh—another Iraqi woman returning from the souk, toward her home. When she arrived in front of the gray metal gate to her courtyard, she abruptly turned, pushed it open, and then, as she quickly closed it, fastened the latch. She hastened across the courtyard toward the villa where she and Latifa lived, quietly so as not to alert anyone who might be inside her brother's villa next door. Then she raced up the stairs, stepped onto the small landing, and opened the front door.

Entering the small foyer, she lowered her abayah and draped it around her shoulders. For a full ten seconds, she stood mute, overcome by the sudden familiarity of a place she knew so well and that she had left only weeks before. It seemed so long ago that she had gone, she reflected. So long, long ago.

Her ears caught the high-pitched wail of a popular Iraqi singer coming from the second floor. "Latifa, are you there?" No response.

"Come quickly, Latifa. We must go at once."

A slim girl attired in a gray smock, hesitatingly descended the stairs, then caught her mother's eye. "Mama, Mama, I was so worried about you!" Latifa flew down the stairs into the arms of her mother, who drew her close, pressing her head against her breasts.

"I was lucky. I will tell you all about it. I heard that you tried to kill yourself."

"It's not true, Mama, . . . it's not true. I would never give up hope for you. Never. You always said that, you know."

Fatima's doubts about Majid were confirmed. "Quick, get your things together," she said.

"Where'll we go?"

"A man, an American, is helping us. We are being followed. They may come at any moment. Bring me another abayah, . . . my old one. Hurry, hurry."

Latifa ran upstairs and returned after a few moments with a large swatch of coarse black material, still a bit satiny, its fabric glistening.

"Put it on," Fatima ordered. Latifa obediently pulled it around her head and draped its folds around her body. Fatima drew the abayah from her shoulders and enshrouded herself with it. They would be no different from two old women who often came late to the souk.

"Let's go. The back door."

"I must bring my notebook." Latifa rushed back up the stairs, tripping once when her foot caught her abayah. Fatima went to the front window, bent low and nudged the drapery ever so slightly so as to see the courtyard and, from an angle, its gate to the street. Through it she could see two men in white shirts peering into the courtyard.

"Hurry," Fatima shouted. "They're coming!"

Latifa flew down the stairs, her notebook in hand, the strap of her radio over her shoulder. In an instant they were out the garden gate into the alley.

"Run," Fatima whispered. "Run as fast as you can. We must get to the souk."

As a young girl playing games with her brothers, Fatima had learned to move quickly in an abayah, raising it ever so slightly in front of her, taking care not to let it trip her. Latifa, however, was not so used to wearing the garment. When they turned from the alley onto Wazeer Street, she stumbled, dropping her notebook onto the packed dirt. As Latifa bent to pick it up, Fatima shot a glance back down the alley and spied the two men running several short blocks behind them.

"Forget it," Fatima shouted. "They'll catch us."

They crossed over the street, into an alley, where Fatima could see the first stalls of the souk. Not daring to look back at their pursuers, she headed for the most crowded area, around the vegetable market. Latifa was keeping up now, zigzagging through the souk, left, then right, then straight for a while, then right, then left, then right, on and on, into the throng of shopkeepers, customers and casual passersby. Surrounded by scores of similarly attired women, Fatima felt secure that the two men would find it difficult to single them out, at least from behind.

The two draped figures huddled over a display of fresh pomegranates from southern Iraq, as if trying to make up their minds how many to purchase for their evening meal. Fatima murmured, "If we are separated, you must go to the corner of Wazeer Street and El Sadik Boulevard. You will see a tall American there. His name is Charles Sherman. Go with him. Do whatever he tells you."

Suddenly Fatima heard a commotion behind them. A woman's cry. Immediately after, a savage curse. Fatima edged her abayah away from her face and watched as a woman pummeled a man about ten meters away, down the aisle between the stalls. The man held her abayah in his hands. The woman, in her outrage, began to wail. The man sauntered away, seemingly heedless of the shame he had wrought.

"Go now," Fatima said in a low voice. "Remember that I love you."

FORTY-FOUR

Baghdad
Early afternoon, Wednesday
Oct. 9, 2002

Peering around a sandblock wall at the end of the alley, Charles had watched Fatima glide down Zankat al Hudh, then suddenly turn left through the gate of her brother's house. Just after she passed into the courtyard, he saw the two men spring from their car. They approached the metal gate and stood peering through it but did not go farther. One of them went back to the car. Probably to get instructions, Charles thought. Then, a full five minutes later, the same man ran back across the street, yelling to the other man. The two of them charged down the street and turned the corner, evidently planning to intercept Fatima as she left by way of the back alley.

Fatima and her daughter must have had enough time, Charles decided. To get out through the alley. From there, into the souk. After ten minutes, and seeing no sign of the men, Charles concluded that they too had left by way of the alley, in pursuit. Tentatively he walked down the narrow alleys toward Wazeer Street, retracing the route he had taken with Fatima. After ten minutes he reached the intersection with El Sadik Boulevard. He again stood in the doorway of the leather goods shop, whose proprietor, he noted, seemed to have left for the day.

A half-hour passed. Charles was seized by a profound dread. They might well already have been caught, he thought, and might even now be under interrogation. Maybe even dead. What folly to have thought that they could just come to Iraq and take back Fatima's daughter! The Iraqis probably knew who Fatima was from the first moment she stepped off the plane. She was contending with professional killers, who knew their calling and possessed all the means to accomplish their invidious mission. And they could easily have surmised that she was not traveling alone. His cover as an Irish journalist working for *Le Monde* might well have been too obvious. He and Fatima had managed to delude themselves—naively, he now concluded—that some magical mix of pure bravura, unswerving love, and merciful Fate would render them invincible. His heart was heavy with chagrin.

Suddenly, far down Wazeer Street he saw a smallish woman, her body draped in an abayah, walking in his direction. She passed by, then suddenly turned back to him and asked, "Charles Sherman?"

"Yes. And who are *you*?"

The voice was Fatima's but lighter, higher-pitched. "Me—Latifa."

"Good God," Charles said. "Where's your mother?"

"She stay in market." The girl began to cry, wiping her eyes with the cloth of the abayah. "She say . . . go . . . find you. I worry police come take mama."

FORTY-FIVE

Baghdad
Early afternoon, Wednesday
Oct. 9, 2002

The two men advanced toward her. Fatima drew her abayah around her face. Glancing sideways, through a small tear in the cloth, she could pick out their profiles. Hard men. Without souls. She stood between them and her daughter. If she waited until they reached her, Latifa would see everything, throw herself upon them, beg them not to take her mother— all to no avail. They might arrest her too. If Fatima ran back down the row of stalls toward Latifa, they would give chase and maybe seize her and take Latifa too. No, it was better that she create a distraction and make herself scarce in the confusion. It was her only chance.

She walked toward them calmly, just another Iraqi woman, one among many in the Alywesa souk. She paused before the shop of a fruit vendor as if to examine some melons stacked high in a neat pyramid on a large wooden stand. As she passed, she leaned against the stand lightly and felt it budge ever so slightly. She peeked past the fold of her abayah and saw that the two men had advanced to the shop just alongside the fruit vendor's. When their big black shoes came into view within a few feet of her, she pretended to stumble. In her feigned fall, she shoved the stand with all her might, toppling it. Its cache of melons cascaded into the dirt in front of the two men. Keeping her body low, she ducked under the adjoining table of fruit and pushed herself along, on hands and knees, beneath the stands, into the next aisle of stalls. Behind her the market erupted. She heard the cry of the fruit vendor, clamorous shouts that must have come from the two men, and a general pandemonium as the souk responded to the "accident." She emerged in the next aisle of stalls, picked herself up, and began to run. She heard the thudding sounds of men running behind her. To free her arms, she yanked the abayah from her head and shoulders, letting it fall any which way. But as it fell, one of its folds caught her right foot. When she tried to free herself with her other foot, she tripped, lost her balance, and dropped to her knees in the aisle. Before she could rise, a large man fell on her, forcing her down and knocking the wind out of her. Then, as she gasped for breath, she heard a voice rasp like a camel's croak, "Fatima Shihabi, you are under arrest."

"I don't know who she is," she responded.

The two men pulled her up, jerking back her arms cruelly. She blinked in the sun and then fixed her eyes on the shorter man. The right side of his neck was thickly bandaged, and he held his head at an angle. "You will come with us," he muttered coldly. They dug their fingers into her arms and half-pulled, half-dragged her through the souk. She allowed her body to go limp, and several times the two men had to stop and adjust their grip on her. Down the center of the rows between the stalls, she could make out the furrow left by her body, like the carcass of a camel dragged to the abattoir, in the dust and the dirt.

When they reached the blue Datsun, the two men bound her with a thick rope, gagged her with a dirty rag, and, without addressing a word to her, threw her in the back seat as if she were so much chattel. Then the men got in and slammed the doors so hard they rocked the vehicle. The man with the bandaged neck, who seemed to be the superior of the two, sat stiffly in the passenger seat while his associate cranked the motor a dozen times before it would start. When it finally turned over, the driver headed the vehicle down Wazeer Street. As they sputtered along, she craned her neck and gazed blankly out the window, noting that most shops had begun to close for the afternoon break. There was almost no one on the street.

It could well be the last time she would see this lovely thoroughfare, she thought, so full of memories of her days in Baghdad. And yet, now that her fate was decided, she was reconciled to it, without the least fear, without even a twinge of hesitation. She would welcome death gladly. At least Latifa would be safe. She had no doubt that Charles would figure out some way to protect her, to get her out of Iraq and to America.

As they approached El Sadik Boulevard, she sat up straighter. She wrenched her head around, frantically searching the corner for Charles and her daughter. At first she didn't see them. Then, just in front of a leather goods shop, she saw the tall figure of Charles bending to a small black-clad figure that Fatima was certain was her daughter. Fatima took a quick breath and held it.

"Well, well, what do we have here?" screeched a voice from the front seat. The man with the bandaged neck angled his torso toward the car window. He studied the two figures with all the curiosity a scorpion might display in examining its prey before stinging it. "Pull over," he muttered to the driver "Not here. Too close. No, over there." He pointed to a space beyond a large delivery van. "There, here, stop. Stop."

The man with the bandaged neck slowly opened the door and gingerly eased himself out of the car. Then he turned back and said to the driver, "Take her to Al Khatabi. I'll meet up with you later." He looked back at her, and for the first time Fatima had a good look at him. He looked oddly familiar. Perhaps it was because of what Charles had described as the man's "cruelty wrinkle." Yes, that was it! It was the man she had seen in the helicopter the day of her escape, the man who had followed her in Paris, who had hunted them down in Talloires. And the bloody bandage around his neck—he must be the man who had killed Omar!

And now he leered at her, his face full of malevolence, his eyes smoldering with hatred. "And now, Madame Shihabi, thanks to you, because of your stupidity in returning to Baghdad, I am able once and for all to settle things with your friend Mr. Sherman." He drew a snub-nosed pistol from his jacket and brandished it in his left hand, turning it back and forth before her. Fatima vainly struggled to free herself and cry out, but her bonds held. The man peered from behind the van down the street to be certain that his prey hadn't departed. Then, he once again turned to address Fatima. "Oh, and one more thing: Don't think you'll ever see your daughter again. Ever. We know about your little Latifa too."

Fatima watched in fear and horror as the man slowly ambled back down Wazeer Street. He was obviously taking his time, and she knew, with every fiber of her being, that he would show his prey no mercy.

FORTY-SIX

Baghdad
Mid–late afternoon, Wednesday
Oct. 9, 2002

The blazing sun scorched Baghdad's buildings, markets and monuments, its concrete and mud houses alike. It seared Charles and Latifa too as they stood absorbed in conversation on the corner of Wazeer Street and El Sadik Boulevard. And, a kilometer away, a sliver of that light struck Fatima through the window of the blue Datsun that was carrying her away to certain death.

"Do you know where they took your mother?" Charles asked Latifa.

"Women Prison, I think." Her English was poor, but at least she was able to communicate, Charles thought.

"Can you take me there?"

"Yes, I go see mama there. One time before."

"How far?"

"Not far. Maybe three kilometer. I show. There." An arm appeared from beneath the shroud and pointed up Wazeer Street.

"Okay. Let's go."

As they crossed El Sadik Boulevard, Charles squinted his eyes against the insistent sun. He felt entirely composed, resolute, as if somehow it had been preordained that he would be in just this place, at just this time and for just this objective. He glanced down at the formless folds of coal dark cloth moving along beside him, two small, sandaled feet venturing out now and then, two steps for every one of his. He felt curiously light-hearted, as if he and his shadow were setting off on some grand quest, about to enter the belly of the beast, from whence only wit and pluck would decide whether they survived or not.

When they reached the other side of the street, Charles noticed an elderly man edging himself along by the street side of the wide sidewalk, a stone's throw down the block. The man, whose bent body and halting gait gave him an air of forlorn decrepitude, wore a dark suit and a fedora angled over his face. He wore a black glove on his right hand, which he pressed to his neck as if massaging away an irksome crick or a rheumatic ache. Almost out of instinct, Charles took Latifa by the arm and steered her into the dusty street, so as to give the man a wide berth. There were no vehicles on the thoroughfare and not another pedestrian in sight. "Hurry," Charles whispered, pressing himself as much as Latifa. "Go fast," he said in case she hadn't understood.

They were not more than ten feet from the man when Charles noticed a flash of white between the man's fingers. When the man looked up, Charles instantly recognized the scarred face. It was the face of the man who had tracked Fatima and Omar through Paris, the face of Omar's killer, the face of a man who would kill Charles and Latifa now without the least compunction.

Charles reached out for Latifa and was about to tell her to run when the man drew a pistol from the inside pocket of his jacket. He pointed it at them, and smiled derisively. "So, Mr. Sherman, we meet again," he said in heavily Arabic-accented English. "I am very happy to welcome you to my country. It's only too bad that you will never leave it . . . alive, that is." The man looked up and down Wazeer Street to be sure they were not observed. "Now, you and your little friend there . . . ." He interjected in Arabic what Charles, hearing the word "Latifa," took to be a question, to which Latifa made no reply. The man continued in English, addressing Charles, "I want you both to come with me. We won't have to go too far. Walk ahead of me here on the sidewalk." He waved them along with the muzzle of the gun. "That's it, that's it," he rasped as they compliantly walked along. Every impulse in Charles's body told him to bolt, but he knew that, odds on, a trained gunman would need only two or three shots from the revolver to down his target, another to finish his work. And then there was Latifa. He couldn't let anything happen to her.

Farther down the block they came upon a narrow alley, in deep shadow cast by two large edifices that appeared to house apartments. The gunman muttered gruffly, "Turn here. That's right. Get going. Move." He let his captives advance well ahead, and Charles did not dare turn to look behind. As they moved down the alleyway, his eyes widened, working to adjust to the shade. Not far along, the alley turned into a small courtyard, bounded on three sides by dingy tenements, their grilled doorways firmly shut against the heat of the day. A crude, wooden staircase led to apartments on the higher levels. It was a sorry place in which to meet his end.

"Get in the back. Against that wall. Yes, over there. Now, turn around." Charles braced himself for the shot. He hoped death would come quickly. But their captor had other ideas in mind. He was like a sly fox captivated by his catch, batting it back and forth, mouthing it a bit, breaking it down, savoring it before finally consuming it. He would fuss a bit with his victuals.

"Why do you Jew-loving Americans attack Muslims?" The question seemed oddly removed from the time and place of the courtyard. With a flourish of the pistol, the man enforced his demand for an answer.

"Why do you think I'm American?"

"Mr. Sherman, we have a complete file on you."

"You probably know the color of my eyes."

"Actually, Mr. Sherman, we know a lot more about you than you'd ever imagine. We knew all along where you were staying in Paris although we didn't expect that you'd discover our people so soon. We almost lost track of you for a while, but of course Professor Shihabi underestimated our technical capability."

"How were you able to do it?" Charles reflected that he knew only part of the answer.

"It was simple enough. From the start, we knew your every step. After you cleverly arranged for Mrs. Shihabi to escape the net we had set for her in Saudi Arabia, we began monitoring her telephone conversations from Saudi Arabia."

"How did you do that?" Keep him talking, Charles told himself.

"It's thanks to your own American surveillance technology."

"What?" Charles replied in disbelief. He would indulge the man's braggadocio.

"Sure. Your own government uses it to monitor telephone conversations in your own country. And of course your Pentagon shares the technology with friendly security agencies around the world, including the Saudi Ministry of Defense. Lucky for us, we have our friends in Saudi too. And our friend Ali helped us listen to Mrs. Shihabi's cell phone conversations, you know, when she was in Saudi Arabia—even, Mr. Sherman, when you called her from your New York office with Professor Shihabi. We recorded the whole conversation. I almost had to laugh. You really did make some empty promises to her, all those lies about going to America. You *are* pretty naïve, you know."

Charles ignored the insult. "Well, then how did you track us all to Talloires?"

"Again, thanks to your own American technology. Ali made sure that we could track Professor Shihabi's—what is it?—oh yes, XzPhone. Quite simply, once we determined that he had GPS, we tied into his cell phone. After that, we knew where he was every time he made a phone call. It wasn't that hard," the gunman said proudly. His pleasure at lording it over his victim was apparent. "You really did deceive Mrs. Shihabi, though."

Keep him talking, Charles thought. Needle the man. Make him think. Make him respect the human being at the business end of the gun. It was what self-defense counselors always advised. "Not at all," Charles replied. "We in America are a haven for all kinds of people. We welcome everyone to our country," Charles replied, "and that includes Jews and Muslims as well as Christians, Buddhists . . . whatever. Except for terrorists, of course."

"What you in America call 'terrorists' are just defending us in the name of the Most Merciful Allah."

"They're killing a lot of innocent people."

"Don't tell me that your puppet Israel isn't killing innocent people—and they are my people, my brothers and sisters in Islam." The man waved the pistol in his left hand and glared. It was clear that he had heard the arguments before, Charles surmised, but maybe for the first time from the mouth of an infidel at his mercy. It was high-stakes poker. Charles didn't dare break his stare into the man's hateful eyes.

Charles suddenly realized that Latifa wasn't beside him. In the duskiness of the alley, his sun-soaked eyes couldn't pick up her amorphous shape. And the man, so focused on his conversation with Charles, hadn't noticed. Charles began to hope that perhaps Latifa had escaped or was at least out of harm's way. He braced himself and, trying to buy time—to come up with a way to outwit the gunman—continued prodding him.

"The most *evil* one of all is your Saddam Hussein," Charles fairly shouted, his voice echoing around the courtyard. "That bastard has done everlasting harm to your country and its people. Why do you permit him to do this to you?"

The gunman's eyes widened in rage, and the furrow in his forehead deepened. Charles sensed the man's trigger finger tighten, and he wondered if he might have gone too far.

"Saddam is the protector, the savior of our country," the gunman croaked angrily. "Without him—" His words were cut short as a mass of black cloth descended from behind him—over his head and face, and tight around his wounded neck.

Latifa! Charles thought. He had planned on rescuing her, but she had come to *his* rescue. Tensed as he was, Charles tried to sidestep the bullet that he knew would come, but he felt a sting, then a throb, as it struck the upper part of his left arm. The man tried to fling off the cloth, but Latifa held on even more firmly, keeping the cloth tight against the man's injured neck. Suddenly the man reached behind him, flung Latifa away and with her the folds of cloth enveloping him.

Charles launched himself at the gunman, knocking him off his feet, and grabbed desperately at the man's left hand clenching the gun. With a supreme effort he caught it, forcing it away and to the ground. He knocked the hand again and again into the paving stones until the gunman let go of the weapon and it clattered away. "Latifa," Charles cried. "Latifa, get the gun." Then he sat squarely on the man's chest and pushed his hands against the gunman's throat. The man squealed in pain, and Charles struck him once squarely in the jaw. It was enough to quiet him, and he lay on his back, breathing heavily.

"Where have you taken Fatima?" Charles asked fiercely.

"To the police station."

"You lie." Charles squeezed the man's neck until he roared again with pain.

"No, no," the man gurgled. "The Woman's Prison."

"Which one? Give me a name."

"Al Rashad."

From his years of reading the poker faces of his fellow dealmakers opposite him at the negotiating table, Charles sensed that his adversary was again lying. Charles pushed hard on the man's neck, until bloody phlegm gurgled from his throat and, along with it, some words. "Al Khatabi," the man choked out.

"Where?" Charles asked again to be sure.

"Al Khatabi Women's Prison."

"What floor?"

"Three."

"Are you sure?"

"Yes."

"Latifa, go get rope, wire, anything to tie him up."

"Yes, I do," she responded quickly. "I come back. No problem." She picked herself up and ran back down the alley. Within a few seconds, she returned. "I forget abayah," she said. It was caught under the man's right leg. She pulled the cloth away, flung it over her head, and darted away.

Charles gazed down at the mangled face of the man who would have killed him, who now appeared to lapse into unconsciousness—brought on, Charles surmised, by the suppurating wound in the man's neck, the weight of Charles's body on the man's chest, and the trauma of their struggle. Charles adjusted his weight slightly, and the man moaned in pain. He would be out of commission for a good long while, Charles reflected.

Latifa had saved him, saved them both. She was too clever for words. She had sized up a situation that had seemed hopeless. She had pursued the only available avenue to their deliverance. She had summoned the strength that apparent weakness affords. And she had wielded the only weapon she had—her abayah. Fatima would have been proud of her.

Fatima. Still straddling his unconscious adversary, Charles began to wonder how he could ever hope to save her, now that she was in the hands of their pursuers—very likely even being tortured by them. But she would never talk. By now, they would have concluded that they would have to kill her. His only hope was to somehow reach her in time. He reached down and looked at his watch. It was two thirty. Where was Latifa? He began to worry about her. Perhaps Mukhabarat had picked her up too.

A good twenty minutes after she left, Latifa returned with a long, hemp camel halter. She had found it in the souk, which had all but closed for business for the afternoon. With Latifa's help, Charles wrapped it around the gunman's wrists, looped it a few times around his feet, and secured it to his neck, which had begun to ooze blood. The man didn't utter a sound, apparently having fallen into a coma. The binding wasn't pretty, Charles told himself, but it was all they could do, and it should hold for several hours. When they had finished, Latifa again arranged her trusty abayah around her shoulders. Before she could drape it over her head, Charles caught her eye and smiled at her. "You wield a mean abayah," he said. She looked at him quizzically. She didn't understand.

"I mean, thank you for saving my life." With her veil no less, Charles again mused. Her weapon of choice. Latifa smiled proudly.

"Welcome—I mean—you welcome. I think mama. She help me. Now we go help her." He reached out and rested his right hand on her shoulder. Then they turned to head back down the alley and onto Wazeer

Street. He felt a trickle of blood on his left hand and reached to touch the sleeve, which was soaked in blood.

"Not so fast, Mr. Sherman." Charles recoiled at the croaky voice that seemed to come out of nowhere. "You see, as they say in my country, when you strike the camel, it always finds a way to bite you back."

Charles froze in his steps and did an about-face. There, some twenty feet away, the still-bound gunman lay on his side. But in his bloody right hand, he held a small but lethal-looking device that he now pointed at Charles. The man must have been conscious all the while, Charles thought. He must have slipped his hand out of its bandage, slipped his bindings, and reached a holster hidden somewhere on his leg.

"It's a ricin pellet gun—very effective, I might add, at short range. You'll barely feel it, Mr. Sherman. Once it bites, you'll have two minutes to beg forgiveness from All Merciful Allah before you descend into everlasting damnation."

Charles had heard of the spring-loaded ricin gun. It was the killing device of preference for the professional assassins of the diplomatic world. It projected into its target a tiny but extremely potent deposit of poison, so tiny that the pellet's point of entry into the body could rarely be found and so deep that it could not be extricated before the victim died.

Charles decided to continue his tactic of distracting his captor. "Allah forbade killing of innocent people. The Holy Koran clearly says that."

"To be sure. But you, Mr. Sherman, you and your brother Americans, are far from innocent. You not only blaspheme the Most Holy One, you massacre Muslim women and children. So, it is my honor, my sacred duty, to . . . ."

Charles felt the deadly pellet coming, and closed his eyes. A sound like a gunshot shattered the quiet of the courtyard, reverberating against the cement walls of the enclosed space. He mentally felt himself all over, wondering where, in what body part, the ricin pellet had lodged. He suddenly thought of Sarah, and a flood of shame passed over him. He should never have left the sanctuary of their sheltered lives. She would never forgive him for this.

When a split-second later he blinked back open his eyes, he was astounded to see the gunman sprawled in the dirt of the yard, blood gushing from a massive wound in his forehead. A few feet away Latifa pulled off her abayah and came over to Charles. She handed the still-smoking pistol to him. "I sorry. He say you. He no look me. I no am. He no see." She held up the black cloth, which had a neat round hole in its center. "I shoot . . . from abayah." She calmly stood before him, trustingly looking him in the eyes. Then she began to cry. It was the cry of a twelve-year-old who had come of age.

Suddenly angry shouts emanated from one of the higher apartments. The staircase creaked as those whose afternoon peace had been disturbed by the commotion in the courtyard came down to investigate. Bare legs and sandaled feet appeared on the stairs. Charles put his hand on Latifa's shoulder. "We have to go. Okay?"

"Yes," she replied. "We go find mama."

The two hurried back down the alley and onto Wazeer Street, which neighboring buildings had begun to throw into partial shadow. They ran along for several blocks before he was sure that the courtyard's inhabitants hadn't pursued them. As they strode along, Charles put his thumb into the air and said, "Again Latifa, you saved me, my life. You shoot good—very good." He made his fingers as if they were firing a pistol. "In America, you could enter tournaments, competitions." He didn't think she understood, but he grinned at her anyway, and she smiled back at him.

After a few minutes, Latifa came closer to him as if she wanted to tell him something. Finally she said, "I play game, video. All my time. Uncle Abdeljelil, my uncle, he show me. I good player."

"I'm sure you are," Charles responded, laughing. "I'm sure of it."

Although his left arm felt as it had when he was young and his father scored a direct hit in their shadowboxing games, the bleeding seemed to have subsided. He was sure that the bullet had passed clean through. Nevertheless, he felt that he should secure his arm until he could have it looked at. He directed Latifa into the shadows of an alleyway. "Latifa, let me have your abayah a second." She quickly pulled it from her head, and handed it to him. He tore off a long strip of the cloth, which he wrapped around the wound. "That'll hold it for a while," he reassured himself.

After steadily walking for about an hour, occasionally moving into the shadows when cars or trucks passed by, they came upon an imposing stone and red brick structure, which dominated a large square bordered by government buildings.

"Al Khatabi," Latifa said, drawing back the folds of her abayah to point to the edifice. "Prison for woman. Mama there."

It now being late afternoon, Charles decided to wait until dusk could cloak his approach to the prison and to allow office workers in the neighboring buildings to head home for the night. Plus, it would give him time to figure out what to do.

"Go, over there," he said, pointing to a shady, tree-filled park at the other end of the square. He took Latifa's arm and directed her to a crude stone banquette, where they sat side by side, looking out on the wide esplanade. Latifa took off her abayah, draping it around her thin shoulders. Entirely self-composed, she gazed at him with a directness that bordered on boldness. She gave him a knowing half-smile that seemed all at once fearless and daring, as if he were her co-conspirator on a school lark. In the flickering shadows, her face reflected an intense beauty— Fatima's air of acute intelligence tempered by a sweetness of disposition, rare for a child of twelve.

"Your mother has given me many adventures," Charles said, smiling back at her.

"Me too," Latifa said, cocking her head in a way that made him think of Fatima. "She different. Not normal. I think so."

"She's a good person," he said, endowing more feeling to the words than he had intended.

"I know."

"Where is she? What floor?" Charles remembered that the gunman had told them the third floor.

"I think she on three floor," Latifa said. "Where I go see her. Where big women stay."

In the early evening, the third floor was ablaze with light. Interrogation was not a nine–to–five business, Charles mused. "They're probably questioning her now," he muttered to Latifa, but she did not respond. She sat quietly, looking straight ahead across the hundred yards or so toward the prison, swinging her spindly legs back and forth, back and forth, under the bench. She seemed engulfed in thought, and he decided not to trouble her further with questions. Each time a car passed on the square, he would lower his head, sometimes pretending to massage his forehead so as to conceal his face. Each time he would refocus his eyes on the imposing, perhaps unassailable, prison across the huge square. Once his eyes fell upon the statue of a military figure, unmistakably that of Saddam Hussein standing erect, arm extended in paternalistic gesture, in the square's center. Iraq's national hero, Charles reflected. At least for some Iraqis. Maybe their Founding Father. Their George Washington.

Latifa, seated beside him, broke the silence. "What you do?" she asked in a tremulous voice.

"Latifa, I just don't know. It looks mighty difficult." He paused. "But we'll figure something out."

What would the great martial artists, the famous swordsman Miyamoto Musashi, have done? he wondered. Outnumbered two hundred to five in the epic battle of Hitari-mayashi, he and his fellow swordsmen had managed to slay forty well-armed and well-trained soldiers to every one of theirs. It was more than a matter of timing, he reflected. To succeed, the act had to be one of pure and utter arrogance—unexpected and decisive.

A plan was beginning to form in his mind. After what seemed an interminable wait, dusk began to spread itself across the sky. In the west the sun's curious alchemy turned its yellow gold into a molten silver fringing the night sky, while a rosy haze suffused the gathering darkness above the prison walls.

"Let's go," Charles murmured. Latifa hoisted the strap of her radio over her shoulder, then drew her abayah up to her head and once again framed her gleaming face. They walked slowly through the park, crossed the avenue, and stood in the shadows of a colonnaded building abutting the square.

He had a chance, he reflected. One godawful chance to save Fatima's life. If they had not already killed her.

FORTY-SEVEN

Women's Prison
Baghdad
Late afternoon, Wednesday
Oct. 9, 2002

The room was practically devoid of detail. Windowless white walls. A solitary light bulb hanging at the end of a black electrical cord from the acoustic-tiled ceiling. A mirror covered the entire far wall. It was probably two-way, she thought, to let others observe the prisoners' torments. Standing before her was a man in a black suit. His coarse, pitted face seemed too large for his wiry body. She sat, tall and proud, on a straight-backed wooden chair in the center of the room.

From deep in her mind, she unearthed the memory of another time she had sat in a chair similar to this one. Was it in this same room? The same interrogator? At the beginning, she had dreaded these wit-matching sessions: the interrogator's questions always at the ready, his steady pressure of innuendo, his relentless abuse, and his tacit, but ever real, threat of pain or of death. Against it, she would project a total indifference to her fate, caring not one whit whether she lived or died.

It had toughened her, her earlier time of torture, a period of almost three months. Her body was muscled and strong, her mind resilient, deft even in distress, and suffused with a deep calm. She was no longer in a realm of implicit resistance but in a country of absolute acceptance. She would acclaim whatever Fate had decided for her. And if they killed her, at least she would have that last flush of joy that the dying experience when they have finally quieted hope and relish the comfort of certainty.

She faced her tormentor without the slightest intimation of fear. "I pity you," she said derisively, gazing into his vacuous eyes. "You have no soul. You already are dead. You are just waiting for death to come take you into her fat arms."

The first slap, more like a punch, struck the left side of her face. "You will not speak except to answer my questions."

"I will give you no information," she said. "You will have to torture me."

"We are not going to torture you, you see."

His response took her by surprise, and for a half-second she entertained a fantasy that Abdeljelil once again had come to her rescue.

"Why would we torture you? We know everything," the man snarled. "We know, for example, that you and your friend—what is his name? Charles, yes, Charles Sherman—tried to kill one of our people in France. We know that you came back to Iraq to take your daughter Latifa with you. You see, . . . Mrs. Shihabi," he addressed her scornfully, "you can't hide anything from us."

"You know nothing."

He hit her face again, harder this time, bloodying her lip. "You forget who we are." The man looked at himself in the mirror, and a vile smile crept over his face. She was sure now that, behind the mirror, someone was indeed observing her interrogation. Then he turned back to her. "Your friend Ibrahim told us everything. Of course we had to work on him awhile before he would cooperate. It took us a little time, but he eventually came clean. Too bad he wasn't strong enough to bear up under our methods of persuasion."

The sadistic methods of depraved minds, Fatima thought. "May Allah never forgive you for this," she breathed between clenched teeth.

"It is you whom Allah will not forgive. It is our right and duty to exact our vengeance. You are a traitor. You have defiled your country, and you have deliberately flouted the laws of Islam."

"It is not against the laws of Islam to tell the truth."

The man angrily turned away and began to pace up and down before her. "Mrs. Shihabi, you are an enemy of Muslims just as you are an enemy of Iraq. Ibrahim told us how you sent foreign newspapers your shameless lies about our country. And we know how you were going to reveal state secrets about our weapons to the Americans." He paused to puff at his cigarette. "Oh," he added as an afterthought, "in case you're worried about it, nobody else will be disclosing those secrets either. Do you recall when you spoke with Mr. Sherman by telephone about the lady who gave you those papers?"

Fatima couldn't hide her surprised look. She hadn't expected this.

"Well, a few days after your conversation she had an unfortunate accident. She fell into a grinder used by the laboratory to refine certain materials. She got a little too close to it, I'm afraid. And in a day or so there will be no one else left to tell the weapons inspectors." The man smiled again at the observer concealed behind the mirror.

Curious though she was about how they obtained their information, she disdained giving them the pleasure of telling her. "You barbarians," she muttered, spitting at the man. Some of her spittle landed on his polished black shoes.

The man looked down at his shoes. Then he raised his head and snarled, "Worthless vermin." He strode to the door, opened it, and looked back at her. "We have something planned for you this evening that you're going to find, shall we say, interesting. This, Mrs. Shihabi, will be the last time you ever come to visit us." He went out, slamming the door behind him.

Fatima composed herself, gingerly felt her swollen lip, and calmly smoothed her hair. She thought of Latifa and Charles, both probably now dead at the hands of the gunman with the bandaged neck. A swell of remorse buffeted her, then swept over her, overcoming her, crushing her spirits, so strong that it almost made her sick. In the end she had failed almost everyone who had tried to aid her, first her dear brother and then Charles Sherman, a man she had truly loved, and now her daughter, who meant more to her than anyone, anything else in her life. How her egotistical effort to improve her lot in life had come to nothing, indeed had entwined others in her own foredoomed fate and destroyed them too.

Fatima thought of her father. His soft brown eyes. His luxuriant beard, at which he was continually pulling. Intrepid in his own way. And *inshallah*, she would meet him in paradise. He had died proud, she recalled. She tried to remember a poem she had written about him just after his death. About the old rifle she had found in his closet. She had entitled it "The Revered Rifle."

The night my father died
I found a rifle in his things.
With trembling arms, I raised it before me,
Wond'ring what its awful purpose was,
Since, by Allah, he had known no fear
While daring danger all his life.

My father fought the battles fair
Against fierce Turks, our tribes,
And, as a child, the English crown.
Feted, ribboned and renowned,
A fighter heedless of his fate,
Mindful only of his charge,
He advanced regularly through the ranks.

Fearless he was in all his cruel contending.
And so he was in my encounters with him—
Moral, reasoned (even heated) quarrels.
He stroked his beard,
And creased his brow,
Calmly challenging accepted facts,
Convictions adamantly held.

For his whole life he set aside his gun,
The metal smooth, black, silken
The roundness of its barrel

Coldly shining.
Primed to fire.

Woe betide his daughter now,
For I . . . I lack my father's arms,
To use in extremes of need.
I just possess this crude device,
A well-thumbed pen—
A pen with which to meet the Others.

Fatima folded her hands in her lap and, sighing with resignation, waited for the interrogator's return.

FORTY-EIGHT

Women's Prison
Baghdad
Early evening, Wednesday
Oct. 9, 2002

Latifa," Charles whispered, squinting to see her face in the gathering dusk. "Do you know anyone who has a car?"

"Yes, Uncle Abdeljelil."

"You mean your mother's older brother?"

"Yes."

"A good man. Your mother told me about him. But isn't he at your home now?"

"No, he now work. Office not far. He go home seven."

Charles held his watch up to the light from the square: 6:45. It would be close.

"Latifa, if your mother is to be saved, we all must help her. You too." Charles smiled at Latifa, although he could now barely see her face. "Here is what I want you to do. I want you to go to your uncle. Right now. Run. Run as fast as you can. Ask him to come here. Right now. With you in his car. See that little road over there?" He pointed to a dark alley, about thirty yards away, leading into the square, now nearly empty. "Wait there, with your uncle, in the shadows. Don't let anyone see you. Your mother and I will come for you. Do not leave—for any reason. Do you understand?"

"Yes," she answered quickly.

"Oh," Charles added, "may I borrow your radio for a while?" Latifa pulled the radio's strap from her shoulder and handed it to him.

"Don't worry, I'll give it back to you."

"And do you have any money?" He rubbed his fingers together. "Just a few coins."

Latifa reached into a small purse from under her abayah and gave him three dinar coins. Then, she glided toward the lane, keeping to the unlit spaces beneath the archways.

With his fingers, Charles dug out a cobblestone from the sand at the edge of the square, feeling its cool round shape in his hand. Then, staying in the shadows of the buildings around the square, he furtively made his way toward the front of the Women's Prison. As he drew closer, he could see two fatigue-clad soldiers, carrying automatic rifles that looked like Kalashnikov AK 47's, standing at ease at the bottom of a long staircase. The stairs led to a Grecian entrance with a revolving glass door.

Charles positioned himself behind an imposing fountain, just in front of a small office building at the side of the square, from which he could observe the comings and goings from the prison. He waited for about ten minutes before he concluded that the men, apparently on duty for the night, had no relief or rotation with others inside. Then one of the soldiers laughed, while the other flicked his cigarette butt into the street and then turned and went up the stairs and through the door. Maybe on a mission for Mother Nature, Charles mused. He would have only a matter of minutes. He slipped off his loafers and pushed them into the front of his shirt.

The remaining soldier, with the characteristic ease of Arab soldiers, leaned against his rifle, languidly gazing around the square. Another quiet evening on guard duty outside a Baghdad building that no sane person would try to break out of, much less into. He lit a cigarette.

As the soldier turned his gaze away from him, Charles moved swiftly—into the semi-shadows of a building adjoining the prison, about ten meters from where the soldier stood. Reaching into his pocket, Charles found the few dinars Latifa had given him. He threw one of them over the head of the soldier, aiming for the front of the office building on the other side of the prison. The coin hit the glass door, tinkling as it fell onto the sidewalk.

The soldier turned his head in the direction of the sound, automatically putting his hand on the stock of his weapon. Charles, now running as quietly as he could along the sidewalk, threw the other coin in the same direction. It too hit the front of the building, this time ricocheting between the door and the metal security grate that covered it. Suspicious, the soldier now turned his body toward the sound and raised his rifle slightly. Racing along, Charles had almost reached him before the soldier caught the sound of Charles's stockinged feet on the pavement. As the man turned to look behind him, Charles half threw, half shoved the cobblestone, which made a dull thump as it struck the man squarely in the temple. He tumbled onto the sidewalk, his rifle clattering as it fell beside him. Charles took it and dragged the man toward the building, where he propped the unconscious man behind a column.

Just as he reached the shadows, Charles glanced up the staircase and saw the glass revolving door begin to turn as the other soldier returned from his mission. The man looked around the front of the prison and then proceeded down the stairs to the street level.

"Psst," Charles whispered. "Psst." He then took Latifa's radio off his shoulder and flicked it on, projecting the melodious wail of an Arab chanteuse into the square. The soldier ambled over toward the building, grasping his Kalashnikov as one would a valise, muttering something in Arabic that Charles could not understand. As he passed the first column, he spied the splayed legs of the other soldier. He leaned as if to say a word to the recumbent soldier, and Charles, coming around the other side of the column, struck him hard with the butt of the first soldier's rifle.

FORTY-NINE

Women's Prison
Bayhdad
Early evening, Wednesday
Oct. 9, 2002

The man in the black suit was back in only a few minutes. As he closed the door to the room behind him, he said almost casually, "Yes, this you will find most interesting, Mrs. Shihabi." His puffy, porcine face came so close that she caught the whiff of cigarette smoke on his breath. "We know you, like all our visitors, know about old Mr. Pest–Killer."

She shivered almost perceptibly as she recalled a story she had once heard of a pesticide-soaked bag being placed over a torture victim's head.

"We have heard that you are very creative, and we thought that you would enjoy being the first to play a new, rather intriguing, game with us today. It is called Mr. Killer–Pest."

"You see, Mrs. Shihabi, this bag"—he held up a brown burlap sack—"holds seven kinds of scorpions, spiders, fire ants, chukka bugs, other poisonous insects, . . . that sort of thing. They are all quite venomous, you might say. They will make you very, very sick—unless they kill you, of course. Whether you die, or you lose your arm, or you just swell up depends on how long we keep your arm in the bag." He now stood before her, leering. "It's ingenious, eh?"

Practically frothing with malevolent delight, the man went on. "But, you see, in honor of your special visit, we have added one more killer–pest . . . fresh from Ethiopia. He's the puff adder. You might have heard of him too. He's the most poisonous snake in East Africa. One bite and your death is certain . . . usually within forty-eight hours if not sooner.

The toxins destroy your body from within. It essentially disintegrates within a day or two, you see."

"Who told you to do this?" Fatima asked.

"The highest authority. There is no higher authority save Allah himself. And it is he who has selected this special means to secure vengeance for your traitorous acts."

"Have you no conscience of your *own?*" She sensed that she might get to him.

Suddenly he stiffened as if pricked by an insult. He glanced at the mirror again. Then he turned abruptly and gazed at her. "Give me your arm."

Resigned, Fatima extended her right arm. The man quickly put the bag around it, pulling the drawstrings tightly above the elbow. He stepped away from her, then turned back to face her. Swelling his chest portentously, he said, "Madame Shihabi, I am pleased to inform you that you have been honored this evening by the presence of a most distinguished spectator at your fateful game with Mr. Killer–Pest. And please, . . . please, Madame Shihabi, play the game well. Your spectator does not like to be disappointed." The man nodded in the direction of the mirror.

Fatima trembled as she glanced at the double-sided mirror, catching the outline of her spare body erect in the chair. For a few moments she stared at her reflection, as if seeing herself in a dream, wondering who might be looking back at her, taking in such lamentable proceedings. Then she turned her eyes back to the evil contrivance affixed to her arm.

All of a sudden, the bag seemed to come alive. Its contours stiffened, then began to crease, fold, then unfold, slowly circling around her arm. A muffled whir began to rise through the burlap, filling her ears. The sound lasted several minutes, then little by little it subsided. Just as the room became quiet again, she heard a hiss. A continuous, menacing hiss. A hiss redolent of malice and hate. It too stopped for no reason, and abruptly. Almost at once she felt a bite on her forearm, which surprised her with its hurt.

She felt faint. As she began to lose consciousness, she thought she heard a sadistic laugh from behind the mirror. She realized that she knew perfectly well who it was. Who it had to be.

FIFTY

Women's Prison
Baghdad
Evening, Wednesday
Oct. 9, 2002

Charles dragged both soldiers into the darkness of an alley alongside the building. The larger man groaned, and Charles hit him again, driving him deeper into unconsciousness. It would be hours before he awakened, Charles was sure. He removed the man's fatigue shirt and trousers, put them on over his own clothes, and donned the man's fatigue hat. He slipped his own loafers back on. Then he picked up the two Kalashnikovs and headed toward the front of the building, checked that his scuffle with the soldiers had gone unobserved, and bounded up the stairs toward the prison's entrance.

When he reached the glass doors, he peered through and saw that they opened onto a large lobby with a main desk at which a soldier sat dozing. At the lobby's rear was a metal grille door, presumably leading into the prison itself. A security camera, suspended from a fixture in the wall, covered the entrance. He would have to pass before the camera quickly and pray that whoever checked the half-dozen monitors in the lobby would fail to notice that he was carrying two weapons rather than one. He pulled the fatigue hat tight over his forehead and pushed through the door. Once inside, he mumbled a word to the soldier on duty, then came around his desk and crouched beside the man's chair, aiming one of the Kalashnikovs at the man's stomach. Seeing the man stretch his foot to press a button on the floor, Charles kicked the foot away, then fiercely looked the man in the eyes. As their eyes locked, the man slowly raised his hands.

Charles glanced around to be sure no one had seen what had transpired. He then mimed opening the grille door with a key. The soldier leaned forward, opened a drawer, and took out a large ring with keys. Keeping the Kalashnikov trained at the soldier, Charles motioned him to move toward the locked door.

"Fatima Shihabi," Charles said softly, trying to give the words an Arab pronunciation. He sensed that the man understood. Just after he said the name, Charles could hear the whir of the camera as it gradually turned its focus from the entrance toward the rear of the lobby. Racing to the wall and reaching up with the other rifle, he wedged its stock in the mechanism, stopping it. He motioned the soldier to open the door. The man turned the key several times, then looked back at Charles as if for further instructions. Charles released the camera, ran to the door, and pushed himself and the soldier through. On the other side, Charles took the key and with the barrel of his rifle urged the man along.

They entered a long corridor, flanked by massive wooden doors. Administration, Charles surmised. As they passed a stairway, Charles pointed at it and showed three fingers. The man shook his head and motioned Charles to follow him. How could Latifa be wrong? Charles wondered. And the gunman in the courtyard had said the third floor too. Unless the third floor was where prisoners were interrogated. Or was it where they were detained? Losing confidence in his impromptu escort, Charles was about to stop him when they reached the end of the corridor, which was barred with a heavy metal grille, then another. Through them Charles could see row after row of prison cells around a large courtyard. He guided his finger to the trigger of one of the Kalashnikovs, remembering from his military school days to confirm that the trigger lock was in the off position.

A soldier guarded the antechamber between the two grilled doors. As they approached, Charles's escort, raising his hands, spoke in Arabic to the guard, who quickly lowered his weapon and took out another set of keys. He opened both sets of doors, and Charles, with the two men before him, forged on, past cells holding female prisoners, several of whom were veiled. A terrible stench of filth and rot and human waste filled his nostrils.

After they passed a half dozen cells, the second guard abruptly stopped. He took out a parcel of keys from a pocket in his shirt and opened the cell door. Charles motioned both men inside. In the dim light, he could barely make out the shapes of three women, all of them veiled, sitting with their backs against the rear wall of the cell. Another lay on a crude metal bed that projected from the wall.

The guards motioned toward the prostrate woman. Cradling her right arm before her, she raised her head weakly from the bed. At first Charles told himself that the frail, spiritless figure could not possibly be Fatima, that he had been tricked. The woman gazed at him, her eyes sunk in their sockets, each like a pool of black water at the bottom of a cistern.

"Charles," the woman said, her voice barely above a whisper.

When he heard her voice, so plaintive and frail, he was heartsick. He had never expected her to be in such a bad state, so soon after being imprisoned. "Are you able to walk?" he asked, keeping one of the weapons trained on the soldiers.

"I think so."

"We must go quickly."

She began to raise herself, then sank back on the bed and started to cry. "I cannot," she gasped through her tears.

"You *must* try . . . for your daughter."

A light flashed in her eyes. "Where is she?"

"She's waiting for us."

Fatima sat upright on the bed, began to stand, then swooned against Charles. "I'm a little dizzy."

As she leaned against him, one of the guards pushed away the rifle. With his fist, he hit Charles in the throat, just below his Adam's apple. Charles leaned forward, gasping for breath. The next punch landed near his eye, and he fell, smacking his head on the stone floor. Both soldiers leapt on him, and one knocked Charles's head against the floor. He felt himself begin the long, slow drift into oblivion.

Suddenly Charles felt yet another weight on top of his two assailants. His vision blurry, he vaguely discerned the outline of another figure tearing at the two men, scratching catlike at their eyes, ferocious in her pent-up rage, relentless and wrathful. For an instant the two soldiers recoiled as their veiled assailant pummeled them, and Charles found himself free to roll out from under them. As he did so, he spotted one of the Kalashnikovs lying a few feet from him. One of the soldiers saw it too, and as Charles reached for it, he lunged, pinning it under the two of them. They each tried to get to the trigger, and the soldier found it first. The rifle fired two bursts, shattering the stillness of the prison and echoing in the corridor. The bullets sprayed around the cell, ricocheting off its stone walls.

Charles felt a stab of pain in his left arm and knew at once that a ricocheting bullet had hit him, this time striking bone and nerve; except for a steady throb, he lost all feeling in his fingers. As he clutched at his arm, he felt the soldier's body atop him go limp. Charles pushed it away and rolled across the stone floor almost to the far wall, pulling the rifle with him. In the dusky light, he saw standing at the entrance to the cell the other soldier, who had finally subdued Charles's defender and found the second rifle. As the soldier aimed it in the half-light, Charles, with his right arm, raised the weapon on the floor beside him and triggered a burst of bullets. Their force blew the man's body through the doorway.

The muffled wail of alarms resounded through the prison.

Picking up the two rifles, Charles ran to Fatima, shouting. "Let's go!"

Fatima struggled to rise, and Charles half-lifted her from the bed, wincing from the pain in his left arm as he did so. Once out of the cell, Charles turned back to the three veiled figures, nodded, and said, "Thank you," knowing that they would probably never understand anything but his gesture. The figure in the middle nodded in return.

Outside the cell, they heard a strange, murmuring din reverberating through the prison. Hundreds of female voices resonated as one, a steady drone of sound, as if an airplane were passing overhead. The community of inmates had become aware that something they had never experienced before was happening: one of their number was escaping. On and on the cacophony echoed, as the female prisoners, many veiled, stretched their arms out through the bars of their cells into the corridor, now ululating words of supplication, of hope, as Charles and Fatima rushed along. When they reached the still unlocked doors to the prison section, Fatima suddenly slumped, barely conscious, clutching at Charles's right arm. He dropped one of the Kalashnikovs, lifted her over his right shoulder, and cradled the other weapon in the crook of his battered left arm. He found her surprisingly light. They charged through the gates into the administrative area of the prison.

"Uh—oh," Charles muttered as a soldier and a uniformed prison official emerged from an office on the right side of the long corridor. The soldier raised his rifle, and Charles pumped the trigger of his automatic weapon, killing the man instantly. The official threw himself onto the floor of the corridor. As they raced past, Charles spotted a soldier peering through the grille of the door to the prison lobby. Before the soldier could get off a shot, Charles fired but missed his target. As the soldier poked his weapon through the grille to return the fire, its barrel snagged on the grill, giving Charles the chance to fire again. The soldier fell where he had stood.

They found the grille door to the lobby locked, and Charles, balancing Fatima on his shoulder, leaned the rifle against the door, reached into his right pocket, and found the key. As he drew it out, another soldier appeared behind the grille and, with a malicious leer and sadistic slowness, leveled his weapon to fire pointblank at the two targets. Locking his eyes onto those of the soldier, Charles contorted his face into the fiercest mien in the kendoist's art. From deep in his throat came the fearsome cry of the kendo combatant. "*Ki-ai!*"

It was enough to startle the soldier and before he could squeeze off a round, Charles, with his good arm, angled the stock of his rifle through a slot in the grill and thrust it at the man's groin, in a swift kendo move that would have made Takeo Matsui proud. The man's weapon discharged harmlessly as he fell writhing on the floor of the lobby. Charles then fumbled to turn the key, but finally did so, and he and his burden finally reached the lobby, now eerily empty except for the groaning man holding his private parts. As Charles bent to relock the door, the man lunged for his weapon. Wielding the rifle stock again as lightly as a bamboo stave, Charles knocked him out with a single blow. He relocked the door, throwing the key into a corner.

A piercing alarm now shrieked through the prison, and from outside, in the streets of the city, came the distant whine of police sirens. When they reached the revolving door, Charles glimpsed a reflection in the glass of a soldier rising from behind the lobby desk, weapon raised. Charles quickly wheeled and fired once, the bullet striking the man in the shoulder, felling him. Other soldiers now milled in the corridor behind the locked door. As bullets careened all around him, he thrust himself through the door, Fatima's limp body over his shoulder.

Once outside, Charles could hear the sirens clearly now, just a few blocks away. Damn, damn, he said to himself. All Baghdad will be looking for us. They've most likely never had a prison breakout before—at least not from the Women's Prison. It was an edge, though only a slim one, he reflected.

At the top of the staircase, Charles slung the Kalashnikov over his left shoulder, his arm now entirely numb and virtually useless, and adjusted Fatima's body. Amazingly light, he thought again. So much energy and force in so slight a frame. As he descended to the street, he jostled her, and she moaned twice.

"Hold on, I'll get you help," he said. He wondered what was wrong with her. He would have to find a doctor between Baghdad and the border.

Charles and Fatima arrived at the alley just as the first police cars entered the square, their whirligig lights flashing off the statue of Saddam Hussein as they rounded the square. Latifa appeared after a few seconds.

"I want know it you. Uncle there," she said, pointing into the shadows. "How mama?" she asked, looking at the dark shape across Charles's shoulder.

"She is very sick. We've got to get her to a doctor. As soon as we can."

Abdeljelil got out of the car as they approached and helped Charles lay Fatima in the back seat, her head on Latifa's lap. Then standing by the open car door, he embraced Charles. "I hear many, many good thing. I hear you try get visa for Fatima, my sister. Latifa now say you save life of Fatima. You good man. You my brother too," he said gravely, kissing Charles on one cheek, then the other.

Touched by Abdeljelil's sincerity, Charles shook his hand warmly. Word travels fast in Arab families, Charles mused, although it surprised him that Omar hadn't mentioned being in contact with his family in Iraq. His thought was fractured by the wail of sirens outside the prison. The police would soon be on their trail. "Let's get out of here," he said, leaping into the passenger seat. Abdeljelil ran around the front of the car and threw himself behind the wheel.

After several attempts, the black Mercedes roared into life and, without lights, headed into the night—down alleys and lanes so dark and serpentine that it was impossible to know where they led, past the shadowed back walls of fine villas, apartments, office buildings, parking areas, occasionally verging into the penumbras of street lights on the main thoroughfares. Once a police car entered an alley far ahead of them, and they quickly turned off the route, forging on through other byways. Several times, Charles was sure that the road ended in a wall or a house, only to have Abdeljelil turn the wheel at the last possible moment and head down some new track, deeper and deeper into the darkness. They seemed to parallel the main road south of Baghdad, on which, once or twice, they saw the flashing lights of police cars, and Charles thought he heard the faint strains of sirens.

After an hour, they arrived at a raised escarpment that afforded a view back toward the city. Ablaze with lights now, it seemed to pulsate with iridescence, like a jar of fireflies shaken in the dark.

He looked back at Fatima. She had stopped moaning and now seemed in a deep sleep. A coma even, he thought. As they passed through a small village just south of Baghdad, he glimpsed her face under the solitary streetlight. It was a pasty gray, and her mouth was crimped tightly, as if she were trying to suppress a terrible pain.

"We must stop," Charles said to Abdeljelil. "Your sister needs a doctor. Her arm seems swollen. Maybe they injected her with poison."

"No doctor," he responded. "Uncle. Not far."

As the car rattled along on the washboard road, Charles felt his own arm throb with pain. He tried to raise it but couldn't. Though he believed the bleeding had stopped, a wide area still felt wet with blood.

They drove a few more kilometers. Then, the road dipped and seemed to follow the course of a deep wadi. Once, as the car bumped its way through a hamlet along the road, Charles saw the glow of a television set, surrounded by pickup trucks providing it power. As they drove on, the headlights caught a horse in its beams, sending it loping off into the scrub brush. Finally Abdeljelil slowed the car, and Latifa, who had fallen asleep with her mother's head in her lap, stirred in the back seat. He pulled off the road into a group of mud houses, arrayed around a railed corral, which enclosed two camels and a donkey. When he turned off the ignition, he left his headlights on for illumination.

"Al Kassim, our hamlet," Abdeljelil announced. "My Uncle Abu live here."

"Good. Good," Charles replied, giving the thumbs-up sign. Exhausted, he could think of nothing else to say that Abdeljelil or Latifa might understand.

Abdeljelil got out and, without knocking, pushed open the wooden door of one of the houses. After a few minutes, he came out and leaned in the car window.

"Okay. Come."

Charles tried to lift Fatima from the back seat before he remembered his left arm. Wincing, he called Abdeljelil, who gingerly picked her up, cradling her in his arms, and carried her through the door into a small courtyard in front of a one-story mud house. At its door, an elderly man, attired in an immaculate white thobe and a red-checkered ghutra greeted them, motioning his nephew to carry Fatima into the main room of the house. As Charles passed him, he said a few words in Arabic, appearing to address Charles.

"Abu say you stay here when you want," Abdeljelil said, as he entered the dimly lit room, his unconscious sister in his arms. He went over to a rude wooden bed against the far wall and gently laid her atop it.

"Ask him if there is a doctor nearby," Charles said.

Abdeljelil and his uncle spoke in Arabic for a few minutes.

"He say village not far had doctor. Now Jordan. No doctor here. Maybe one hour. Road very bad. He near Najaf."

"She won't make it. Ask him if he has medicine, anything," Charles said, half in anger and frustration. "She seems to be having a reaction to a poison, as if it was put into her arm. Look, look at it." He pulled back the sleeve of her blouse.

Abu came close and studied Fatima's arm, now grotesquely distended, in the light of a kerosene lantern. He examined its glossy skin, cupping his hands around its areas of dark purple. The swelling seemed to reach high on her upper arm. After several minutes, his face took on an air of profound concern. He shook his head several times and spoke in Arabic to his nephew in a doleful tone. Then Abdeljelil turned to Charles. "He say viper. Bad viper. You can see bite. Very bad poison."

"Can you get anti-venom, medicine, anything?" Charles asked desperately.

The two men spoke again for several minutes. Finally Abdeljelil. "No many medicine. Not here. More, you go Najaf."

"She's fading, she's dying," Charles answered. In the few minutes while they were talking, Fatima's condition had appeared to worsen. Her breathing had become more labored. Her brother placed his hand on her forehead, and Fatima groaned. She began to turn from side to side. Delirious, she even tried to get out of the bed. As if wrestling with death itself, Charles thought. After several minutes of frantically tossing back and forth, her body relaxed, and she opened her eyes. She looked first at her brother and then at Charles. Her eyes glinted from the light of the lantern, which Abu had put on a rough-hewn table by the bed.

"I'm sorry, Charles," she said, her voice weak.

"Just rest. You're going to be okay."

"There's a saying in Arabic, you know," she said, her dark, deep-set eyes shining. "Autumn love has no future." She winced a little from the effort of saying it.

"Yes, I know, you once told me. I don't believe it, though. Love is timeless. You've taught me that. You don't know where or when you might find it. It's like a lost penny. You never know where it will turn up."

"You'd make a good poet, you know," she said, pausing to collect her strength, " . . . I mean a *feminist* one, of course," she added weakly, her eyes crinkling.

"You're going to have to help me." Charles smiled lovingly.

With her good arm she drew a scrap of paper from a pocket of her shirt. It fell on the caked mud floor. As Charles picked it up, she said, "It's for you . . . to read later." She began to cough uncontrollably.

Then she closed her eyes and was silent for a time. Latifa uttered a sob, then caught her breath.

Fatima slowly opened her eyes again. "Look after Latifa," she said to Charles with sudden urgency.

"We'll look after each other. She's saved my life a couple of times already." Charles took Fatima's good hand in his and pressed it reassuringly.

"She is my treasure," she said, gazing at her daughter.

"I know," Charles said.

"And don't let her wear any veils," Fatima added, teasing again. Spoken with the certainty of death, Charles felt.

"You mean visible or invisible?" He grinned at her.

"You know what I mean."

"I think I do."

"And don't *you* wear a veil either."

"Don't worry. They won't fit me."

"I mean the invisible ones." She began coughing again, and he saw a spot of blood appear on the blanket.

"I know." He paused, sure now that she was dying. "You showed me how to take mine off." Her smile tried to break into a laugh. Her dark eyes gazed at him.

"You taught *me* . . . a few things too, you know." She paused to get her breath. "Like how one person's love can make all the difference in your life."

"I don't know that I made any difference in yours," he said with a touch of irony.

"Your love made me live in a way I had never before. I never knew how to love a man until I met you." The exertion of speaking brought another round of coughing, this time longer than the others. Charles wiped a trickle of blood from her mouth.

"My love for you has changed me a lot too, you know, . . . in some pretty basic ways."

"You are a good man, Charles. I do . . . love . . . you . . . ." she said, her voice trailing away.

"I love you too, Fatima," Charles said, taking her hand again and squeezing it. He leaned over her and kissed her forehead, coldly moist from the poison in her body. The kiss seemed to rekindle something within her, and she turned her eyes toward Latifa. Fatima spoke to her in Arabic, and Latifa listened intently, nodding several times. Once Fatima shifted her eyes toward Charles, and he could tell she was speaking about him. He could only guess at the nature of their exchange, but from the fervor in their bright eyes and the look of utter devotion on their faces, he knew that mother and daughter had communed, for the last time, in the most profound and loving way.

Latifa leaned over her mother and kissed her cheek. With that, Fatima closed her eyes and breathed a long sigh, as if she had freed herself from some enormous weight. Her body relaxed, her features became placid, and the lines in her forehead smoothed. Charles held her hand a long time, finally bowing his head and letting his tears fall freely. Latifa again leaned over the bed, kissed her mother's forehead, and then, resting her head on her mother's strangely unmoving chest, released her tears in heartsick sobs. Abdeljelil and his uncle stood silently, heads bowed, at the foot of the bed, their profound grief concealed by their impassivity.

For most of the next hour, they stood by Fatima's deathbed, gazing for the last time on her beautiful visage, her olive complexion now blanched and ashen, her lips still as in a photograph but pursed as if about to make one last point in the ongoing argument she had carried on with life, or, perhaps, about to recite one or two more lines of verse, before she embarked on her long journey, her leave-taking for another country. It was a face in which one could read peace, and Charles was consoled to know that never again would her soaring spirit be trammeled by the torments of her oppressors. She truly was free at last.

Without acknowledging the others, Charles bowed his head one last time, placed his lips against Fatima's cold forehead, and pressed her lifeless fingers against his own. Then wordlessly he walked to the door of the abode, cracked it open far enough to let himself through, and gently shut it behind him. Once outside, he was startled to find himself in total darkness except for a crescent moon low on the horizon and a luxurious tapestry of stars stretched across the dome of the sky far, far above him. It was the night sky of the desert that Fatima must have seen every night of her childhood, he reflected, the stars speaking to her and her father like old friends. At one with the earth and sky, she too would have been spellbound by the immensity and grandeur of the scene, her imagination fired by such a panorama of matchless beauty, even as the same night air would have chilled her.

He held his wounded arm in the crook of his good one and slowly let his feet take him away from the house, past the car, and onto the rutted road. He stopped, glancing back at the dark outline of the house, a sliver of lamplight squinting from a missing chink in its mud wall. For a long time he stood, his eyes drawn upward, deep into the vast universe of stars above him. At last, with tears streaming down his face, his heart bursting, he flung out his good arm heavenward and choked and howled in rage and pain and sorrow: "Why? . . . Why? . . . Why?"

He felt his body, wracked with sorrow, collapse beneath him, and he fell to his knees, his hand still high, as if beseeching the impassive heavens. He bowed his head prayerfully and then threw himself onto the desert track. The dirt and sand tasted cold and acrid as they mixed with his tears.

FIFTY-ONE

Kassim, Iraq
Thursday, Oct. 10, 2002

The morning after Fatima's death, an elderly woman came from the nearby village and washed Fatima's body, then wrapped it in a coarse white shroud. Later that day, in keeping with Muslim tradition, Charles carried it to a shallow, unmarked grave that Abdeljelil had dug on the upward slope of the wadi. They held a brief ceremony, during which Abdeljelil, in a low, dirgelike chant, recited a passage from the Koran. Remembering the paper Fatima had given him, Charles reached for it in his jacket with his left hand. Bolts of intense pain passed up and down his left arm. His upper arm was a mass of clotted blood. Around it had coalesced the cloth of Latifa's abayah he had used as a dressing. Wincing, he cradled his left arm across his chest.

He again reached for the paper, this time with his right hand, and pulled it out of his jacket pocket. He read aloud the lines of a poem she had shakily penned—when and where he could not imagine.

"Enrich me with the flood of love that wells with you
    and take pity on this tinder in the fire your passion has
    kindled,
And if I ask to see you in reality,
    grant it, and do not answer: 'Thou shalt not see!'
O my heart, you promised me patience in this love,

Therefore endure, though you be anguished and
   tormented,
For love is life, and if you perish in its rapture
   your reward is to die and be forgiven.

'*Umar ibn al Farid*'

Then they buried her. Charles placed alongside her body a small
wooden box, with the poem she had written in their hotel room in Annecy. Latifa placed a handful of sand on the shroud, then remained a long
time at the side of the grave. Abdeljelil and his uncle bowed beside the
grave, reciting prayers as they slowly filled it with sand and rocks. Finally
Charles put his good arm around Latifa's thin shoulders and drew her
gently toward him. To be sure, he thought, theirs was going to be a long
and profound relationship. He gave the girl a reassuring squeeze.

"We must go. Soon." Abdeljelil's deep-set eyes glinted at him with
concern.

Latifa raised her head and with a quizzical expression asked her uncle
something in Arabic. He shook his head determinedly and gazed across
the desolate landscape, a forlorn look in his eyes. Latifa glanced at
Charles, then looked away. Charles knew better than to ask the nature of
the exchange but guessed that it concerned him. He could only surmise
that Abdeljelil's absence from his work and from his family's villa, immediately after his sister's escape from prison, would be noticed. And Saddam's vengeance could be swift and merciless.

FIFTY-TWO

Sahra al Hijarah Desert, Iraq
Early morning, Friday
Oct. 11, 2002

It took them the better part of the night to get to the border with Saudi Arabia. They bushwhacked across the seamless expanse of desert flanking the highway south, picking their way past escarpments jutting out of the desolate flatness, rejoining the road only when their impromptu route proved impassable or when they had to cross a bridge over the occasional wadi. And when the lights of an approaching vehicle loomed over the horizon, Abdeljelil quickly extinguished their headlights and turned the car back into the brush. With infinite finesse he coaxed the Mercedes along, slowing to a crawl to traverse more vegetated terrain, from time to time backing up to go around an outcropping, now and then diverging far from the highway down timeless camel trails that he ferreted out, more by instinct, Charles sensed, than because of some past excursion through the region. Along the way they came upon a large city far off on the horizon to the east, its ambient light suffusing the desert for miles around. Charles thought he saw light glinting from the dome of a mosque, a sparkling diadem at the center of a luminous setting.

"Al Najaf. Special place. Holy Ali. Husband of Fatima, daughter of Prophet Muhammad." Abdeljelil said, his smooth, handsome face radiating pride. Charles nodded appreciatively. Expecting a comment from Latifa, he turned and saw her curled on the back seat, in a deep slumber.

His left arm began to throb again, and he felt blood trickle down his forearm. "How far to Saudi Arabia?" he asked, pronouncing the words precisely so that Abdeljelil could understand.

"Three, four hours. We go slowly."

"No problem. You drive very good, . . . very good."

Abdeljelil beamed at him.

But the trip took almost seven hours. Seven hours of bumps, jolts and swerves, which jangled their nerves even as they crunched their bones. Several times along the way, Charles thought he would pass out from the excruciating pain in his left arm. He worried that the wound would start bleeding again, but his makeshift bandage held. Finally they saw the several buildings and gated barricades of the border crossing to Saudi Arabia. Abdeljelil again switched off the headlights, and they silently studied the complex. Charles heard a rustle in the back seat and felt Latifa's breath on his neck.

"They will know who I am," suddenly came an Arabic-accented voice out of the darkness.

Charles at once caught the drift of Abdeljelil's thoughts and realized the import of his earlier discussion with Latifa.

"We go through the desert," Charles said insistently.

"No. I stay in my country . . . with my family, with my wife, my children. I leave, I cannot come back. Saddam kill me."

"We can walk."

"No. Too dangerous. They watch . . . everywhere. You must go many miles, too far, get lost in desert. No good. I have plan."

"I trust you."

"We go. Say nothing." Abdeljelil said a few gruff words to Latifa in Arabic. She made no response.

Abdeljelil turned the car back to the highway, switching on the car's headlights when its wheels spun on the graveled pavement. They proceeded down the road at a normal pace and after several minutes came to the first barricade of the border crossing. Two Iraqi soldiers lounged in the well-lit inspection area, smoking and talking, at the open door of an office. Spotting the car, the soldiers casually waved it down. Abdeljelil abruptly stopped the car just before the gate and, without turning to Charles, got out. He straightened his shoulders and, with a confidence

Charles had not seen before, swaggered over to the two guards. They continued their conversation for a while and then lackadaisically turned their attention to him.

Abdeljelil drew out his papers from his jacket and handed them over. The guards eyed them a bit cursorily, suddenly looked at each other, and deferentially gave them back. They offered him a cigarette, which Abdeljelil took, then accepted a light from one of them. The three talked for a long while, laughing genially from time to time, as if they were standing in the square of a sleepy village, two brothers batting the breeze with their city cousin. For an instant Charles doubted his decision to leave his fate and that of Latifa in the hands of her uncle. A Baathe party official to the core, Charles thought. All too willing to save his own skin. But there was nothing that Charles could do now.

After a good fifteen minutes, Abdeljelil, gesturing in the direction of the car, addressed the guards in a manner that suggested he was disclosing some special confidence. One of them kept smiling while the other, with suspicion written all over his face, angled his body toward their distinguished visitor from Baghdad as if to better catch his words. When Abdeljelil had finished, the guard frowned. He shook his head, muttered a few words to the other guard and, with his right hand, motioned Abdeljelil into the office. Abdeljelil turned, looking toward the car with a pained expression in his eyes. Then, drawing himself up with self-importance and with a fury that would have frightened any but the most callow functionary, he moved his right hand across his chest, roaring so loudly that Charles and Latifa could hear it. "*Khloss!*"

"What means "*khloss?*" Charles whispered to Latifa, whose breath he felt at his left ear.

"It finished, . . . over."

"What does he mean?" Charles asked, frantic. Fear gripped his heart.

"He go . . . tell Saddam . . . soldiers bad guys."

"No, no. He can't do that." Charles grasped the door handle and pulled at it with his good arm. If he bolted now, he could run into the darkness. The border couldn't be that far. But then he stopped himself. He couldn't just leave Latifa.

"No go. . . . Wait." Latifa touched him lightly on the shoulder. "My uncle . . . smart. He talk good."

Then it dawned on him. It *was* clever, Charles thought—the threat to walk out of the room, to bring in higher authority to settle matters. It was the hallmark of a good negotiator who has nothing to lose in the deal, this the deal to save their lives. And who better to finesse that deal than an Arab with the street-smarts of the souk? But it was always a last-chance stratagem. He was developing a new respect for Fatima's brother.

The suspicious guard raised his automatic weapon and held it point-blank at Abdeljelil's head. The other guard, seeming to reprove his comrade, pushed the rifle away and directed his words at Abdeljelil, this time with none of the warmth of their earlier repartee. Then the three fell back into animated discussion, their hands telling Charles what their words could not. He could well imagine what threats, what promises, what arguments and what exhortations Abdeljelil might try, in order to secure their freedom. But in spite of his entreaties, the recalcitrant guard continued to shake his head, more and more adamantly. Charles began to sense that the sticking point was Latifa. No doubt persuaded by the power of Abdeljelil's status, the prospect of retribution if they crossed a party member and the promise of a large bribe, they would let Charles through, but as for the child of an enemy of the regime, they were under orders. Orders were orders, and orders from Saddam or his sons were orders like no others.

Charles could tell that Latifa sensed it too as he heard a faint whimper from behind him. Then suddenly the back door clanked open, Latifa's feet scraped on the gravel, and she ran the thirty feet around the metal gate and into the inspection area. She threw her arms around her uncle, who quickly drew her to him. With his hands raised, he had been in the midst of making a point but now glared at the guards. He drew his hands across his throat menacingly and glanced down at the elfin figure embracing him. Latifa cocked her head at the two guards imploringly. An image of Fatima, standing at the window of their hotel in Annecy, flashed through Charles's mind. Abdeljelil then fell silent, like the most astute negotiator he was, letting all his arguments and the emotions of the moment weigh on the minds of his fellow protagonists. It occurred to Charles that the guards might be from the region, Shiites possibly, maybe even relatives of relatives of Abdeljelil's family.

With an almost imperceptible nod, the holdout guard caved. At once Abdeljelil bounded back to the car, Latifa running in his wake. "Give me all money you have," he whispered at Charles. "*All*. Fast." Latifa jumped into the back seat.

Charles winced as he shifted his position and reached for his wallet with his good arm. He emptied his wallet of every Euro he had. He was sure it was the equivalent of at least five hundred dollars U.S. He handed the sheaf of bills to Abdeljelil, who ran back to the guards and pushed it at them. They took it, counted it, and ambled into the office as Abdeljelil ran back, got into the driver's seat, and revved the car's engine. The heavy metal gate of the first barricade swung up, then the second gate. Without so much as a fleeting glance at the guards, who stayed inside their post, they passed through the border crossing and, almost before they knew it, found themselves on the other side.

Abdeljelil pulled the car off onto the sandy shoulder of the highway. He got out and came around to the passenger side. He opened the door and solemnly stood beside it. Then, pointing down the highway, he said, "Border crossing Saudi Arabia not far. Maybe half-kilometer."

"Come with us," Charles again said as he stepped from the car. He already knew the response.

"No. You go . . . with Latifa."

"They will know what you did."

"No, guards no talk. I go home now, to my wife, my family. I be okay."

"This is your car. How can we return it to you?"

"I have many car. In my country I big man. You must take."

"You are a brave and good man."

"Take care Latifa."

"I will. She will come back some day."

"I hope, I hope. You go now. Border Saudi Arabia not far." Abdeljelil pointed down the highway. "Go hospital for that," he added, pointing to Charles's bloody left arm.

Charles put his good arm around Abdeljelil and kissed him firmly on both cheeks. He took Abdeljelil by the shoulder and held it in his right hand, gazing into his dark, kind eyes.

"Be well, my brother," Abdeljelil said, his eyes brimming with tears. They embraced again, and then Abdeljelil turned to Latifa and spoke to his niece in Arabic. Uncle and niece held each other for a long time. Then Latifa, crying, appeared to plead with her uncle to come with them. He virtually ignored her entreaties. Then, without a further word, he turned on his heel, and, stately and proud, walked back along the highway toward the Iraqi border. Charles and Latifa watched him until his figure merged with the semi-gloom of the gathering dawn.

"He is a good man," Charles said, still scanning the shadows for Abdeljelil's figure in the murky air of early morning. A filet of cool desert air swept over him, and a profound sadness crept into his heart. Sobered and recoiling from the trauma of their trip, he vowed never to forget Abdeljelil or his fateful decision to come to the aid of his sister. Whatever had been negotiated at the Iraqi border, Charles was sure that Fatima's brother had been obliged to make the supreme compromise: He had given up his life to save theirs. Latifa too had understood that, and she too would never forget.

Charles opened the passenger door for Latifa. "We'd better go," he said with manufactured cheeriness. "We've got a long day ahead of us."

The two of them got back in the car. He had to crank the engine a few times before it would turn over. Finally the car roared to life, and he maneuvered the car back onto the highway. He was almost overcome by the profound relief he felt. He looked over at Latifa, who had settled herself in the passenger seat. "Welcome to the free world," he said.

"I hope . . . maybe I like," she replied wistfully.

Brave words, he thought, from a child whose life had been so completely changed in just a day, who had lost her own mother, who had left her family perhaps forever. Thoughts of Fatima then began to surface in his mind, and tears welled in his eyes and began to course down his cheeks. He looked away, out the car window. He tried not to think about the unbelievable pain in his left arm.

The sun was rising now, over the desert. Its rays had begun to fall on every dune, every wadi and oasis, every escarpment in the desert's sandy universe, defying the desert's mystery and insulting its intimacy. Brilliant rays of sunlight streaming through the desert she once loved. Bountiful rays they were, he thought—rays of promise and of hope she once cherished. Rays that now cheered her final resting place, the grave of Fatima Shihabi.

FIFTY-THREE

Riyadh, Saudi Arabia
Friday–Monday
Oct. 11–14, 2002

The trip to Riyadh from the Iraqi border was more difficult than Charles could have imagined. Entering the Kingdom of Saudi Arabia without a visa was no small matter, and it took several long telephone conversations between Jameel Zawawi and the Saudi border officials before they could be persuaded to let the two travelers from Iraq cross the frontier. The monotonous drive through hot, barren desert, filled with scrub brush, sapped what remained of their energy. Latifa slept for the entire trip, while Charles tried to concentrate, forcing his feet to press the pedals and his eyes to focus on the ribbon of road before them. All the while Charles's physical condition continued to weaken. And when toward late afternoon they arrived at some mud huts that marked the outskirts of Riyadh, he had to summon his last ounce of strength to pilot the car to the center of the city, then to Jameel's office on King Saud Boulevard. When they finally arrived, Charles was too weak to leave the car and had to send Latifa to get Jameel. But by the time Jameel came down, Charles had passed out, his body slumped across the front seat of the car.

Jameel quickly called an ambulance from King Faisal Hospital, not far from Jameel's office. Two medics came immediately in a small van, and within minutes they were wheeling the still unconscious Charles on a small gurney into the hospital's emergency room. Jameel and Latifa, who had followed the ambulance in Abdeljelil's car, waited outside the room in a small antechamber. Taking the opportunity, Jameel questioned Latifa about all that had happened in the past several days. Initially shy before this personage so imposing in his blue cape fringed with gold, Latifa soon warmed to his charm and told him everything, omitting not a single detail.

After a good hour, a doctor appeared. "Mr. Sherman apparently has suffered a great loss of blood. He's a lucky man. He could not have survived much longer without medical care."

"He's pretty strong," Jameel said, looking first at Latifa and then at the doctor. "Will he be okay?"

"He's had multiple gunshot wounds in his left arm. The bullets passed through the flesh, but one bullet struck bone and perhaps a nerve. It will be a long time before he can use the arm again. He will need rehabilitation for it, and possibly surgery after the extent of the damage can be determined. Except for that, his vital signs seem satisfactory."

"When can we see him?" Latifa asked pertly.

"Now is okay if you wish, but only for a few minutes. He's regained consciousness, but he's still groggy. We've pumped his body with a lot of medicine. We'll hold him for a day or two to make sure he's on the right track."

When they came into the emergency room, Charles was half-sitting, half-reclining, in a hospital bed, several intravenous tubes connecting his arms to pouches of liquids hanging around him. He had his eyes closed, but he opened them as his visitors appeared.

"Hello, Jameel." Charles was surprised at the weakness in his voice.

"Hello, my friend." Jameel's eyes had lost none of their twinkle after so many years. He came to the side of the bed and took Charles's hand. "It's good to see you."

"It's been a long time."

"We've missed you in the Kingdom. You meant a lot to us."

"Well, you always said I was your brother. With all this Saudi blood in me"—Charles gestured toward the pouch of blood above his head—"I guess, now maybe I am."

Jameel's face crinkled with delight, and he squeezed Charles's hand. "You haven't lost your sense of humor—in spite of the challenges you've had recently."

Charles turned his head toward the only window in the room. His eyes filled with tears. Then he turned back toward Jameel. "She didn't make it, Jameel."

"I know." Jameel paused for a few moments, then added, "Latifa told me." He strode over to where Latifa was standing, near the foot of the bed, and pulled her toward him. His own eyes watering, he continued, "She was what you in America would call a 'classy lady,' Charles. A real class act, you know."

"I know, Jameel. I loved her."

"I'm not surprised. She seemed perfect in all respects except for one thing she lacked: the love of a man. And you gave it to her."

"I'm not going to let the memory of her die," Charles responded. He turned toward Latifa, who had kept her post at the foot of the bed. "I'm taking Latifa to America with me."

Latifa beamed a smile at Jameel and came over to him, to the side of the bed. He gave her a grandfatherly hug, grinning all the while, the gold caps of his fillings flashing. "You know, Latifa," he said, "you very much resemble your mother. She was a beautiful woman, I'm sure you know."

Latifa simply nodded her agreement. Then, cocking her head as Fatima would have done and staring boldly into his eyes, she said, "Thank for help mama." It was a genuine, self-assured gesture worthy of a young woman twice her age.

The doctor on duty appeared again and asked that they take their leave, so that Charles could be administered further tests. As they bade their farewells, Jameel said, "Of course, my wife Sada and I will be pleased to have Latifa stay with us until they let you out of this place. And when they do, I want you to join us. And you may use my office as if it were yours. Mr. Mir will be pleased to see you again after so many years. We'll fix you up with a phone. We even have computers now. Times have changed since you were last in the Kingdom, you know."

"Thanks so much, Jameel. Latifa's in good hands, I know. I'll call you when I'm to be released."

Mid-afternoon the next day, Charles felt strong enough to leave the hospital and, against his doctor's advice, decided to do so. He telephoned Jameel and gratefully accepted his offer of an office and lodging. Jameel immediately came to pick him up, and at Charles's request, brought him directly to the office. He told Mr. Mir to give Charles anything he needed, particularly access to a telephone.

Charles's first call was to Sarah. Still early morning in New York. He woke her up.

"Just wanted you to know I'm alive. I'm with Jameel in Riyadh."

"That's wonderful! I've been worried about you."

"I'll be back in a few days."

"I've missed you."

"I know. I've missed *you* too. It's been a tough time."

"I look forward to hearing all about it."

"I can't wait to tell you. It changed me, . . . the experience did, I mean."

"Not the same old Charles Sherman?"

"You'll see what I mean."

"I can hear something different in your voice. No, I mean I really can. What's happened to you?"

"I'm not sure that even I know. It's been difficult. I'll tell you every-thing when I get back." He felt fragile, vulnerable even, yet determined. A vision of Fatima flashed through his mind. She would have teased him about his veil showing.

"Of course, Charles," she said, "I'm anxious to hear about it."

"I'll call you when I know my schedule for the flight home. I'll be coming through Paris."

"Be careful. Please be careful. I can't wait to see you!"

"Me too. . . . I mean, I can't wait either." He was losing it. "Sarah, I have to sign off."

"Charles, I love you."

"I love you too."

It had been a strained conversation but, in a way, a reaffirming one. He was going to have to feel his way, but he was confident that something deep within his makeup had changed. And Sarah was going to help him take off his veils.

His next call was to Claude Vergier. It was with some foreboding, especially after all that had happened.

"Charles, where are you?" Claude asked at once.

"Saudi Arabia, in the offices of a lawyer friend of mine," he replied. "Long story."

"I'm glad you called. I have what you need."

"The name will be different."

"What do you mean?"

"Mrs. Shihabi won't be coming after all. I will have her daughter, Latifa, with me."

"No problem. I'll work it out. Just go first to the French embassy in Riyadh. They will issue her certain *lettres de passage*, just like the ones Madame Shihabi had. They're papers for stateless people to let them travel to France. Come to Paris, spend a few days with us, and we'll get you and Latifa on a plane to the States. It hasn't been easy, with all the restrictions after September eleventh, but I've got it all worked out. It was a friend of my brother, you know, at your embassy here. Our government is raising a few objections to your president's threat to go it alone in Iraq, but my brother's friend was happy to do him a favor. Latifa will be allowed entry into the United States."

"Claude, I cannot thank you enough."

"*C'est normal.*" Charles knew that Claude was smiling. He was an angel, a miracle worker, Charles had told him. And, as self-deprecating as he was, he knew it.

After another two days of solicitous care on the part of Sada and her servants in the Zawawi household, Charles felt well enough to get on the plane to Paris. As Claude had promised, Latifa's papers were in order. Buoyed by a splendid send-off by Jameel and Sada, the two travelers set off on the next phase of their journey.

FIFTY-FOUR

Air France Flight 010
Friday, Oct. 18, 2002

Would you like another martini, Mr. Sherman?" asked the flight attendant. "We won't be taking off for another twenty minutes, so you have
a little time."

"No, thanks. I have a little left. One's enough for me . . . at least for
the moment," he added.

"How about a soft drink for your young friend?"

Latifa looked up from her new notebook and laid down her pen. Her
frown of concentration faded. "No thank, I okay too." Her dark eyes
moved quickly to Charles in the seat beside her and fixed him with a
conspiratorial glance. Then, putting on the headphones of the Sony
Walkman that Charles had bought for her in Paris, she turned back to her
writing.

"No, we're doing just great. We're happy to be here," Charles reassured the attendant.

"I hope your arm isn't bothering you," she said, looking at the sling
on his arm. "How did you break it?" She seemed genuinely concerned.

"It's a long story. A bit complicated, you know."

"Well, we hope you both have a good flight," she added cheerily.

Charles settled into the leather-cushioned seat. Three full days in Paris
had proved strong solace for their sorrows. They had stayed at his favorite hotel, the George V, where Latifa had been in continual amazement
over the *grand luxe* of her room, the fountains and flowers and frou–frou
décor of the public rooms, and the continual availability of *citron pressé*,
the lemonade to which she had taken a liking. They had strolled the

principal shopping areas of the city, and between the two of them, they found various conservative clothes for a young woman of Latifa's age, of which Fatima would have approved. One afternoon he had even steered Latifa past the Hotel St. Simon, where he ventured a look inside, imagining Fatima in her blue silk suit, seated once again on the banquette across the lobby where he had first met her.

The time together let them bond to a degree that delighted Charles. Not surprisingly, Latifa possessed many of the same qualities of her mother, not the least of which was her determination. Once or twice, Latifa and her protector even came to loggerheads over a particular blouse or skirt that seemed too *adult* or too extravagant for the young Muslim girl. And more than once he had to employ all the persuasion he could muster to get her back to the hotel in the evening, as she begged him to let her pursue her exploration of the captivating city. Nonetheless, other of her mother's traits, including her spirit, intelligence, and wit, had made Latifa a most agreeable traveling companion. And so, after three days, they had reached an understanding that was both sincere and profound. And they were utterly devoted to each another.

He would wait to talk with Sarah about Latifa's future. With her mother and Omar dead, and Abdeljelil almost certainly dead, who would raise her? He had promised Fatima to take care of Latifa, and without the least hesitation he now would do so. There was always adoption. He'd have to talk to Sarah about it. Indeed, he couldn't wait to tell it all to Sarah, to tell her the whole story, everything that had happened, all of it. And she would understand, he knew—she was that way.

She would have liked Fatima, and Fatima her. They were two sides of the coin. Sarah and Fatima. Fatima and Sarah. Women for whom freedom—of thought, of choice, of action—mattered more than anything else in the world except for the ones they loved. Women who had redeemed him from himself. Through their love they had changed him profoundly.

It was Sarah who had prepared him for his journey to his inner self. Years ago she herself had made that journey. And she had taught him what it meant to choose a different path, being true to himself. In her mind what mattered most was the freedom to explore that vast inner world of individuality. She had recognized them for what they were—the veils of capitalistic success, material possessions, and even conventionality itself—veils that served only to mask the predicament of the human condition—his predicament, he thought. And she had made him see those veils too.

Fatima's freedom was of a profoundly different sort, he reflected. It was the freedom to project oneself onto the great world at large, to affect the "Others," as she would have called them. It was the freedom to cajole them, even shame them—with words and ideas, to make them understand. It was the freedom sought by those who storm the barricades, foment the revolutions, save humanity from itself, and make the world a better place. It was Fatima who taught him the meaning of *that* freedom—and in the process altered his values so fundamentally that everything he thought he believed in was now called into question.

She had challenged him in ways no mega–merger deal ever had. He knew it the first evening he had spent with her in Talloires. In no way had she been taken in by the razzmatazz of the Charles Sherman Show. An Arab from Baghdad, no less—she possessed all the strength—of character, of beauty and of love—to make *him* pay attention to *her.* To bring him up short. To buck him so hard he hardly knew what had hit him. She had held a mirror to his eyes and forced him to see who Charles Sherman really was, and then ever so slowly to take off his veils, and in the bargain to become fully human.

His bandaged arm began to throb, and he leaned forward and tried to relax his shoulders. As he resettled his bulky body in the first-class seat, a piece of paper fell from his pants pocket onto the floor between the seats. With her sharp eyes, Latifa spotted it, and unhooking her seatbelt, she leaned down, picked it up, and handed it to him. He gave her an appreciative smile, and she returned it. He then unfolded the paper and studied it. It was the "gift" that Fatima and Omar had given him in Talloires—their translation of Fatima's poem "The End of the World," written out in

Fatima's elegant, cursive script. Holding it before him, he read it and then read it again.

At the very top of the paper, near the title, were penned in Fatima's handwriting the words "Dedicated to Ana Lucretia Maldonado." A champion of human rights in Guatemala, Fatima had described her. In a country long beset by the worst abuses of human rights imaginable. Living with the same fears that Fatima had confronted. Balancing the conflicting demands of her family, her freedom, and her future as Fatima had done. A woman he had to meet, he decided. And one day soon he would call on her. He carefully folded the paper and put it in his wallet.

The grind of the plane's motors brought him back from his reflections. He glanced over at Latifa, who had fallen asleep. The glimmering light from the window emphasized her high cheekbones and soft, beautiful face. She truly did resemble Fatima, he reflected. He would do everything he could for her. Make sure that she had the choices that Fatima would have liked her to have.

As the plane rose in the sky over Paris, he caught a glimpse of Montmartre. Atop its fenestrated flanks soared the alabaster dome of Sacré-Cœur, with all the contours of a Middle Eastern mosque. Farther on the horizon, there was the Arc de Triomphe, and then, anchoring the azure sky, a sweeping panorama of Paris. Not without reason was it the City of Love, he mused. It was there that he had begun to learn what love meant. And what it meant to be loved.

Latifa stirred, sleepily opening her dark, lustrous eyes.

He could no longer see Paris.

EPILOGUE

23 Wall Street
Late afternoon, Wednesday
Oct. 8, 2003

"Hello, Metta." Charles rested his chin atop the stanchion around Metta's cubicle.

"Well, Charles Sherman. *Bean venue*, welcome back."

"Metta, please don't take this the wrong way after all these years, but you really should work on your French. It needs a lot of work."

"*Nooo probleeem, messur*," replied the unsinkable Metta. "Actually my financé and I are heading over to Paris next month, . . . just for a week though." She looked at Charles for a reaction.

"You don't say. That's terrific. You'll have a great time. The French will love you."

"Why, *mairrzee*, Charles. We certainly do miss you around here."

"*Merci*," Metta. "That's *merci*," he said, giving the word as much of a French pronunciation as he could muster.

"I'll miss you too, Charles."

"I just thought I'd come back and say good-bye to a few people before Sarah and I leave for Geneva. Is Art in?"

"He's in his office. I dropped off a document in there a few minutes ago."

"Look, Metta, keep working on that French. I'm going to test you the next time I see you. Take care of yourself."

"You too, Charles. *Aw revere*. I mean *oh revoy*. Oh, Charles, whatever, you know what I mean, . . . you know what I mean. *Naisay paw*? Don't you?"

Already halfway down the corridor, Charles winced in mock chagrin. He would miss Metta. He wished he could take her with him. Hansen, who had taken over most of Charles's projects after he left the firm, was standing in the doorway of Art's office as Charles approached.

"Well, look who's here. Charles Sherman, Freedom Fighter Extraordinaire. Hello, Charles. Congrats on your new position. It does sound cool, I have to say."

"I do expect it to be interesting," Charles replied, perhaps a bit too seriously, as he breezed by and into Art's office. "Hey, Art. Would you have a few minutes for me? Sarah and Latifa are waiting downstairs. We're headed off to Geneva this evening."

"Why sure, Charles. Frank, close that door, would you?" Art rocked back in his leather chair. He worked a paper clip back and forth between his fingers. Charles thought of Jameel with his worry beads. "I can't believe it's almost a year since you left. You surprised a lot of people, you know. We all thought you were a lifer. And you were that close, . . . that close"—Art held the tip of the paper clip in his long, elegant fingers—"to locking up Morgan as a client. Witherspoon still hasn't gotten over it."

"That's *not* true, and you know it."

"Well, of course it's true. Witherspoon always thought highly of you." Art appeared flustered.

"You knew that after 9/11 things weren't the same for me, didn't you? You knew that it made me look at life differently, but I couldn't bring myself to make a change—that is, until Fatima Shihabi came along. It was a case tailor-made for me, with the emotional momentum to attract me in the first place and then let me escape the gravitational pull of the only world I knew—and loved, I might add." Charles saw the faintest hint of a smile creep across Art's face. Then Charles added, "And I'll bet that Witherspoon knew it too. Don't deny it, Art. You taught me too well as a dealmaker to read the faces of those I'm dealing with. You knew I'd never be the same after Fatima Shihabi."

"No, no, Charles, the credit is entirely yours. Law practice is not only about practicing law, you know. We're all entitled to live the lives Fate has in mind for us, to realize our full potential if you want to call it that. And that means you and me and Fatima and Sarah and everybody else on the face of the planet." Pausing, Art glanced at a photograph on the far corner of his expansive desk, a photograph of his daughter dressed in a business suit, her eyes sparkling with intelligence and vivacity. "You weren't the only one affected by September eleventh, Charles," he said.

Art's daughter had been at a meeting high in the South Tower that awful day. They had never found her body.

"I'm sorry," Charles said, bowing his head. The effect on him of 9/11 paled in comparison to a parent losing a child.

Art sighed, then suddenly turned his head back to him. "It's true. You *were* primed for a change. I just, shall we say, nudged you along a bit." His face broke into a genial smile, and he paused, gazing out the window, the same view Charles had always had from his office. "And don't bother yourself about Witherspoon. He's done quite well for himself. He's got that attack dog you liked so much on Goldstar barking for him."

"You mean Christopher St. George?"

"The one and only."

"Shit. Witherspoon could have done better." Charles studied the face of his mentor. "Maybe I should've stayed, after all," he added, flashing a grin.

Art stretched back in his leather chair. "Well, so you're off to the High Commission on Refugees—number two in the legal department, eh? I understand that the UN isn't the easiest agency to work for. A lot of politics, you know."

"There were certainly enough politics just to get hired. But if I can ride it out, I'll move into the top spot when the general counsel retires. Sarah's happy about it. She can't wait to go skiing. And she can paint anywhere."

"I'm glad you two lovebirds finally tied the knot."

"Yeah, somehow everything changed after I got back from Iraq. But, of course, you knew that it would . . . change, I mean." Charles smiled at Art bemusedly.

"You've told Sarah the whole story, I suppose—subject to the usual concerns for client confidentiality, of course." Art studied his face as if trying to read any messages hidden in his expression.

"She knows it all, . . . and she knows how much I appreciate everything she's done. I feel as if I've rediscovered what a wonderful woman she is."

"That she is, Charles. That she is. Give her my best." Art paused, then asked, "How's Latifa doing?"

"Well, there's been an interesting development. She's going back to Iraq, to live with her uncle."

"I'd have thought that she'd had enough of all that."

"Now that Saddam's gone from power, the family just wants to go on with their lives. Her uncle had been high in the Baathe Party, you know. Saddam's henchmen beat him up pretty badly, tortured him practically out of his mind. He'd have been killed, but Saddam wanted to see him suffer for as long as possible. Curiously Saddam's vengeance actually saved him. He was let go in the general prisoner release last October only ten days after they threw him in prison. He was fortunate, although the torture messed up his body. Funny thing was, when we invaded, we threw him back into prison as a suspected collaborator with Saddam. He was released again just last month. He's a pretty remarkable guy. I got to know him a bit. Latifa adores him."

"When does she go back?"

"She'll spend a few days with Sarah and me in Geneva, then go on to Baghdad. The two of them have really taken to each other, almost like mother and daughter." Charles glanced at his watch. "Oh, God, I'd better go. Sarah's waiting for me downstairs." He quickly stood, as did Art, who came around by the side of his desk. They shook hands affectionately, and then, on impulse, Charles embraced his mentor.

"Thank you, Art. I mean it. Thanks for everything."

"Not at all, Charles," Art said warmly, his eyes glistening. "Your time at Lloyd & Forster will long be remembered. Look, *do* give our regards to Sarah. My wife misses their evenings at the opera. Anne enjoyed their conversations so much, you know, . . . those evenings when you were at the printer with Witherspoon."

Charles stepped away, in the direction of the door, then turned and looked at Art. "Tell the Silver Fox I was asking for him."

"I surely will."

Charles grasped the door handle, hesitated for an instant, and again looked back at Art. "I forgot to tell you. We're adopting a Guatemalan child, from the northern highlands. The papers arrive in Geneva next week, and we pick her up in mid-November."

"You've become quite the family man," Art teased, sitting back down behind his desk. He seemed small and wizened, and his expression a little wistful, as he fixed his eyes on his protégé. He then nodded, softened his features into a smile, and added, "Close the door behind you, Charles, will you? Thanks."

When Charles passed Art's secretary's desk, he happened to notice that Art's phone was lit. It could be Witherspoon, he thought. He had a fleeting vision of Christopher St. George listening in, reposing in the red wingchair that always stood before Witherspoon's desk, the very one where Charles had sat through so many conference calls on deals for his former client.

When Charles reached the lobby, Sarah greeted him with a full kiss on the lips. He hugged her and then leaned to hug Latifa.

"Sorry to be late, guys. I was with Art."

"I *thought* you might be there awhile." Giving him a wise and knowing look, Sarah took his hand and pressed it in hers. Then the three of them, hand in hand, went up Wall Street, merging into a horde of home-ward-bound office workers and their supervisors hurrying to catch the early train to the suburbs.

The afternoon sun had leached the chill from the autumn air. Chased by a light wind from the east, the air felt fresh and clean against their cheeks. More like a day in early spring, Charles thought. Latifa must have felt it too, he sensed, for she quickened her step, bounding ahead, her treasured notebook swinging at her side. As they marched along, past Federal Hall, he looked up at the bronze statue of George Washington, impassively monitoring the rabble in briefcases from his command at the top of the stone staircase. Slowing his pace momentarily, Charles studied the familiar face. He fixed in his mind George's noble profile, his sturdy constitution, and his steadfast bearing as the Street's foot soldiers of finance paraded before him. It would be a long time, Charles reflected, before he would see that august figure again, . . . if ever.

And then, practically before he realized it, George winked. At him. He was almost sure of it. He shot a glance back at those resolute eyes, at that revered countenance, veiled with its usual straight-faced serenity. Must have been the light, he told himself.

Bemused, Charles took Sarah's arm and stopped her abruptly, in the middle of the sidewalk. When their eyes met, she gave him a wide, confident smile, which he returned. As they stood there, in the midst of the throng milling around them, he gave her a long hug, and when Latifa came and gazed up at him, he pulled her to him as well. Then, the three of them turned as one, and with Charles's arms encircling both Sarah and Latifa, they strode along, their heads high and their hearts full of gladness.

It was the springtime of their new lives.

A NOTE ABOUT THE AUTHOR

DJ Murphy graduated from Harvard University and Georgetown University Law Center. As an international corporation lawyer, he worked for law firms in New York City, Paris, and midwest America, representing large multinational companies. He also worked *pro bono publico* to assist refugees seeking asylum from political or religious persecution. In 1999 he retired from the practice of law in order to teach and to write. He taught for five years as a Visiting Professor at Ecole Supérieure de Commerce in Bordeaux, France. This is his first novel.

The author contributes ten percent (10%) of net royalties he derives from this book to the United Nations High Commission on Refugees.